Jack Curtis was bor̲ _____ _____ ___ ____ ___ _____
time between Lond̲__ ___ ___ ____ _ ___ _ ___ __ ___
Country. His acclaimed novels, *Crows' Parliament*, *Glory*
and *Sons of the Morning* are all published by Corgi.

Also by Jack Curtis

CROWS' PARLIAMENT
GLORY
SONS OF THE MORNING

and published by Corgi Books

CONJURE ME

Jack Curtis

CORGI BOOKS

CONJURE ME
A CORGI BOOK 0 552 13593 3

Originally published in Great Britain by Bantam Press,
a division of Transworld Publishers Ltd

PRINTING HISTORY
Bantam Press edition published 1992
Corgi edition published 1993

Set in 10/11pt Linotype Plantin by
County Typesetters, Margate, Kent

Corgi Books are published by Transworld Publishers Ltd,
61–63 Uxbridge Road, Ealing, London W5 5SA, in Australia
by Transworld Publishers (Australia) Pty. Ltd, 15–23 Helles
Avenue, Moorebank, NSW 2170, and in New Zealand by
Transworld Publishers (N.Z.) Ltd, 3 William Pickering Drive,
Albany, Auckland.

Made and printed in Great Britain by
Cox & Wyman Ltd, Reading, Berks.

To Ysanne

One

Abra –

Zeno placed his hands together, palm to palm, finger resting on finger, thumbs aligned like a man praying, and raised them to Marianne's nose. She went cross-eyed trying to hold focus.

Slowly, as if anxious to keep her attention, his hands drew apart; he might have been describing the length of some object. Not knowing which hand to follow, she looked straight ahead. And then – she might have willed it into existence – the something began to appear between his palms. As if he were unravelling wire. As if some bolt of silver light, some shaft of energy, had arced between terminals in his fingertips. It glittered.

Marianne smiled. She was enjoying the moment. Everything was slightly muzzy, and she liked that. There was a small candelabrum on the table just to her left: five candles. Each pod of flame, touched by the breeze, trembled slightly; together, they threw a corona of soft light, a halo that hovered on the edge of her vision. She knew that she looked particularly lovely in candle-light. Beyond that dusky glow lay an elderberry darkness. She could fantasize that the room had fallen away and the little scene was being played out against a backdrop of infinity – a table, the remains of a meal, snifters of brandy, two candle-lit faces, a moment of after-dinner entertainment.

Zeno smiled too. His hands moved further apart, still level, still held aloft on either side of her head, but out of sight. He looked like an evangelist calling sinners to redemption.

Then he clapped.

She stared at him, wide-eyed. His palms lay on her cheeks. His arms were locked, biceps creasing his shirt sleeves, tendons rigid, the heel of either hand propping her jaw. All of a sudden, he was holding her up.

A gusher of blood welled in her ear. It ran between the middle fingers of his right hand, then over his wrist. It became a long slick, going glibly down his forearm and trailing off the point of his elbow in a flow so constant that it seemed solid. A needle-thin stalactite releasing a stutter of thin drips.

– *cadabra*.

Two

There was a running sea. Cross-currents brought line after line of waves slantwise across the bay, moving fast, booming against the base of the sea wall, then throwing up a vast white fan of spume that hissed as it rose. Further out, the water was slate-grey under slate-grey weather. Near the horizon everything merged to an eerie point of erasure – neither sea nor sky.

Nick Howard sensed it before he saw it. His car topped the headland and there was that blankness: no cloud, no horizon, no sense of distance that landmarks give – the world wiped clean. Then he crested the hill and saw the town cupped in the bay, seeming almost deserted from that distance. He saw first the sea, the sea wall, the storefronts clouted by spray, the line of hotels, cheap restaurants, amusement arcades, chandlers, boat yards . . .

He was there to lay a ghost.

He checked in at a seafront hotel – the Palings – as he had been told to do. His luggage consisted of a small leather grip. Clean shirts, clean underwear, shaving gear. He wasn't expecting to stay long. Once in his room, he opened the grip and started to put his shirts into a drawer, then stopped as if suddenly losing enthusiasm for the job. He went to the window and leaned against the sill. Windborne threads of spray built a delicate lattice-work against the glass.

To lay a ghost . . .

Nick didn't believe in an afterlife. He knew that hauntings have less to do with the dead than the living. We carry the past with us; we summon our own spectres.

9

A wave of anxiety struck him, though he couldn't connect it to anything; it was as troubling as those moments of sadness that sometimes overwhelm us on waking – vague, nagging depressions, inexplicable until memory overhauls the feeling and reminds us why we feel bad. Nick remembered what was making him anxious. He remembered Louise standing just outside the door of their house, bringing Michael to say goodbye. The boy had raised a hand and wagged it cheerily. His father's business trips were nothing new to him.

Louise had kissed him, and asked, 'When? Friday?'

'If not, Saturday morning, for sure.' It hadn't been necessary to concoct much of a lie. The trips were nothing new to Louise either.

Nick shuddered, as if someone had pulled a hair along his spine. There was no reason for anxiety . . . except that he had lied. It was courting bad luck.

He remembered a game he'd played long ago with some friends. A game of worst things, worst fears. Each in turn had owned up to the awful imagining that wouldn't go away. One of them had said, 'Someone I love could be dying at this very moment.' It had never occurred to him before, but he'd thought of it often since. He thought of it as he stood by the window in his hotel and watched hawsers of foam thud across the sea wall.

Further out, a small, blue, clinker-built boat was clouting a passage through the whitecaps. Its wheelhouse was a crude plank-and-awning affair, like a sentry-box. Nick couldn't see how it could possibly make progress. Irritated by the sluggishness of the craft, he discovered a little spurt of energy in himself: enough to help him stow the rest of his clothing in drawers and cupboards, and arrange his shaving gear on the sink surround.

When he went back to the window the boat was almost out of sight, just about to round the point on the north side of the bay. Its little blue nib of a prow dipped repeatedly; it travelled but didn't move; then it was gone.

Nick went to the bed and lay down. He felt lethargic

again, but also edgy: the upshot of having nothing to do but wait. He wanted to go for a walk. He wanted to be somewhere else – another town, another time. He wanted to go home. But he had to wait.

He lay on the bed for two hours as the room grew dark, listening to the wind shredding on the cornerstone, high-pitched and reedy, as if he were out to sea and hearing the wind in a high rigging; then he slept.

In his dream, the seven of them were sitting in a circle. He remembered the place – a big room, like a loft, lots of big cushions, a bed very low to the floor, a kitchen area behind a screen; he couldn't remember who lived there. They were smoking, the joint going round from hand to hand, except the dream changed it to a little package with many wrappings. Each of them removed a wrapping and read out the message written there – a fortune stogie.

A voice said, 'Someone I love could be dying at this very moment' – reading the message. In the dream, he knew who had spoken. When the phone woke him, he forgot instantly.

Zeno said, 'Nick? Nicholas?'

The wind whickered. The room's deep twilight deceived the eye, making objects seem to move, stealthily, then grow still when looked at.

'Nick?'

If there was a bulb in the bedside lamp, it must have fused. Nick held the phone to his ear, unable to speak, like an actor who hears his cue and turns to stone.

'Nick . . .'

Seven of them, sitting in a circle. A sunlit room; a game of 'worst things'. Three women, four men.

Nick said, 'Who is it?'

'Nick.' The voice issued his name on a falling breath. 'I thought you'd find me. I thought you'd come.'

'Sam?' Nick's voice was shrill; he could have been issuing a warning. 'Sam? Is it you?'

The voice gave an address, instructions on how to find the place; a warning of its own. 'Don't tell anyone you're coming here. Don't tell anyone.'

'No.'

'You didn't give anyone the name of the town? Or let anyone know which part of the country . . . ?'

'No.'

'It's our secret?'

'Yes.'

'Our secret,' the voice repeated. 'It always was. It still is . . .'

Nick listened to the dialling tone without hearing it. After a while, he hung up the phone. The dusk thickened, still cheating the eye.

A vase drifted across the surface of a chest of drawers, then wavered and went back. Ghosts loomed and dwindled on the blank TV screen.

The world was suddenly too close, too dangerous. Ghosts and secrets. Lies and bad luck.

When he stepped outside, a warm wind buffeted his face and deckled his face with a mist of spray. He walked parallel to the sea wall for a hundred yards or so, then began to climb a hill that led back into the town. It was a featureless place, once you left the seafront. Narrow streets, small shops, houses that all seemed to date from the forties and fifties apart from two low-rise developments – grey, stained façades, half-lit stairwells – that stood side by side like bad ideas abandoned.

Close to the top of the hill, the road swung round to the right; a few detached houses had been built just below the crest. Nick continued to climb, finding a narrow path and the stile that straddled it, just as he'd been told. It wasn't a tough climb, really, but it took Nick's breath. A month or two past forty, he was carrying twenty pounds of excess weight and didn't usually take any exercise beyond walking to and from his car.

His eyelashes were furred with moisture; when he reached the top of the path and turned round, the lights of the town fractured in his vision, spreading in tall rays that pulsed like an aurora borealis. He ran his sleeve across his face then climbed a second stile and began to traverse the brow of the hill.

He was crossing a field now and the ground under his feet was cloying, each step a little mud-wallow. He was sure he'd followed the directions he'd been given correctly, but there were no houses up there; no streets. He came to a barbed wire fence and stood still, baulked, not knowing what to do. He could still see the lights along the harbourfront, but up on the hill the darkness was total.

'Dewer Street,' the voice had said. 'Number forty-nine.' Nick tried to think back along the list of directions. He knew he hadn't gone wrong, but repeated the instructions under his breath: *A stile, a lane, another stile . . .* He parted the uppermost and middle strands of barbed wire and climbed through, snagging his topcoat. He twisted to free himself, but the ground he'd stepped on to sloped sharply downhill. As his foot slid away, he heard his coat tear. He sat down heavily, hands out to brace himself, and felt the ooze where cattle had churned the turf. His legs threshed as he backpedalled, looking for a foothold, and he fell again. A thick, soupy wetness seeped through to his thighs.

The only thing to do was start again. He began to edge downhill, trying to keep his balance on the wet slope. The lights along the seafront were still visible but their glow, when he looked away from it, made the hillside darker.

He started to go through a wood, black and boisterous with wind, the trees making a steep angle against the slope of the ground. Again he fell, travelling several feet on his backside, before his outstretched feet hit a nest of roots.

'Dewer Street, Dewer Street, *what* fucking Dewer Street? I've footslogged across farmland, now I'm like some storybook orphan, lost in the wood.' He spoke the words out loud, trying for a jaunty tone, and at once the sound of his own voice terrified him.

What am I doing here? he thought. How in God's name did I get here? He'd expected the instructions he'd been given to bring him directly to a house. Now it was as if the walk up from the sea had never happened; as if he'd gone to sleep in his hotel room and woken up skidding between tree-trunks in the dark.

He pulled himself up and continued downhill, slithering a few yards, colliding with a tree, resting, pushing off again. The wind whooped and bellowed in the leaf canopy. He came to a small stand of silver birch and paused there to get his breath, one outstretched hand braced against the pale bole of a tree. It stirred as a big gust shook the branches and he pulled his hand away, startled, as if his touch had brought some dead thing to life.

He must have fallen ten times or more in getting down to the road. Below the waist, his clothing was sodden, and slick with mud. He stood still, panting as if he'd been pursued. A web of scratches that he hadn't registered during his plunge through the wood now began to sting his face and hands; each of them wept a line of bloodbeads.

It was clear that the road was a loop, rising from the seafront on one side – the side he'd taken to ascend – and dropping down to the other end of the harbour from where he now stood. His trip across the fields and through the wood had simply brought him to the end of the road farthest from the stile.

He went back to the seafront. He went back to his hotel room. The phone rang before he could take his shoes off.

'Nick? You couldn't find the place?'

'Where in hell are you?'

'Dewer Street. Number forty-nine.'

'What game is this? Why did—?'

'Where have you been, Nick?'

'I did what you said. I wound up in the middle of a wood.'

'A wood?'

14

'Above the town there's a—'

'Yes. My God, what were you doing way up there?'

'You told me—'

'Dewer Street.'

'OK. Where *is* Dewer Street?'

'You're there, Nick. You're there. Your hotel is in Dewer Street. It's number eleven. I'm at forty-nine. Not far; not far at all.'

Nick opened his mouth and closed it again. After a moment, he said, 'Why the runaround?'

'Runaround? No, it's easy. You're eleven; I'm at forty-nine. Just along the front – direction of the point. All you have to do is follow the numbers.'

'Give me time to change.'

'No time for that.'

'I fell in the woods. I'm—'

'No time for that.' The voice was insistent. 'You've wasted time.'

'What difference can it make?' Nick asked. 'I just—' A double click and then the dialling tone.

Outside again, Nick headed towards the point. It's strange, he thought, that I can get nothing from the voice. Surely I should recognize it. People change, their appearances change; hair turns grey, jawlines sag, features become blurred by lines; silhouettes thicken. But voices stay the same, don't they?

He realized that he could have got things wrong. Maybe the voice belonged to someone he'd never met. And if that was true, everything became more mysterious and frightening than he'd thought.

He turned his face from the wind and the streamers of spray it carried, checking numbers as he walked.

His hotel: eleven. Seventeen, a hardware store. Twenty-five, a launderette. There was a bar that didn't show a number, but if you counted along it had to be thirty-three. Once more, he was walking out of the town. He passed the street that looped round towards the wood. Further along, he could see where the buildings stopped. On the seaward side, the wall ended and a cliff rose steeply, cutting off all sight of the ocean. Where the lights of Dewer Street stopped, and the seafront lights were checked by the shoulder of the cliff, the road continued in darkness.

You bastard. What game is this?

Nick slowed his pace, thinking he might turn back. Then he saw the clumsy, white numerals on the double gate of a boatyard, two curves and two slashes, put there by someone with a paintbrush too big for the job. The last place but two on Dewer Street.

He went in, expecting to find a house beyond the yard. There wasn't one: just a dozen or so boats and a couple of storage huts. There was a little light from the street. Nick picked his way between chocked-up hulls, walking deeper into the yard.

He said, 'Hullo . . . ?'

A fizz, a hiss. In the deeper darkness farthest from the street came a ball of light like St Elmo's fire. It swung from side to side. A little beacon; a lantern to light the way.

'Hullo . . . ?'

And there was another – swinging like the first, crackling softly as if energy were being shed. While Nick watched, the globes of light turned blue. Each described a low parabola in the air, leaving behind a delicate blue-white trail.

Then there were three. And now they were emerald, shimmering with a pale, icy radiance that almost hurt the eye; three globes of iridescent green rising and falling in lazy loops, left to right and right to left, so that they kept a perpetual motion, one ascending as another fell away, one always at the zenith, all of them constantly changing places.

Now they began to move with greater speed, as if they had found orbits of increased power. The globes themselves blurred with their own tracks and traces, so that their passage through the air drew permanent shapes of domes and arches, a vivid green cathedral.

'What is it?' Nick asked. 'What do you want?'

The globes turned red; curves and spires now etched in flame as if the Devil had touched them with his finger.

Then suddenly they flared to fiery white, purged and pure, all-but blinding; and there in the midst, God's own weapon of vengeance turning over and over through the glare – a glint of steel – then flickering off into the dark.

'What do you—'

Nick heard a sound like someone drawing breath, then took a hard punch to the arm, though no-one was near enough to hit him. When he looked, a slender knife was stuck in the meat of his bicep.

He said, 'Oh . . .' then took a step backwards, still peering at the place. He put up a hand to grasp the haft, making a little push-pull motion, as if he might loosen the blade. It made the pain come in.

He backed up another step, and his shoulders rapped the stern planks of a lithe racing yacht. So intense had been the white light from the globes, that the pattern of their passage through the air was etched on to his retina. The cathedral still burned in the sky like a vision vouchsafed to a saint.

Zeno caught the globes one-handed, a juggler's expert catch, then let them drop to the ground as their brilliance faded.

Well, he thought, that was fun.

Marianne Novaks had been fun as well. His mother had always said, 'If there's something you have to do, you may as well do it with a will.'

Truth to tell, he'd given Marianne a bit of a runaround too. The first night, he'd called her and made a date at a small restaurant two streets back from the sea. You walked down steps to a cellar hung with fish nets and glass floats. A bit kitsch; but it was quiet at this time of year, and the food was good. He'd given her an hour, then sent a message that spoke of unavoidable delay.

The next night, he'd sent her back to the same place,

the same time, the same table. After an hour and a half, a girl had arrived with a single red rose and a memorized rhyme: 'Don't just sit there feeling blue; Call three-oh-nine, oh-six-oh-two.' The girl had smiled a toothy smile and showed the swell of a lightly freckled cleavage as she'd handed over the flower. When Marianne phoned, he'd told her how sorry he was. She'd said, 'I'm only here because you asked me to be.'

'Not quite true,' he suggested. 'You were curious, weren't you?'

'I'm sorry if this sounds overly tetchy, but I can't help feeling that I'm being fucked around.'

'No, really. A meeting out of town. I was sure I'd be back in time to keep our date.'

'What do you want?'

'To see you.' A long pause during which Marianne didn't ask why. Zeno answered the unasked question anyway: 'You know the reason.'

'So what's next? I come back tomorrow night? Same table, or can I choose where to be stood up?'

'No.' His laugh had seemed genuine – apology and anticipation, mixed. 'Let's forget the restaurant. I'll be back early tomorrow – plenty of time to cook. You like fish?'

'Yes.'

'It's the perfect location for fresh fish. Come to my place.' And he'd given her an address.

As he was hanging up, she said, 'You know, I didn't recognize you at first.'

The next evening she'd arrived and there he was: all smiles, renewed apologies, champagne, sole *bonne femme*, and an after-dinner trick she'd never seen before. Would never see again.

He'd watched her arrive at the restaurant; of course he had. He'd also watched her leave. On the second night, he'd even gone into the bar and looked on as she shredded the paper napkins and worked her way through a few glasses of Chablis. A runaround. Yes, it was; though not much of one. It was just a way of delaying things for a while. Delaying the moment. Not for pleasure's sake; not that. No: these were old friends. He hadn't seen them in years. No-one would want to say a quick 'Hello, good-bye'.

He thought that Marianne's patience would support two nights alone in the cellar restaurant. Nick Howard was a different matter. A busy man; a family man. So Zeno had sent him for a wander in the woods – it just delayed things a little; and, as with Marianne, it was a disorientation ploy. The technique always worked with an audience. Direct their attention somewhere else. Give them something else to think about. Make them uncomfortable, dizzy, not sure what they're seeing. Then work the trick.

Nick Howard had walked into the boatyard tired, confused, his face stinging with scratches. Half an hour before, he'd been splashing through mud, free-falling down a wooded hillside; now he was standing amid chocked-up hulls in darkness, waiting for something to happen. Then came the fiery globes. And then the knife.

Nick's arm was across his body, his fist clamped on to the haft of the knife. His head was dropped in a brief bow. He looked as though he were making some obscure act of obeisance. Zeno flickered another out of the darkness: pinpoint accuracy, but the timing was unlucky. He couldn't have second-guessed the moment. As the blade whickered across, turning once in the air, Nick yanked the first knife out. He yelled and twisted away from the pain in the instant that the second knife arrived. It quivered and sang in the polished boards of the yacht. Nick heard it but didn't see it. He had moved into cover on the other side of the hull. Zeno wondered if Nick had been strong enough – careful enough – to keep a grip on the knife when he pulled it out.

He moved towards the yacht, going to the right. At the same time, he sent a green globe arcing away to the left. It hissed like a hot iron plunged into water. From the other side of the yard came a clatter of falling planks, then the sound of Nick pulling at the gate.

Exits and entrances . . . Zeno went into one of the storage huts that abutted the wall of the boatyard and emerged into the street. He saw the double gates gape and fall back, then gape again as Nick struggled to make them open. He waited.

The wind was a little stronger now, the sea a little rougher. Even so, you could hear other sounds behind that rush and roar. A saxophone rose and wailed along with the wind, then fell back to allow a voice to come in. The music came from the bar that Nick had passed. From the doorway, a spillage of pale pink light spread like a slick into the wet street. A bus taking five passengers into the next town rolled through the livid puddle, spreading flounces of colour. For a brief moment, the drumming of its engine beat back the tide.

It might have seemed logical for Nick to try to make it to the bar – safety in numbers, a telephone call to the police; or to run at the bus, waving his arms, forcing the driver to pull over. Zeno wasn't too worried about that. There were too many questions that Nick wouldn't have wanted to answer: Why are you here? Why did you lie? What made you come? Who did you expect to meet?

The gate gave and Nick emerged into the street at a run. He looked back towards his hotel. Zeno stood there, silhouetted against the lights, his face in darkness. The two men stood square to one another for a moment.

A ribbon of airborne spray looped across the street at Zeno's back, carrying an arc of rainbow as it broached the seafront lights. The sax slowed down. The bus went past.

Nick seemed to peer at his adversary a second – as if he might discover on the other man's face an expression that would let him know what best to do. The face was dark. Slowly, Nick backed off. Then, like someone issuing an invitation, he turned and began to run slowly into the shadows where the sea wall merged into the cliff.

Zeno tried to read the motion for what it was:

indecision, perhaps; a man too wounded to move quickly or decisively. Or a lure . . . Suddenly it occurred to him that, despite the puzzlement and shock he must be experiencing, Nick might have come up with a plan.

Try for the car, Nick thought. You're not badly hurt. Try for the car. Unfamiliar ground – of course it is. So use the darkness as a cover; darkness and the sound of the sea. Find a way of circling back to the car.

His other thought was, Who the hell is it? *Who?*

His bicep throbbed and he favoured the arm as he ran, holding it low and tensing the muscles from wrist to elbow in order to lessen the shock to the wounded part. The knife was gripped in his usable hand. He loped across the last few feet of paving where the seafront safety rails were embedded in a concrete stanchion and the cliff took over from the wall.

It seemed that as soon as he began to climb, he was in total darkness. The path he was on lay a good five yards back from the cliff's edge, but he couldn't see that. The invisibility of the cropped turf was the invisibility of sea and sky. He could hear the ocean and smell it, too; he could feel the wind battering his cheek. But he ran in blackness; ran through blackness.

A thorn bush whipped his legs. He pitched forward putting out an arm to save himself, and felt the rough crust on his upper arm shift and a sudden posset of blood break from the gash. Zeno heard his cry – scarcely an arm's length away, or so it seemed. With the lights of the town behind both men, the pursuer gained the advantage. Zeno stopped and peered furiously into the dark, as if sheer concentration could summon up his quarry. He saw the faintest of silhouettes, black on a deeper black, rise a short way ahead and his arm snapped back and forth like someone cracking a whip.

Nick stumbled again; a sudden cramp had caused his leg to buckle. He hopped twice in order to give the muscle a chance, then put his foot down, expecting it to hold up.

A razor-line of pain rose from his calf and tore into his groin. He crouched, still hobbling forward, and put his hand to the place. He could feel the knife-haft and soft gouts of blood that came in time with his heartbeat and lapped across his hand.

He dropped the knife he was holding and grabbed the knife in his leg, as if he'd suddenly decided it was the better weapon. The gesture took him off balance and he fell, rolling twenty feet or more down the slope towards the road. When he came to rest he simply held his calf, hard, making a tourniquet with his hands. His mouth was jacked open in a silent scream. The pain went through him in a rush, then came round again. He felt sick and faint. More than anything in the world, he wanted to yell. Yelling would help to let the pain out.

Nick's fist tightened on a clump of grass. He turned over, trying to come up on his knees, and tears fell straight from his eyes on to the back of his hand. He waited. His only advantage was that the fall had taken him off the skyline and out of the faint glow from the town lights. Footsteps ran across the roof of the earth – *spat, spat, spat*, as boot soles hit the skim of mud coating the path. Nick cowered in a cave of darkness and heard them go. Soon there was nothing but the wind and the echo of rollers barging the underhang of the cliff.

He waited a full ten minutes – maybe longer, since he might have passed out briefly; he wasn't sure. He realized that the fall had more or less dislodged the knife – it was hanging at a sharp angle from the muscle in his calf – so he teased it out of the wound, using a thumb and forefinger to lend a lightness of touch. It dropped on to the grass and was instantly lost.

With one hand clamped to the injury, Nick began to move downhill: backside to heels, knees up, then flexing and starting again, like a rower moving the wrong way. From time to time he stopped – either because it hurt more than he could manage, or because his injured leg spasmed so violently that he lost control of it. When he reached the bottom, he stood upright and took a few paces along the road in the direction of the town. His foot squelched in his shoe. He imagined how he must look and could only see, in his mind's eye, a creature boltered with blood. Blood up to the wrist like dye, blood smeared on his face where he'd wiped his tears away, blood soaking his clothes all around the open wounds, and a trail of blood leaking from his heel like an awful snail-track.

He was light-headed, falling into a dream for a moment as he walked. His footsteps seemed to ring in his ears like hammer blows to an anvil; each step a mile; and he heard Louise say, 'We looked everywhere. No-one had seen you.'

Cords of spray in his face brought him round. He'd walked clear of the cliff's shelter and was holding on to one of the guard rails in the sea wall. The wind was still flinging the sea into the street, but the tide was on the ebb. A strip of pebbly beach was visible.

Nick looked towards the hotel and saw his car parked on a patch of asphalt to the left of the entrance doors. Between that point and the place less than two hundred yards away where the cliff began, several flights of steps went down from the sea wall to the beach. One opposite the hotel; another close to where Nick was standing. Up on the seafront, he was visible to anyone. The last thing he wanted was a helping hand, a concerned voice.

He went down the steps in a series of clumsy skips and hops, making it to the shingle in a sudden rush as he missed his footing. In the lee of the wall, he took a breather, leaning against the rough concrete, one hand to his injured leg. The wound in his arm had opened up with the fall, but didn't hurt nearly as much; it was just a wet throb. The streetlamps above him gave enough light to show a clutter of wet rocks and the snaky line of foam where the tide was drawing back.

He fell every few yards or so – not big tumbles, but the rocks were wet and slick with seaweed, and the light was poor. The only method was to walk in an ungainly crouch, his good arm stretched out to take his weight when he next slipped. The skirts of his raincoat were heavy with moisture. Each time he fell, he stopped for a breather; each time the rest grew longer.

He closed his eyes. Louise and Michael were standing at the door as he hobbled towards them, clothes bloody and torn. Louise said, 'We looked everywhere.' She was frowning, and holding Michael's hand as if Nick's appearance threatened the boy in some way.

He realized that he would have to tell Louise where he'd been, and why he'd gone there. He'd have to tell her everything. That was his worst thing: to have to tell.

Between the steps by the cliff and the steps by the hotel, Nick fell more than twenty times. The rhythm of the waves on the shore was the rhythm of his pain – it washed over him with a fierce repetitive pulse, drawing back to his calf and his shoulder in a rasping undertow, then flooding him like black foam. He sat on the bottom-most of the steps that emerged close to the hotel and laid his cheek against the wet wall, needing to cool himself. One hand was in his coat pocket, clutching his car keys as a refugee might grasp some precious keepsake of home.

Gain some strength, he thought. Then climb the steps. Cross the street. It's dark; the street is wet with spray – the buildings are wet. Even if someone is there, my soaked clothes won't appear strange.

Get into the car. Drive slowly away. Get five miles; five miles will be more than enough. Then stop for some preliminary first aid. There's an emergency box in the car – tape, gauze, antiseptic, paracetamol. Then drive home. Drive straight home. Tell Louise everything. Maybe, in the end, it will be a relief to do that.

He drifted into dream again. He was home. It was a mild afternoon, sunlit; through the window, he could see Michael playing on the lawn. He felt OK. His arm and leg still pained him a little, but he was warm and rested and knew that he had made the right choice. Louise sat in the big chintz sofa in their living room, her head canted slightly to one side as he told her about the worst thing.

It seemed she could hear him, though he couldn't hear himself. The words floated from his lips in an appalled silence: for your ears only . . . He got to his feet. Louise said, '*Nick*,' – sharply, reprovingly, and he turned to the sound.

'*Nick!*' And he turned to the sound.

Zeno's hand was flung upwards – hold that pose, watch the birdie. There followed a soft explosion. A sheet of chalk-white magnesium light flared up inches from Nick's face and everything disappeared into the glare. He turned, stumbling on the rocks, arms out like a man struck blind. The world was white. He stared and stared and before him was nothing but blankness, nothing but void, as if someone had wiped his vision off, as if his eyeballs had been peeled.

Something settled on his neck, a flutter, then it crossed. Like when Louise stood behind him to adjust his black tie before they went out to some formal dinner or another. Left over right; one end longer . . . His ears popped as the tie tightened.

A toecap took him at the back of his injured leg and he went down as if to pray. A knee smashed in between his shoulder blades and his head snapped back as Zeno yanked on the garotte.

For a moment, it seemed his sight returned. He could see Louise, her face solemn. Behind her, through the window, Michael was running across the grass. Just for a second; then they were both expunged.

The cord sank in the flesh of his neck. The sea was a vast, enveloping roar that banged in his ears like a barrage. Inch by inch he was being dragged towards it, pulled by a fierce undertow. The pain was everywhere now.

And all he could see was starburst, bomb-blast, flashfire, the heart of light . . .

Three

Every time he sat in a prison cell, Sam Pascoe started to sweat. He would anticipate the fear before he reached the cell itself. Bars behind him sliding back into position with a soft rumble; the trek along bare corridors; then the heavy door with its Judas window. He would go in, sit down, and try to disguise the moment of terror.

This time was the same. A web of moisture formed in his armpits, beads on gossamer, and a tiny seepage ran from the hollow of his throat down to his belly. He didn't speak; he was waiting for the tightness in his chest to disperse. Instead, he busied himself with some papers, taking them out of his briefcase and setting them down on the table as if they had to find a precise order.

He glanced round the cell with lowered eyes – a man trying to find something without seeming to look.

A wooden bench, he thought. Four strong legs, slats on top. A simple construction. It isn't here; it never will be. I'll never see such a thing again. Nonetheless, he looked – as someone will look both ways before crossing an empty road.

He straightened the papers again, and smiled. It just took a minute, then he was fine; the tremor went out of his hands. Anthony Stewart wanted to respond with a smile of his own, but his mouth couldn't find the right shape.

'Well, Tony . . .' Sam had almost forgotten the fear. 'We have a date for the trial. There are a couple of things I want to ask you about: details, you know; possible tripwires.'

Stewart began as if some mechanism had been triggered. He spoke short, choppy sentences, with eccentric pauses. 'I spent that evening at my mother's house. With my mother. I spent . . . I often visit her. Well – once a week . . . I often—'

'The report—' Pascoe cut in. 'The report that someone saw your car that night . . .'

'A mistake. Listen, they know. What time she died. I wasn't there. I was fifty miles away. I go once or twice. A week. Every week. Have done since my father died. I took her some chocolates. Sat with her in her room. The TV's up there. Everything's up there. Fridge. Little oven for warming things through. Magazines and snacks. The telephone. She doesn't use the rest of the house. Not much. We sat up till late. She never sleeps. A nap or two during the day. We ate the chocolates. We watched TV.' The smile came back and fluttered round his face, looking for a place to settle. He said, 'OK?' as if Pascoe might have a little more work to do before he could know the story as well as Stewart himself.

Pascoe read out the licence number of Stewart's car and the time at which it was seen. Stewart shook his head. He was sitting on his hands, like a schoolboy.

'You can ask my mother,' he said. 'Anyone can ask her.'

Pascoe had already done that. A day nurse had taken him upstairs. Amy Stewart had been sitting up in bed to watch TV. A woolly fug of body smells and cooking residue clogged the corners of the room. The windows were shut tight.

'He comes every week,' she'd said. Her eyes hadn't strayed from the TV screen. 'Anything to get away from that bitch of a wife.'

Pascoe slotted the papers back into his briefcase. Stewart stood up and followed him to the door, then held out a hand, a man at his own front door offering farewell to the last guest to leave: Good to see you. Thanks for coming. Take care . . .

A green Volvo had been appropriating Pascoe's parking space of late. He had left a note on the windscreen a couple of times, but to no effect. His office was in a glass stump – ten storeys that took the light but gave none back; a dull gold tint on all sides. You always felt eyes on you, whether people were looking out or not.

Five minutes later he was standing behind that copper sheen, invisible, resting his forehead against the glass wall of his office and staring out at the dull city view. A line of cars idled on one of the main thoroughfares, stretching as far as he could see, each windscreen glossed by the low afternoon sun. Like Pascoe, the drivers were hidden beneath the glow. The line jerked forward, rolled a few yards, then stopped.

'You saw him again. What do you think now?'

Pascoe had heard George Roxborough come in, but hadn't bothered to turn. He said, 'Who drives a green Volvo?'

'What?' Roxborough joined him by the glass wall.

'Does anyone in these Chambers drive a green Volvo?'

'I don't think so, no.'

'Good.' The glass beneath Pascoe's forehead had grown warm with contact. He shifted slightly and found a cooler patch. 'Do you fancy Stewart?'

'Take the case on?' Roxborough had wanted it from the outset. Murder with a margin of doubt. A door, booted off its hinges; jewellery taken, and some loose cash; the whole house reeking with blood, the walls striped with it, the ceilings stippled with it, furniture drenched by it; and then, in the bedroom where the flow ended, Mrs Anthony Stewart awash in it. It felt good to Roxborough. In Chambers, the betting was Stewart at 3–1. Roxborough had already taken the bet; why not take the client too?

'Because?' he asked.

'Personal, George.'

Roxborough didn't ask for more. Pascoe was famous for it. One theory was that he had to see out periods of crippling depression – could feel the onset and would go away to weather the storm. Another theory was that he drank. Now and then a bender, and nothing he could do to

28

stop it. Everyone knew the reason. Or thought they did.

Well . . . There had been terrible depressions. There had been nightmarish binges. Sometimes the one came first, sometimes the other. And, in truth, there didn't seem a lot of difference between them. Black holes that drew everything in – light, music, joy, any kind of pleasure in any kind of activity, good thoughts, good memories, ambition, hope for the future . . . Drew them in, and himself along with them, so deep that it seemed he would suffocate, go blind, go deaf, go mad for lack of light. Long ago, he had found his own definition of depression – endless pain in endless darkness.

It happened less and less now. Mostly, it was a sweat bead along the backbone and a tremor in the hand as he approached the cell, or a sudden, hard pain under the heart when he opened his front door on to silence.

George Roxborough was looking for the catch. 'What? He's changing his plea?'

'No. He's telling the same story.'

'His aged mother still says the same?'

'His aged mother still says the same.'

'But the police have his confession.'

'A metaphor.'

'What?' Roxborough's question was borne on a tiny plume of laughter.

Pascoe delivered the explanation in the manner of the accused: 'All that blood. When I found her. I'd never loved her. I felt guilty. As if my lack of love. Had killed her.' A tight stutter, tuneless and thin. In his own voice he said, '*As if* . . . A metaphor: you see?'

If Roxborough did see, he wasn't prepared to say so. 'Will the mother testify?'

'Can hardly wait.'

'Is she credible? Will she hold up? How does she sound?' It was three times the same question.

'Don't worry, George.' Pascoe provided the answer: 'She's safe enough.'

A fat man in a beige suit puffed up to the Volvo. He was

carrying a box; the lettering on the outside told the world that he'd bought state of the art in CD players. He opened the tailgate, then paused for breath. When he'd loaded the box he re-locked the car and walked away.

'Did he do it?' Roxborough asked.

Pascoe had left the window. He was sitting at his desk flipping through the Yellow Pages.

Roxborough was puzzled. 'What are you looking for?'

'Found it.' Pascoe put the straight edge of a ruler alongside the page and tore, then laid the ruler at right angles and tore again, removing a half-page box ad. He said, 'Yes. He did it.'

Roxborough said, 'Maybe I could talk to you over the weekend. Go through the statements and some of the evidence; take a look at what the prosecution's got.' He paused, as if Pascoe were refusing payment for some small professional favour. 'You're sure?'

'He's yours, George. Enjoy him. Not the weekend.'

'You're going away . . .'

'Leaving in about ten minutes.' Pascoe had found a large sheet of cartridge paper in his desk drawer and was stapling the display ad at the centre to give it proper prominence. He seemed absorbed by the task.

'Why?' Roxborough thought it best to be specific: 'Did he kill her?'

'He'll stick to his story, George; and his mother will stick to hers. You'll get him off; it's a cinch.'

'No, it's not; but I'll have it anyway.' A pause. 'Tell me why.'

Pascoe laid the stapler flat to the paper and whacked the spring-loaded handle; then he held the mounted ad up for inspection. 'Well, there'd be lots of theories, George. A moment of blind rage; a need for change; a rush of shit to the brain. All the same thing, really.'

'Why do *you* think he did it?'

Pascoe smoothed a couple of wrinkles out of the torn yellow page. 'I think his mother told him to.'

★   ★   ★

George Roxborough took the Stewart file with him when he left. Pascoe swung his chair round to face the wall. In one hand he held a page from a newspaper, in the other a letter.

The news clipping said that the body of a man had been found on rocks at the sea's edge and that the man had been identified as Nicholas Howard. It gave Nick's address, said he was married, and mentioned that he had a son, aged four. It also mentioned that he had been murdered.

Because it was a local paper, the story had taken the full front page under a twenty-two point headline. Pascoe had obtained the paper after seeing a report in a national journal; there, the death had been dispensed with in a short paragraph. Centre-page was a picture of Nick, a reconstituted snapshot. He had a moustache. Pascoe thought it looked silly – as if Nick were out to impress.

He reread the letter. It mentioned a name: Lori. It made reference to the past. It contained a story – briefly told – that Pascoe had heard before, and had hoped never to have to hear again. It asked him to go to the Palings, a hotel close to the ocean some six hours' drive away, and wait there for a telephone call.

The newspaper report told him that Nick's body had been dumped by the tide on a rocky inlet. He was pretty badly mashed by the wave action against the rocks, and he'd been in the water a few days, but it was still possible to see the stab wounds in his upper arm and his calf, and the strange torque effect of the ligature marks on his neck, dark like a trace of rot in fruit.

Pascoe knew he would have to go. All that was strong in his life, all that compelled him, came from the past. His life, day to day, didn't interest him much; the past had a fierce power. He almost never had a dream that was puzzling to him. He knew who the people were; he remembered the events. Each dream made perfect sense: each little playlet of betrayal, of loss, of unspeakable horror, of death. As the images began, he would be drawn back, screaming silently, as a lost swimmer is drawn into the undertow. All the places were known to him. All the faces were known to him – the desperate eyes, the mouths howling in the dark.

Lori. He saw her in close-up, though she didn't know he was watching. Tear-tracks where her make-up had run; she came into the bedroom, her skirt caught up like an apron to hold all the pills.

He remembered a big room, a loft. One of them had said, 'Someone I love could be dying at this very moment.' A game of worst things.

He put the clipping and the letter in an inside pocket, carefully, as if the most important thing was to put them out of sight.

He wondered who had killed Nick Howard. He wondered why.

The sun was weak, almost below the rooftops. The tint on the glass walls was a dull, ochre sludge. Pascoe opened the boot of his car and rummaged round in the small tool box he kept there. Finally, he came up with a tube of Locktite. Reversing the cartridge paper, he smeared the entire contents of the tube on to it. Then he walked over to the Volvo, gripping his homemade poster by the tips of the uppermost corners, and pasted it carefully on to the driver's side of the windscreen, taking care to ensure that it was completely flat and wrinkle-free.

The cars trickled forward, a sluggish flow of hardware, noise and stench. By the time Pascoe had filtered in among them, the cartridge paper was welded to the Volvo's windscreen like a steel plate. The Yellow Pages ad stapled to it showed a smiling mechanic holding out a telephone: BLACKSTONE GARAGE – EXHAUSTS: BATTERIES: TYRES: REPLACEMENT WINDSCREENS.

It was risky – of course it was – to go to the inlet where Nick's body had been found, but Zeno couldn't resist the impulse. Still, the police had finished their work three days before; he reasoned that he was more likely to be seen by ghoulish sensation seekers.

In the event, no-one was there. Maybe the weather didn't suit them.

There was a thin chill in the wind. It whickered round the headland and pushed breakers across the mouth of the inlet. Zeno clambered towards the sea until he came to a big V-shaped cleft between two damson-coloured boulders. One was smooth and long with an arched back like a cat's. The other reared up, it's broad bulk curving seawards; in the early light, it had the appearance of an elephant seal pushing through the surf. Zeno had no way of knowing, but he felt sure that this was where Nick's body had jammed, face up, arms wide, pleading for discovery.

He sat astride the cat's back and worried at how things had gone wrong. Some mistake he'd made? Or some freak event? Nick had floated back like a scrap of malicious gossip. If Zeno had known the one detail that the police had decided not to reveal, he would have been closer to an answer. A mistake, a freak event – both these things, and some bad luck.

The blue clinker-built boat had put to sea that night with Zeno and Nick aboard. Nick's body had been under a tarpaulin at the back of the plank-and-awning wheelhouse. Zeno had made a long curve, holding a steady course to follow the line of the bay. Beyond the point, he caught the heel of the wind, and the little craft had stalled, shuddering; the gale had banged on its timbers, as if great doors were being slammed all along the hull.

Zeno had swung the prow into the weather and locked the wheel, then hauled Nick to the side. Nylon cord lashed his wrists to a concrete land anchor – sailor's knots round the deeply set iron ring. Nick went first, trailing over the side like badly wrapped ballast. Then Zeno got both hands to the land anchor and made a dead lift, raising his knee to take the weight; a squat and press brought it on to his shoulder. Nick's bulk hauled him seawards, and in the same moment the little craft rolled in the swell. Zeno was running when he hit the side. He felt his feet lift and for a moment saw nothing but blackness – the night was so dark, the ocean so dark – and heard nothing but the roar of wind and wave. The anchor flew away into the blackness and Nick rose like a big fish hooked hard, then was gone.

Zeno put about and ploughed back towards the lights of the town. He wouldn't return to harbour: even on a night like this, he wasn't inclined to take the chance. He'd anchor in one of the sheltered coves along the coast and chug back late the next morning.

He noticed that the concrete had left rough grazes on his hands, little puckers of skin in white lines; they stung. He would bathe his hands in warm salt water, then smooth in lots of lanolin. Zeno looked after his hands, as any craftsman might take good care of the tools of his trade.

Zeno's mistake – with Nick – had been dropping him where he did; in theory, well out to sea, but in fact close to a bar that shelved up before dropping away to the beach. The bad luck was the weather; in calmer conditions, he might have taken more notice of charts and landmarks. The freak event came two days later.

The land anchor had swung down to the shelf, trawling Nick in its wake. It had scraped along, dragged by the undersea currents, and Nick had followed, his arms arrowed towards the anchor, wrists lashed, ankles lashed – a perfect shape for swimming. Finally, the anchor had settled; it lay in calmer water, wagging to and fro, with Nick's body floating above it, echoing the motion. His hair wafted like weed. His eyes were plump and white; they stared off into the black fathoms as if some deep mystery lay there that concentration could unravel. All things being equal, he was set to stare at that mystery until sea creatures had picked him over to the bare bone. Two days later, a pleasure craft killed its engines directly overhead. That was the freak event.

Two girls and a man – just visitors and just having fun. They dropped anchor on to Nick's legs, fouling the rope that bound them. They played some music and drank a few beers. One of the girls unpacked tuna steaks and a salad.

An hour later, they raised anchor and left. The man had felt the resistance as he cranked the winch – gathering in the anchor-chain as the links straightened and rose from the water; then it went; the chain dipped and wound on smoothly.

Underwater, Nick's body had grown taut between the land anchor and the sea anchor. He looked like a pennant flying in a stiff breeze. The sea anchor had lifted him almost to the vertical and the ratchet slowed for a moment. The tendons in Nick's wrists stretched and the skin concertinaed against the rope. For a few seconds, nothing happened. Then Nick's hands popped off the wristbone, still tethered to the iron ring. The ragged wrist-ends with their spikes of bone rose beseechingly, and he turned over twice, shaking the pleasure boat's anchor.

For the rest of the day, Nick drifted with the current. Fish nudged and bumped him, pausing to feed. That night, rolled and shoved by the tide, he came to the inlet. A wave dumped him between the cat's back and the seal. Water poured off him like a drawn curtain and there he was, in the dawn light, staring inland with empty eye-sockets, his wrist-bones white as tusks.

That was the detail the police hadn't released. It was something that might allow them to tell a false confession from a true one, or let them know the same man was at work if more such killings occurred. One theory, of course, was that the hands had been removed to prevent fingerprints being taken; though since Nick's pockets held ample identification, it wasn't a theory that held up for long.

The signs of Nick's murder were as clear as the day. No-one considered that the loss of his hands might have been an accident.

Zeno was depressed. Things were a muddle. He'd sent a

letter to Sam Pascoe and another to Sophie Lanner. Now Nick's murder had been reported. Of course, there was a strong chance that neither Sam nor Sophie knew. Even so, the possibility made him edgy.

He'd been sure that they would all come in time; curiosity would draw them. But Nick's death would make them afraid, and fear would keep them away.

A natural funnel in the rocks suddenly filled with water that soaked his shoes. When he looked left and right, he saw that the tide had drawn round him, covering lower-lying sections of beach on either side. He got down from his perch and splashed through ankle-deep water to the tideline, then walked a mile along the cliff path to the place where he'd parked his car.

Now it was time to go home to Carla. She wouldn't ask where he'd been or what he'd been doing; she never did that. Their life together was based on mutual love, mutual trust. For Zeno, it was a new life, a miraculous life. And, in truth, everything he had done – everything he ever did – was for her.

Four

Sam Pascoe arrived at the Palings at nine-thirty. He could hear the ocean, but couldn't see it. From a headland five miles away came the flash and fade of a lighthouse. Pascoe sat by the window and watched it until the compulsion of counting off the seconds from beam to beam grew too irksome.

There had been seven of them in the group: himself, Luke Mallen, Charlie Singer, Nick Howard, Sophie Lanner, Marianne Novaks, Susan Hart. They'd all been about the same age – late teens or early twenties in 1970. Sophie and Marianne had been the youngest – both still at college. The rest were starting out on careers, though none of them took it too seriously. It was the seventies: they listened to music a lot, they talked feverishly about revolution, they made a case for taking drugs, and took them.

They were all friends of Charlie Singer, that's how the group had formed. Charlie had a private income from somewhere. It enabled him to have a flat: a place to hang out. Charlie's loft was where they'd played the game of worst things. Sometimes, other people would drift in and out of the circle, but the seven remained constant. Now and then there were lovers among them; now and then not. Sex was no big deal: they were all friends. They slept together, they listened to music together, they took trips together – and often that was what they liked to do best. A tab of acid would see the night away; a profusion of dreams; things they might have done, might not have done –no-one could remember. One time they all had a memory of having been to the ocean, but none of them could say for sure it wasn't a dream. Maybe someone had mentioned the sea, or described the sea, and they'd all gone there in imagination. Charlie's car was low on fuel the next day, so who could tell?

Thinking about it all, Pascoe suddenly experienced a rush of *déjà vu*. He was lying in a corner of Charlie Singer's loft next to a girl, though he didn't know who she was. Brilliantly coloured butterflies were hovering on a silk drape, their wings slowly stirring. They were so close, so detailed, that he could see the dusting of dark powder on their backs. The iridescent peacock whorls on their wings fixed his eye; they seemed to shrink and grow and glow in the dim light.

The girl smiled a wet, pink, wraparound smile. She knelt up, disturbing the sky, and the butterflies lifted off in a slow shirring of wings, shedding soft grey particles, heady as pollen. She unbuttoned her blouse and shrugged it off. When her breasts fell free, they seemed, to Pascoe, to cast a faint, warm glow. They were flecked with butterfly dust.

She stretched to shuffle off her jeans; and then she crouched over him and laughed. The sound had a rich, echoing resonance that turned in the curl of his ear. She took his hand, which was light and riddled with nerve-endings, a nest of live wires, and drew it into her groin. He stroked her between the legs and felt everything, saw everything, tasted everything, smelt everything, as if his fingertips were all sensation.

She took hours to remove his clothes, days to lower herself on to him, sinking and sinking as if she were fathomless. Her breath on his face made him feverish. Then she drew back, sitting upright, spreading, until they were coupled so deeply that he touched her at the quick.

He opened his eyes, swimming back from raw sensation, and saw her above him, flat belly, lean waist, her ribcage jutting, her whole torso stretching up, reaching up, breasts hard and lifted, arms above her head, her face in darkness. He thought she grew from him like a tree.

At that moment, the acid dream had fallen away and

he'd seen everything clearly. The silk shawl draped on the back of a screen; the embroidered butterflies that seemed to flutter and settle as light caught the rich material; the girl above him, rocking back and forth, eyes closed, bound up in her own pleasure and the drug's wild clutter of images.

He'd heard laughter from beyond the screen, and music, and a light played liquid shapes across the ceiling. For just that instant, he remembered, everything had been pin clear. Then he was tripping again, floating, growing inside the girl like a great tap root while she swayed above him, branches and arms and leaves and hair.

Pascoe was dizzy with recollection. He closed his eyes and opened them again to try to check the sensation. The girl – who had it been? Marianne, he thought, or Susan. Yes, probably Sue. He went to the window and counted revolutions of the lighthouse beam – something mundane to slow him down.

He reached the low thirties, and stopped counting. His eyes were fixed, his mouth slack, as if he were in the first stage of a trance. The phone rang three times before he noticed it.

'Sam?' The voice was low – not quite a whisper. Pascoe struggled to recognize it. 'Sam . . .'

'You sent me a letter?' A half-question.

'That's right.'

'And you want – what? Money? Is that it?'

'Money?' The word was returned to him broken-backed. Because it was a whisper, Pascoe couldn't tell whether the speaker was insulted or amused. 'No, Sam, not money.'

'Do I know you?'

'We had a mutual friend.'

'Who?'

'Lori Cosgrove.' Pascoe didn't respond. 'I thought we ought to have a talk about Lori. About what happened to her.'

'To what end?' Pascoe said, and realized at once how pompous the phrase sounded – lawyer-speak.

This time there was no mistaking the voice's amusement: little, throaty huffs of laughter, then a mincing version of Pascoe's tone. 'To what *end*? Well, let's see . . . To the end of guilt, perhaps. To the end of remorse. To the end of loose ends. To a satisfactory end.'

'For whom?'

'For wh*oooom*?' The voice parodied him again. 'Well, for me, of course.'

'So it is about money.'

'If you want to think so.' Something there – something Pascoe knew but couldn't fix on. The controlled whisper drained the colour and tone from the voice, leaving it featureless. Pascoe wondered if a surprise would make the caller forget himself, and was tempted to make a sudden mention of Nick's death, to see what that would do. Not a good idea, he decided; it might be his only advantage. Best to let it be thought that he knew nothing.

'Do you want to meet, or what?' Pascoe tried for a tone of weary impatience.

'Sure. Of course. Pop round. I'll be here.'

Pascoe had already decided that if there was to be a meeting, he'd insist on a place of his choosing. Neutral ground. He said, 'There's a bar just a few doors down from this hotel. Half an hour from now.' He hung up before he could hear any objections, then immediately took the phone off the hook.

If it wasn't money, what else could it be? Someone who knew about Lori Cosgrove . . . Pascoe had never told anyone. But there had been six other people involved. How many times had they shared the burden? How many others had heard about the worst thing – husbands and wives perhaps, lovers and children, friends, therapists, priests . . . ? If it wasn't money . . . But then why was Nick Howard dead?

Pascoe looked at the telephone lying on the bedside table; a loose end. He fell on to the bed and closed his eyes. Out of the darkness behind his eyelids, he saw Lori, her skirt bunched to hold the pills. She had emptied every bottle she could find. Treasure trove. They were among trees on a warm night – all seven of them. You could hear the cascade of night wind through the leaves. Marianne Novaks reached for the field glasses. She said, 'Let me see.' Pascoe remembered the intense clarity of the moment; the drug had made everything vivid and slow.

He slept, briefly, his face close to the bedside table and the silenced phone. In his dream, Marianne handed back the glasses and said, 'Look . . .'

When he focused, the curtains were drawn in Lori's window. Then they parted with a theatrical flourish and there stood Lori, cheeks rouged and powdered, a broad band of penny-sized freckles over her nose, springy plaits jutting from either side of her head. She had gathered her gingham pinafore into a hammock and tilted it to show a profusion of chocolate bars. She smiled a gappy smile that made Pascoe want to laugh. He was laughing when he woke.

The room had grown cold. He felt stiff, as if the soft sea air had got to his joints. The telephone lay in his line of vision so he lifted it and stretched to replace it.

The voice said, 'Sam . . . Sam . . .' Still there; the man had never hung up, so when Pascoe took the phone off the hook, the line had remained open.

'Were you laughing or crying, Sam?' He had listened to Pascoe's sleep and Pascoe's dream.

'Sam . . .' Dead leaves in an eddy of wind; a husk; a dry whisper.

When he got to the bar, he was one of four, including the barman. A man and a woman were sitting in a booth by a window, staring at the glass like travellers on a train watching the landscape slip by. All they could see was their own reflection.

Pascoe sat at the bar in order to be visible. He ordered a whisky and a beer, side by side, and angled himself so that

the door was directly in his eye-line. He was thirsty: the
beer went down in a couple of long swallows. He sipped
the whisky; after a while he ordered another and drank it
slowly. He watched the door, feeling he might lose
advantage if his concentration slipped.

Nondescript music was filtering into the bar like bad
air. Beneath that, Pascoe could hear an intermittent drone.
After a while, he realized that it came from the couple by
the window. They were talking to one another, but
looking at each other's reflection in the window, as if
anything more intimate would be too great a risk.

The barman said, 'Are you Sam Pascoe?'

Sam put his glass down too heavily and gave an
involuntary laugh. Famous for a moment. The well-
known Sam Pascoe spotted in a bar in the little coastal
town of Longrock. He said, 'You've got a message for me.'
It wasn't a question.

'An address,' the barman said. He gave Pascoe a slip of
paper and told him how to find the road.

'Who left the message?'

The man shrugged. 'Someone called. Just to say that he
couldn't make it – that he'd see you later.'

'How did he identify me?'

The barman seemed to take an interest in Pascoe for the
first time. 'Something wrong?'

'No, just curious. How did you know me?'

'He said I *wouldn't* know you.' Pascoe didn't understand. The other man lifted a hand as if to indicate the bar
and, beyond it, the town. 'I know everyone else.'

Pascoe put the slip of paper in his pocket. He said,
'Why didn't you tell me before – when I first came in?'

'He said there was no hurry. He said to let you have a
few drinks.'

'You know him well?' Pascoe asked. 'My friend?'

'I don't think so.' The barman shook his head slowly. 'I
didn't recognize the voice.'

There was a three-quarter moon behind thin scarves of

dark cloud. Pascoe let a bus go by, then crossed the street and leaned on the sea wall, supported by his forearms, hands clasped. He might have been offering a prayer for guidance. He could see a line of white, fifty feet off, as the waves tipped on to the shore and drew back with a low hiss.

Do it, he thought. What is there to lose?

The barman's directions were good; no chance of getting lost. A road on the edge of the town; a house that stood on its own, all its windows dark. Pascoe laughed out loud. 'Jesus,' he said, 'what a set-up. I'm not going in there.'

He walked down a short path to the front door. There was enough light from the streetlamps to show that it stood at a slight angle, inviting him. He took a few paces to the right and looked in through a window. The room he saw was bare to the floorboards.

He stepped inside. The bang of the front door as it closed echoed along the hallway, then more distantly in rooms beyond. He waited. No-one came. He went from room to room, and each of them was empty. Upstairs, all the doors were closed save one. A finger of buttery light fell into the stairwell.

What am I supposed to do? Pascoe thought. I know what drew me here, but not what drew me so *far*. The town, the hotel, the phone call, the bar, this house . . . Each a logical step, but each one stranger than the last. You take one step and then you take another. How do you know when to back off? And now I'm standing outside this room in an empty house and expecting to die.

When he went in, the glow was candles, and a table was set for one. Alongside the place setting was a bottle of Chablis on ice. The cork had been drawn and a linen napkin draped over the neck. The ice-bucket was wrapped in a pale membrane of dew.

A plate with a thin golden rim was covered with smoked salmon. Elsewhere on the table: bread, a crisp salad, a camellia in a narrow vase. The centrepiece was a tape-recorder.

Pascoe looked round the room. Apart from the table and a chair, there was only a tall pine cabinet in one corner – an old-fashioned wardrobe, he reasoned, since this had obviously been a bedroom. He felt edgy with his back to the door, so he crossed the room swiftly and opened the cabinet. It smelt faintly musty: the mildew of old clothes; but it was empty now.

He sat in the chair, because that way he could face the door. Or you could leave, he thought. With the food in front of him, he felt a sudden rush of hunger – saliva swamping his jaw. He pressed the play button on the tape-recorder, wincing as he did it. No explosion came, if that's what he'd expected. Just the voice, as before; husky, slow of speech.

'I'm sorry to do this to you, Sam. A device . . . It probably seems silly to you – a bit elaborate? But I couldn't meet you in the bar. Surely you see that? The things we have to talk about demand a meeting place that's a little more discreet. No? Also, I guess it's by way of a test. You wonder if I'm going to ask you for money – a sort of withdrawal against my collateral. The collateral being Lori; being what happened to Lori . . . Well, perhaps I am. I just wanted to make sure that we'd be alone when we met. So – I'll have watched you come here, watched you go into the house; and I'll have satisfied myself that you came alone. If you've done that once, then, of course, you'll do it again. And I bet you did; I bet you came alone. Lori is too much of a secret to share, I know that.

'Give yourself a glass of the Chablis, Sam. Have you tried the smoked salmon? You've come a long way. You must be hungry.' The laugh came again, hoarse, a whisper of mirth. 'You don't have to worry. The food's good. There's nothing wrong with the food.'

Pascoe found himself pouring a glass of wine. He put the bottle back amid the ice and lifted his fork – then replaced it.

'The thing is, Sam, it's a little late now, don't you think? Maybe we've done as much as we can do today. It's

44

the weekend. Why hurry things? So I'll see you here tomorrow. Eight o'clock – would that suit you? Eight tomorrow evening. We can talk then. Is that—'

Pascoe reached out and hit the stop button violently. Christ, he thought, I'm being given the runaround. He laughed in anger and the candle flames hopped. What game is this? Why not just: twenty grand in a locked briefcase, leave it at the hotel in the following fictional name and go away for ever. Then your secret's safe. Until the next time.

Someone I know? Or simply someone who knows about me? And knew about Nick . . . so probably knows about the others. If I stick around long enough, will they all show up in Longrock like some sort of gruesome convention?

Without knowing he was doing it, Pascoe took a sip of wine and followed it with a mouthful of smoked salmon. He registered the after-taste and sat still, waiting for the convulsions to start. After a moment he drank some more, then topped up his glass. He put some salad on to his plate.

At one point he looked round, seeming to be momentarily taken aback by his surroundings – as if he'd woken only to find that he had entered the dream he'd been dreaming. Then he laughed and shook his head.

In a strange town, in a house stripped bare, in the complete stillness of an upper room, Pascoe sat alone eating his supper by candle-light.

Not far away, Zeno sat with Carla, enjoying a meal that she had prepared. She was a wonderful cook: of course she was; nothing about her was less than wonderful. She had made liver, with little dumplings to soak up the gravy. Zeno lowered his face to the plate and sniffed the deep, nutty tang of the meat, then raised his eyes to Carla's and smiled a wolfish smile. He looked like a tracker who had just crossed a promising spoor.

The house was in woodland above the ocean. Some

nights, they could feel the tremor of breakers in the roof timbers, as if their bedroom was far out to sea. They would make love – everything he wanted, everything he'd taught her – and then he might lie awake, watching her face while she slept, wondering how something so perfect, so fragile, could be preserved from harm.

Carla stood behind him to fill his glass. With the other hand, she stroked his face. She spoke his name as if calling a blessing on the food.

Zeno closed his eyes and the moment overwhelmed him. He began to cry: happy that he owned what he owned, fearful that some quirk of luck might take it from him. Carla drew his head back, cupping his jaw, and his tears ran into her hands.

She stood close; he leaned back on to her. The little paroxysm of his weeping shuddered between her hip bones and she knew it was joy, pure joy, and fear of loss.

Pascoe was leaving. He didn't know whether to snuff the candles – as if there was a right thing to do. He decided to leave them burning.

He returned from the door on an afterthought and pressed the tape-recorder's play button.

The voice said, '. . . OK, Sam?' Just that. Pascoe waited for several minutes, but the tape spooled on in silence.

Five

Longrock had once been a fishing village – a harbour, a few houses close to the shoreline, others lining a couple of narrow streets that wound steeply upwards towards farm-land. You could find those pictures in books – sepia tones of boats on the foreshore; of the harbour just after a catch of fish had been landed. Men with Ahab beards and calico shirts mended nets; women in long aprons and cotton bonnets stood in line at trestle tables, fish in one hand, gutting-knife in the other.

No-one remembered those days. The place had grown, but hadn't really prospered. There was no fishing any longer . . . a little farming. Most of the people who lived there worked in bigger, noisier, richer towns nearby. Young people drifted away looking for signs of life in the cities and never came back. Each evening, the streets were near-deserted.

The town had shops and bars and one cinema and, up on the hill, set in its own grounds, a hospital for the mad.

There had been a time when families might come to spend a brief holiday in the town – staying at the Palings perhaps, or one of the other hotels that offered a sea view. Not now. Five miles up the coast, just a little way inland from the lighthouse, investors had built a complex of hotels, a marina, a shopping mall, a Water Funland under a vast geodesic dome, tennis courts and a nine-hole golf course. Between them, the hotels offered a casino, an olympic-sized pool, three banks, beauty parlours, con-ference facilities . . . Out there on the headland was everything anyone could want. Well, almost everything.

You'd see a stream of taxis, some nights, bringing hookers ordered up by the conventioneers. The hookers came from one of the bigger towns nearby. They worked by the hour and added their cab fares and travelling time as a surcharge.

Wallace Ellwood was always happy to pay whatever they asked. He covered the cost on expenses; and, anyway, if his appetite for girls was large, his appetite for food was correspondingly slight. His restaurant and room service bills were small; no-one had ever queried his expenditure.

He always stayed at the Windrush – the smallest of the hotels. People knew him there. They thought he was a businessman with interests in the area that had to be checked on from time to time. In a manner of speaking, he was. The doorman, the desk clerk and the night porter turned a blind eye to the girls who found their way to his room; there was always a hefty tip when he left. Privately, they considered he was just a little . . . well . . . greedy; but what the hell? If it's tax-deductible . . .

Ellwood got out of the shower and wiped a hand over the film of steam on the bathroom mirror. He stepped on to the scales, though he knew what the result would be. His weight hadn't shifted more than a pound since his early twenties. He was stick thin. You couldn't have tweaked the flesh up anywhere on his frame. But it wasn't an attractive body – hairless and slick from the shower, he resembled something that had lost its shell. The skin bore a greyish tinge, dull, as if it would dry to an ashy roughness. His hair was gun-metal, a long widow's peak that lay pasted to his head by shower-water. He liked that effect, and would get it again, later, with gel. His face was long, just as his body was long – bony nose and a small mouth.

From the bedroom came the clink of a fork on china. He felt himself stir and dropped a hand to cup his balls. He enjoyed his trips to Longrock. Clean air, ocean views, time out from the stress of city life . . . A little business satisfactorily concluded. Things had grown somewhat trickier of late, but then what was life without the occasional difficulty to spice it?

Again, the clink of a fork; then a coffee cup lifted and set down. How exciting it was, that . . . *availability*. He glanced at the mirror, steam cooling on it now, his image warped by running moisture, and watched himself grow hard.

The girl didn't look round when he walked into the bedroom. She was sitting at a table, dressed in his gown, and concentrating on her room service order – juice, coffee, a slice of melon, toast, hash browns and scrambled eggs. The client pays for the client's ways.

Ellwood went to stand beside her – so close that, when she did turn, her lips almost brushed the tip of his cock. She looked up at his face, then down again. Ellwood stroked her hair, then extended the gesture so that his hand lay on the nape of her neck. His fingers tightened, just a fraction, and he moved a step closer.

'Busy day, honey,' Ellwood said. 'No time for a proper breakfast . . .' He cupped the back of her head. Crumbs of egg lay in the corners of her mouth. '. . . just a snack.'

Sam Pascoe went back to the house that morning; with him was a young man who wore a rash of acne and a small, gold ear-ring. Pascoe had tried each of the town's three estate agencies. The last one was the right one.

The young man's name was Davenport. He was concerned about the loss of the 'For Sale' sign. 'It's been empty for a while,' he said. 'People aren't moving into this town, they're moving out.' He unlocked the front door and ushered Pascoe in. 'Wish it was me,' he said. 'Wish I was moving out.'

The rooms seemed larger by day, and shabbier. There were patches of damp; here and there a handspan of scabby plaster. One of the windows was broken.

'The town's dying, you know? It's dying street by street.' Davenport seemed taken by the image. 'Building by building,' he said. 'We could do you a deal on this property, you know? The vendor's keen to sell.'

'Who's that?'

'Some retired guy.' A shrug. 'Used to come here for the sailing. Offloaded his boat, too. Place is too quiet even for a retired guy, you know? Wanna look upstairs now?'

Go back to that little restaurant, back to the place where you first met . . . The gloom of candle-light, soft shadows, cold wine. You spoke in whispers, sometimes half-heard, because what you were saying, what you were hearing, was too risky for absolute clarity. The place might have been full, but you seemed the only ones there. Secrets went to and fro, not always understood. Go back next day in the morning. It's cold, like a barn. A clutter of tables and chairs, stale smoke, the whining roar of a vacuum cleaner.

The room was bare apart from the big pine cupboard. Pascoe opened it and found a card table inside, folded up. It didn't seem big enough for candles, plates, salad, ice-bucket, tape-recorder . . . The window was curtainless. He could see the curve of the sea wall and a black acreage of water.

Davenport wandered in to join him. He opened and closed the pine cupboard. 'Left behind . . .' he said. 'What business are you in?'

'Law,' Pascoe told him. 'I'm a lawyer.'

'Not thinking of setting up shop in Longrock?'

'I'd be buying the place for my mother.'

'Retirement,' Davenport said. 'Thought so.'

'Can you phone from here?' Pascoe asked him.

'What?'

'Could I make a telephone call from here?'

'You want to call someone?'

'No. Is the phone connected?'

Davenport shrugged. 'Who knows?' he said. 'Seen enough, or what?'

They walked back towards the ocean with a thin drizzle blowing into their faces – rain so light that the wind lifted and curled it, like smoke. Pascoe said, 'You couldn't let me have the key?'

'Take a second look?' Davenport guessed.

'That's right. I'll get it back to you tomorrow morning.'

'I've got others, you know?' The key was linked to a plaque with a freepost number on it. 'Turn it in before you leave.'

'OK. I'll probably be gone tomorrow.'

'Wish I could say the same. I go this way.'

They paused before parting. Pascoe said, 'Why don't you?'

'Oh, yeah,' Davenport said, 'I'll be there. Pretty soon, now. Up to the city. More money there, you know? More style, more speed. Plenty of girls. Plenty of stuff to do.' He looked edgy, as if already the bus was leaving without him. 'Sure, I'll be up there. Soon as I get set.'

'I understand,' Ellwood said. 'I understand why you did it.'

'Do you? Good.' It made Zeno edgy to have Ellwood in the house. Carla had gone out for a while. 'A business meeting,' Zeno had said. She'd seen Ellwood before – he was part of the lie that Zeno told her; but Zeno preferred that they meet at Ellwood's hotel, or maybe in the little ornamental park in the middle of town.

The lie was this: Zeno's parents had died leaving him a large, invested capital sum. Ellwood was the family lawyer; he advised and oversaw the investment. Now and then, they would meet to discuss a change in the portfolio. Zeno might have to sign some papers. Zeno felt safe with the lie, even though he knew that Carla loved him too much ever to doubt him.

Ellwood said, 'I understand because I know how you feel about Carla.'

'Don't mention her,' Zeno said. 'Don't talk about her.'

'But, listen: you have to be careful. Do you want some coffee?' Ellwood made the offer as if Zeno were the guest.

'What are you telling me?'

Ellwood got up and went into the kitchen; when Zeno joined him he was pulling things out of a cupboard, looking for filter papers. He said, 'It's enough. OK?'

'You don't—'

Ellwood turned, swiftly, and his hand knocked against the stacked contents of a cupboard shelf. Cans clattered to the floor along with a packet of rice that split, shedding grains towards the four corners of the room. 'Look,' he said, 'it's all right. Do as you please. No-one minds. I don't mind. But not now.' He found the filter papers and put one into the compartment above the coffee jug. 'How long have you been in Longrock?'

'Six months.'

'Right. A couple of months should do it; a couple more. It's a slow process. Let's just keep our minds clear till then, OK? After that . . .' Ellwood shrugged.

Zeno said, 'It was an accident. I've told you that.'

'Yes. I know. What do you do? Fill this with water? Half fill it?'

'A couple of inches off the top. It was Nick's fault.'

'I know.'

Zeno took a coin from his pocket, palmed it, produced it, palmed it again. His equivalent of a nervous tic. Ellwood smiled. 'You could have been one of the best.'

'I do it for fun. Amateur night.' It was a lie. Ellwood had seen him work. 'I don't know why Nick turned up here. It was like he'd tracked me down. Who knows what he wanted? We had a few drinks. We talked about . . .' For a moment, it seemed that Zeno might be about to say 'old times'. Nothing so easy. No – nothing so free and easy. He said: '. . . the past.'

'Ah, yes; the past.' Coffee was chugging through into the jug. Both men watched it. Unobserved, the coin flickered into view and vanished once more.

'We went down to the beach for a walk. I didn't want to talk about that stuff. Then he got angry. OK' – Zeno held up an empty hand – 'we both got angry. I'm not even sure how . . . Well, I hit him, I know that. Hit him hard. But even so . . . He fell back on to the rocks. That must have knocked him cold. Maybe it even killed him. I just walked away. Just walked away. He was washed up three days later.'

Ellwood knew something that Zeno didn't – a police report that said: no hands. He took a mug from the kitchen dresser and poured himself some coffee. 'Sure,' he said. 'You told me this before.'

The coin appeared, was flipped into the air, and disappeared in flight. Zeno's life was all deceit.

Ellwood said, 'You've got a job to do here. Things are going well. No complications – right? Don't make things difficult.' Then, as if it were connected: 'And Carla? How is she?'

Zeno produced the coin from thin air and tossed it on to the kitchen counter. It rang like a bell. 'Carla's fine.'

Ellwood nodded – the merest threat in his eyes. He said, 'You're so lucky to have found her.' He walked across the kitchen, rice grains crunching under his feet. It was a minute or two before Zeno realized that he'd left. The mug of coffee was untouched.

Ellwood took the seafront road back towards the headland and his hotel. He was driving too fast, his wheels snaking in the wet from time to time, his windscreen wipers banging back and forth like an argument.

He thought: You'll do as you're told, you sorry bastard. You've got too much to lose.

Zeno got to his hands and knees and started to sweep rice grains into a mound.

He thought: Say one word to Carla, just one – I'll kill you for sure.

Ellwood's car gunned down the seafront road as Pascoe was walking towards the bar. He watched the rear end fishtail slightly as Ellwood passed the boatyard and took the hill that led away from Dewer Street.

Boy racer, Pascoe thought, and smiled. Everyone's anxious to get out of this town. As he thought it, the impulse to leave was suddenly strong. He felt at risk, and he felt out of control. His bizarre dinner of the night before seemed beyond explanation. He had gone back to the Palings and sat in his room watching the lighthouse beam as before. The light had flickered in his vision and he'd let the room grow dark around him.

He glanced at the window where the couple had sat the night before, half expecting to see them staring out, looking for their own faces. When he went in he was alone in the bar, but he could hear voices from beyond a door at the back of the room – a man and a woman shouting at one another, though somehow they didn't sound angry; their yells were punctuated by a series of soft crashes. After a moment Pascoe realized that they were stacking bottle crates on opposite sides of a room. He sat on a stool and rapped a coin on the bartop.

The barman looked out. He said, 'Did you find your friend?'

'Not a friend,' Pascoe told him, 'a business acquaintance.' He asked for a drink. The barman poured it swiftly, then turned his back on Pascoe; he was looking for something on a shelf behind the bar.

Pascoe had ordered whisky, knowing that it was too early in the day for him. The first sip made him heady. He said, 'I heard you had a murder locally. A body washed up near here – was that it?'

The barman turned; he was smiling. 'You with the Press?'

'No.'

'I don't mind. We had them down here for a couple of days, but things soon cooled off. No-one knew the guy. Could have died anywhere.'

'I suppose so. They put his picture around the town.' Pascoe had noticed the posters – DID YOU SEE THIS MAN? – and Nick smiling lopsidedly in the snapshot, the kind of fuzzy grin that told you others had once been in the photo, smiling smiles of their own. It was the same picture the papers had used.

'Yeah,' the barman shrugged. 'No-one knew him. He wasn't a local man. What're you – back-up story? Feature article?'

'Nothing like that,' Pascoe said. 'I'm curious, that's all.' He finished his Scotch and asked for another. There was a warm flush in his cheeks that he was beginning to enjoy. He saw his hand go out for the fresh drink, and heard himself speak, as if he were sitting alongside. 'Where they found him – is it nearby?'

'Not really. Then again it's not far.' The barman was trying not to grin. Who was this guy kidding? He waited, wanting Pascoe to do a little work for the information.

'How far?'

Now the grin arrived. He drew Pascoe a pencil map on the back of a blank bar receipt. Out of the town, taking Dewer Street to the west. After three miles a picnic-parking area and a coastal path to Lowland Head – twenty minutes walk, maybe – and just beyond that, the inlet.

Pascoe nodded and took the map, then got down from his stool. His feet touched the floor without seeming to make proper contact. Two whiskies, he thought. Good Christ, I'm getting old.

The barman raised a hand and Pascoe echoed the gesture, believing the man was saying goodbye. He found himself holding a letter. It was what the barman had been searching along the shelf for earlier; now he slotted it into Pascoe's raised hand.

'Came this morning,' he said. 'Don't worry. Those other journos lived in this bar. Morning drinkers, just like you. Stayed out at the big hotels on the headland, but they liked it better here. Local people, local colour. I used to take messages all the time.'

When Carla got back, Zeno took her into the sitting room. He'd made her some China tea because she particularly liked that. A small, green pot with a plaited cane grip and two dinky cups without handles. The tea was orange-yellow. Big flakes of leaf floated to the bottom. He told her he'd had an idea – it was that they move away from Longrock. Maybe she'd like to try London for a while. At least, somewhere livelier. He was worried that she might grow bored. Wouldn't she prefer theatres, galleries, designer stores, new friends, something *happening*?

'Just pack up and go?' she asked.

'Just go. Someone else can pack.'

'You don't like it here any more?'

'I could use a change. Don't you feel that way?'

'You go,' Carla told him. 'I'll stay.' And although it was a joke – of course it was – the panic in his eyes was broad and unmistakable.

'Just for you.' He was backtracking so fast that he stumbled over the words he'd left behind. 'I thought you might feel like a change, could use a change, be somewhere where something was *happening*.'

Carla smiled and shook her head. 'I like it here; don't you? I can see that the time might come when I want to get away. It usually does. I suppose that's when I'll go.' After a moment, she added, 'Then we'll both go – won't we?'

He sat beside her and put his head on her shoulder while she stroked his hair. After a moment, she unfastened two buttons on her blouse and, taking him by the wrist, slipped his hand inside. He held her breast lightly, his fingers barely curled, his eyes closed. He might have been asleep.

He said, 'Never leave me.'

In the same instant, blurring his words, she said, 'Show me something.' He didn't move. She said it again, the merest hint of a plea in her voice, knowing he wouldn't be able to resist that. 'Show me something.'

Carla sat in a chair: an audience of one. She was alone in the room. Her eyes were on the partly open door. A wooden trunk on wheels came through, seeming to move on its own. The lid flapped up, hiding what lay behind. A hand appeared, writhing, thumb to fingertips to make a tulip shape, and Carla saw that the hand was streaked orange and white like a flower. It moved left and right, waving in a gentle breeze; then it burst into flame with a soft *whoosh*.

Another hand appeared and stole the flame. The first hand was unmarked, the second ablaze. For a while the hands switched the flame to and fro, one grabbing one giving, until they came together in a folding, writhing motion and washed the fire off. It ran along the edge of the lid like quicksilver.

And introducing –

Zeno stood up behind the lip of fire. His face was ebony, his nose a great beak, his hat bore a curling feather. *Scaramouche.* He drew his sword and swept it along the lid, removing the flame which he put into his pocket. Head back, he swallowed the sword, then blew a tall plume of flame to anneal the blade.

He gave a courtly bow, stooping below the level of the box lid. Then he turned and stepped out of the box. When he turned again, the mask was gone, the hat was shiny and tall to match his tails, and the sword had become a cane. He came in front of the box to do a little tap dance, the cane touching the floor to the left, then the right, then left again as it softened and became a white scarf that he looped round his neck until it slithered down his arm, pink-eyed albino, tongue flickering. He gathered it like a ribbon, loop over loop, and flicked it into the air; it fell back a shower of silver spangles.

A globe grew under his downturned palm, shimmering with rainbow colours like a vast soap bubble. Zeno stood with both arms extended. The globe began to move, coming from under his hand and travelling along his arm. A second appeared and followed the first; then a third – all of them travelling along the cross of his outstretched arms, over his shoulders, behind his head, towards the other hand.

He gathered them as they arrived, turning his palm the

right way up, and they crossed and looped between his fingers, moving so smoothly, so fast, that they teased the rainbow out into an arc and swam along it, falling and rising, Zeno's fingers flying, his face behind the whizzing globes bathed in the radiance of the zodiac.

He gathered the brightness in and stepped back into the box.

And now a volunteer from the audience . . .

Carla stepped up. Three steel hasps hinged to the lid, three steel loops screwed to the box. Three padlocks in readiness. She flapped the hasps over the loops and ran the padlocks through, snapping them shut. Then she went back to her chair.

Brrrrum. She did it under her breath, tongue rumbling behind her teeth. *Brrrruuuuum.* A drum roll. The box fell forward and the lid flapped open. You could see that the padlocks were still fastened tightly through the loops. The box was as empty as a whore's promise.

Carla sat in the room alone, applauding till her palms stung.

Pascoe found the inlet easily enough. The rock shaped like a cat was almost underwater, but the bull seal was rearing out of the foam, its bulky, plum-coloured back gleaming in the wet light. There was only the slightest mist of rain in the air: just enough to make cobwebs of Pascoe's hair.

He imagined Nick Howard's body flung up on the stony beach and wondered what three days in the water had done to the face in the snapshot. For a moment he felt angry, as if Nick had been a real friend, a brother even; as if love were involved and he ought to be looking for vengeance. Then he realized it was fear he was feeling.

Tonight, he thought. I'll go back to the house tonight. That's all. Any more of this peek-a-boo shit, and I'm gone. What's it for – this elaborate tease, this now-you-see-me-now-you-don't? In the same moment as he wondered that, he was taken with the terrible sense of vulnerability that comes with being watched, almost an ache, as if a hand was already reaching out to touch his back. He turned at once, his heart looping in his chest, the flesh on his shoulders puckering. No-one was there.

Of course, he thought – a tease. A game of who am I, what do I know, what could I tell? It was what they had done to Lori.

First a woman's voice: We know what you're doing. We know all about you. You think no-one knows; but we know. You can't hide anything from us . . .

Then a man's voice: We know all about you. We know what you've been doing. We know everything . . .

Then a woman's voice . . .

Pascoe saw what was going on. Whoever it was, he thought, it's someone who knows everything.

The letter the barman had given him was unopened in his pocket. He feared it might say: Joke over. Forget it. Go home. He also feared that it might not. He slit the envelope and read the message:

How many angels can dance on a pin?

There was only one place to go and he went there.

The key gave him an advantage. The idea, he thought, was not to get there too early, in case the house was being watched. And not to get there too late, in case he found another meal for one, wine nicely chilled, service not included. Best to time it, if he could, so that he caught the son of a bitch setting the table, candles and all, like some lovelorn dope out to seduce the Princess Goldenheart. Eight o'clock? OK – arrive at seven.

Now that he'd seen it in the light, the house didn't seem as mysterious. He remembered the broken window and the ragged plaster; he remembered the faint odour of damp. The door was not on the latch this time. He used the key and stepped through into the hallway, listening all the time. Just inside the door, he paused to listen better. All he could hear was the rustle of his own breathing.

He'd bought a torch at a local hardware store, though where there were windows the light from the streetlamps was so good that he barely needed it. Its white roundel helped him up the stairs and along the corridor. The door that had been open on the previous evening was now shut. Pascoe directed his torch beam round the jamb looking for the slightest gap, but didn't find one. He opened the door and went in.

When he saw what he saw, his torchbeam sped about the room like a mad eye. He wasn't trying to light anything with it. The sodium glow from the window showed him everything: the table laid for two, crisp napkins, wine in the ice-bucket, a fresh camellia, the candles unlit.

He fell against the door and slammed it, the sound reverberating through the house like a sudden shout; there was a roaring in his ears as if he were underwater, and for a while he felt he would black out for sure. He fought his breathing to keep it under control.

He forced himself to look at the table, to see what was there. Wine, yes; food, no. The cork still in the wine. No candle-light. Things half done: still in preparation . . .

Jesus Christ! He's in the house!

He must have heard me come in, Pascoe thought; *must* have heard. He moved away from the door and stood behind the table. Then, on an afterthought, went to the pine cupboard. The door was latched by a hook and eye device that fitted tightly. As he pushed up the shank of the hook, Pascoe heard it grate, steel on steel. It made a noise like road drills; like jack hammers. The door opened on a little draught of mildewed air, like bad breath. The cupboard was empty.

As he latched it again, Pascoe heard a sound from deep in the house. It might have been a door that creaked, or the uncarpeted stairs. He held the torch like a club and waited, but the sound didn't come again.

Well, he thought, this guy wants to have dinner with me and he wants to do it privately so that he can issue a blackmail threat. Not a pleasant idea, but not a lethal one either. Why don't I step out into the corridor and shout 'Hello'? Or take my place at the table and wait for him to join me? What's he going to say? What's the worst? 'A lifetime of monthly payments, or you can kiss your career goodbye. Don't take it too hard. Think of it as a kind of insurance. You have insurances, don't you? Just another debit when your pay cheque comes in.' And what am I going to say? 'Hands up, it's a deal?' Or maybe, 'Take my career, cash it in for pennies, then feed them up your ass till they come out of your ears.' But isn't that what's happening here after all? A business deal, just a little more crooked than the rest.

Then again, Nick Howard was on posters everywhere you looked.

Pascoe opened the bedroom door – just enough to enable him to slip through – and shone his torch into the corridor. Then he walked to the uppermost stair and played the beam down into the stairwell. Dust particles, disturbed by his own feet, danced down the shaft of white light.

He opened his mouth to shout and heard the bedroom door behind him click shut.

For a moment, he could do nothing but try to convince himself that it hadn't happened. When he turned, the door was closed. I could stand here for ever, he thought. I could wait on this spot until doomsday, never knowing whether to go back into that room or downstairs and out into the street. He went a pace towards the door and stopped. For one wild minute, he thought that he could see the whole thing clearly. He would open the door and step through and immediately someone would throw the fuse-switch. The lights would come on, and there they'd all be: Marianne and Luke, Susan and Sophie and Charlie Singer, chorusing *Surprise*, throwing streamers, and laughing fit to bust.

But in his sudden bright imagining of the scene, he saw another face: Nick's ragged flesh foraged by the sea's meat eaters, his mouth clogged with silt, his eyes scoured by salt.

The vision checked him for a moment, then he went on, going at speed for the door as if he might walk through it. You take one step, then you take another.

As he stepped through, he said, 'OK, you bastard . . .' but there was no-one to hear him. The wine had been uncorked. There was *salade Niçoise* in a big, glass bowl. The candles were burning – so recently lit that he could see the white wick at the core of each flame.

He looked towards the pine cupboard. The hook and eye were still in place. Even so, he strode over and opened it. Nothing. He closed it again, quickly, and fixed the catch. Then he put the breadth of the table between himself and the door, standing behind his chair as if at some formal dinner, waiting for the honoured guest to take his place.

A card caught his eye: a new addition; it was propped against one of the candlesticks.

With the compliments of:

THE GREAT ZENO

Illusionist : Magus : Escapologist

Despite the tension he felt, Pascoe almost laughed out loud. He lifted the card and reread it, then turned it over. The back bore a line drawing of one hand in the classic position for palming an object, a second in the 'open' position – to show whatever was hidden. The revealed object was a question mark. At the bottom of the card, the line:

How many angels can dance on a pin?

I'm to be given a magic show, Pascoe thought. And, even

though he could feel the pulse crashing in his wrist, he sat down at the table and poured himself a glass of wine. Cabaret time. He took a sip and sat back, trembling slightly, his eyes fixed on the bedroom door, waiting on the big entrance.

'Come on, then, you daft bastard.' He spoke the words out loud. 'Amaze me.'

The door didn't open. No-one came in at the door. But someone entered the room.

And introducing –

Zeno stood in the room. His face was bone white, his mouth red, his eyes dark scorch marks.

– the Angel of Death.

The fact that he'd sat down was Pascoe's only piece of luck. He rose, seeming to move in inch-by-inch slow motion, a great bellow of fear issuing from his wide-open mouth, and his thighs hit the rim of the table, upending it.

For a long, suspended moment, everything was in the air: candles, candlesticks, plates, the glass bowl, everything; and Pascoe rising, his hands going up for protection, his howl of terror burgeoning in the room. Zeno's first knife took a deflection, catching the rim of a plate as it turned in the air. Pascoe was aware of it without properly understanding what it was – a chip of light amid the airborne debris. He flung out a hand, the palm in line with his throat, and felt a shaft of pain go through his wrist and up into the elbow.

Instinct was taking him forward, trampling broken glass, his shins cracking the chair-rail; he went full-tilt, as if to come close to death would be his only hope.

Zeno had unshipped another knife, but didn't have time to throw. Pascoe half fell as he came within reach, crashing into Zeno at the run, his arms wrapped round, his hands palm-out against the impact. The knife was still embedded between wrist and knuckle. They hit the wall, and the slender blade went straight through the flesh.

Zeno gasped, a flush of sour breath in Pascoe's face.

The knife had speared Pascoe's hand, then taken Zeno to the left of the spine, cutting in more than two inches before it stuck. They wrestled, both wanting to get free, and the knife turned in Pascoe's hand as it turned in Zeno's back, opening their wounds. Pascoe's face was close to Zeno's; their foreheads knocked; red lips brushed Pascoe's throat. Too close to see features clearly, even if they hadn't been blurred by the death's head make-up. But Pascoe could see the eyes, wild, rimmed with red and black.

Zeno clamped his hand to his back, gripping the knife, then spun away, drawing the thin haft clean through Pascoe's hand. He continued to clutch his back. His mouth was an O of outrage and his tongue lolled out as if he had tasted his wound and found it foul.

Pascoe didn't remember getting to the door, or opening it, or stepping through, or closing it after him; but he was in the corridor. He half fell, half rolled down the stairs, whooping with pain and fear, his head whacking the wall. He cannoned into the front door and found himself going for the lock with his damaged hand. It was crimped like a claw and streaming blood.

Outside, he ran up the short garden pathway to the street, then turned downhill, towards Dewer Street and the sound of the sea. He was sobbing and calling out, though he didn't expect anyone to hear; his calling was nothing more than a reflex. His hand was burning, glowing orange-white like iron in a furnace. He held it above his head, to help staunch the bleeding, and to cool it in the night air.

He thought: If I stop running, if I stop calling, I shall fall and faint and bleed until I die. The thought kept him on his feet. He ran downhill towards the sea with great, galloping steps, calling and crying, his bloody hand held aloft like a banner.

Zeno stood in a corner of the room, his back bent and his hand to his kidneys, like an old man feeling the strain of an uphill walk. He was sobbing with rage and talking through the tears.

'Now what . . . ? Now what . . . ? I don't know what . . . he should be dead . . . can't tell Ellwood . . . can't tell Carla . . . no-one to talk to . . . no-one to talk to . . .' His mouth was stretched with anguish, like a Greek mask, and the words emerged as a long, incoherent, fluctuating cry.

Bad luck. Bad luck that Marianne recognized him; but once she had . . . He had to protect himself – himself and Carla; had to protect them from the worst thing.

Think. *Think*. First things first. He was wearing black for the Angel of Death: black jeans, black shirt, a black silk blouson jacket. He stripped off the jacket and shirt, then put his hand back to the cut as he crossed the room. He could feel the blood filling his palm and running across his knuckles. He found a napkin among the wreckage and refolded it in case there were glass slivers; he clamped it to the wound and, holding the shirt around himself like a cummerbund, tied the sleeves tightly across his belly. Then he put the jacket on and zipped it to the neck.

He took a candle and went downstairs to the bathroom. Taped up behind the old-fashioned cistern was a small, flat make-up box: some Leichner sticks, cremine, tissues. He lit the candle and set it close to a small, mirror-fronted cabinet, then smeared some cremine on to a tissue.

The flame hopped and settled. In the dim, yellow glow, Zeno brought his face up to the mirror and wiped his lips. From the pocket of his blouson, he took a polythene bag and dropped the used tissue into it; then he took another and wiped his eye.

He'll come back, Zeno thought. He'll run away now; but he'll come back to Longrock soon. And he won't tell anyone. No, he won't tell a soul.

Lips smeared like a mouth much-kissed. One eye bright, the other dark and dead.

I'll see him then, Zeno thought. I'll see him when he comes back.

Pascoe came out of the shadows and into the lights of Dewer Street with his legs failing him and his breath like fire in his throat. He slowed and stopped, falling sideways to support himself against the wooden gates of the boatyard. For a moment, he stayed there, doubled up, fighting for air and hugging his hand to his chest as if it were a small, hurt animal. Then he pushed himself upright and walked on. His frenzied charge downhill had taken almost all his strength. His feet dragged. He felt consciousness come and go – a soup of sounds. The sound of his heart, the sound of breakers under the sea wall, the sound of a saxophone rising and falling along the wind.

The couple by the window saw him first. Their conversation dried on their lips. They stood up and looked back into the room; the looks meant: guess what's coming . . . He started for the bar, and the barman met him halfway because it was clear that he wasn't going to make it.

Pascoe had already decided what lie to tell, and now he told it to himself once more, the words fighting with the fuzzy clarion of bells and drums and horns that filled his head.

The hospital doctor looked about as tired as she could be this side of sleep. She cleaned the wound and sewed it top and bottom. A nurse bandaged it. The doctor administered a tetanus shot and wrote a prescription for tetramycin. Pascoe couldn't stop shivering.

'Walking on the beach at night, slipped and fell, hand out to break the fall – broken bottle.' Pascoe couldn't understand why she was giving him his story back in précis, then he saw the nurse writing. 'That right?' the doctor asked. They both looked at him.

'That's right.' His teeth chattered.

'Get it checked by your own doctor, take these—' she held out the prescription. 'Get some sleep.' He smiled but didn't speak.

'You're shaken up. I could give you something to calm you down. I'd sooner not; I try not to use that stuff.'

'Don't then.'

She nodded and went out of the booth. A few seconds later, the barman came in and walked Pascoe back to the reception area.

'I owe you one,' Pascoe said.

'Forget it. I had a good time with those other journos. Livened the place up. I like you guys.' Pascoe sat down. 'What part of the beach was you on?'

'Up towards the cliff,' Pascoe said, 'off Dewer Street.'

'Uh-huh,' the barman screwed up his eyes, as if in thought. 'Except the tide must have been in, wasn't it?' Pascoe didn't respond. 'No, you must have been further along than you thought. Closer to the hotel, I expect. There's always some beach clear there, even when the tide's up.'

'Closer to the hotel . . .' Pascoe added it to the lie.

'That's it . . .' The barman turned towards the door. 'Come on. I'll take you back.'

'I'll get a cab,' Pascoe told him. 'Thanks.'

'Yeah? Are you waiting for someone?'

'That's right. I'm waiting for someone.' Pascoe stood up and extended his left hand for a backhanded shake. 'I'm grateful, really.'

The barman walked backwards to the door, as if he expected Pascoe to change his mind.

He waited in reception, watching injured people come and go but none of them with vermilion lips and burned-out eyes, and a wound to the small of the back. The doctor who had attended him went through at the run, beeping from a top pocket. Pascoe's heartbeat lay in his hand – strident, like cymbals crashing; pain came with each crescendo.

He reached into his right-hand pocket – a crossover draw – and found the card, with its two hands, one open, one closed.

And introducing now . . .
The audience was breathless . . .
And introducing –

Pascoe waited another hour, but he didn't come.

Six

Ellwood had driven almost three hundred miles, taking the motorways towards London. Fifty miles short of the city, he'd taken an exit that had brought him, almost at once, into open, flat countryside – a vale that lay between hills so distant that they were blue smudges behind the early evening mist. From time to time he'd had to check the map, open beside him on the passenger seat; on one occasion he pulled over in order to read directions he'd scribbled on to a sheet of the Windrush hotel notepaper.

By the time he found the place, the sky was gathering a rich blue along the horizon, about to deepen into dusk. He left his car in a gateway and walked about half a mile along a lane bordered by willows. On the other side of the trees, the river moved noiselessly, slow as lava, its thick surface flooding with dull fire in the last of the sun.

Ellwood saw a figure at the water's edge, and stopped for a moment, giving in to an old habit of wanting to see without being seen. The man was bringing line in, slowly, the tip of the rod just above the vertical and angled to the right. A metal lure, triple-hooked, glittered as it came into the light. The fisherman gathered some line left-handed, switched the tip of the rod from right to left and cast again, sending the lure snaking out beyond a growth of reed close to the opposite bank. Slowly, he trawled the spinner back again.

Ellwood walked off the path and across the grassy patch that led to the riverbank; the bottoms of his trousers began to drag as they soaked up the wet. The fisherman made another pinpoint cast, dropping the lure so smoothly that the water seemed to fold over it.

'You found me.' He spoke without turning.

Ellwood stood a few feet back and to the left. 'Your directions were good enough. What are you trying for?'

'Today? A pike.'

'Just one?'

'Well, I'll take what comes; but there's one in particular, yes. A real bruiser. Sometimes you can see him lying up in shadow close to the bank. I thought he was a length of willow branch at first sight. I've been looking for him in this swim for more than a month. He's here, all right, but he's wary. This spinner flips through the water like a roach in trouble. It seems that he won't make an effort for it, so I've been trying to put it right past his nose. Even if he's not hungry, he might just lose his temper with it. Loose emotion, Wallace; wasteful feelings. Gets people into trouble.'

'He's out by those reeds is he?'

'Something is.'

Ellwood hadn't seen Tom Carey for more than five years. It seemed that the man had put on weight, though the pockets of his fisherman's waistcoat were stuffed with equipment, so it was difficult to say for sure. Then Carey turned and smiled, briefly, before making another cast, and Ellwood could see the puffiness round the eyes and pudgy jowls lapping the man's collar.

As if reading Ellwood's thoughts, Carey said, 'It's been a while.' Guessing at other thoughts in Ellwood's head, he added, 'I've been retired all that time. Retired from the church; retired from *everything*.'

Ellwood caught the emphasis, but chose to ignore it. 'Surely no-one retires from the church.'

The lure came out dripping. Carey gathered line and described a long loop with the tip of the rod. He was dropping the triple barb into the same hand's-breadth of water every time.

'I don't invoke the body and blood of Our Lord, I don't comfort the torn in spirit, I don't give praise with the saved, I don't snatch brands from the burning.' The spinner flicked back, just below the surface, churning the river's reflected gold with a silver spoon. 'I don't interpret the word of God, I don't preach, I don't baptize or give last rites. I don't do shit.'

'Do you pray?'

'I pray to catch the old thug lying out there by the reeds. Huckleberry Finn prayed for a fishing rod – remember that? Gave up praying because he never got one. God doesn't seem to favour fishermen which, given the day jobs of most of the disciples, seems bloody unfair.' Carey lodged his rod on a V-bracket that was pushed into the softer ground at the bank's edge and took a flask from one of the waistcoat pockets. 'Perhaps He thinks the symbolism of it all is a bit corny.' He took a swig from the flask and offered it to Ellwood. 'Fishing,' he said, 'you know . . .'

'You think God has a sense of humour?' Ellwood tapped his tongue with the neck of the flask to find out what he'd be drinking, then took a long pull. It was brandy.

'Sure, I've always thought so – I mean, why else would we have Alzheimer's disease. Pray for what?'

'For whatever you want.'

'There's nothing I want.'

'That's impossible.'

Carey laughed. He took back the flask and gave himself another drink, then lifted the rod and made a neat cast. His laugh grew louder. 'Don't say things like that, Wallace; you'll make me frighten the fish.'

'We need you, Tom.'

'Ah . . . Yes, that's different. That makes you the one who's praying.' Carey felt the lure dip and struck fast, taking the rod to the right, but the line went slack. 'Getting angry or getting hungry?' he wondered. 'Either will do.'

'You'll get some good sea angling down there,' Ellwood said.

'Sure.'

'He's jumpy. He needs someone to talk to.'

71

'What's all this magic stuff?'

Ellwood shrugged, smiling. 'The Great Zeno. He's very good: I've seen him work.'

'Where did that come from?'

'Ask him.'

'I haven't seen him in – what? – eighteen years, Wallace. What makes you think he'll talk to me?'

'He will. He always did. Anyway, you might not have seen him recently, but you've been thinking about him.' A few months earlier, Carey and Ellwood had spent the best part of an hour on the telephone. A long string of questions from Ellwood; good guesswork from Carey. Ellwood had been researching his man. 'What have you got to lose?'

'Tranquillity. I'm getting too old for disruption in my life.'

Ellwood said, 'Sixty-two . . . three . . . ? You're a young man still. You must think about those times, don't you? The way it was . . . Everyone with a sense of purpose, everyone with a point of view?'

The river closed over the lure like a soft fist. 'I don't care much for the past, Wallace. It isn't what it used to be.'

'Anything,' Ellwood said. 'Anything you want.'

A sudden outraged energy shook the reeds and churned the surface of the water. Carey struck again, hitting hard, and the fish was on. He reeled in, raising the rod at the same time, then lowered it to give slack. Ellwood could see the tension in Carey's shoulders; his rod arm was buffeted and yanked by the furious power that flowed up the line.

Carey reeled in, dragged on the rod, dipped it and reeled in again; the graphite sections curled and quivered. The fish was swimming hard downstream, pulling towards the far bank where it might find cover among blackthorn bushes; if the line tangled in reeds or on a low branch, he'd be lost. Carey fought the fish but tried to give him leeway; a little at a time would land him safely.

He reeled in again, and the pike broke water, frantic

with rage, sending gobbets of gold skittering over the surface. Then he went deep, swimming at the rod so that Carey almost forgot to own the advantage. He took line swiftly, bringing the fish to the overhang of the bank, and landed him with a small gaff.

Ellwood stepped forward to take a look. The fish lay still, as if Carey's hand on its shoulder was a comfort and a solace. The crisp gills were pink with air and blood; a bramble of teeth lay along the ugly, undershot jaw.

Carey worked the barb out with hook-scissors, then reached into a pocket and took out a little curved wood-and-horn club.

'Do you know the name for this? The correct term?' He handed it to Ellwood who looked, then handed it back with a shrug. 'It's called a priest,' Carey said. 'You see: there are symbols everywhere here. What I'm about to do is a sort of irony.'

His hand lay on the fish like a benediction. He brought the ribbed horn down hard, clubbing twice. The pike leapt in his grasp, then went limp: something for the slab.

'Terrific,' Carey said, 'baked with fennel and a little white wine.'

'Was it him?' Ellwood asked. 'The one you wanted.'

Carey shook his head, smiling. 'Less than half the size,' he said. 'And not one tenth the trouble. The one I'm really after would walk up the bank on its fins and bite me on the ankle.'

The sun was going under the horizon. A long shadow spread upriver, turning the water from gold to lifeless pewter. Ellwood said, 'I have to get back, Tom. What's it to be?'

'What do you want me for, Wallace? Just to calm him down?'

'Like I said: he needs someone to talk to.'

'Someone who'll afterwards talk to you . . .'

'We'd like to know what he's thinking, yes. What his plans are.'

73

'You tell me that Nick Howard's dead,' Carey was dampening some cloth to wrap the fish.

'He says it was an accident.'

'And was it?'

'No.'

'Anything I want . . .'

Ellwood smiled, grey eyes in a grey face. 'Forgotten pleasures, Tom?'

'No.' Carey folded the cloth over the pike's head, over its crimson gills, over its bright eye, as if preserving the dignity of the dead. 'No – but I'm sure you'll think of something.'

Ellwood didn't bother to rejoin the motorway; he took country roads, liking the onset of deepening blues across the vale. If a slow-moving vehicle threatened to hold him up, he overtook it without bothering to look too closely for any oncoming car. He passed a truck going into a blind curve, and came off the crown of the bend in the almost-dark without a qualm. He didn't believe in a charmed life, but he knew nothing would harm him that day. It was a system of risk that he followed like a creed. It worked off feelings – high or low. On bad-luck days, take no risks; on good-luck days, you can do any damn thing you like.

On a long, straight stretch of road, in the deepening dark, he saw approaching headlights flicker along a stand of trees. In a couple of beats, the other car would turn into the straight and head towards him. Ellwood killed his own lights and steered on to the wrong side of the road, at the same time slowing his speed by half. He was chuckling under his breath.

The oncoming car came into the straight. Ellwood waited a few seconds, then snapped on his lights and gunned the engine, hearing his tyres squinny on the metalled surface. He drove at the other car as if he'd go through it; but he'd left enough room for the driver to have time to see him – enough time to make a decision.

Ellwood flicked the wheel over, feinting towards his

own side of the road, then came back on collision course. Maybe the other driver was shitless with shock; but maybe he'd thought of switching lanes. Ellwood grinned: now you don't know what the fuck to do for the best, do you? He held it steady, foot flat down and about three seconds left. Lights flooded his windscreen, cataract-white, and then were gone as the other driver made his choice. The two cars passed in a blurred roar – engines, a wailing horn, twin slipstreams that crashed and slammed between them.

Ellwood took the curve that led out of the straight without losing any speed. His car shimmied, but stuck to the camber. The smile on his lips would have cut tin.

He said, 'I knew you'd do the right thing.'

The western approach to the city was flyovers and grey tower blocks and six-lane snarl-ups. The sky glowed – a soup of neon and bad air. High up in the one clear strip, you could see the twin lights of planes as they hung above the airport, dropping stack by stack.

A road snaked up, taking the traffic on a two-mile elevated section that led into the heart of the city. Halfway along, on the fastest stretch of road, a thirty-storey block had been built. You could see into the dim stairwell that rose through the building's core. On either side, windows glowed like beacons.

Ellwood lived there, in an apartment that was a little above eye-level with the cars. He would stand at the window sometimes, enjoying a cup of coffee perhaps, and construct epic games of chicken. It would be a summer evening, the sky choking on purple and crimson and livid yellow, one man travelling west on the east-bound carriageway, taking the middle lane, cars and trucks weaving round him while he drove a dead straight line towards the setting sun.

Your vision swamped by purples and yellows, a smell of burning . . . On a good-luck day, you could drive it blind and live.

He ignored the slip road that would have taken him

down to the street and the building's entrance level. Instead, he drove another three miles to one of the city's mainline stations and began to cruise.

The streets around were bright and everything was on display. The police in that area called it the Meat Market. Those who weren't paid off made arrests from time to time: it was just a token. Ellwood liked to go there. It meant he could find a different girl each time; someone he'd never seen before; more importantly, someone he'd never have to see again.

He chose a tall one with a Cinderella wig and a skirt like a bandage. She slammed the car door and ran her hand along the inside of his thigh. 'Pull round the corner,' she said, 'down there. It's a dead end.' She told him what she wanted to do for him. Ellwood shook his head and turned the car round. He bulled his way into the main road traffic.

'Oh, shit!' She looked for the door handle. 'Listen, I don't go out of the district, you understand? If I travel, I'm losing money.'

'I'll pay you for that,' Ellwood told her. He mentioned a sum.

The girl shrugged. 'Yeah? OK.'

Ellwood drove back fast, running lights, overtaking on the inside. The girl was silent. When he glanced across at her, he saw that she was asleep.

Much later, she slept again, her face in the pillow, her ass still lofted in the air. Ellwood put a foot to her flank and pushed her on to her side. She woke and looked at him fuzzily. He said, 'You're losing money. Isn't that right?'

She went to the window and looked out at the torrent of headlights while Ellwood phoned for a cab; the vehicles were close, seeming to pass almost under her nose. 'Can they see me from here?'

'I expect so,' Ellwood said.

She laughed and stepped closer, bringing her nakedness up to the glass – just a torso cut off at neck and thigh.

76

Ellwood imagined himself driving the elevated section and seeing her there, backlit in his window, faceless, flesh on a rack.

Welcome home . . .

Seven

Pascoe's doctor had unwrapped the wound, then turned the injured hand over and back several times, as if looking to find fault with the work. The line of the cut was puckered; the stitches were like a comic grin.

'Clean,' the doctor had said. 'Your luck was that you landed on a bottle that had been sluiced in salt water.' Now Pascoe was living off a diet of pain killers and antibiotics. The other comment the doctor had offered was: 'Don't drink.'

Just the one, Pascoe thought. Everyone gets a drink at the end of the day. He made it a vodka, and left room for a splash of tonic water.

He'd been back three days, but hadn't been anywhere near his office. He'd phoned his secretary to say that he was ill. Two minutes after he'd finished speaking to her, George Roxborough had called.

'What kind of ill?'

'I cut my hand. It's infected. I've got a fever.'

'Because you're in court on Thursday.'

'I won't be there, George. It's nothing.'

'Depends on your point of view. I think your client takes it seriously.'

'He was caught flatfooted with some bargain basement crack. He's a long way down the chain: either a token arrest or a sacrifice. It's just a committal hearing, George. Put it on offer. Someone will have it.'

'What's his defence?'

'The police are lying.'

'Are they?'

'On this occasion they don't need to.'

'You don't sound like a man with a fever, Sam.'

'Did you go to see Tony Stewart's mother?'

'Yeah. Everything off pat – time of arrival, time of departure, the chocolates he brought her, what they saw on TV.'

'And you've spoken to Stewart . . .'

'Of course. Same story there. If they both hold up, the prosecution could have a tough time. They've got little enough, apart from his confession. Confessions aren't worth shit these days.'

Pascoe had been unbandaging his hand for a peek – a small compulsion he'd fostered and now couldn't check. 'Have you thought about that – the fact that their stories are a match?'

'Thought what?'

'The TV programmes, George. It's a nice touch, isn't it? If Stewart can give the same details his mother gives . . .'

'She videoed the programmes for him: is that what you expect them to say? He went over later and watched them.'

'No video, George. The day nurse will testify to that. No record of any video – no purchase, no rental agreement. She definitely didn't have a video.' A tiny pulse had moved in the cut, like the tick of a clock. Pascoe had blown on it, silently. 'No, the TV details are terrific. I'd play that up if I were you.'

'He called his mother. She told him what she'd watched.'

'Doubtful. His account is altogether too colourful. You can only give someone an outline, really. Second-hand versions sound like just that. His doesn't.'

'What then?'

'He had the TV on while he killed her.'

A silence; Roxborough had either laughed or cleared his throat. He'd said, 'You think so?'

'Watched some, killed her, watched the rest.'

'Jesus. You really think so?'

'Tony Stewart,' Pascoe had said, 'is a peculiar little guy.'

Pascoe sipped at his vodka, winced at the strength of it, sipped again. He'd been sleeping a lot, as if dreams could be a way out. Or a way back. He thought about the times they'd had, the seven of them. The men would be easier to trace than the women, because women changed their names; they became Mrs Someone Else. Surely, they would all be married now. And divorced, most likely.

If it wasn't a member of the group, it was someone who'd heard their story; which meant that one of the women could be involved as an accomplice. But if it was a group member it was a man – so either Charlie or Luke.

Someone who wanted to use the past for profit. That was the rational view. Pascoe had worked with that sort of greed before; indiscretions for sale, guilt at a cut-price rate. Some people paid for ever, some people paid for a while and then got angry. Twice Pascoe had defended the angry, trying to make a jury understand how a killer could also have been a victim.

The rational view would also encompass Nick Howard's death, especially if Nick had been one of those who got angry. Stab wounds, the press report had said. Well, sure; but stab wounds could as easily indicate a fight as a deliberate killing.

Pascoe could make sense of all that. But there were things that stood apart from the rational view. A table set for one in an empty house, a painted face, a figure that had walked straight out of the wall. And there was no doubt what the intention had been on that occasion: not extortion, but death.

A letter took me to Longrock, Pascoe thought – a mention of Lori Cosgrove. Make that the first-known fact. One of the group, or someone close to one of the group. OK.

Someone killed Nick Howard. We don't know why and

we're not sure how, but he's dead and that's another fact. OK.

And someone left me a calling card: The Great Zeno – illusionist. Candles lit in an empty room, a bottle uncorked, a sudden appearance with knives and a winning grin. Magic. Jiggery-pokery. That's a fact as well.

The men would be easier to trace . . .

Pascoe dialled a number and took another pull at his vodka. Each time, the strength was more familiar. The phone rang and rang. Pascoe checked the time: seven-thirty; people leaving for dinner parties, for the start of the movie, for curtain up. Except Rob Thomas, who didn't like people and didn't want to be entertained and never went anywhere.

After another full minute of ringing, the phone was lifted. Rob sounded more weary than resentful.

'I need to run a couple of people to earth,' Pascoe told him.

'The usual provisos, Sam.' Thomas meant: If they're wanted, please don't tell me. If they're violent, tell me at once. If they're missing children, forget it.

'Charles Singer. Lucas Mallen.'

'Where do I look?'

'A place called Longrock – south Cornwall. It's about as far west as you can go without drowning. You should also look in a town called Claydon, which is—'

'I know Claydon,' Thomas said. 'Used to be trees and fields. Now a dormitory town: in the sense that it seems to have gone to sleep.'

Trees and fields, dairy herds on the outskirts . . . A cobbled square at the centre, with an auctioneer's block and sink-holes for the portable cattle pens farmers used to ship in on the last Friday of every month. A brand-new shopping mall. A palais de danse. The police station had a peace sign splashed on the brickwork.

Pascoe remembered how some of them – maybe all seven, maybe not – had walked beyond the town limits with wine and cheese and fruit. There was a conical hill

81

with a copse low on its flank. It was a midsummer day and they had dozed under the leaf-cover. The birds had stopped singing each time a helicopter went over, low and loud, towards the USAF base ten miles away.

'Who are they?'

'People I used to know,' Pascoe told him. 'So they'd both be about my age. That's the best I can do.'

'Married, single, kids, professions, known associates, physical peculiarities, hobbies and pastimes, likelihood of a police record . . . what?'

'No,' Pascoe said. 'Sorry.'

'Oh, well; at least you didn't give me Smith and Jones.'

Lawyers need people to help them with this task and that. The people in question are usually ex-policemen; the tasks are often confidential. The people who help often have friends of their own who are still policemen. Each has something to sell, or else they want to buy. It's a brisk trade, all in all.

'You'll find them on some computer or another.'

'Not me,' Thomas said. 'Someone else might.'

'Call in some favours,' Pascoe suggested.

'A favour works both ways.'

'There's a drugs case at my Chambers – crack dealer; no-one special, not much stuff. I suspect he'll name a few names if the approach is right.'

'You'll talk to him—'

'No. George Roxborough. The guy was set up – I don't think he's realized that yet. When he does, he might well feel annoyed.'

'I'll offer it as barter. Not even computers can do everything for you, Sam. There'll be a fair number of Charles Singers and Lucas Mallens.' He paused to consider the names. 'Maybe fewer Mallens.'

'Nationwide, yes. In the specific areas I've mentioned, not so many. The age group will limit our choices, too.'

'If they've moved away . . .'

'Ah, well,' Pascoe said. 'If they've moved away, it's tougher.'

'Unless you can afford to hire a team to check every forty-year-old Singer and Mallen in the country – yes, it is.' It was Thomas's way of saying that a favour only gets you so far. To make the rest of the journey takes money.

Pascoe knew how difficult people are to trace. The note from his wife had said: *You won't be able to find me. I've changed my name.* She'd been right. He'd spent a year looking. Rob Thomas had helped. You can only find the people who aren't hiding.

'Let's give it a try,' Pascoe said. As an afterthought, he gave Thomas the names of the women, too. Why not? Computers don't understand workload.

'I'll ask,' Thomas said. 'If they're on a file, they're yours.'

'Shall I call you at home,' Thomas asked, 'or at the office?'

'Neither,' Pascoe said. He gave Thomas the address and telephone number of the Palings Hotel.

Pascoe took his drink to the window and looked down at the park across the street: a place where the local kids had fun. Only last week a gang rape had occurred in one of the jungly dips and dells. At other times kids wandered in and out with their little tubes of solvent, their little packs of crack. You could always hear a bass-line wafting out of the park. Now and then the police would amble along and bag up everyone there. It didn't make much difference. In that neighbourhood wrecked children were a renewable resource.

Pascoe didn't invite many people back to his flat. Those that came usually asked him why in hell he chose to live there. His usual response was to make some gag about living over the store.

When he had been sure that Karen wasn't going to come back to him, Pascoe had sold their house and traded down to the place by the park. The difference had gone into a bank account – as if waiting for Karen to claim her share. It would have been possible for Pascoe to buy better; he had nothing to do but work and he made a lot of money. He never moved though. It wasn't that he liked the area, or found it colourful, or even that he couldn't summon the energy to move.

He lived there because he didn't believe he deserved any better.

Eight

Zeno stood back in the shadows and watched them drift in, his audience, his faithful few, his fans.

Stage right – the wooden trunk. Stage left – a large card, mounted on an easel and advertising the act: THE GREAT ZENO – plain, black playbill lettering inside a border of curlicues and flourishes. A vaudeville touch.

The lighting was lousy, but then it always was: two fuzzy floods in the slips and a spotlight that was usually a beat or two behind him. The male nurse who had volunteered for the job could never remember his cues. The space had been used for storage, then as a common-room, before the hospital authorities had made an entertainments area of it, and the back of the little stage was dim. Zeno hated that. The audience might think it an aid to trickery. However, it gave him a chance to see them in . . .

Did they have nothing else to do? Did they have nowhere else to go? There were one or two newcomers. Some looked at the stage with bright-eyed expectation; some with indifference; some with a disbelief that seemed to be fostered by anger.

Other faces were more familiar. Zeno checked them off as they took their seats: The Lady with the Flower, Mac the Cough, Birdie, The Wandering Jew, Dog Face, The Man with the Big Bow Tie . . . The regulars brought things with them – a skein of knitting, a sandwich, the sporting pages. It seemed that they might have come to meet one another again. After all, they appeared at every performance. Did they see themselves, perhaps, as a little family, bonded by Zeno's routines, reunited each time they came to see a show? They weren't like casual trade, come in to get out of the rain. A captive audience, they turned up sleet or shine, snow or swelter. Did they look, each time, for a missing face – a death in the family – and nod at one another to acknowledge the loss, and record it with slow, sad smiles?

Zeno looked for signs of this, but found none. They never looked left or right, or smiled or spoke. Eyes fixed on the stage, they made themselves comfortable and waited to be amazed.

Zeno delayed until the shuffling had subsided, then stepped out of the shadows and worked his first trick through the ragged round of applause.

He fanned a pack of cards, palmed them, fanned them again in the opposite hand, flung his arm up and produced in their place a cane with a red silk pennant attached that he knotted and unknotted with a duck and swerve of the wrist.

The cane became a rope, the pennant a flame.

He was spinning rope cowboy-fashion, the noose a loop of fire that turned in the air with a soft rustle and rip like a flag in a freshening breeze.

He widened the noose, so that it hung beside him, a fierce zero, then stepped through a couple of times before throwing it into the air and bringing it down a shower of red-gold streamers.

Pascoe, he thought. Now you're a danger to me. And a danger to Carla. A danger to our life together, you're a shadow cast on it; a stain on it. You're a piece of the past, and I don't want any of it – not the piece that's you, not any other; I want to take a cloth and wipe it away. I don't want Ellwood, either. And soon enough, I'll have done what he wants me to do and I'll cross him out: like an old address, like a wrong number. Carla and I will leave one night. I'll tell her my brother died; I got the money. We'll leave under cover of darkness, like deserters – a new address, a new number.

He was working the box, having shown them it was empty. Three globes crawled along the lifted lid and swarmed into his hands. He juggled them as they hissed with white-green light. Someone remembered to dim the floods, but the spot danced round the stage, trying to find him.

Carla had come into his life like a hurt creature that he had to care for. People would have called her plain, but she wasn't that. Maybe she didn't worry as much about her appearance as some women. She wore her blond hair parted simply and hanging to her shoulders; no lipstick, no mascara, no painted nails; and her clothes were always practical, never glamorous. Some people looked first towards her legs – people who had spotted the slightly exaggerated swing to her walk, almost a lurch if her leg was giving pain that day.

They would slip away one night and never be found. One minute there, the next minute gone, like magic.

He had found her on the beach, in the lee of a breakwater like a piece of flotsam. She had come to the ocean, she told him, because it was as far as she could go. Everything had been left behind, and willingly, though it was scarcely a sacrifice, since there wasn't much to leave. Rain had pearled on her face along with the tears, and she was soaked to the bone. He'd taken her in because there was simply nothing else to do. They had walked up the beach together across steep shingle and loose sand, her lameness all the more noticeable. Childhood polio, she'd told him, and linked her arm through his as if that was the way they always walked.

The lighting man finally remembered to kill the spot. In the dull gold glow that remained, the globes whizzed and sang, making towers and trees in white and green and red, making profiles and pillars, making arches, making skyscapes, making all the shapes you see when you're dazed by an open fire. The audience was utterly still, like night animals ringing a camp and staring in.

Carla had stayed. She never asked him a question; he

never asked one of her. They had decided to make the past a dreamless night. When he first made love to her, she shook and shook but begged him not to stop: feverish, it seemed, with fear and need. She hung on to him like someone in fathomless water, tired beyond measure and past all hope.

The next day, she cooked him a meal, as if that were her part. She gathered his clothes for washing. She cleaned the house.

He flung the globes so high, they made ropes to the roof; then, one by one, they fell darkly back, made invisible by the brilliance that still crackled in the air like a thousand flash bulbs. The audience were blinded, as Nick Howard had been blinded.

Zeno waited for the lights. He thought he might find the lighting man after the show and slap him a couple of times to wake him up. The floods brightened slowly and the spot tracked him across the stage with aggressive reluctance.

He palmed an egg and produced it; dry-washed his hands and it went. He produced it again – twice the size. A red silk square covered it and he bunched the cloth with both hands, working something precious, something delicate, from the bottom to the top.

A white dove. It left his hand and circled the stage, then returned. At the back of the stage was a board – four vertical planks about six feet tall. Zeno wheeled it forward into the light, then stopped it centre-stage where it stood upright and seemingly unsupported, like a closed door. At eye-level – two wooden pegs.

Zeno tethered the dove with a red leather thong. The pegs stood the wrong way for a perch, allowing a little purchase, but not much, so its wings beat to keep it upright. Zeno twirled the red cloth in a rapid flourish and the silk was suddenly fire that burned tightly round the dove in a scorching yellow and orange hoop.

The dove seemed to soar from the board, though in truth it moved no more than an inch or two, head lifted, breast like a prow, its wingbeats fanning the flame. Zeno was walking away – down stage towards the audience. Behind him the dove's wings clattered in motionless flight.

He smiled and turned, the knife arriving from nowhere and settling in his fingers. He threw and the tether parted. The bird seemed to be in mid-flight as it left the board, but that was an illusion. Like a creature that remembered food better than fear, it circled and came meekly to hand. Zeno folded the dove into his hand, into the silk, into invisibility.

'You conjured me up out of nothing,' Carla had said.

They shuffled out: Dog Face, Mac the Cough, the Man with the Big Bow Tie . . .

Zeno stood back in the shadows to watch them go. They never noticed him there. When the show ended, Zeno ended too; magic ended; the world fell into place. So why was there still a man at the back of the hall, watching the stage as if the finale was yet to come; as if the fire might blaze again, the dove fly back?

Zeno saw who it was and shock kindled in his chest. He swayed on his feet, his eyesight blurring, his ears filling with the sound of the sea.

Here was the best trick of the evening. Out of nowhere, Father Tom Carey, in his priest's grey polo shirt and clerical collar – just as memory held him – one hand half lifted in greeting or else in benediction.

Nine

Pascoe was sweating even before they opened the Judas gate. Roxborough stepped through and nodded a greeting to the prison officer. London was getting a few days of Indian summer, so everyone was in shirt-sleeves; fans whispered in the reception room.

A dark plaque of moisture discoloured the back of Pascoe's shirt. He knew it was there and the knowledge made him feel grimy. The surgical half-glove and cuff that protected his stitches was itchy; its colour had gone from grey to greyer still. Roxborough was swinging his briefcase like a pendulum.

'Saw the mother again,' he said. His voice was low because the officer was only a step or two ahead. 'I believed her.'

'You did?' Pascoe measured his pace against his colleague's. He was carrying a boulder in his chest; breathing was becoming a complicated and difficult business.

'I became a juror, you know? Projected . . . I listened to her as a juror would listen—'

'You hope—'

'And I believed every word she said.'

'Remember – it's bad to be disbelieved; it's lethal to be disproved.'

'She's got it by heart. Not too glib, but not shaky, either.'

Pascoe stopped for a breather. They all stopped. He said, 'It's a gift, George. From me to you.'

Stewart was there with a handshake and a shy smile. When Pascoe told him that George Roxborough was taking over the defence, Stewart transferred all his attention immediately, as if Pascoe had been switched off.

'Have you seen. My mother yet?' The fragmented sentences made him sound deferential, like a man who expected all the time to be interrupted.

Roxborough's smile was all reason and reassurance. While Pascoe sat on the sideline, he listened to Stewart's halting but word-perfect tale with the sympathy and good grace of any juror.

Outside again, and back in Roxborough's car, Pascoe opened a window to let the slipstream dry his shirt. It was close to lunch time, so they found a pub near the river and sat with their beers in the shade of a scallop-edged umbrella.

Roxborough said: 'Shall I say when you're coming back?'

'Tell them a week or two, if you like. I'll phone from time to time.'

'It's being called annual leave,' Roxborough told him.

'Is it? That's good.'

'But it's being thought of as depression or a binge.' Roxborough sipped his beer. 'I can tell them it's not a binge.'

'Tell them what you like,' Pascoe said. Then: 'I don't mean to sound waspish, George.' He shrugged. 'I need time out. I can't say why.'

'What was happening back there? At the nick.'

'I sweat. My hands tremble. I have trouble getting my breath.' The crisis he was describing was nothing new, though he realized that Roxborough didn't know that and would probably assume that it was Pascoe's reason for wanting time off. So much the better. He persisted with the truth. 'It's been getting really bad for a while now. After Karen left, I . . .' He broke off and shrugged. 'I just find it difficult to go into prisons.'

'Just prisons?'

'I think so, yes. I haven't tried much else.'

It wasn't to do with Karen directly, Pascoe knew that; although it had become acute since she had walked out, the source of the problem lay elsewhere. He didn't mind, though, if Roxborough saw it as a symptom of loss.

'I took a call from Rob Thomas. He says you want Paul Arthur Maynard thrown to the wolves.' Polly Maynard – caught with his bag of crack selling a night's sleep to the wrecked heads in cardboard city.

'The opposite. I'm suggesting he might like to deal. Trade some time for a handy name or two.'

'And what will Rob do for you?' Roxborough finished his beer and stared into the glass. The dregs of foam winked as they shrank. 'Karen's not coming back – even if you should find her, she wouldn't come back. It's been years.'

Pascoe shrugged, letting him think wrong thoughts again.

'What do you want me to say to Polly?' Roxborough asked.

'Make him angry. Tell him he was set up.'

'Was he?'

'Must have been at some time. Aren't we all?'

The summer went all the way down to the coast. Pascoe drove a Saab automatic that was the best ride in the world on an open road. He started out of the city before dawn and reached Longrock just after ten. The sea was a brilliant blue; turquoise where it rolled over shelving rock. He parked outside the Palings and walked towards the hotel entrance, expecting nothing, the mid-morning sun warm on his back. What he saw made him shout out loud.

A light blue Peugeot was pulling out of a parking space nearer to the hotel, Sophie Lanner at the wheel. She looked left and right, then worked the wheel fast with the heel of her hand and drove down Dewer Street in the direction of the boatyard.

Pascoe ran a few paces after her, arm raised like a

policeman. People looked round, and a car coming towards him braked sharply before he waved it on. The Peugeot took the hill where the sea wall gave way to the cliff, topped the rise, and was gone. He started back towards his own car, then realized he was too late for that. And as he stalled on the impulse, he saw that the moment of recognition was bound to have been self-deception. In thinking about the past, he had summoned a ghost. The woman in the car had simply looked like Sophie Lanner; or, more accurately, the Sophie he remembered.

He registered in the hotel and the clerk asked about his hand as if Pascoe were a member of the family.

'Better now,' he said.

The clerk remembered a man coming into the lobby like a chainsaw victim, blood on his shoes, blood stiffening his clothes, blood in his hair from holding his hand aloft.

'Much better,' Pascoe added.

They had given him the room he'd had before. A view of the ocean; to the right, a long, thin spit of land, raddled like a withered arm and scabbed with patches of red-brown bracken.

Coming back was all chances. The chance that Rob Thomas would put Longrock together with one of the names that Pascoe had given him. A chance for surprises. A chance to renew old acquaintance. A chance to die. He would start by revisiting a couple of familiar haunts.

The barman was a faceful of smiles: one as Pascoe walked in, one for a beer on the house, one for the letter he set down alongside the drink.

'You're soon back.'

'One or two things to do,' Pascoe told him.

'Loose ends,' the barman suggested. 'Leads to be followed up.'

'That sort of stuff.'

'You know something the others didn't know, that it? The guy washed up in the inlet – why he was here; who he saw.'

'Did he see someone?'

'Well, he was a long way from home. Why should he be here unless it was to see someone?' The barman was playing newshound and he had another sort of smile for that: knowing, sly.

'Maybe he needed time on his own,' Pascoe said. 'Maybe he was looking for a door.'

'A what?'

'A door – a way out, an exit.'

'Running away.'

'It's possible, wouldn't you say?' Pascoe asked the question as if he really wanted the barman's opinion.

'Someone killed him . . .'

'Strangers kill strangers, don't they? It happens all the time.'

The barman thought Pascoe was leading him astray; a newshound anxious to cover the scent. He said, 'Listen, what do I care?' He tapped the letter as if Pascoe might not have noticed it.

'You know a lot of people locally?'

'I know the regulars,' the welcoming smile returned. 'People like yourself.'

'Luke Mallen. Or Charlie Singer . . . Charles . . .'

The barman thought for a moment, head to one side like someone scrutinizing a photograph.

'No. Who are they?'

'Not sure,' Pascoe lied. 'Names that came up.'

'Something the others didn't know.' The barman gave himself a tot of brandy. 'There are things that I know, too. Things that didn't get into the papers.'

Pascoe's look said he doubted it. The barman didn't seem hurt by Pascoe's scepticism. He looked over the rim of his glass and said, 'No hands.'

It sounded as if he'd pulled off some act of deftness. Pascoe shook his head, as if to say: Too fast; I didn't see it; go again.

'The guy washed up near Windrush Head. The hands were missing. Someone had chopped them off.' All good stories were exaggerated in the telling.

Pascoe tried to evaluate the information. He could make no sense of it. 'How do you know that?'

This time the barman's smile was knowing. 'It isn't only journalists that drink in this bar, you know. Policemen too.'

Pascoe put the letter into an inside pocket and got down off his stool. As he walked away, the barman called after him: 'It's not the door . . .'

'What?' Pascoe looked towards the street and back again.

'It's not finding the door that's important.' He laughed and threw the dregs of Pascoe's beer into a sink. 'Ask any husband . . . It's finding the key.'

He went to the inlet to open Zeno's letter, just as he had before. The breeze was laden with salt and rotting seaweed. The coastal path hemmed him in: blackthorn and bramble; gorse flowers like the first, quick rash of flame in a forest fire.

It's a trick, he thought, and I don't know how it works. He tries to kill me, he fails, I go away. But then I come back again – and that's supposed to be a surprise, supposed to give me some kind of advantage. What do I find? A letter at the bar, as if it were my poste restante address. However the trick works, I don't like it. This son of a bitch is thinking my thoughts.

Sam,

I expect you've been looking for me, just as I had to look for you. The difference between us is: I know where to find you. 'Baskin & Somers', an office near Chelsea Bridge. It didn't take much research. Or else, it seems, that bar on the seafront. I couldn't be sure that you'd book in again at the Palings, though I expect you have. I bet I could find you there.

So there we are – I know how to get in touch.

We'll have to meet again, Sam, don't you think? Well, of course you do; why else would you have come back? Here's a proposal – let's meet in a public place. Wouldn't that make you feel easier? Let's do that. Let's make a date.

I'll leave a note for you in the usual place.

The wind made the page crackle, sending a sub-text in rapid morse. Pascoe was motionless, his eyes on the letter, although he'd read it twice. He knew that someone was standing very close, directly behind him, also motionless.

When he turned, Sophie Lanner was holding a gun on him.

Some gulls were riding a thermal close to shore, their hoarse, weeping cries overlapping like the weft in cloth. He couldn't be certain which he'd heard – the gulls or Sophie's voice. He stood up, folding the letter, and then he heard her clearly.

'Sit down, you bastard.'

The gun tracked him as he rose, then again as he lowered himself. She was holding it two-handed, left hand angled slightly to cup the weight, arms straight, feet braced. It looked as though she knew how to shoot.

Pascoe folded and refolded the letter – hands out front and carefully in view. He said, 'I thought it was you. Then I persuaded myself that it wasn't.'

'Did you? Why?'

'I'm not that accustomed to good luck. Where in God's name did you get that?' He nodded towards the gun.

'Well, your luck's changed. And the only reason I haven't shot you and kicked you into the ocean is because other people might know about the letter.'

'Someone sent you a letter . . . ?'

'Fuck you, Sam.'

'And you think it was me.'

Sophie laughed, her mouth curving in a broad grin that Pascoe at once remembered. She was tall, and slender still, her hair the ruddy gold he'd recognized her by as she drove away from the hotel. Her figure might have been a little heavier – breasts and hips – but the merest amount; enough to make a woman of a girl. The narrow face and broad brow seemed to be without lines.

'Yes,' she said, 'I think it was you.'

Long legs; a pair of Levis cinched with a webbing belt; a touch of make-up to lift her cheek-bones.

'What are you looking at?' She waggled the gun impatiently, as if bringing a meeting to order.

'I'm sure you got a letter,' Pascoe conceded. 'It wasn't from me.'

'Then why are you here?'

'Because I got a letter too.'

He sat on a clutter of pebbles facing the sea, his back to Sophie. She sat on the pebbles facing Pascoe, maybe twenty feet behind, the gun in her lap. She read both the letters he'd received, then read them again. From time to time, she glanced up to make sure he hadn't moved. One hand always lay close to the gun. She looked at the card he'd given her: *The Great Zeno : Illusionist : Magus : Escapologist.*

She turned it, one-handed, as a gambler turns a playing card.

How many angels can dance on a pin?

'I thought it had to be you when I saw you getting out of your car at the hotel. I just kept driving. I didn't know whether you'd seen me or not. I didn't know whether you'd recognized me or not. I turned round once I was over the brow of the hill – parked the car in a side-street and walked back towards the quay. I saw you go into the bar, then go back towards the hotel. I went to my car and waited, just in case. When you passed me, I followed.'

'What did you think I wanted?'

They were conversing in muted yells – having to compete with the rush and hiss of the tide.

'When I first got the letter? Money, I suppose.'

'What do you think now?' Pascoe had told his story. Without looking back to catch her reaction, he'd stripped off the surgical glove and held his hand up in the breeze, as if the wound still carried heat.

'Turn round,' she said. 'How can I tell whether you're lying if I can't see your face?'

'If you believe that, you'll believe anything. I've looked into the steady gaze and winning smile of many a skilful liar.'

'I suppose you mean women.' As Pascoe got up and walked across the pebbles towards her, Sophie raised the gun a few inches from her lap. 'I said turn round. I didn't ask you to join me.'

Pascoe ignored her. He sat alongside her but facing the opposite way. 'No. I was thinking of a man called Drew Bellamy.'

'Who?'

'He murdered his wife. Cut bits off her – afterwards, or so the autopsy showed, though I couldn't see it providing the foundation of a reasonable defence.' She looked at him, waiting for the sense of it. 'I became a lawyer when I grew up.' He leaned over to reclaim his letters and the card. 'What did you become, Sophie?'

'Rich.'

The gulls had drifted down, six or so, to distribute themselves about the foreshore, each on its own boulder. They had the appearance of a sparse but intrigued audience. In retrieving the letters he had come close enough to take the gun, but she hadn't seemed to notice.

'And Nick is dead?'

'Yes. Nick's dead.'

'I don't understand – what happened to you in the house, I mean. And the food . . . you said . . . ? Candles, wine – what was it?'

'Chablis,' he told her. ''Eighty-nine. Great year, but it's not really drinking yet.'

She said, 'I'm not sure I'm ready for jokes. I don't think we've got there, OK? I don't know what to think. There's still a fair chance I'll shoot you.'

Pascoe picked the gun out of her lap, tossed it in the

air to reverse it, then held it out to her butt first.

'What makes your clients trust you?' she asked. 'If you had to pick one thing?' She had ignored the proffered gun, leaving Pascoe straightfaced, his clever gesture hanging limply from his hand.

'My fees are ruinous.'

She stood up, then bent over and took the gun from him without really bothering to look. 'If it wasn't you who sent the letter, if you're telling the truth about things, then who was it? Who's Zeno?'

'I'm telling the truth,' he said, 'and you believe me. Otherwise you wouldn't have let me take the gun.'

'It's not loaded.' Sophie muttered the words and made a vague pass with her hand, as if her mind were elsewhere. Already, she was walking back towards the coast path, her head bowed like a beachcomber hoping for a treasure trove.

The bartender had become his brother. He was judging Sophie as a potential addition to the family. She asked for a beer, and that seemed to give him some confidence. There was a question that Pascoe had been wanting to ask.

'How rich?'

'As rich as you like. There's a bar at the hotel, isn't there?'

'Yes. But sometimes I find a message waiting here.'

'From Zeno.' She made the name sound exotic.

'That's right. As rich as you like is a hell of a lot of money. Where did it come from?'

'I married it.' Sophie drank some beer, then ran her tongue over the residue of foam on her lip. 'Too high a price.'

'You're divorced.'

'In a manner of speaking.'

'What manner?'

'Separated.'

'From the man, but not from the money,' Pascoe guessed.

'Are you talking to me about my own life?' Sophie asked. 'Are you passing judgement?'

Pascoe nodded – not an admission, but an apology. 'It's none of my business.'

'Damn right.' She snatched the bar menu from its little metal holder and read it carefully twice.

Pascoe said, 'Are you hungry?'

'No. I'm not.' A pause. 'I'm regaining my temper.'

'Well,' he said, 'I was out of line. On the other hand, you were waving a gun in my face not long ago. It didn't make me angry, but it did make me curious.'

Sophie shrugged. 'It's just . . . you spoke as if you had the right. As if you knew me.'

'I used to.'

She ignored the remark, but circled back to one of her own. 'The letters that you've had – from Zeno – all typewritten?'

'Yes.'

'But did they sound like anyone you knew?'

Pascoe thought about it. 'Not really, no.'

'Because it seemed to me that the one I got sounded a bit like you. Which is why I thought what I thought when I saw you outside the hotel.'

'Which is why you came after me with a gun.'

'It was—'

'Unloaded, but I didn't know that. Why do you have it at all?'

'You're asking about my life again.'

'Well,' Pascoe flapped a hand as if clearing smoke. 'I tried to hear a tone of voice in the letters, yes. I couldn't get a fix on anything. There's a sort of continual smirk between the lines, but I can't pin it on anyone.' A thought struck him. 'He sent the letter to my office – not difficult, since my name's on the letterhead. But what about you? Whoever it was knew how to reach you. That must tell us something.'

'Yes, I'd thought about it . . .' Sophie showed him an envelope; the letter had been forwarded through two previous addresses. 'I was still Lanner when I lived at the first place; in fact it's the address *you* might have had for me.'

Pascoe shook his head. 'Me . . . anyone. It's possible that someone else got to hear about Lori – someone outside the group – and the someone has decided to use the information.'

'For money.'

'What else?' As he said it, Pascoe knew that he no longer believed that. He chased the theory anyway – for Sophie's benefit. 'It's been a long time. It's almost certain that someone has shared the story: The Death of Lori Cosgrove, a melodrama, as told to—'

'Melodrama . . .' Sophie was gazing down at the tabletop, dipping the bottom of her glass in a spillage of beer and printing circles on the fake wood-grain; her voice was so low that Pascoe barely heard her repeat the word.

'So it could be someone we've never met – someone who only knows one of the group.'

'Or it could be that accomplice working with the person who first gave the information.'

'Or it could be Charlie. Or Luke.' She didn't respond, so he explained: 'Nick's dead; it wasn't me . . .'

'Yes,' Sophie said, 'I'm not stupid. I see how the options narrow.' Pascoe heard the irritation in her voice and wondered which name had struck a nerve. She gave a half-smile and said, 'Charlie was just the type to bring a rabbit out of a hat.' Pascoe summoned a picture of the man: nimble Charlie; nervy Charlie; witty, charming, fast-talking.

As if supplying Charlie's alibi, she added: 'It could have been a woman. Could have been me – or Susan, or Marianne.'

Pascoe lifted the hand he'd shown to her on the beach: the stitches decaying, like a sprig of rusty wire. 'I was there, remember. I've met him.'

Sophie shuffled along the bench seat and stood up. When she slung her bag over her shoulder, Pascoe could see the sag of the gun.

'Show me.' She took a pace or two backwards, as if impatient to be away. Pascoe was taken by surprise. The barman noticed her sudden movement, and looked from one to the other, a shadow of anxiety on his face.

'Show me.' Sophie turned and walked towards the door, confident that Pascoe would follow.

Of course he'd always intended to go back to the house. He'd transferred the key the estate agent had given him to his own key ring as if he owned it.

They walked up the hill side by side, going briskly – prospective buyers about to view their tenth of the day. Sophie was wearing a tweed jacket, nipped at the waist, an oyster-coloured blouse in some slubby material, and a string tie with a lapis toggle. The tie lifted in the wind like the tails of a kite.

'And what about you?' she asked. They weren't talking about the house; they wouldn't do that until they got there.

'You can ask, but I can't?'

'You were making judgements. There's a difference.'

'Married once; not now.'

She smiled like someone who'd just been reminded of a good joke. 'The whole world,' she said. 'The whole wide world.'

She stood just inside the front door and looked at him. A shiver twitched her shoulders and ran from her neck to her cheek in a lick of pink. She put her fingertips to her face.

'It could be you.'

'It's not.'

He turned his back and went up to the room. It was empty apart from the pine cupboard. When he looked more carefully, he could see tiny fragments of glass and china in corners, or caught up in cracks between the floorboards, or close to the skirting-board where a broom wouldn't go.

Sophie stepped in and stayed by the door to look round.

102

One arm hung straight down by her side, weighted by the gun. Pascoe spread his hands like a salesman, wares out for inspection.

'In here?' she asked.

'Look around,' Pascoe said, turning to face the window.

A room bereft of furniture apart from an old cupboard. Sophie saw the shards, bright as mica, in crevices. On a wall next to the door, and on the floor close by, were bloodstains that someone had scrubbed at: pale streaks and splashes higher up; cartwheels below.

She put out a hand and traced the mazy outline of a gout that had weathered-in like watered silk. 'Why did you stay?'

'To eat? God knows. It was odd. Like hypnosis, but no-one was here to do it. I didn't know what was going to happen, but I wasn't too worried. It was all strangely reassuring, because it looked like a joke. The table set for dinner, wine, the rest of it. I went along with it – my side of the joke. I sat down and ate the food and drank the wine and waited for my host to show up.'

'But he didn't.'

'Not the first time.'

'And when you came back?'

'I was frightened then. When I realized how close he was – in the house, playing games – things half done, the wine unopened, the candles unlit. I went out of the room for a moment; when I came back, those things *had* been done, but no-one was in here to do them.'

'Magic.'

'Yes.' He looked at her to catch the smile that came with the remark, but there wasn't one.

'The Great Zeno: Illusionist, Magus, Escapologist.' She was looking at the bloodstains again. 'You knew Nick was dead, but you didn't feel threatened?'

'It was the atmosphere,' he said, and walked over to where the table had stood. He had the excited, absorbed look of an archaeologist locating an important site. 'Food, wine, the promise of good conversation – that was what the set-up said. I was curious, not frightened. At least, not at first.'

'Set-up's right.' Sophie seemed to relax into belief. She said, 'What do you plan to do now?'

He turned to answer and as he did so, saw the gun come up. A jumble of thoughts turned in his mind, but none of them got said: You think it's me . . . Why now . . . ? You're the accomplice . . . A shawl with embroidered butterflies . . . It isn't loaded . . . It isn't loaded . . .

The sound of the shot in that enclosed space was so vast that Pascoe couldn't tell whether he'd been hit or not. Like swinging inside a great bell as the clapper struck. The rip of cordite peeled his eyeballs. He stood still, shocked into patience, waiting for pain to arrive. Sophie's eyes were blurred by fear and looking over his shoulder. He turned, following the line of the gun. The cupboard door was open.

'Jesus Christ, I'm sorry, I didn't, the door just, I was scared. I didn't know I was doing it.' She said it all in a rush, all on one note, her eyes still on the swinging cupboard door, the gun still raised. He gave her a while, then stepped forward and took the gun away. For what seemed like minutes, neither of them spoke; then Sophie said, 'I didn't know I was doing it.' Her tone was no different from before.

The bullet had entered the cupboard door at about head height, a bright star of raw wood that collapsed to a black hole at its centre. When Pascoe pushed the door further open, he saw that a second hole, more ragged, had been punched through the side of the frame.

Behind him, Sophie said, 'It opened.' She looked over Pascoe's shoulder at the cupboard's deep recess. A size for hanging robes, evening dresses, overcoats. 'It swung open for no reason. I remembered what you'd said about how he was suddenly in the room.'

Pascoe looked at the hook and eye catch. It was intact, but the hook might not have been properly secured. He tried to think back to the night when Zeno had made his grand entrance. Surely the fastening was secure: he'd checked that – hadn't he? – before sitting at the table. He'd checked the cupboard. He'd looked inside, for Christ's sake.

He stepped in and said, 'Now shut the door.' The musty smell was sharp in his nostrils, and it was dusk inside the cupboard but not full night, because the door wouldn't quite close on him.

He said, 'Push,' and shuffled back, knocking his heels against the panelling. Sophie shoved the door twice, trying to make the hook and eye marry, but there was more than four inches in it. He stepped out again.

'I remembered what you said: one minute you were alone in the room, the next he was in here with you.'

'Yes, sure . . . Well, wherever he came from, it wasn't out of the cupboard. It's too small and, in any case, I made sure that night. I looked inside.' He went towards the door. 'We'd better go.'

'Don't you want to check the rest of the house?'

'I do. What worries me is that the people who live round here might not think gunfire a more or less routine event.'

'Could have been anything.' It seemed that Sophie wanted to think that too – wanted to erase her mistake by muddling it with other possibilities.

'You think that's what they're saying? It's more likely that they're asking each other why they heard a gunshot from an empty house.'

'People mind their own business. Some sort of bang: they won't care.'

'A moment ago, you were so jumpy you were shooting at a door. Now you want a tour of the place.'

'I'm OK now,' Sophie said; and in truth, she looked perfectly calm. She tweaked the gun from Pascoe's grip, making him hop back, then put the safety on. 'I'm fine. I want to see.'

The rooms were empty, save for the tiny pockets of detritus that clutter every unoccupied house. A light bulb on a mantelpiece; a stack of newspapers; empty wine bottles in a kitchen cabinet. They went down a hallway where damp patches, speckled with brown decay, bloomed on the wallpaper like orchids.

Dark heel-and-toe prints on the floor.

Further on, a bathroom door carried a smudged handprint in the same dark stuff. The handprint opened the door on to other trophies. A smear of Leichner red at eye-level on the mirror; a curl of black on the lip of the sink.

Sophie licked a fingertip, then reached out and touched the trace of red. 'What did you say about his face?'

'Like a Death's Head. Black eyes, the rest white. Red lips.' Pascoe was looking at the mirror, his face, Sophie's face, her finger resting on the smear as if she were finding a place on a map. The mirror squeaked and she brought her hand to her face like someone holding a flower.

'The smell of the greasepaint,' she said. 'The roar of the crowd.'

'What does it tell us?' Pascoe asked.

'Tells *you* nothing. Tells *me* that either you're a terrifically careful liar, very skilful, very well-prepared, or else you're definitely telling the truth.'

'What have you decided?'

'You're telling the truth. Not because of your cut hand, or the crazy story, or the blood, or the make-up round the sink.'

'No.'

'No. The way you looked when you were in the room upstairs.'

'How did I look?'

'Like you'd just jimmied the lid on a coffin.'

The bloody footprint in the hall was like a pointer, telling them to turn back towards the heart of the house. Sophie stepped over it, hurrying towards the front door, towards the light, the street outside. Pascoe felt the urgency in her to be away.

She reached the door and the look on her face was exactly that of someone who almost leaves the house before remembering – what? Keys? Shopping list? A burner still alight on the stove?

'It doesn't work.'

'What?' He had put a hand to the door-catch, waiting for her.

'We see his dressing room – down there; the bathroom, where he put on the make-up, got ready, whatever. We see the stage – the room upstairs with a table laid for one, candles and the rest, all set for his big performance.' Sophie walked over to the staircase and peered up. She frowned and looked back down the passageway.

'Between the dressing room and the stage,' she said, 'walks the Great Zeno – Illusionist, Magus, Escapologist. Come on . . .' She started up the stairs, Pascoe following. 'Now we don't believe this Zeno is a spirit, do we? A supernatural being? A big glop of ectoplasm modelled like a man? No: we think he's real; just like you, just like me. Can't walk through walls, or suddenly materialize from plain air and candle smoke . . . Then he must be exactly what he says he is – a magician; a conjurer. Flesh and blood. Blood – you've proved that much. So: down there, in the dressing room, he puts on a gruesome face' – she opened the bedroom door and stepped inside, then turned to Pascoe as he followed – 'and then he turns in a performance so brilliant that he almost leaves his audience for dead.' She wheeled round, one arm outstretched. 'Right here, on the stage.'

Pascoe waited. Sophie squinted at him, seeming to expect him to supply the rest of the scenario. He said, 'Go on . . .'

'OK.' She looked round the room, inviting him to do the same. 'Between the dressing room and the stage – what? The wings, of course. Some means of making an entrance. But it's not the door. So where is it?'

This time, Pascoe did survey the room. 'Not the window, of course,' Sophie said.

As his gaze moved on to the cupboard, he saw her smile. 'We know that's impossible,' he said.

'Well, no, it's not. In point of fact, it's not. When we were leaving just now, I realized.'

'But you couldn't come close to shutting it when I got inside.'

'Exactly. That's the issue. Come over here.'

She took him to the cupboard and opened it, then took off her jacket and held it sideways as if the shoulders were on a clothes hanger. When she tried it inside the cupboard, one shoulder overlapped the door frame by several inches.

'When I saw this cupboard, I couldn't work out what it was for. Dishes, maybe; knick-knacks. One thing for sure – it was too narrow to be a wardrobe. I couldn't close the door when you stood in it facing front, so how could clothes hang in profile? But then I thought: So how did he get into the room – suddenly, in the way you described, one minute not there, the next minute *there*. From a hiding place, from something in the room; it had to be. Not the cupboard; except it *had* to be the cupboard. All conjurers have a magic cabinet, don't they? And I suddenly remembered, when I took the gun back from you, that you stepped back for an instant – maybe you thought I hadn't finished firing – you stepped back to the wall alongside the cupboard. And when I thought of that, I saw you standing there. Do it.'

Pascoe stood in place. He couldn't see round the cupboard. Front to back, it would have held him with inches to spare.

Sophie found it, though it wouldn't have taken anyone long. A simple push-and-release spring fixture on the side panel that stood nearest to the corner of the room. It opened on to a space behind the shell – all part of the cabinet. She slid into the gap and found a little brass grab-handle to close the panel with. Pascoe watched her smile disappear and he stood alone in the room.

He opened the cupboard, and it was empty. Sophie's

voice said: 'I've had to push the inside panel forward slightly. It slides. You don't notice, because you're not looking for it. Close the doors.' He closed them. 'Now shut your eyes.'

When he opened them, she was standing beside him, her finger pointing at his head, thumb cocked.

'Bang,' she said; a half-whisper. 'Bang, bang, bang. You're dead.'

The barman served their drinks and hurried to the next customer. It was Happy Hour and business was brisk; the men of the town were getting a couple in before going home to their wives.

Here's a proposal, Sophie read. *Let's meet in a public place.*

'You think he means it?' she asked. 'I don't.'

Let's do that. Let's make a date. I'll leave a note for you in the usual place.

'What are you going to do? Sit here and wait like an army bride? Why do as he says?' She looked round the bar at the pack of married men. She seemed to be the only woman in there. Two boys, scarcely old enough to drink, bragged at one another with whisky. The old man in the corner seat hadn't moved since Pascoe and Sophie had first arrived at the bar; he was making a beer last all afternoon. No-one was wearing Death's Head make-up and a wicked smile . . .

Pascoe said, 'Do you remember Charlie Singer's flat?'

'Yes. I remember it. A big area – just one room, really.' She closed her eyes to get a better view. 'A galley kitchen; a bathroom with a glass roof and stained-glass panels . . . There were screens separating part of the space – one cut off a little study area, another the bedroom. Charlie used to move them round according to how he was living his life at the time – open or secret. Umm . . .' Her mind's eye went round the space. 'Not much furniture.'

'Do you remember a shawl decorated with butterflies that used to hang on one of the screens?'

'No. Why?'

'It's a very strong recollection for me. The shawl draped across the screen that separated out the bedroom – and a pattern of butterflies. They were sewn in staggered rows to give room for the spread of their wings. Very bright colours; glowing colours.'

Sophie smiled. 'A lot of acid went down in Charlie's flat. I expect we all have some vivid pictures of that place.'

'But the butterflies aren't one of yours?'

'Not butterflies. I remember some pink and green mice that used to do a rather camp version of "My Way".'

Pascoe laughed. 'You always had good jokes.'

'You're saying I haven't lost my touch?'

'All the evidence isn't in, yet. The joke about the gun was a great start.'

'Well, to begin with I let you take it away from me. I wasn't concentrating. If you thought it had been empty all along, you looked stupid, not me. Also, if I told you it wasn't loaded, I got an advantage. Maybe you'd make a move. Then I'd know you had sent me the letter.'

'And if that had happened? If I'd made a move?'

As before, the accusatory finger, the cocked thumb. 'Bang.' When Pascoe shook his head to show disbelief, Sophie said, 'Don't ever bet something you can't afford to lose.'

The barman was doing a terrific job of see no order, hear no order, so Pascoe went to the bar to get refills. Sophie noticed that they were both doubles. She said, 'If it had been straightforward blackmail would you have simply paid up?'

Pascoe said, 'I didn't have a plan, Sophie. You're the one who arrived with a gun.'

'What happens,' she asked, 'if this guy tells the world about Lori Cosgrove?' Pascoe shrugged. 'Come on, Sam. Didn't you say you're a lawyer? What happens?'

'We killed her,' he said. 'In effect, we all killed her. What do you *think* would happen?'

*   *   *

For a short while longer they talked together, heads close, sharing secrets. When they left, the husbands were still laughing and drinking, but you could see they were edgy; they had entered the two-drink time lapse between 'overdue' and 'dangerously late'.

The old man in the corner seat was still nursing his beer; and now he was smiling to himself.

Not only Sam, he thought, but Sophie Lanner too. He felt like a trapper watching his quarry feeding close to the snare.

Ellwood had said, *Don't make things difficult.*

Not difficult – simple. That was the whole point. A simple life, a new life; life with Carla. No muddle, no mess, just the slate wiped clean, the past wiped clean.

Ellwood gets what Ellwood wants. I get what I want. As if offering a toast to the notion, he raised his glass and swallowed the last of his beer.

The Great Zeno – Illusionist.

Pascoe and Sophie walked back to the Palings together in a pale afternoon light that gathered greens and golds along the horizon. The sea was still.

'We could go and see Nick Howard's wife,' Sophie said.

Ten

Wallace Ellwood was sitting as still as stone in an office on the Embankment. A lighter was chugging upstream, flat-bottomed and ugly, riding the current with graceless ease. He watched its progress through the early evening murk – the way the bow-wave spread evenly to the banks. You could have struck flints off his jaw.

For twenty minutes he had listened to Hilary Todd telling him things he already knew, and he was tired of it. Thick circlets of hair sprouted from Hilary's cuffs, as if to assert the manliness left in doubt by his name. He walked up and down as he spoke, using his arms a lot and growing redder in the face as he warmed to his subject.

You cheap piece of shit, Ellwood thought. The best part of you ran down your father's leg.

The burden of Hilary's message was caution, security, tidiness. He said, 'Longrock . . . Longrock . . .' He might have been trying to recollect a place he'd once driven through. 'Longrock . . . And the old man's safe? Safe and secure?' His fixed look demanded the correct answer.

Ellwood nodded, but it wasn't enough for Hilary. He continued to stare, eyebrows raised.

'Safe and secure, yes.'

'It's just' – Hilary gestured expansively, rolling his wrists – 'just that we'd hoped for faster results, Wallace. No criticism . . .' His sincerity disappeared into a smile that would have slain small animals.

'Good.'

'Sorry?' Again the eyebrows twitched.

'Good – I'm glad. That it's not a criticism.'

'You're good at your job, Wallace, and you've spent a long time building contacts, structures, networks of people who've been useful to us from time to time, and will be again, I'm sure. You're usually unorthodox in your methods, in fact your whole approach is decidedly maverick, but you almost always get what you're after. What *we're* after. Your private life has always been something of a cause for concern, but there we are: radicals never tread a well-worn path, do they? You're loyal in an eccentric sort of a way, and although I've come to see that your real interest lies in personal pleasure, I've always believed that hunger is a sharper spur than honour. We've always needed people like you. We need you. But no-one's indispensable, Wallace, so don't look at me like something you found in your lunch, because I know a lot of things about you. The fact is, I can hurt you. Another fact is, you can't hurt me. While things are like that – best behave, OK?' The smile came back, brilliant as a blade. 'And you're sorting things out down there – have I got that right?'

'Yes.'

'Good. They say the old man's mad. He might well be. But the English make a habit of madness, don't you think? A form of privacy; a means of escape. I don't want that old man to escape just yet. There are things I need to know. After that, he can be as mad as he bloody likes.'

'We're getting there,' Ellwood told him.

'Are we? Good.' Hilary drew the *oo* sound out like a delighted child.

'He's doing a lot of talking.'

'Is he? Good.'

'It's going well.'

'Good. Well, we haven't asked questions of you until now; we haven't pried. You have the authority, the contacts, the set-up. Just . . . We'd hoped for faster results.'

'Not long,' Ellwood told him. 'You'll get what you need.'

Hilary smiled. 'Good. Good. Good.'

Wallace Ellwood's true home was the City of Dreadful Night. Like every wilderness, it had its flocks and herds. The nocturnal creatures were the most exotic: feathers and furs in electric hues, hides chased with silver, each specimen marked about the eyes with black and lilac, about the lips with pink or crimson or mauve.

Ellwood cruised to and fro, watching the girls as they grazed in shop doorways, or on the kerbside, or lodged on stationary cars; their fodder was cigarettes and loaded candy. He cut one out with a *parp* on his horn and she came to the nearside door of the car as if she were trained to the hand.

She was frightened and angry when he started to take her away. Then he mentioned money, as usual, and gave her a dab of coke on the back of her hand to keep her quiet.

Later, he brought her back to the street blank-faced and wide awake. She sat stiffly, as if concentrating on keeping her body together. Hilary Todd had made Ellwood very angry, very tense, but he wasn't feeling too bad now. The girl got out of the car before it had quite finished moving and clattered away into the dark, knees together, arms wrapped round. Ellwood reached over and closed the passenger door. When he looked up, two men were standing by the car, one by his window, the other directly in front. He might have driven at the man blocking his way, except for the fact that he treated Ellwood to the merest glimpse of his gun.

The man by the window was a tall redhead. He ambled round to the front of the car and made a show of looking at the number plate, then walked slowly back and tapped on the glass. He had the loose-limbed, flowing walk of someone who is savagely fit.

Ellwood brought the window down three inches. The redhead smiled and leaned forward in order to be better heard. He said, 'Hello,' and waited a moment. He might almost have been expecting an answer.

Ellwood looked straight ahead at the man with the weapon. The redhead didn't seem to mind the averted gaze. It gave him the opportunity to speak directly into Ellwood's ear.

'You've been taking some of my girls off the patch.' His voice was low and strangely gentle. 'Now, some of them wanted to go and some didn't, but what they wanted isn't all that important. It's what I want that counts. And I want them close to home. Economics – that's the key. I don't know what you're giving them, but I don't think it all comes back to me. That's not good. They turn a fast trick in the car – I know what that costs; I can judge my income. I can judge my investments. I can judge my returns. Some people run a business one way, some another. With me, it's high output, quick turnover, good cash flow. So I like them on the patch, working hard and working fast.'

'I'm intrigued,' Ellwood told him. 'Good business theory, good business practice. Fascinating. Fuck off.'

'Another thing . . .' The redhead's voice still held the same hushed note of confidentiality. 'One or two of them have come back hurt. Now that's not so much the problem. I mean, a girl of mine will always work unless she's unconscious or got her snatch in traction. But if there's any smacking to be done – I'll do it.'

'Good,' Ellwood said. 'That's settled, then.'

The redhead smiled. He stood back a short way and put his arm through the gap Ellwood had left between window and door-frame. He didn't seem to want more space. The man at the front of the car lay on the bonnet, belly down, facing the windscreen. When he extended his arms, the muzzle of his gun was the only thing Ellwood could see. The redhead took Ellwood's nose between his thumb and the side of his fist.

'This is what I want you to remember.' As he spoke, he rotated his fist slightly. Ellwood felt pressure at the bridge of his nose like a headache building. 'Take your money somewhere else. And your dick. And your bad moods.'

Something stringy and cartilaginous popped high in Ellwood's nostrils. A rill of blood hurried across the redhead's wrist.

'Remember this, too. If I see you round my girls again, I'll have you hurt. Not this – really hurt.' Still barely more than a whisper, though the voice betrayed a hint of the effort the redhead was making.

Ellwood's eyes were watering freely. He looked straight ahead, mouth open, blood and tears gathering on his jawline and running down to his chin, then to his throat.

'I won't see you again, so I want you to remember.' A couple of wet firecrackers exploded somewhere deep in Ellwood's face. The man draped on the bonnet laughed from behind the glass. The redhead withdrew his hand. His cuff was soaked.

'OK?' he said. 'Understand? That's good.'

Ellwood put the car into gear, his other hand welded to the wheel. He made a part-turn, reversed a few yards to gain clearance, then drove slowly out of the street. Not once did he look towards the redhead and the other man. Not once did he touch his face.

He drove half a mile down the main thoroughfare, then turned off into a side-street that led to a quiet square. The square was built round a tiny park and ringed with plane trees. He parked the car under the trees and cut the engine. Then, leaning forward slowly, shoulders rigid, he covered his face with his hands, and howled into the darkness, wounded and murderous and mad.

Eleven

He was working the box and they were loving it. You could tell by the stillness, the sense of apprehension. They never applauded, or cooed, or gasped. The Lady with the Flower, Dog Face, The Man with the Big Bow Tie. They were all there. Birdie. The Wandering Jew. Mac the Cough. He made the globes flow along the rim of the lid, like lightbulbs on a theatre marquee. As each globe reached the end, it hopped on to the floor and came to heel. They *loved* it. You could sense the bated breath.

He asked for a volunteer and someone hopped up on to the stage: the perfect candidate in his white smock and trousers. He held out the strait-jacket and Zeno shrugged into it, standing to face the audience and hugging himself while the straps were buckled. Then he turned, to let them see how the man linked the buckles with a chain and the chain with a spring padlock.

More chain went round his thighs and ankles, padlocked into place. He raised his chin and the man snapped a steel collar round his neck. From a ring on the collar, a long chain went down to his ankles and up his back to his neck again, padlocked to the other chains in turn. He could move by hopping a few inches, nothing more.

The man helped him into the box and closed it. He padlocked the cast-iron hasp that held the lid, then bound the box with three chains and padlocked those. Then he clambered off the stage. Everyone looked at the box. In the utter stillness, the Lady with the Flower began to cry.

Someone walked on stage – a clown in a check suit three sizes too big. On his head, a fez; on his face, a sorry smile. He was peering into the audience as if he didn't know where he was. After a moment or two, he spotted the box. It was clear that he was made curious by it. He walked round it a couple of times, then tugged at one of the chains. The fact that it wouldn't budge seemed to quicken the clown's curiosity. He tried again, yanking at the chains, at the padlock, at the lid of the box, but everything held.

Now he was really angry. He went off-stage and reappeared with a crowbar. Huffing and puffing, he thrust the bar under one of the chains and levered down. His mouth was stretched in a great big grin of effort, his eyes squeezed shut. Nothing.

After a moment, he switched his attention to a padlock, getting the crowbar through the steel hoop and twisting furiously. It wouldn't give. In a fury, he swung the crowbar like an axe, whacking the locks, trying to knock them off. It was pointless.

The clown looked at the box in disgust. He knew there was something in there: something valuable, something priceless, perhaps; but he also knew he wasn't going to get it. He tossed the crowbar down and left the stage.

Stillness again. The box centre-stage, like a totem. As they watched, the lid hopped. A chain unfixed and snaked to the floor, its links ringing. Then another, then the third. The lid hopped once more and the padlock on the hasp rattled and fell. It was easy work for the lighting man; the spotlight took every eye to the box, the rest of the stage was dark.

The lid flapped back. A shadow flowed through the audience – everyone's head lifted, everyone leaned forward.

In a deafening silence, Zeno stepped out of the box and strode towards them, his grin like a fanfare, his arms held out like someone come to save.

Father Tom Carey met him after the show. He was a regular, now, along with the others; a fan. Together, they walked through the town and down to the foreshore.

There were three or four points of foam round a circlet of offshore rocks, otherwise the water was flat to the edge of the world.

'How do you do it?' Carey asked.

Zeno shrugged as if he wasn't sure. Then he said, 'Usual thing. I do this trick, do that; all the time, I push the box around the stage in a sort of haphazard way – carelessly – so it seems to end up in a random position. Well, it's over a trap. Lateral thinking, you see. People say, If he can get out of one chain, he won't be able to get out of two. If he gets out of two, he'll never manage the rest. Then there's the strait-jacket, the connecting chains. They think of the obstacles one by one. But they all come off together, backstage, where there's someone with a key.'

'What about the box,' Carey wanted to know. 'It's locked and chained, but you get out of that.' He thought back. 'Is it the clown?'

Zeno squinted against the breeze. They were walking below the harbour wall where he'd killed Nick Howard.

'Yes, it's the clown. The trick is to pretend to test the locks and find them impossible. In fact, they're being undone. But you don't see that.'

'I didn't see it,' Carey agreed. 'The clown's good. Who is he.'

Zeno looked at him in puzzlement. 'It's me.'

They walked past the town and into a patch of sand dunes and marram grass. Carey said, 'We've known each other for a long time. When did it start – the magic?'

'No,' Zeno said. 'We knew each other a long time ago. It's a different thing.' Carey let it go. 'It began as fun. I was travelling. I went to Greece. I was living on a beach on one of the islands. A man there taught me to juggle. He used to be with a circus. It started there. You just need fast hands. Most of it is tricks.'

No it's not, he thought. It's magic. It's wonderment. It's having life on a line. I don't know how to say those things and be properly understood.

Carey said, 'It's good to see you again.'

'Why are you here?'

'Aren't you pleased to see me?'

They sat down in the lee of a dune. Sandgrains whispered through the stalks of marram grass. When Zeno leaned forward and put his head on his knees, he heard the sound as voices softly singing. He saw a church interior, dark and cool; he sat in the confessional and said everything there was to be said. On the other side of the grille, Father Carey, listening.

Carey was looking out to sea. He seemed a little petulant – waiting to have his question answered.

Aren't you pleased to see me?

Zeno remembered the lingering smells of incense and wood polish; the tall windows; the darkness of the confessional, curtains drawn to keep the knowledge of sin from everyone but the priest.

Forgive me, Father, for I have sinned. It is a week since my last confession.

Every week, without fail. He would tell all there was to tell. Her name. What they did. What they talked about.

Lori.

And Father Carey would say: *The woman is married. It's a mortal sin.* But they both knew it wasn't the issue. What he and Lori did wasn't important. What they said – that's what he went to confession to unload. The things she told him. The secret things.

Zeno remembered how he would leave the church unburdened, clean of knowledge, clean of secrets. He remembered the feeling of lightness, as if he'd been emptied out.

He said, 'Why are you here?'

'Friends of yours asked me to come,' Carey told him. 'They thought you might like to talk.'

'Wallace Ellwood,' Zeno said. Carey didn't speak. 'Nick died by accident; we had a fight.'

'When did I ever judge you?' Carey asked.

Never, Zeno thought. You never did. If he closed his

eyes he could imagine the grille between them, could hear the distant singing, could feel the darkness where secrets must be told.

Yes, I'm glad you came. I didn't know I needed you until now. But there are things you have to hear. Things you have to help me understand.

Zeno said, 'I've met someone. Carla. I found her one day on—'

'No,' Carey said, 'wait a minute. Not like that.' He shuffled round, taking himself out of Zeno's vision, until they were sitting back to back. Their shoulders touched. Slowly, Zeno leaned backwards, head lifted, and let his confessor take the weight. Eyes open, he saw the sky: washed-out blue-grey and gulls on a thermal. Eyes closed, he saw the grille: behind it, shadow-fragments and a voice that would forgive anything.

'Now,' Carey said, 'begin again.'

Forgive me, Father, for I have sinned. It is twenty years since my last confession.

Twelve

They left Sophie's Peugeot in the car park at the Palings and drove eight hours up country to a sad waste of time. Louise Howard talked a lot, but she had just the one subject. Her eyes were dark and withdrawn as if she could only look inward.

She said, 'Not that he died. I mean, people do. He was fit, I think. He used to go to a gym, sometimes. His company paid for health insurance – regular check-ups and so forth; but you know – people do; unexpectedly, or else they get ill with something that can't be cured. No, that's not it . . . To be murdered. Not just die, but be murdered.' Her cuticles were livid where she'd picked the soft skin off. 'You're friends of Nick's, is that it?'

'We knew him a while ago,' Pascoe said. Then, as if it gave him some obscure form of authority, he added: 'I'm a lawyer.'

'It's too damn late for that,' Louise snapped, then frowned at herself because what she had said made no sense. 'Why are you here? The funeral was days ago.'

Sophie saw the opportunity and took it. 'We got that wrong. I'm sorry. We'd hoped . . .'

'Too late. The police finished with him and we buried the rest.' She shuddered, thinking of it. 'A road accident – you can cope with that. A fall, a disease. It makes no sense to be murdered; none at all. He was a businessman on a trip. He shouldn't have been anywhere near the place.'

She knew nothing about a letter. She knew nothing about any meeting. Sophie talked a little about their friendship with Nick. She mentioned other friends –

122

Charlie Singer, Sue Hart, Luke Mallen, Marianne Novaks. Lori Cosgrove. They watched her face. Louise knew nothing about any of them.

She went with them to the door. 'I don't know what happens about his will. I don't know what happens about his insurance. I've got a child to bring up. He was murdered; maybe that changes things.'

Pascoe said, 'The will isn't affected. It makes no difference.'

Louise looked at him as if she had just worked out the reason for his visit. She said, 'If only he'd just died, like other men.'

Pascoe said, 'Where do you live?' It was one of a million things he didn't know about her.

'London,' she said.

'It's two hours to London, six more to Longrock. Do you want to go home?'

'No, I don't. You live in London too, yes?'

'Yes.'

'Then why don't *you* go home? I'll come with you.'

They drove and talked. Sophie was able to glance at him from time to time as she spoke – the passenger's privilege, to look at the driver while the driver must look at the road. He had a slightly blunt profile that became good-looking when you saw him face-on. Green eyes, pepper-and-salt hair, dead straight and a little too long. When he finger-combed it back from his forehead, it would flop the wrong way, then slowly fall into place, layer by layer. A tiny sickle scar, like a Turkish crescent, marred the line of his cheek-bone. She hadn't really looked at him closely till now.

Stupid to think it might be you. But what put the thought in my head? We didn't have a leader, exactly. That wasn't part of the game. But there had to be an energy source. It was you. Luke had wild schemes, but you could make things happen. Charlie had secrets and sorrows; you had ambition.

She said, 'You wanted to blow up a train – remember that?'

'I wasn't serious.'

'Like fuck. You had the whole thing worked out: time, route, everything. You'd even got hold of some detonators.'

'Military target.'

'Oh, sure; I understood the reason.'

'It would never have come to that.'

'Why not? We did other stuff.'

'Minor acts of sabotage.'

'Yeah – other stuff. We burned down a building. Blowing up a train was on the agenda too. Definitely on our things-to-do list.'

Pascoe didn't respond for a moment; when he did, he sounded weary. 'What a joke. We were a joke. Sneaking around the USAF base at night with blacked-up faces. Sugar in petrol tanks, peace symbols on the walls, tyres slashed, some poor sod with third-degree burns. What did we hope to achieve?'

'It was exciting,' Sophie said. 'I wish we *had* blown up the fucking train.' There was silence between them for a moment. As though she were reading his thoughts, she added: 'But I wish we hadn't killed Lori.'

The worst thing rode with them down to London.

Carla set food in front of the two men, then went back to the kitchen to fetch her own. When she joined them at the table, Father Tom said grace. They ate the meal slowly, a simple pasta dish with salad, followed by a sorbet and cheese. Father Tom congratulated Carla on her cooking. She maintained that it was nothing – criticizing herself for its plainness. Father Tom pointed out that all food is a sacrament. This seemed to satisfy Carla. She smiled to herself as she cleared the plates away.

Carla hadn't asked any questions about Tom Carey. She had simply accepted him as a friend of Zeno's. Tom had heard all about Carla, however.

Zeno had said, 'I've never known anything like this – never felt anything. Women – you know; there have been women. I've led an unsettled life. Ellwood has used me for something, now and then. I've had this job and that.'

'The Great Zeno,' Father Tom had said. 'Illusionist, Magus, Escapologist.'

'Sometimes. I don't always like to do that. I've done casual work – enough with the retainer I get through Ellwood. Conjuring – magic – you can't do it as a business if you really care. It has to . . . build up. It's delicate business.'

'All tricks, you said.'

'Yes, it is. Of course it is. All tricks. But you can get tired. The show can begin to look tired.'

'So you'd gone from job to job, from place to place. And then you met Carla.'

Down on the beach Zeno had finally opened his eyes and taken his weight off Carey's back. He'd stared at the slow curl of the breakers and told the priest about the moment when he'd found Carla.

'I took her back with me. It was the only thing to do. She needed my help. It was as if she could only be safe with me, only be protected by me, and somehow, against all the odds, she found me – down there on the edge of the sea, as if all her past had washed away and I was the only chance of a future. No past, do you see? No *past*. We loved each other at once, it seemed to me, in the moment that we met. I didn't know things like this could happen. It's too powerful to describe properly. It wraps me up. Do you understand?'

Carey had said that he did.

'It consumes me and I live off it. Does that make sense to you?'

'It does.'

'It eats me and it feeds me. Do you see?'

'Yes,' Carey had said. 'Yes, yes.' They had still been back to back, so Zeno wasn't able to see that Father Carey's face was filled with fear.

Now they sat together face to face while Carla cleared the table and brought coffee. After that, she excused herself and went to bed. To compensate for her lameness, she hoisted her left hip slightly as she walked. The effect was oddly erotic; she was wearing denims and the globes of her buttocks rolled with the movement.

Zeno shifted in his chair and put a hand to his kidney region, wincing. When Carey glanced at him, an eyebrow raised, he smiled: 'My back. It's nothing new.'

Carla had disinfected the wound and dressed it. She hadn't asked him about it; she hadn't spoken at all. It still troubled him slightly; he could feel the scar pulling and there was a deep ache in the wound at times.

It was all-but dusk; they were making do with the light from the candles that Carla had placed at either end of the table. Zeno poured two brandies. He rolled a coin across his knuckles and back.

Carey smiled. 'Fast hands,' he said.

'That's right.'

'Tell me about it – your magic show. How did that start?'

'I suggested it, the hospital authorities agreed. Simple as that. I give one show a week. Enough for them, and more than enough for me. A captive audience. I'm one of several volunteer acts: a barbershop quartet, an amateur dramatic group . . . Most of the time, they just watch TV.'

'What do they think?' Carey asked. 'About the Great Zeno?'

'They're all mad,' Zeno said. 'Who knows what they think? The nurses bring them in. They watch the act. They go out again. Now and then one of them throws a fit. Did you understand what I was saying to you earlier? About Carla?'

'Of course. Of course I understood. And the old man's there? He comes to the show?'

Zeno smiled. 'One of the regulars. I call him the Man with the Big Bow Tie.'

'How long, do you think?'

'Did Ellwood ask you to ask that?'

Carey smiled. 'I'll talk to Ellwood. You can talk to me – just like the old times. How long . . . ?'

'He talks about the past. It's a jumble of stuff. His childhood, school, the war . . . He hasn't said anything yet. I don't . . .' He paused. 'Ellwood asks too much. I want to stop all this now. It was different before I met Carla.'

'Just this one,' Carey said. 'Then perhaps you can stop.'

A thought came to Zeno. 'Tell Ellwood,' he said, 'that if he involves Carla, I'll kill him. She isn't the past.'

'You want to wipe it out,' said Carey, 'don't you? You want to kill it off – just as you killed Nick.'

'It was an accident.'

'No it wasn't. However it happened, whatever brought him here, you wanted him dead. He's the past, and you fear the past. Why lie? What are you afraid of?'

Everything, Zeno thought. Everyone who can bring the past back to me and threaten the future with it; threaten my freedom and the chance to be with Carla. Anyone who knows about those times, about the group, about Lori.

'Lori . . .' Carey might have been reading his thoughts. 'Do you think about that?' Zeno looked away. 'Well, she was a stupid woman,' Carey said. 'What happened was bad. But it was in pursuit of doing good – a good cause. One of those vexed questions. The church used to fetter itself with theological conundrums of that sort. Remember? How many angels can dance on a pin?' He laughed. 'Seen any of the others?'

'What?'

'Others from the group.'

'No.'

It was almost dark outside the room. The sickly glow from the candles dyed Zeno's cheek; the coin glittered back and forth across his hand: just chips of light. They were talking without being able to see one another's face. Carey got up and found the switch.

Zeno was looking directly at him. 'Lori told things to me. Told me secrets. I came to confession and told them to you. You told them to someone else.'

Carey said, 'That's how it worked.'

'All in a good cause. A new world; a new future.' Carey was silent. 'That's all I'm asking for now,' Zeno said.

Sophie peered out of the window of Pascoe's flat, presenting only her profile, like a fugitive. A helicopter was quartering the park, its vast, chalk-white searchlight hauling through bushes and trees, walkways and knolls, like a net dragging the dark. The sound of its rotors hummed on in the window panes.

'You like living down here?' she asked.

'People have asked me that before.' Pascoe was making omelettes. He had scarcely been aware of the chopper. Sometimes they were looking for muggers, sometimes they were just reminding the area's lowlife that there was a war going on.

He'd offered Sophie wine and she'd asked for whisky. When she moved away from the window and returned to her chair, it was there at her elbow, along with some chilled mineral water. She topped up from both bottles, eighty-twenty in favour of Scotch.

Pascoe said, 'Do you drink a lot?'

'It's a good technique – countering a question with a question, especially a *leading* question. A form of professional foul for you, I imagine.' When he smiled, she smiled back. 'Still, I'll trade you an answer for an answer. I used to drink a hell of a lot. That proved dangerous, so I cut down and drank a lot. It wasn't as dangerous, but it was quite a responsibility: quantities to check, schedules to keep, you know . . . a reputation to maintain. Now I just drink heavily from time to time – binge. Between binges, I sip. This is sipping. Why do you live down here?'

Pascoe brought the omelettes to the table, along with a tomato salad and some bread.

'Do you know about the *Marie Celeste*?'

'Sure. A ship found floating in mid-ocean. No-one aboard. As if the entire crew and passengers had left on a second's notice. Meals half-eaten, ovens warm . . .'

'That's right. One morning I went out, had an average sort of day, returned home to the *Marie Celeste*. It was as if she had simply thought of the idea, got up, taken a coat and left. In the living room there was a book she'd been reading, still open. A cup of coffee, half-finished; it was cold. She'd been going to make grilled scallops – all the preparation was done. They were marinading in the fridge. The implements she'd used were in the sink.' Sophie watched as he reconstructed the picture in his head, going from room to room. 'It was almost dark by the time I got back. I realized she must have been gone a while, because the lights were switched off. She'd left the radio playing; just forgetfulness, I'm sure. I came in and it was too dark, really, to see the furniture, or the pictures, you know, but there was music playing, a cello piece, very slow, very rich. I looked for her in every room, and wherever I went I could hear the cello.' Pascoe wandered over to the table where the Scotch and water stood and poured himself a drink, then brought the bottle over for Sophie. He said, 'Maybe you'd like some wine?'

She shook her head. 'No thanks. I rarely drink for pleasure.' She had eaten her omelette; now she leaned over and took a forkful of his. It was untouched.

'All her clothes were still there, it seemed. Shoes. Jewellery. She hadn't taken books or records or any of the bits and pieces round the place that were hers. No knick-knacks, no geegaws, no keepsakes. There was a box of Tampax with just one missing. Afterwards, I thought that was funny. As if she imagined that by walking out she could become immaculate. I remember saying to someone later: "She got it wrong – it doesn't work like that. Things have to be said; there are things I have to hear, have to know." But that was the end of my marriage – everything still there in the house except my wife; the cello playing,

129

myself still wondering why she'd gone out in such a hurry and when she might be back.'

'You're divorced now?'

'No – separated, like you.'

'Why no divorce?'

Pascoe started to eat. His story was over, except to say: 'Because I haven't seen her since.'

'What?' Sophie opened her mouth to laugh, but the laugh became a cough. She smoothed it with whisky.

'She wrote to me, via a colleague at the office. I wondered about that, and came to the conclusion that it was a method of demonstrating that she was alive.'

'In case someone thought you'd killed her?'

He shrugged. 'I suppose so.'

'What was in the letter?'

'PO box number for forwarding her mail; a cheque to cover her share of the mortgage for three months – giving me time to sell the house; permission to sell her property and use the proceeds for a percentage of the legal fees; a request for a couple of what she charmlessly referred to as personal items.'

'Efficient lady.'

Pascoe nodded. 'I hadn't the first fucking notion who she was. Not the first. I'd lived with her for six years.'

'She'd lived with you.'

'Also true.'

'Nothing about the sudden departure? I couldn't bear it another moment – reached breaking-point – felt trapped – any of that stuff?'

'No.'

'You wrote, asking her? To the PO box.'

'Sure. Silence.'

'The stuff she wanted you to send her . . . ?'

'Photographs in a double frame – her parents; two of the many things we didn't have in common, it seems.'

'What else?'

'Her diaphragm.'

Sophie looked at him, wide-eyed and straight-faced.

When she trusted herself to speak, she asked, 'What was her name?'

'Karen,' Pascoe told her.

Sophie lifted the bottle and charged her glass. 'Karen,' she said, and took a sip. A tear popped up in her eye, but still she didn't laugh.

Thirteen

Pascoe woke and looked round furiously. For a moment nothing was familiar, then things swam together: books, pictures, furniture. He'd never slept in his living room before. The phone rang and rang. When he lifted it, there were voices, a man's and a woman's. He recognized the man as Rob Thomas. The woman said, 'No, you've got . . .' then paused in confusion. It was Sophie, barely awake.

Pascoe said, 'It's OK, I've got it. Rob?'

'Sam.' There was high amusement in Thomas's voice. 'Who's she?'

'What's today?'

'Tuesday.'

'Tuesday? Madonna.'

'I called you at a hotel by the sea, then I called your office, but I find you in bed with a blonde. I've got something for you. Something you expected, something you didn't.'

'You found them?'

'Yes and no. Easier if we don't do this over the phone, Sam.' Thomas gave an address in Soho. 'Bring Madonna. Tell her jeans and a T-shirt's fine.'

While Pascoe showered, Sophie looked for the coffee. There was nothing left to eat.

The flat was small. He could hear her clattering round in the kitchen. She heard him start the shower. Those little domestic moments passed them by; it had been too long for both of them.

He came back fully dressed and picked his coffee up as

if he always found it there. Sophie was looking down into the street. She said, 'There's a dead body by the park railings.'

'No there's not,' Pascoe said. 'She just sleeps late, that's all.'

'You must have really hated yourself when you bought this flat.'

It was one of those unlikely events – a wind in the city. Sophie opened the car window, pretending that because the air was swift it was also fresh. Cyclists wearing surgeon's masks did trick riding through the sheet-metal maze formed by a mile of cars.

'Did you look for Karen?'

'Yes.'

'You didn't find her?'

'No. She told me she'd changed her name. I gave up after that. It makes tracing someone damn-near impossible.'

'But you wanted to find her . . . ?'

'Yes.'

'What for?'

As she spoke, the traffic found a free twenty yards and snaked forward, engines howling. He was switching lanes, cutting in on an angry-looking Toyota sports, and she thought he probably hadn't heard her. They came to the fringe of Soho and went stop-start through the grid of streets to a car park.

'I can't remember,' Pascoe said.

Rob Thomas buzzed them in to a narrow door between a café and a pornographic bookshop. The first three floors were film production companies. The fourth was an office and a lavatory. They were much the same size. Thomas was at the door, peering over Pascoe's shoulder to get a sight of Sophie; behind him, a man was sitting at a VDU, his hands moving over the keyboard so rapidly that his fingertips seemed to crackle.

'Your dope dealer was a good trade, Sam. I managed to get extra credit for myself out of the deal.'

'He named names,' Pascoe suggested.

'Yeah. He named names that named names. A big net; they hauled it in like a trawl. The real stuff.'

'This is Sophie Lanner,' Pascoe said.

'Not Madonna.' Sophie looked from one to the other, trying to spot the joke. Thomas said, 'She was on the list.'

'That's right.'

'You found her,' Thomas said, 'I found Charles Singer. But he didn't come as part of the trade. He wasn't on the computer.'

To the police programmers it's just 'the computer'. It will list you if you've ever been convicted of a crime. It will list you if you're wanted in connection with a crime. It will list you if you've been the victim of a crime. Otherwise, you won't be there. According to circumstance, it will offer certain information. About victims it tends to be discreet, but criminals are turned upside down and shaken. If you love your mother, the computer will know. If you love chocolate chip ice-cream more, the computer will know that, too.

'Where did you find him?'

'The dope dealer was a real bonus,' Thomas said. 'You couldn't have known it would work out like that, but I thought you deserved a little extra effort. So I came to see Alex.' He stepped aside like someone drawing a curtain.

The man at the keyboard looked over his shoulder and smiled a fat, dreamy smile. A moon face. He could have been stoned for the best part of a decade. When he spoke his voice was mild and thoughtful. Sophie felt that she'd caught someone in the process of being born again.

'It's right here.' Alex flopped a hand at the screen. A stream of double columns flowed upwards, red gas-plasma ribbons. He stopped the text and scrolled back a little way. 'That him?'

The same address: the loft. Stripped floorboards; scant

furniture, the screen with a butterfly shawl. Pascoe laughed out loud. He said, 'I don't believe it.' Then: 'Yes. Yes, that's him.'

Alex looked rueful, almost sad. 'He's in trouble.'

Like Pascoe, Sophie was staring at the address. The words made a picture and the picture was the past. She said, 'What trouble? How do you know?'

'He owes his limit and more on three credit cards and one charge card,' Alex looked apologetic. 'They've been asking for the money for close to six months. At first they were impatient. Now they're getting angry. All told, he's in for about nine thousand. How I know – this address is part of the creditors' file kept by one of those companies.' The smile returned, lazy and broad. 'I hacked in and stole it. In fact, I hacked in and stole them all.'

The same address. Perfect; impossible.

Why? thought Pascoe. Why, Charlie? Staying is so much tougher than moving on.

'Here's what you probably didn't expect,' Thomas said. 'Singer's not on the police computer, though it sounds as if that's a matter of time.' He handed Pascoe a sheet of paper. 'She was.'

Marianne Novaks. An address; description; items of basic information.

'Missing persons index,' Thomas observed. 'You're not the only one looking for her.'

Pascoe handed the paper to Sophie. He said, 'Thanks, Rob.'

'No . . .' Thomas shook his head and laughed. 'The guy's still talking. I'm in credit, you're in credit. I hope they manage to get him straight to solitary.'

Alex had gone back to work, eyes on the screen, fingers fast but pianissimo. Pascoe looked round the room. There were racks of floppy discs, print-outs, file indexes categorized by district and social grouping. He said, 'What is all this?'

'Customer listings – credit card companies, chain stores, subscriptions, hire-purchase outfits, travel firms—'

'All stolen?'

'All stolen. I'm writing a program that gives a customer-by-customer profile. Income, spending patterns, fixed commitments, holidays, possessions, that sort of stuff. Then the company direct-mails them. A one per cent response is good.'

Sophie leaned over his shoulder and peered at the screen, as if expecting to find someone she knew. 'Who do you work for?'

'Today, a time-share lottery. Yesterday, mail-order CDs. Tomorrow – who knows?' He glanced back for a moment, then smiled, seeming to register her properly for the first time. 'You're Sophie what?'

She saw what he was about to do. 'Lanner,' she said. 'Sophia.'

'I'm assuming London.'

'Yes.'

He keyed the index, then went to file, *clackety-clack*. People and places hurried across the screen, then a block settled into focus, the cursor winking alongside. Alex scrolled through, slowly. 'Sophia . . . There won't be too many of you.' He sat back. 'There you are. Hampstead – very nice.'

Sophie looked at her name and address on the screen. 'OK,' she said. 'Tell me who I am.'

Alex took the cursor to a window at the top right-hand corner of the screen and keyed the number that had appeared next to Sophie's name. Secrets fell in to view like flags unfurling, banner after banner, red on black.

Alex smiled his meaty smile. 'You're rich,' he said. 'How do you feel about a time share in the Algarve?'

Newspaper wrapped round her legs and she kicked it free. Pascoe was walking slightly ahead of her – in a hurry, or else showing the way.

'Sam? *Sam!*' She raised her voice, but she was damned if she'd trot after him like a submissive wife. He looked back, then slowed down at once; he seemed surprised to see her there. 'Marianne's address. That's near Longrock, am I right?'

'I'm not sure exactly where, but close – yes.'

'Does that put them together? Marianne and Zeno. Are they a pair?'

Pascoe shrugged. 'Reported missing by a Peter Novaks. Was that her father's name?'

'I don't remember.' Sophie stopped, letting Pascoe walk on because he was striding past the entrance to the car park. He came back looking preoccupied and vague.

'We left it here? They all look alike.'

As he edged the car broadside into the traffic, the wind was bringing a twister of garbage down the cross-street. Instinct made Sophie duck as remnants from its aftermath rattled against the windscreen. She said, 'You don't get weather in cities, just trash-attack.'

There were two routes open to them: one directly west, the other veering north. Pascoe took them out of the central streets, then filtered on to a through-road that ran straight as a die out of the city.

'We're going to Claydon,' Sophie said.

Something in her voice made Pascoe say, 'I am. You don't have to.'

They were taking the elevated section that led to the western approach roads. Sophie hunkered down in her seat and turned her face to look at the streets below. Pascoe thought she was sleeping and put some music on, keeping the sound low. She let him take her twenty miles beyond the city boundaries before she said, 'No, that's OK. I've nowhere else to go.' Then she did sleep, a Brahms piece on the tape deck, the landscape greening round her, the wind cleaner with every mile.

Almost everything had changed. The centre of Claydon had been ripped out and rebuilt – once narrow streets and redbrick buildings, some even plaster and beam; now, the new brutalism – slab-built office blocks, concrete walk-ways, a shopping complex like a gulag. At one time

Charlie Singer's place had been on the fringe; now it was fifty streets in.

Strangers in a strange town. The street, at least, was the same. Pascoe parked outside and they sat in the car looking at Charlie's building.

'Going back's dreadful,' Sophie said. 'I feel as if I was here yesterday, and everything was the way it used to be. Then I went away for a day and now I've come back to find this. It's what death is like – the future without you.'

She got out and ran across the pavement to the door. When Pascoe caught up with her, she was ringing Charlie's bell for the third time. 'He's not in.'

Pascoe rang the other two bells. Sophie said: 'What difference will—?' As she spoke, a voice came through the microphone grille next to the door.

Pascoe glanced at the name tag by the bell. 'Mrs Anderson? Algarve Tenancies. We telephoned.'

He pushed the door when the buzzer sounded. Sophie walked up the hallway, beyond the door of the ground-floor flat and out of sight. She listened while Pascoe and Mrs Anderson had a conversation thick with misunder-standings and apologies. Pascoe promised to return to his office and recheck the files; clearly a mistake had been made. He walked to the street door, opened and closed it, then went up to Charlie's flat. He found Sophie lounging against the wall, arms folded.

'What difference does that make?' she wanted to know. 'We're in the house, but—'

Pascoe slipped the lock with a credit card. He said, 'Lawyers know things that lawyers' clients know,' and pushed the door open to let her in.

The place was dim and still. The window blinds were down all round the flat, though the slats had been raised to give a little light. A chill had gathered in the air, and a stale smell.

It was as it had been – a couple of rugs on the vast floor space; a wallhanging; a new sound system – unchanged apart from that. The kitchen was a fifteen-foot counter running along one wall with a stove, a fridge, a sink, cupboards above and below. The rest was almost all open space. A desk behind one set of screens, a bed behind another.

The desk top was empty. The bed was littered with clothes hangers. Pascoe got on to his knees and peered underneath.

'Suitcases,' Sophie guessed his purpose.

'And they're not here.' He emerged, then disappeared behind the other screen, taking Zeno's letters out of his pocket and laying them on the desk top, before searching the drawers for matching paper. He found unpaid bills, bank statements, junk; a fistful of post-it notes, which he pocketed. No typewriter. When he went back into the main room, Sophie wasn't in sight.

'Remember?' her disembodied voice asked him.

He did and he didn't. The room was familiar and because of that unutterably strange. They would sit on the floor, the seven of them, propped on cushions, shaping a new world order from dope and indignation. They built castles in the air and dynamited them. They built banks and barracks and parliaments, prisons and courts of law, and blew them all to hell. Sometimes they argued; but on one part of the agenda they all agreed. Everything must change. And so it had.

'Remember?' Sophie asked. She came out of the bathroom and started towards the kitchen. 'There's a circular stained-glass panel in there – an elephant. I recalled it as being bright red with jewelled eyes.'

'Is it?'

'I must have been tripping at the time.'

He went into the bathroom to look and found a grey elephant in a sketchy blue-green jungle. When he came out, she had disappeared again.

'It was non-stop tripping, wasn't it, Sam? That's how it seems to me. Tripping and talk. Now and then, we slipped out and broke the law. I liked that part. It was exciting.

Fuck the revolution. I did it for the buzz. I liked it better than sex.'

He found her behind the bedroom screen, sitting on the bed with her back to the wall, arms round her shins, her chin propped on her knees. When he came in she looked directly at him and started to laugh delightedly, as if he had just surprised her with a terrific joke.

'Rescue me, Sam. I'm in a fucking time warp.'

'He's moved out.'

'He hasn't been there in some while,' Pascoe said. 'That doesn't mean he won't go back.'

They were driving out of the town, climbing towards a ridge of hills. The houses were sparse now; the town had spread, but not this far. Just back from the road, two ponies were kicking their heels up in a paddock.

'What will you do?'

'Ask Rob Thomas to top and tail each day with a phone call. He might get lucky.'

'If Charlie's running away from bad debts, he isn't likely to answer the phone.'

'Everyone answers the phone. It might be good news.'

'It might be the Grim Reaper.' They were still climbing, travelling along minor roads now, with woodland on either hand. The wind was still up and louder than it had been before.

'On the other hand, of course, Charlie might be down in Longrock waiting for us.'

'Is it Charlie?'

'I don't know.'

'You came pretty close. You fought with him while he tried to kill you.'

'It could have been Charlie, yes. The greasepaint was a disguise. The years between were a disguise, too. Behind that mask of make-up, it could have been anyone, but—'

'Something you recognized?'

Pascoe tried to recall the moment, the sense-impression, then he shrugged. 'Not really . . .'

'Charlie was always the private one,' Sophie said. 'The one with secrets.'

'Was he?'

'Sure.' Pascoe glanced sideways and surprised a half-smile on her face. 'He wasn't easy to get to know.'

'It's impossible to know anyone. Isn't that one of the lessons we learn?'

'You mean Karen.'

'I mean anyone.'

In the pale afternoon light, the ridge was resolving itself into beech woods and bald escarpments. Below them, a rash of new-growth conifers; lower still, a pocket-sized plain.

'We're going to Lori's house,' Sophie said.

'Yes. We're going to Lori's house.'

The plain was man-made and cordoned off. A straggle of conifers came right down to the fence, one or two with signs nailed to them. You could see some hangars in the distance and, on the left, low blocks of administrative buildings; the main entrance was on the other side of the complex – two miles away, or more. Sophie got out and went to the wire.

After a while, Pascoe lowered the car window. He said, 'Let's go.'

Sophie turned round, bouncing her shoulders against the wire and calling to him. The wind brought her words along. 'How stupid we were. How stupid. Not stupid to have done what we did – no – but to think it would make a difference. Wasn't that stupid, Sam?' He pretended he couldn't hear, but she knew better. 'We sabotaged their trucks, we painted slogans on their buildings, we played tag with guards and dogs, we cut their wire, we torched an entire fucking admin block up here, Sam – remember that? And how stupid, how fucking *stupid* to be doing it for something as wasteful as a good cause.'

He said, 'Get in the car.'

'We thought it could change. Did we think that? Did we

141

really think—?' She threw her hands in the air, scattering tactics, ideals, blueprints for the new world. 'What lamebrains, Sam; what a bunch of deadheads.' He looked away, but her voice came down the wind, high-pitched and passionate. 'What sinners we were. Acid and accidie. All the shit we talked. All the fucking *shit*, Sam. Jesus Christ, we could have been having a good time. We could have been doing it all for *fun*.'

Pascoe looked at her through the open window. She had borrowed a blue woollen scarf that he'd forgotten he owned, and tied it loosely under her chin. The wind lifted the fringed ends and wagged them in front of her face. She said, 'I'm not going up there. I'm not going to Lori's house.'

The officers' residences were just below the hill, strung out in a long line, and a good way apart to give space and privacy. At the backs of the houses, the beech wood took over where cultivated ground ended. Visitors would drive along a narrow macadam lane, past the double gates, the slick lawns, the Stars and Stripes on a pole. That was one way to see your friends. Another way was to leave the car parked in a pull-in on the approach road, close to a phone box, and walk past the lane to a track that led up through the beeches. You could see the backs of the houses – french windows, dining-room windows, bedroom windows; and you could see people going to and fro in the rooms. With a pair of field glasses you'd have been able to tell what they were eating for dinner.

Pascoe reached back to grab Sophie's arm pulling her up on to the slope where the track met the road. She was pale and tight-lipped. After they'd gone a few yards, she muttered something and barged past him to lead the way.

Lori had lived in the fourth house. Sophie stood exactly opposite and stared down at the windows.

Pascoe said, 'I saw her in the bedroom window. Then suddenly she was outside. When I thought about it, recently, I seemed to see the window as a stage. You know

– the curtains were parted by some mechanism or other and there she was like the star of the show. Then outside.' He paused, struggling for recollection. 'In among the audience. It was like a dream.'

'Was it?' Sophie laughed. 'I remember things you can't imagine. I remember her dying in front of my nose. I remember flying from the branches of a tree and the flight took all night, and Lori was miles below me, barking like a dog.' Her voice became matter-of-fact. 'Sure it was like a dream. We were all out of our fucking heads.'

The USAF base presented any number of targets: trucks, buildings, fences, airstrips. Lori was a target too; less obvious than most, more vulnerable than all of them. Lori was in love with someone, and it wasn't her husband. She saw her lover as often as she could; and the times between their meetings were a blank misery to her – she got through them on Valium and trust. The relationship made her happy, but it made her desperate too. There was no way of avoiding it and no way of solving it. Her vague hope was that the obsession would pass, leaving her as she was before. At forty-three, she was too old to change her life, also too old to turn her face from passion.

Like all relationships, this one had rules. She could phone him, but he could never phone her. They could meet on some days, but not others; some evenings, but not others. They could go for a drive, but only in his car. All the rules really pointed towards one paramount rule – nobody must find out. But someone had.

First a woman's voice: We know what you're doing. We know all about you. You can't hide anything . . .

Then a man's voice: You think no-one knows, but we know. We know all about you . . .

Then a woman's voice . . .

'We threw petrol bombs through the windows of an admin block down there, and that was to change the world; we knew it was – we'd learned it off by heart.' Sophie had tears in her eyes. 'But Lori: oh, Sam, that was the real thing. That was for fun.'

Fourteen

If you want to know how to like a man, ask his friends. If you want to know how to hurt him, talk to his enemies.

The man who had broken Ellwood's nose was named Ronald Morton, but his friends, like his enemies, called him Mort. There are times, of course, when friends and enemies are almost the same people; or they can change day by day. Ellwood sat in the red, plush booth of a pub, half lost in the daytime dark, and drank large whiskies with DS Sean Dolan who used to be Mort's friend and was now his enemy.

'It's a matter of balance,' Dolan said. 'Thus far, no further. We're like the Monopolies Commission; if one person has all the action, there's no real spirit of competition, is there? No free market economy.' He was laughing as he spoke. The topic was the way Morton had cornered the market in prostitution in that area of London. 'Fixed prices,' Dolan continued, 'docile labour force, ultimate control of product. No good. Democracy is being able to haggle over the price of pussy, or it's nothing.' He was enjoying himself hugely. 'My shout.'

He shouldered his way to the bar, a big man in a suit he'd slept in and spilled things over; a stake-out suit. Ellwood wondered how much he'd taken from Morton over the years, and why he'd been cut out now. Dolan came back carrying, in one hand, more whiskies, and a beer chaser for himself; he used the other hand for cigarettes one after the other, a copper's occupational therapy. He sat down, answering Ellwood's question as if it had been spoken out loud.

'I was in and out of the Vice Squad. Thought I'd try a

spell on Serious Crimes. Over there it's sex and violence sometimes; in Vice it's sex and violence all the time. It's best to stay with what you know. Specialize: the secret of success. By the time I was back on the strength, someone else had cornered Morton's market. Only to be expected, of course. So I made a couple of friendly suggestions – welcome home present, that sort of thing. No go. I offered to turn a pair of blind eyes, just the way it used to be; but he was already getting his protection.'

Dolan drank the whisky and the beer and put the glasses down in plain sight.

'Fucking toe-rag. Nautilus triceps and a bankful of money . . . I went round to see him, he laughed at me. I went round again with the thought of giving him a slap – couldn't get near him; enough soldiers for a fucking army. So I nicked him: lifted him from a boozer just down the road from here. I walked in off the street with a couple of over-excited noddies I found in a squad car. Injured pride, you see.' He lit a cigarette, cupping his hands round the flame of the match as if he were hiding it. 'Big mistake. Made everyone angry. I'm still living it down.'

'I can imagine.' Ellwood wanted to tell the end of the story himself. 'Feel like another try?'

'What? I'm leper-spit to everyone; don't ask.'

'No . . . Don't do anything. Just tell me how.'

Dolan said, 'I'd better have another drink.'

Ellwood went to fetch them. The barman looked over his shoulder to where Dolan was sitting and waved Ellwood's money away. When Ellwood put the drinks down, he said, 'But you still have some influence.'

'Jesus,' Dolan said, 'be a sorry day if I couldn't get a drink on my own patch—' He did the whisky in one and tapped the glass against his teeth. 'Bad temper, you see – that's my problem. A tendency to act on impulse. If I'd thought things through, I might have found a better way.' He pretended to ponder what the better way might be. 'Well . . . you could try him at the gym.'

Someone came in through the tall doors, bringing a hot

stench of fast food and ash wrapped in a scarf of diesel.

'He's a big guy with red hair,' Dolan said, but he was laughing through the joke. He could tell that Ellwood had already met Ronald Morton. A long bruise, a finger of shadow, lay beneath Ellwood's eyes and across the bridge of his nose.

Dolan wrote an address on a matchbook and pushed it across. 'How did you find me?' he asked.

'Someone who asked someone who asked someone who—' Ellwood shrugged. 'Bread on the waters.'

'I fancy your line of work,' Dolan told him. 'Closed shop, I suppose.'

'You picked the wrong decade. Everyone likes everyone else, trusts everyone else, agrees with everyone else. There's only the Arabs left to hate, and everyone hates them equally. They even hate themselves. All in all, there isn't much to do.'

'Pity. It strikes me that I'd've been good . . .'

Dolan let the unfinished sentence wash to and fro with the mares' tails of smoke while he brought back more drinks.

'. . . you know, at *international* sex and violence.'

Ellwood didn't really have the time to spare. A careerist would have set it aside – one thing at a time; don't let your feelings run you off the rails. Ellwood wasn't like that. He knew all the stuff about professionalism, about 'ambition does the job and nothing else'. Now Hilary Todd was hot for results, he should have been down in Longrock trying to keep everything sweet, with Ronald Morton listed as a bad debt to be collected some time in the future.

Ellwood knew that stuff, but it made no sense to him. He worked off instinct. Instinct makes a snake strike. He worked off emotional equivalents. Cancel pain with pain was a good example of that.

It was just before noon when he arrived outside the gym: a classy façade with a green and gold awning midway down a Chelsea side-street; the restaurants close by served hors d'œuvres and seven brands of mineral water. The timing was calculated on known factors in Morton's life. People who work-out seriously work-out every day. Evening would be Morton's busy time; evening and night. Peddling pussy, doing a little business on the side – a girl could usually deal you a sachet of crack before she put her head in your lap. Morning would be for sleeping.

Morton showed up at four o'clock, the quietest time in the gym. Three guys with him, two wearing warm-up suits like Morton's, one in jeans and a T-shirt under a leather blouson. Ellwood watched from his car. They weren't really expecting anyone; it was male bonding Ellwood was looking at, not a man needing his minders, but the guy in the blouson was there to ride drag, just in case.

Ellwood gave them fifteen minutes to change and start the first circuit. He got out of the car, also wearing warm-up greys and carrying a nylon hold-all. The aviator Raybans were his only concession to fashion.

The previous day, he'd gone to the gym and asked for a membership form; afterwards, he'd wandered through the place, reading their brochure and nodding as if he cared. A briny odour of sweat was carried past on billows of injected air and muzak.

'See your card?' The receptionist had her hand out, the other still resting on a keyboard.

'No,' Ellwood told her. 'I'm for the physio. Private session.'

She opened an appointments book and ran her nail down the list. Ellwood read 5 p.m. upside down and tapped the name alongside.

'Phillips.'

'Right.'

'You're early.'

'I know. Sometimes he gets a cancellation.'

'Not today.'

'But I can wait?'

'Sure.' Her eyes went back to the green glow of the

screen and her hands came together again, ten glossy hoofers doing an old routine.

In the changing room he stripped, took his towel, then walked up three fake marble steps and round a dogleg that took you into the fake marble shower room. Five shower-heads on each wall, then a dogleg to take you out. He stood under one of the jets for a minute, then emerged with his towel draped over his head and walked naked to where he'd left his bag and clothes. He turned modestly to the wall to dry himself off. In the course of half an hour, he did this six times.

Most of the lockers were standing open, their keys in the locks. Seven were shut.

A man came in on his own, showered and left. Ellwood sat with his towel round his waist, his back to the room, turning the pages of a magazine – relaxing after his work-out.

Another man came in, then three together. Ellwood tensed. He walked to the wall of mirrors and sinks and hairdryers and glanced past his own reflection at the newcomers, then, reassured, went back to his bench and his magazine to wait them out.

After they left, he stood under the shower again. As he emerged, draped like a fighter approaching the ring, the minder in the blouson came into the changing room. Ellwood went to his bench and stood ass-out to the room, scruffing his hair. The minder glanced at Ellwood's nakedness – water pearling his shoulders and tracking down to the tuft in the small of his back – then looked away. A moment later, the other three arrived.

Standing, Ellwood bent over to dry his feet. In that position, he was timelessly vulnerable: a turtle belly-up, a landed fish. He heard a yell from the shower as someone fooled with the hot and cold control; the accompanying laugh was Morton's – as hushed and discreet as his speaking voice. It faded into the hiss and drub of water.

The minder went past and peered at himself in the

148

mirror. Maybe his wife had told him, You're putting on weight, or else, Your hair's getting thin. Naked as truth, Ellwood stood close behind so their images nestled. The gun had been in his sports bag; now he held it in clear view, like someone offering a gift, and the man turned with his mouth wide open. Ellwood slipped the silencer between the parted lips and shook his head, as if to say, I understand: you're lost for words.

Together they walked past the mirrors, past the lockers, away from the shower, to a urinal and a row of cubicles at the very far end of the room, each cubicle with its fake marble walls, its fake marble crapper. Like a careful partner, Ellwood led them in the dance, their steps perfectly in time, their costumes wildly mismatched. He turned his wrist like someone neck-reining a pony and backed the man into a stall, then fired immediately.

The minder was flung off the gun. A starburst of brain and brainpan hit the wall; the dead man put out his arms in a scarecrow gesture and sat down heavily, then started to topple forward. Ellwood caught him under the jaw and pushed him upright, pulling the stall door shut in the same moment. The body flopped forward again, the head thudding against the door and holding it closed. Ellwood went back to the shower. He walked up the three steps and round the dogleg.

Morton was washing his hair. His head was thick with lather that flowed down over his shoulders and both hands were raised, fingers flexed to massage his scalp. One of his companions was standing face-up to the shower jets, eyes screwed shut; the other was looking puzzled, slightly askance, because the person joining them in the shower was odd in some way – that purposeful walk, and one arm hanging straight from the shoulder. By the time he isolated the oddness, he had taken a bullet in the throat and was almost dead. He hit the floor, *thud-slap*, and spun on the water slick. The others seemed not to notice. Ellwood stepped up to the second man and presented the gun to his tilted head. He shot once while the man was standing, then again after he'd gone down.

This time, Morton turned to the sound. A foamy delta of shampoo was sliding across his shoulders and down his chest. He thumbed water out of his eyes and saw Ellwood, gun up and ankle deep in a swill of blood and suds.

Ellwood smiled. The band of bruising from cheek to cheek and over the bridge of his nose was shiny as shellac in the spray; it glistened like warpaint. He said, 'Hello, Mort.'

It was a day for dancing. They performed a little pavan, delicate steps on the ersatz marble floor – first back, then side to side, then back again; one arm raised to kill, one raised in fear.

Ellwood found himself under one of the shower jets, the gun held straight out and clear of the spray; the man he was going to kill was edging sideways towards the dogleg exit as if the music had stopped and the dance could now be broken.

Their voices clashed.

'What do—'

'Do you . . .' It was Ellwood who continued. 'Do you know any French, Mort?' The man stopped backing off for a moment, as if the strangeness of the question had over-ridden his fear. 'Do you speak the language at all?'

Ellwood brought his man down with a bullet to the hip and advanced on him with the gun held straight at his face. Morton clutched at his wound, blood seeping through crevices in his grip.

'*Parlez-vous français?*' Ellwood shook his head, confirming Morton's lack. 'Not a word of it? Well, that's a shame.' He brought the gun closer to Morton's face and the man raised his hands and covered his eyes.

Ellwood shot him in the balls. Morton screamed and flipped on to his side, knees up, hands clamped between his legs. 'It's a shame,' Ellwood told him, 'because you won't really get the joke I'm about to make.'

Morton lay curled, knees to chin, hands hidden, eyes wide, like a child who waits for sleep while scary shadows gather in the room. Water drummed down on him, turning vermilion as it sluiced his groin and ran into the drainage hollows. Ellwood put the silencer into Morton's ear and squeezed off his last shot. The dead man's head leapt from the shower floor and slammed back down. A great cloud of blood billowed like a halo round his tousled head.

Ellwood stooped as if the man could hear him. He said, 'You're fucking dead, Mort.' He laughed. 'Dead, Mort. You don't think that's funny?' He spat, landing the gobbet on Morton's cheek. 'I said you wouldn't get it.'

He stood under the shower for a few moments to wash off some splashes of blood. When he was through, he turned all the shower jets off. The blood that ran on the ersatz marble was richer and slower without the water to thin it.

Rinsed clean, he went to the bench and towelled his hair, then took a piece of card with a Letraset message on it from his bag, along with some masking tape. Going back to the shower, he fixed several strips of tape across the entrance, from eye-level down, and attached the card. The message read: 'WATER DISCONNECTED FOR TEMPORARY REPAIR. PLEASE BE PATIENT. TEN MINUTES, MAXIMUM. MAINTENANCE OFFICER.'

When he left, the girl on the desk smiled vaguely. An hour or so later, she completely misdescribed him to Sean Dolan, who was happy to record her string of errors. He looked at the tumbled bodies, at the shower floor like an abattoir, and thought: I knew I was talking to an angry man; I didn't know how angry. His second thought was, Back to the way things were – I can start from scratch. He smiled as the body bags came out.

Once Morton was dead, Ellwood forgot him completely. Within two hours he was travelling west through the city, headed for Longrock, the afternoon sun throwing lines of light off crane jibs, scaffolding catwalks, tower block windows . . .

Fifteen

A gull rolled on the wind, then banked on stiff wings and slid across half a mile of sky.

Carla said, 'I come from a family of strangers. No-one knows anybody. We remember each other's names; that's about as far as it goes.' She was a better listener than storyteller.

'My parents are dead,' Zeno told her. 'Each was an only child. I'm an only child as well. Sometimes I think it might be a gift; like being the seventh son of a seventh son.'

He stood in the canvas wheel-house of the blue clinker-built boat, edging inshore with the push of the current. He anchored just off a tiny beach the shape of a Moorish moon, and pushed a two-seater inflatable over the side, then hung a rope ladder, going down first so that he could hand her aboard.

Once on the beach, she slipped out of her clothes and waded back out to sea. She lost her limp when the water reached her waist – buoyed up, she turned and waved to him and he waved back like any husband.

He spoke to her because she couldn't hear him. 'I love you . . . I've never loved anyone in my life before. I killed two people. I killed them because of you. Because of us. There are others I have to kill, then we'll be safe.' His obsession with her was limitless; all he knew or cared about was love and how to preserve it. Her vulnerability produced an ache in him, and a fierceness that made him want to stave off the entire world.

Carla raised one arm and pushed forward into a slow crawl that brought her in with the tide. Her lameness grew as she walked back through the waves, shoulders swinging against the undertow. He gathered her in, waterbeads running everywhere, her hair sleek to her skull.

'I love you,' was all he saved of his confession.

She kissed him, and drew him on, kissing him blind while he got out of his clothes, kissing him when he entered her, his shadow blocking the sun and turning the light under her eyelids to mauve dusk.

She lay beside him and heard another moment from his confession. 'I've never loved anyone in my life before.'

When she said the same thing to him, he gasped and she felt his body leap alongside hers, like something diving. 'You conjured me up out of nothing. Until I met you, I was nothing. I'd gone so low that I didn't know what to do, so I hitch-hiked, just heading for the sea, and then I walked through the town, and then across the beach to the tideline, and that was as far as I could go.'

There were veins in her eyelids like the veins in the wings of a moth. He watched her as she drifted into sleep, then he got up and walked to the very edge of the little beach. He remembered the fevered look in Marianne's eye. She'd been drunk, of course, but more passionate for that. It was that passion, that desire to be free, that had made him send the letter that brought her back.

I sometimes think it would be better . . . Wouldn't it be better to tell someone – to own up, not to have to live with it, each day, every day? I know what it would mean . . . But each day, every day! Don't you think about it? Don't you dream about it? I think about having to live with it for the rest of my life. I'm not sure I can. Her fingers had laced and unlaced, as if that pattern were the clue to what should be done. *The rest of my life; I'm not sure I can live this way that long.*

If one could do it, all could do it.

*   *   *

Carla lay on her stomach, arms straight above her head and pointing inland, like a marker to buried treasure.

Zeno lay a little way apart from her, falling in and out of a dream. All seven of them sat in a ring, making decisions, like a family in conference. Sam Pascoe said, 'We could blow up a train.' Zeno shivered and woke.

Carla was damp from their lovemaking. Little badges of sand dappled her skin.

'Never leave me.' He spoke not knowing whether she could hear him.

From where he stood, Ellwood could see the dip in the coastline that marked the cove. He might have caught a glimpse of the blue boat as it lifted on the swell, but he wasn't looking for it. He stared out from his room at the Windrush Hotel and saw only the sea and the sea was just a gigantic blankness to him.

Tom Carey sat at a room service table, working his way through everything on it. He said, 'Some things I know, but not enough.'

Ellwood had returned to Longrock with a face like a ghost-dancer and an unforgiving deadline. He had called in on an open line to Hilary Todd's PA, a too-attractive, over-ambitious girl named Annie Roland. The idea had been to simply report his return, but Annie had scrambled the call and patched him through. Hilary had been spikily dismissive: 'Soon, Wallace. I don't think I trust your set-up down there. You've made promises you don't seem able to keep. Your friends in this department are growing fewer. Time you were put out to pasture.' Hilary was eight years Ellwood's junior; maybe ten. 'You were good in your day, Wallace.'

Carey said, 'It's one thing to be his confessor. He's fallen into that routine readily enough. He's disturbed. For one thing, he's terrified of losing the woman. He's crazy for her; crazy in love. He thinks about the past and he thinks about the future; never the present. As for me – I'm learning piecemeal. The Man with the Big Bow Tie –

who's that? You want me to be confessor and confidant; keep him balanced. But I won't work in the dark.'

Ellwood smiled. You've always been in the dark, he thought. You believed you knew what was going on – back then, when you played the radical priest, when you sat in the confessional and listened to the information he brought. You knew nothing. You passed the information on for the sake of your stupid cause; your lost cause. You thought I believed what you believed; you thought I betrayed my own. But in truth, you knew nothing. Now here we stand, years later, and you believe you know who I am, what I believe, whose side I'm on. You know nothing.

Carey continued to eat. Ellwood watched like a man peering into a cage. 'In that hospital up on the hill, where Zeno gives his magic show, there's a man called Sir Harold Piper. His diagnosis is paranoid schizophrenia. There are a number of theories about the illness; one says it's a means of retreat from a situation, now or in the past, that the patient is emotionally incapable of facing; another maintains that the whole thing comes down to biochemistry in the end – chemical imbalances causing mad flights of fancy, voices in the head, crazed ideas.'

Ellwood's gun-metal hair was glossy in the light from the window. His skin looked papery; ready to tear.

'I don't know which is right. I don't care. But that old man either was or wasn't a double.'

Carey looked up, briefly, as if Ellwood had finally said something of interest.

'Just after the war, the Allies set up a number of secret organizations in various countries. Italy, France, Holland. Stay-behind groups. They had two purposes. The first was to train a secret army – a terrorist group that would go into action in the event of a Communist take-over. The second was to infiltrate public life – become politicians, judges, financiers, and to recruit people in the same areas. That way the threat from inside could be identified and defeated.'

Carey was pouring coffee. He glanced at Ellwood, eyebrows raised, and pointed to an empty cup. Ellwood ignored the gesture.

'Well, all that's coming to light now. Perhaps any secret kept long enough is at risk. Newspaper articles; television documentaries; they're all over it, nothing we can do. But that old man up there on the hill knows something else. He knows that the Brits wanted their own insurance. Never very good at trusting our friends, were we? Not great believers in the League of Nations.' Ellwood laughed at the phrase. 'So some members of those secret armies were ours and ours alone. And so were some of the recruits. Insiders – they spied on the spies; they reported just to us. The idea was to have the upper hand. The idea was to act alone. Friends are fine, but they're not *family*, are they?'

'Piper helped set up the groups,' Carey said. 'Is that it? And he arranged to plant the insiders.'

'Yes.'

'And he might have been doubling . . .'

'Life was so much more interesting during the Cold War, don't you think?' Ellwood went to and fro in front of the window like a shark in a tank. 'Spies who spied on their friends, people in high places who worked for two masters.' He paused. 'Priests playing politics.'

Carey ignored the jibe. 'Who would he have told?'

'Moscow is what we assume. Just as part of a regular report. It wouldn't have been of much use to them, of course. Except they'd have known who to look out for. It's possible that they made use of the information at the time of elections; we might be able to trace a couple of smear campaigns to information of that sort; a couple of assassinations too. Still, it's likely that things most often worked to our advantage. The insiders usually managed to give us the edge when we needed it; paid for themselves in cash quite often – a lot of their value was industrial espionage. The point is: they're still there; and they're still useful.'

'What's changed,' Carey wanted to know.

'We've only come to suspect Piper in the last month or so. There was all sorts of traffic when the Berlin Wall came down; trade-offs; exchanges of information. It's taken time to evaluate. Piper's name appears in places, and in contexts, that make him look more colourful than he ought to be – more active, more important. There doesn't seem a lot of doubt. It's a question of who he told and what he told them. He had more to offer than just the insiders, but they would have been his most interesting gift. We assume that the Russians will use it if they have it. Now's their best time. After *détente*, the information's of little direct use to them, but—'

Carey got the point: 'They can sell it.'

Ellwood shrugged. 'Sell it . . . Offer it as evidence of good will. They need business partners. The USSR Ltd is close to bankruptcy. What better than a few favours, now that they need people's trust along with their money?'

'And if they find out? The Italians, the French, the Dutch . . . ?'

Ellwood said, 'They might already have been told. Only Piper knows for sure.'

Carey had eaten asparagus, cold beef, salad, cheese. He was paring the skin from an apple. 'He goes up there and takes rabbits out of a hat . . . *Shazam* . . .' His tone of voice meant: what else?

'He's a lock expert, apart from his other talents. I've used him for a few things since the seventies. Just now and then. He treats his act as a hobby, but in truth he's remarkable. I've seen him do Houdini's water-can escape, the handcuff escape . . . Each time I've used him, it's been to do with his skills in some way or another. Usually locks.'

'What does he unlock for us this time?'

'He brings us Piper's notes. They're compiled by a Dr Harris. Piper sees him three times a week – three sessions. Piper rambles on, the doctor listens; he tapes the sessions; later he files the transcripts. The files are locked.' Ellwood had taken to walking round the room to some arcane pattern of his own devising. 'Analysis, confession . . . they're much the same, I'm sure you know that. We can't act on this until we know the truth. A wrong move could be worse than no move.'

'What's Piper saying?'

'Not enough. There are lots of hints, lots of leads, lots of reasons for suspicion. Not enough hard information. Not yet. It's all a matter of time. Sadly, time is what we don't have.'

'Don't you know?' Carey asked. He was smiling a crooked little smile. 'Don't *you* know whether he was a double or not?'

'It's not moving quickly enough,' Ellwood said. The mysterious route he was following round the room brought him back to the window – light and clear air that still baulked him like the false exit to a maze. 'We'll have to hurry it up.'

'Don't *you* know, Wallace?'

'I don't know everything,' Ellwood said. 'Whatever made you think I might?'

'So that's what we're all doing down here.' Carey had quartered the apple, now he raised a segment to his mouth, trapping it between his thumb and the knifeblade, like a navvy. 'Peering into the head of a man who's lost his mind.'

'He hasn't lost it. He's buried it somewhere and won't say where it is. Don't worry. We'll dig it up. Just keep an eye on the Great Zeno.' Ellwood laughed, as if he'd just invented the name.

'He's afflicted by the past,' Carey said. 'He killed Nick Howard.'

'I know that.' Ellwood flapped a hand at the information. 'I wouldn't use him again, in any case. Too unstable, now. He was always a little weird, wasn't he? I don't care who he kills, as long as he waits. There's a deadline on this.'

Ellwood's unknowable route had brought him to stand

directly in front of Carey. He smiled down – a challenge or a threat.

We'll dig it up.

You couldn't picture him as a child, Carey thought. You couldn't imagine who his parents were. *What am I looking for?*

Ellwood's smile said everything. The bar of bruising over his cheeks made his pale eyes paler still.

I'm looking for his soul. It isn't there. And I must have known that for twenty years or more.

As soon as Carey left, Ellwood made a phone call. As soon as he put the phone down, it rang.

'Well, now . . .' Hilary's voice was honey on a comb. 'I'm looking at a report that speaks of four bodies. One of them a pimp called Ronald Morton. All of them shot in an exclusive gym that's currently trying to think of ways of saving its reputation. One dead in the lavatory, three in the shower.' He paused to reflect on that. 'An efficient touch, really – they can just scrub the place down. No need to redecorate. Now' – his voice grew brisker, like that of a man arriving at the purpose for his call – 'the other name that features prominently in this sordid story, Wallace, is your own.'

Dolan, Ellwood thought. You sorry bastard.

Hilary could have been telepathic. 'Don't blame Sean Dolan,' he continued. 'It wasn't malicious. Just too much booze and too much mouth. Are you there?'

Ellwood counted four, then said: 'Yes.'

'That's good. For a moment, I'd thought I'd lost you. Well now, Wallace . . .' His tone drifted into vagueness for a moment, the temporary distraction of someone consulting ill-organized notes.

Have fun, Ellwood thought. You're digging a very deep hole.

'Wallace . . . Do you know how to spot a drunk? I'll tell you: he'll have a reputation for it. People will know. You'll hear about it a lot. Do you know what you've got a reputation for, Wallace?' Hilary waited, as if expecting an answer. The line between them ticked. Even the silence was gathered on to spools.

'Now, I know you're quick to anger, Wallace, but let me tell you something you might not know: so am I . . .' His voice was sweet and soft as a lullaby. 'I've been having a difficult time with Special Branch. I've been having an even more difficult time with the Serious Crimes Squad. You've been swimming in sewage, Wallace, but somehow it's my office that smells of shit.'

Ellwood had devised a shorter version of his earlier walk round the room – a route circumscribed by the length of the telephone lead. His voice was easy, but his legs were stiff as stilts.

'What's your suggestion, Hilary?'

'There are two theories here, Wallace. The first is that you're so far down the road with Piper that we leave you alone. The second is that you're a liability and we should throw you to the wolves. That's the one I like best. There's always the possibility, though, of letting you solve the Piper problem, and *then* having you eaten alive. Who knows, Wallace? Maybe that's the clever choice.'

'And what's the decision?'

'We're leaving you alone, Wallace, for just a little longer. But you're on a killer deadline down there; you're almost out of time. We've been getting a lot of strange feedback from Europe. Not only that – the Americans have been asking a few questions we'd sooner not answer. It feels like everyone knows some secret and we're not being told. And maybe that's because it's *our* secret. We're all very edgy, Wallace. And in the middle of all this, you take time off to settle a score with a ponce.' The voice was still low; a hint of laughter, perhaps.

Ellwood turned like a soldier at drill and walked a tightrope to the window. The sky seemed to be full of birds. He said, 'Anything else?'

'Results,' Hilary said.

Ellwood waited through an extended silence, then heard

the dialling tone. From the window, he could see the horizon, so clear, so hard, it seemed possible that you could step down from it on to the rest of the world.

He wanted, under his hand, the button that would destroy everything.

For five minutes he stood still, letting the view swim out of focus. Then he made a call. After that, he made another. When the phone was lifted at the other end, he spoke rapidly, anxious to hold the other person's attention.

'This is Wallace Ellwood. I need your help – I'm sure you know why. I don't expect it to come free.' The view from the window slowly reassembled itself. He nodded. 'Yes, I can meet you there.'

What he was doing was risky, he knew that; but there was little enough to lose.

The first call had summoned a girl. She found the door slightly ajar and went in to a man lean as a knifeblade, with black-grey hair, glossy and flat to his skull. He was sipping whisky, one hand on the bottle-neck, a wide smile of welcome crinkling his bruised cheeks.

He said, 'Show me your tits.'

She laughed. One hand went down the buttons on her blouse.

He said, 'I hope you're broad-minded . . .'

Her laugh grew louder. She said, 'Listen – I'm a prostitute. I do everything.'

When she left, she carried her shoes out into the corridor, like someone in a hurry, and stood with her face close to the lift doors. She wasn't laughing.

Ellwood had gone back to the window. He was naked and perspiring slightly, his body giving off a faint musty smell that he liked. Longrock had dissolved to a cluster of lights along the bay. The sea was almost invisible. Apart from a pale ribbon of aquamarine along the skyline, everything was a single shade of blue.

Perfect. Ellwood raised his fist and cocked it sideways, thumb poised like someone holding a joystick.

The girl rode down in the lift in a silence so complete that she seemed to be holding her breath.

Ellwood let his thumb drop – *click* – on the doomsday button.

Sixteen

Three squad cars and an ambulance passed Pascoe's door in convoy. He paused, seasoned to the city, until the sirens faded a little. Sophie held out a cup of coffee and he switched the phone to his left side. In front of him were the post-it notes he'd found in Charlie Singer's flat. He read what was written on them to Rob Thomas – a list of names, phone numbers, other jottings that made no obvious sense.

Thomas said, 'Some of this stuff sounds like sleep-talk.'

'I'm giving you all of it. Use what you can.' Some of it was indecipherable. Pascoe read out a few more numbers. He added, 'Holland, Carlton, Shakespeare.'

'Do you want me to read the entire works?' Thomas asked. 'Or just the Sonnets?'

'I'll be in Longrock,' Pascoe said. 'The number I gave you before.'

'That's fine, Sam, except you're out of credit.'

'Bill the office,' Pascoe told him.

'Are you sure?'

'Bill the office.'

In the corner of his eye, he could see Sophie pulling his blankets off the sofa. There was something brisk and fussy about the way she folded them. He said, 'You didn't have to come back. It's only a cab ride.' The previous evening she had gone to Hampstead to collect some clothes. She'd returned in an hour.

'If I go home, I'll stay there. I haven't lived there long, so it's free of memories.'

'Sounds like a good place to be.'

'That's right.' She stood by the door with her coat across her arm while he made a final call.

George Roxborough said, 'No-one's missing you, Sam.' A long sigh came across the wires. 'I've gone back to smoking. This case is making me jumpy as hell. The police have virtually moved in with Stewart's mother. Going through her story again and again.'

'That's terrific,' Pascoe said. 'They'll have her word-perfect by the time you come to trial.'

The wind had stayed strong, but where Pascoe lived it carried a whiff of sulphur. They drove out of the city with the windows closed. Sophie's face was also closed.

'I had nightmares.'

He nodded, eyes on the road. 'I heard you.'

'It was just like . . . Lori was coming out of the house. She seemed to float. Then down the garden, then out among the trees. We were all shouting at her, but she couldn't hear us. I was in a tree – you know, I'd climbed up – it was full of fruit; I don't know what. Different fruits on one tree.' She went back to the beginning. 'It was just like an acid-rush.'

It took them almost an hour to get clear of the city. She said, 'There weren't any fruit trees, were there?'

'No.'

'It was dark in the trees but Lori was white. I could see her but I couldn't see anyone else.'

'She took her clothes off,' Pascoe said.

'I remember.' She was holding the piece of paper Rob Thomas had given them – Marianne's address. After a moment, she took a map from the pocket on the car door.

'How close?' he asked.

'To Longrock?' She looked at the scale. 'Close. Five miles, perhaps.'

'You could still go home,' Pascoe said.

'I sat in the tree and ate the fruit while she died.'

Peter Novaks was in good shape for seventy – upright, a

long stride, a full head of hair. When he spoke, Pascoe could detect a faint whisper on the lung.

'Always if the weather turns warm this late,' he said. 'It's just an allergy; something else will kill me.' When he spoke about Marianne his voice took on a dull, depressed tone.

'When we were in Claydon? In that case, you probably knew her better than I did.' He grimaced. 'I was away a lot. It was called making a career. At the time it seems like the only thing to do. I certainly thought so. Then all that ended. The career ended – or someone else took it over. My wife got cancer and died in fewer than three months.' He laughed and the wheeze was there, a little louder. 'The trick is, they make you believe you'll be young for ever – or at least for long enough . . .' He looked at Sophie as if she might have been about to say something. 'You've no idea where she is?'

'We came here hoping to find her.'

'To the police, she's just a statistic. People disappear all the time, it seems. Did you know that?'

Pascoe said, 'It's common.'

'Not to me.' They were sitting in a garden that gave sight of the sea. The house had a low thatch and stood on its own just under the brow of a hill. 'A runner – I heard one of them say that.'

'The police have seen everything,' Pascoe said. 'Missing persons . . . to the authorities they're like buses – there'll be another along in a minute.'

'What happened?' Sophie asked.

Novaks shrugged. He looked away towards the ocean. 'She'd come home from time to time. Stay a month, perhaps. She became an archaeologist, did you know that?' Pascoe and Sophie shook their heads in unison, feeling foolish. 'So she travelled a good deal. Then, between jobs, if she wasn't lecturing or didn't prefer to be in London, she would stay here. We liked each other, you see. We got on well together.'

A row of clouds like spitcurls touched the skyline. The

temperature dropped and the garden fell into shade.

'What happened is that she went out and never came back. They found her car at the railway station. That's what makes them certain she's a . . . *runner*. What they don't seem able to ask themselves is why she should run. Put that to them, they shrug.' He gestured towards the house, suddenly anxious because his misery had made him forget that they were guests. 'Can I offer you something? A drink?'

Pascoe said no. There were questions he wanted to ask, but couldn't without seeming too eager. They were friends, calling by on the off-chance. He would have to rely on the old man to remember anything important. He allowed himself a tiny prompt. 'We wrote to say we might be coming down here.'

'Did you? She always gets a lot of mail while she's here.' He thought of something. 'She didn't reply, I suppose? Say anything that might—'

'No.' Pascoe had hoped for news of an unusual letter.

'It's difficult, you see . . .' Novaks bent forward in his chair as if to concentrate; he wanted to say exactly what he meant. 'To the police, it's just another case. Another *runner*. They look for patterns, and they find them. This person, another person, fifty others . . . How can I make them see that Marianne is different? Why should they believe that? They would have to understand the whole pattern of our lives – this family, how we were together, what mattered to us. I say: "Why can't you see? She wouldn't go out and not come back. She wouldn't disappear. She wouldn't just *go*." Why should they believe it? They'd have to know what I know. I can be sure. *Sure*. I *know*. But they look at the patterns. They see another runner.'

The clouds were galleons now, sailing towards them against the ebb of the tide. Peter Novaks raised his head. Sophie had known all along that he'd been crying.

'How can I make them understand?' he asked. 'How can I make them see?'

He got up, abruptly, and went into the house. For a moment, it seemed that he might have lost patience with them for some reason – friends with no good news. Then he reappeared, carrying a card folder. Inside were broadsheets he'd paid to have printed. A studio photograph of Marianne, a headline: HAVE YOU SEEN HER?, a brief physical description.

Novaks gave them a broadsheet each. 'It was all I could do,' he said. 'It's not knowing, you see. I could bear it better if only I knew.'

The sky was slate-grey and black. The first drops struck the car with a metallic clatter; a fistful. A moment later they felt the edge of it. Then the whole storm hit them with a bang like iron against an anvil. Pascoe put the windscreen wipers up to double speed and peered through the deluge. It was like being under water. Shapes loomed in the ramrods of rain – hedges, a fringe of trees, the road like a sudden brown river, bearing them off.

He wouldn't speak, no matter what she tried. In the end, she sat in silence, isolated by rain and the sound of rain, watching dim silver forms advance on them through the downpour.

It was early evening, but the storm made a false dusk. Pascoe's hotel room was a deep blue cave. He sat by the window, steadily sipping whisky. Sophie was at the door, waiting to be acknowledged. She had come to his room to solve the mystery of his sudden depression.

'What I saw,' she said, 'was an old man who had left everything too late. Did that upset you? Your life isn't over . . .'

A rumble of thunder, like cannon-fire, close to the headland; gusts of rain and sea-spray hit the window.

He said, 'There was a group of women called The Mothers of the Plaza de Mayo. They carried pictures of their husbands, their sons, their daughters, their grandchildren. They held the pictures as they paraded round the

Plaza. This was Argentina, nineteen seventy-eight. The pictures were of *Los Desaparacidos* – the Disappeared. Thousands of people had been kidnapped. It started with those who were thought a danger to the regime. Pretty soon, they took anyone. You just had to be in the wrong place at the wrong time, or look like a suspect, or be related to a suspect, or have a name something like a suspect . . . it didn't matter. They took children, pregnant women, innocent people by the truck-load. They were tortured as a matter of course. Some were tortured to death; some were tortured, then executed. A few survived. It went on for seven years. I was down there for a couple of weeks.'

Sophie had closed the door. She was sitting on the bed so that he wouldn't have to look at her as he spoke. 'Why were you there?'

'I'm a lawyer. Various human-rights organizations were asking for volunteers. I don't know . . . remnants of a radical conscience? What do you think?'

'A lot changed in eight years,' she said.

'After Lori died, everything changed.'

'What else happened?'

'There were places you could go and places that were forbidden. I was in a place called La Plata trying to get some tape-recorded statements from a number of relatives of people who were among the Disappeared. It was the wrong place to be. Some soldiers picked me up. They beat me where they found me – in the street, in full view. It made no difference. I was yelling at them, telling them who I was, trying to show my passport, my ID. They took me to a place that Amnesty files on the Disappeared call police station number five. One of them – maybe the officer – must have begun to worry. They put me in a cell and went to find someone. I didn't know that. I thought I was waiting to be tortured. Do you want a drink?'

He got up and fetched another glass from the bathroom. Through the window, Sophie could see grey curtains of rain and grey acres of sea beyond.

'I was there for about three hours. Three hours, I think. I could only hear screaming. And sometimes footsteps. The cell had a small window, high up, over the metal door; hardly any light. I could hear men and women screaming all the time. It never stopped. I sat in the cell and waited for my turn. Then they let me go.'

'How many people?' Sophie asked.

'No-one knows for sure. Ten thousand . . . more . . . They were taken away, held without trial, killed. No-one knew where they were. After they'd been picked up, they simply disappeared. People are still looking – mothers, wives, husbands.' He took a breath as if something had caught in his chest. 'Brothers, sisters, children . . .'

The rain was drummers drumming. Pascoe and Sophie were dark silhouettes in a darkening room.

'I'd been beaten up, so there was a minor diplomatic incident.' He laughed. 'Our man had a word with their man – that sort of thing. It was pointed out that I'd been picked up in a no-go area. Of course, I had a tale to tell. But so did everyone else who went down there. Everyone knew what was happening; or at the very least, everyone suspected. But the important thing was that nobody *saw*. It was the year Argentina won the World Cup – a lot of people saw that.'

The storm had trailed out to sea; now it began to wash in again. Thunder rattled the windows.

'Before I left, I went to the Plaza de Mayo. The Mothers were going round and round, holding their placards, their photographs – smudged faces and the name inked in underneath. The square was thick with soldiers and men from the security forces. The Mothers didn't look at them. They carried pictures of the people they loved round the square because it was all they could do.'

Sophie said, 'Marianne's father is like that.'

'After the demonstration was over, they dispersed in the side-streets. I asked one of them about the picture she'd been carrying. It was her son. But others had disappeared – her daugher-in-law and her grandson. She said, "I

169

expect they are dead. I expect so. I think I could bear that. What's unbearable is that I don't know."'

He set the whisky bottle aside. Sophie found the cap and screwed it on. 'No criticism,' she said.

'No,' he said, 'take it away. I must be pretty drunk; I just don't feel it.'

'What did you do . . . ?' A stalk of lightning arced into the sea, thin and fizzing with energy. Its brightness blanched her eyes; she was blind until the thunder broke overhead.

'What did you do after Lori died?'

'After Lori killed herself,' he said, 'after we killed Lori.'

'All right. After that.'

'Well, for one thing, I went to Buenos Aires.'

'Is that what it was?' she asked. 'Penance. A sin-offering?'

His voice thickened, as if the whisky had suddenly caught him up. 'What did you do?'

'I got married,' she said. 'Sin-offering, for sure.'

Seventeen

The thunder was making them edgy. Mac the Cough kept up a nervous *hek-hek-hek*. The Lady with the Flower swayed like a wobbly doll. Moments of restlessness all over the audience. The Wandering Jew went from chair to chair until a nurse settled him down near the back row. It was like being in a stable when the horses have sensed a fire. The Man with the Big Bow Tie sat perfectly still while Zeno brought fire from his mouth and doused it in his pocket.

All these crazies, Harold Piper thought. All these sick people, frightened of a storm. He did a rapid calculation in his head; crucial geometry. Something to tell Dr Harris about.

Zeno swallowed a flower. A second later, he drew from his mouth a long cord decorated with tiny triangular flags.

I like that, Piper thought. I like that trick.

Head back, Zeno pulled the flags out hand over hand. They mounted into a little pile at his feet like bunting after the parade.

Birdie uttered a soft chirrup like a nestling half asleep. Piper laughed silently. All these lunatics, and me among them. What safer place to be? He developed a proverb to please himself: Hide a prophet among children and a wise man among fools. Dog Face was all done up in her Sunday best, cheeks feverish with rouge, eyes glitter-flecked green. Her lipstick went from nose to chin.

Do you know what I know? Piper's silent laughter was a knot in his throat. Do you know who I am?

Zeno put coloured dye in three balloons and inflated them, then hung them from a board. His knives flickered

171

along the spotlight, whirring like wings. From one balloon, a gusher of blue smoke, from another a gusher of red; from the third a white dove.

I like that, Piper thought.

Lightning sizzled across the bay, a brilliant improvisation. The audience shifted and looked up, like animals startled at their feeding.

You don't know what I know. You don't know who I am. He made up a joke to amuse himself. Question: Why does a crazy act crazy? Answer: Because he can.

Twelve – he counted – thirteen . . . fourteen. And then the thunder came. He calculated the triangulation and fixed on the heart of the storm. Zeno had climbed into the box, strait-jacketed and chained, and a nurse was fixing the outer chains in place. They were breathless, as always. After a moment, a clown came on stage and wrestled with the padlocks. He gave up, but didn't exit through the wings as usual. He hopped down off the stage and wandered through the audience, grinning amiably.

A nurse stepped forward; another hurried down from the back of the hall. An anxious chatter started up among the audience, heads turning, eyes swivelling, hands held up to fend off the unknown. The clown hurried along the rows of chairs, then pushed through until he reached the empty seat on Piper's left. He sat down. Piper fussed with his bow tie, arranging the loops, tightening the knot. The clown had a polka-dot version that spun like a propeller. The nurses stood at either end of the row, anxious at first, then reassured by the clown's sparkling grin.

They sat together, waiting for something to happen. The clown leaned over towards Piper to offer a confidence and nodded towards the stage: 'He'll never get out of that, you know.' Piper looked worried. 'I've checked the locks. It's hopeless. He'll never see daylight again.'

Piper looked from the clown to the stage and back again.

'Except . . .' the clown whispered, and tapped Piper on the knee. A silver key lay in the palm of his right hand.

When he closed his fist and wiped it with his left hand, the key dissolved – both hands, palm up, were empty.

Piper laughed. *You don't know what I know.*

The clown produced the key once more, hidden from everyone except himself and Piper, and winked broadly. He went back to the stage and tried the chains again, shaking them two-handed, then turned to the audience, arms wide in a broad gesture of defeat. He left the stage and everyone watched the box. A minute passed, maybe two. The chains fell off. The box opened. Zeno stepped out to a rumble of distant thunder and one man's furious applause.

You don't know what I know.

The nurses went in among them, talking low. A couple were crying. *Hek-hek-hek-hek-hek* went Mac the Cough. The Lady with the Flower hugged herself.

You don't know who I am.

Sir Harold Piper smashed his hands together and brayed a curious two-tone laugh. I like that clown, he thought.

Dr Leonard Harris firmly believed that what some people called madness was flawless logic to others. He also believed that in environments where madness is expected, madness will be found. An asylum permits insanity, the theory went, so people opt for that.

'I like that clown,' Sir Harold Piper said.

Dr Harris nodded. The Great Zeno's show was useful therapy: a talking point, in fact. Harris approved of the outside world coming inside.

'While I was watching the show,' Sir Harold said, 'I made a couple of interesting calculations. The lightning helped – and its distance from the thunder described in seconds.'

'What did the calculations tell you?'

'Most of my work was done towards the end of the war. It was difficult to know who your friends were.' The answer was nothing to do with the question. 'After the war,' he said, 'the world was a house with lots of doors and windows. Some of the doors were locked all the time, some were locked part of the time, some couldn't be locked because they'd been broken down. Some of the windows had curtains that were always drawn, some had curtains that were occasionally drawn, some had no curtains at all. It's like a fairy tale, isn't it?'

Dr Harris agreed that it was.

'Lots of different families lived in the house. Some were friendly all the time, some were friendly now and then, some were never friendly. Except . . .' Piper grinned, because here came a twist in the story. 'Except no-one behaved as they should. The friendly families might not have been friendly at all. The sometimes friendly ones might really have been *least* friendly when they seemed *most* friendly. And ones who were never friendly might not have meant quite what they said. And you never knew who was from which family. And you never knew which families might be unfriendly tomorrow. And you never knew . . .' Piper's voice took on a deep, sepulchral tone, because this was the scariest part of the story. 'You never knew who might be knocking at your door. You never knew who might be peering in your window.' He wagged a finger. 'Judas was a family man, you know.'

Harris smiled as he wrote that down.

'You don't know what I know.' A sad shake of the head; a sorry frown. 'You don't know who I am.' Piper got up and paced to and fro for a bit. He asked, 'Are you ready to take this down?' Harris nodded, smiling cheerfully. 'This is some of it – some of what I know.' Piper continued to pace, but his eyes were closed with the effort of recollection. 'The thermal reduction, expressed in degrees, of a flame transferred from mouth to air if continued to infinity would extinguish the sun. The angle of incidence, expressed in degrees, between the horizon and the lightning if continued to infinity would engulf the earth. The sound of two such forces passing each other in deep space, in deep magenta space, in the holy blue of space, would disharmonize the music of the spheres. Do you know who I am?'

Dr Harris shook his head.

'Moloch, the Butcher of Children, the Slayer of Innocents, the Great Architect, Gog and Magog: one flesh.'

Dr Harris maintained the pretence of writing. In truth, everything was being recorded on tape and the doctor was making a series of loops and whorls on his pad. Sir Harold Piper insisted on a scribe, pad and pen ready to record his revelations.

'You never knew who was who,' Piper said. 'At times you couldn't even say who you were yourself. Like all these crazies – the people who live in this house. It's the same for them. They don't know who they are, which families they belong to.'

'Who do *you* think they are?' Dr Harris asked.

'Sometimes friends, sometimes not,' Piper said tetchily. 'Enemies pretending to be friends. Experience has taught me that it's difficult to tell one from the other. You have to pretend to believe them. You have to pretend to be their friend. I'll tell you something, though: I like that clown.'

Forgive me, Father, for I have sinned . . .

'She didn't see me at first, but I saw her. Then my gaze drew her eye and she looked across. She had gone for a walk by the sea, and stopped at the bar for a beer. That's what she told me afterwards. It was as simple as that. I didn't know she lived close by – lived there sometimes, anyway; her father's house. It was just a coincidence, neither good luck nor bad, that's what I thought at first. She didn't know what I was down here for. Then she started to talk about Lori. She was troubled by it. Meeting me only made it worse. She said she wanted to tell someone – confess. A way of lightening the guilt. I thought she meant like this – talking to a priest, or else a friend. Just talking it out. Then I could see she meant something else. A clean breast; facing the music; owning up. She talked in that childish way about it. Coming clean. She said that a lot; she kept on saying *clean*.'

An image persisted in Tom Carey's mind of the leper cured by faith. His imagination clothed Marianne Novaks in rags and a grimy turban. She threw her leper's bell away; arms raised, she shouted, 'Clean . . .'

'I knew what it would mean if someone told the story. The end of everything. The end of my future with Carla. I called her and made a date, but I didn't turn up.'

'Why not?'

'I was wondering what to do.'

'No,' Carey said. 'You'd already decided what to do.'

'I was trying to find the means of doing it.'

'The means?'

'You have to find a way to make it real. Like a story that you make up as you go along.'

'And you found a way . . .'

'She was quite angry to have been stood up. Impatient – as if talking to me was just the first step in a process she was anxious to begin. Funny – our meeting had stirred all this up in her, but she hadn't even recognized me at first glance.'

'But you met again, the next evening.'

The storm had ushered in a day of winds. Sand hissed in the marram and little inch-high twisters ran on the crests of the dunes. Great gouts of shadow and shine flooded the sea. Carey and Zeno sat out of the wind, out of sight.

'She got a little drunk as the evening went on. She seemed to be enjoying herself – as if she'd forgotten all about Lori and confessions. I'd lit some candles; she looked very attractive in that light. I think she might have been going to flirt with me.'

'But you found a way . . .'

'It was all a magic show. I did a couple of tricks. She was intrigued. She said, "I didn't know you could do things like that." Simple palming, manipulation, coin sleights, just basic stuff . . .'

'Where was Carla?'

176

'I didn't take Marianne home.' Zeno looked shocked. 'A house that's up for sale. I pretended to be a prospective buyer; I had the key copied. I told her I'd bought the place, but hadn't moved in. She thought it was fun: a table laid in an empty room, candles, sleight of hand.'

'You enjoyed it too.'

'That's right, I did.'

'And you killed her. You killed Marianne.'

A long silence. Then Zeno said, 'That's right, I did.'

Together they went to Ellwood, taking with them a photocopy of the transcript of Piper's last session with Dr Harris. Ellwood read it carefully, then started again at the first page.

Zeno sat in a chair close to the window, his face turned away. Carey asked where the bathroom was, and Ellwood pointed towards the bedroom door without taking his eyes from the text.

Everything was very quiet. Somewhere in the hotel, a piece of machinery hummed then stopped. Ellwood turned a page.

A girl lay on the bed, asleep, face down, a sheet covering one shoulder, one flank, one thigh. When Carey closed the door she gave a little hoarse cry, inaudible outside the room, and her hand fluttered on the pillow like a trapped bird. The room was dim, curtains half drawn; he could see a cheek-bone and an eye still smudged with a remnant of make-up.

Carey stood like a shadow in the room. He thought of sleek shapes he had fished.

A breeze lifted the curtain and the girl turned on to her back, hands up like someone at gunpoint, legs slightly parted. Amid the stripe of black hair between her thighs, Carey saw a delicate pink lip as it opened, damp and slightly furled, salty as a mollusc.

The little cry came again – a moment she couldn't escape from in the dream.

Carey stepped closer, paused, then came close enough

177

to touch. Small-breasted and slender-hipped; her arms were too thin, but her thighs were perfect: long and lean.

He knelt by the bed and watched her. He breathed on her nipples to make them swell, and touched one with the uttermost tip of his tongue.

She turned towards him, knocking his face with her elbow, and he got up at once and hurried into the bathroom. When he emerged, she had turned on to her side, knees up, face sunk into the pillow. The arch of her ribs stirred slowly. Carey stood in the room until he was sure they were breathing in unison; finally, he left.

A moment after he closed the door, the girl leapt in her sleep, then woke. At once she raised her head, looking this way and that, eyes wide and suddenly startled, as if her dream had joined her in the room.

Ellwood's second read had taken him to the last page. He said, 'I like that clown.' Zeno appeared not to have heard. 'I like that clown. What do you think?'

Zeno asked, 'What do you want me to think? What do you want me to think *about*?' His mind was on other matters. He'd left a message for Sam Pascoe in the usual place, but there had been no response. Carey had made him think about Marianne. Thinking of her had made him anxious about Pascoe and Sophie Lanner. Carla had changed her mind: 'Perhaps it *is* time to go, after all. Do we have to stay here?' When he'd wanted to leave, she'd urged him to stay. Now her restlessness made him want to have everything finished quickly.

'How close can you get to him?' Ellwood was thoughtful, glancing back through the transcript, pausing here and there.

'As close as you like.'

'Good,' Ellwood said. Almost under his breath, he added: 'I like that clown.'

'What the fuck does he mean – enemies pretending to be friends, it's difficult to tell one from the other, you never

178

knew who was who? What the fuck does he mean?'

Ellwood was sitting forward in his chair, staring at the transcript. Carey was watching Ellwood. Zeno had gone.

'It could mean exactly what you think it means,' Carey told him.

'Have you read this?'

'Yes.'

'What do you think?'

'I think he's mad. Paranoid, schizoid, whatever you said they said he was.'

Ellwood threw the transcript down. 'It's not going fast enough.'

Carey suddenly saw past Ellwood's anger to something less likely. He said, 'Are you in trouble, Wallace?' He glanced at the bruising on Ellwood's face, then away again. 'They're looking for a double; was it Piper? What are you in this – poacher or gamekeeper?'

'Don't worry.' Ellwood shook his head. 'All I'm suffering from is a cretin called Hilary Todd. He thinks of intelligence work as a time-and-motion study. I can handle assholes like him. In the meantime, I'd like to find out who that old man up on the hill really is so we can all relax and get on with the business of dividing up what's left of the world and its resources.'

Carey took his drink to the chair where Zeno had recently sat. 'He killed Marianne Novaks.' Ellwood stared. 'From what he said, I think she must have died before Nick Howard.'

Ellwood steepled his fingers and touched them to his lips. 'What else did he say?'

'I think he liked it. It frightened him, but he liked it. He did it to preserve himself and Carla, but that aside, he liked it.'

'Don't let him stray,' Ellwood said. 'Don't let him jump the fence.'

Carey swallowed his drink and turned away, his fingers laced tightly round the glass. 'When I came here, Wallace, I had no way of knowing—'

'Don't let him stray.' Ellwood's voice was frost over iron.

'When we went to Charlie Singer's apartment, do you remember, you came round the screen and I was sitting on the bed and I laughed at you.'

'Were you laughing *at* me?'

'In a way, in a way . . .'

Pascoe thought back. He recalled the laughter – how loud and long it had been. She had said, 'Rescue me, Sam. I'm in a fucking time warp.' And laughed some more.

'Was I funny or stupid or both?'

'Nothing like that.'

'Well . . . I don't know what made you laugh.'

She said, 'I remembered the butterflies.'

Almost as she spoke, he saw that it had been her. She was the girl in the acid dream, naked and swaying above him like a tree. She laughed at him now as she saw the moment flower in his mind.

'Why didn't you tell me?'

'You might have thought I was still an easy lay.' She got up on an elbow, the better to look at him, and saw his eyes go first to her breasts, then to her throat, reddened by soft bites. Their legs nudged under the covers. They were both chasing the memory of the butterflies.

The storm had stayed with them almost through the night, fading then circling back again. Pascoe had been thoroughly drunk. They had talked some more, but after a while he went over to the bed like a man on stilts and fell his length, feet over the edge, his face between the pillows, asleep before he landed. Sophie had gone to his chair and sat there keeping watch, a night nurse making light work of the rest of the whisky. When the last of the storm emptied out of the bay and a pale glow seeped up from the horizon, she had finally slept.

Later, Pascoe had woken and sat on the edge of the bed, head bowed, as the ache in his temples slowly expanded.

He had scarcely noticed her. In the bathroom, he'd stripped off his clothes and stepped into the shower, shuddering. I know these mornings, he'd thought. I know about mornings like this. Bit by bit, he'd brought the heat control up until the water was scalding his skin to rosy pink.

He'd emerged and walked back into the bedroom without a thought, naked, dripping water, slightly feverish as his body cooled. Sophie had watched while he'd stretched out on the bed. His careless nakedness had left her faintly insulted, faintly amused. Her own hangover was an altogether milder affair. In other days, she would have given it no more than three on the Richter scale. She had put her head to one side and drifted back to sleep.

It was almost noon before she'd woken again. Someone had been trying the door. When she'd opened it, two women had been there with bed linen, soap, towels. She'd smiled winningly, and asked them to try much later. Then she'd closed the door and had done what she'd been planning to do since Pascoe walked out of the shower, bollock-naked, ill, and paying her no mind. She'd taken her clothes off and lain down next to him.

'It was you,' he said. 'Why didn't I see that before?'

'You were out of your skull on acid. Why should you remember anything?'

'I remember the longest fuck in the world.'

'Was it?'

'That's the way it seems. Butterflies all over the room. I was rooted in you. I thought I would touch your heart.'

'I'll take that as a metaphor.'

His finger touched the swell of one breast, between her nipple and her ribcage – a little welt of scar tissue, about an inch long, puckered and white. 'I don't remember this.'

'No,' she said, 'you wouldn't.'

Their appetites for each other startled them. She lay full length on him and spread her legs, slowly, to tease him. He turned her over and she lifted her knees until they

181

rested on his shoulders. She said, 'Just keep doing that, keep moving like that, don't stop, do that, just keep doing that,' and put her head to one side, arms out, a crucifix. A blush welled up from her breasts and spread on her throat.

'It was all such crap, wasn't it, Sam? Sex and revolution; acid and revolution; rock and roll and revolution. We talked about the Establishment, about Capitalism . . . We thought we were in control. A joke. *They* were in control – always have been, always will be. We thought we owned those things – no. They sold us the sex, they sold us the drugs, they marketed the music, they packaged the entire fucking culture. Everyone with a poster of Che on the wall, everyone tripping, everyone talking shit. And us too – running about the place being baby Weathermen. I wish to Christ we'd blown up that fucking train.'

'Who are "They" now?' He answered himself, smiling. 'They're us.' His second question sounded as if it had been prepared for some time: 'Who else was there – among the group? I mean, sex-for-the-asking was pretty much part of the doctrine.'

Sophie laughed delightedly. 'It's a bit late to be jealous, isn't it?' She thought about it again. 'Or a bit early . . .'

'Who?' he asked; and knew the answer before she gave it.

'Charlie. Just now and then.'

They had kept the curtains closed, but daylight filtered through the weave. Lines of light rippled on all the walls, as if it were high tide in the room. Pascoe told Sophie some more things about Argentina – about how he couldn't go into a prison without wanting to scream and run.

'It got worse when Karen left.'

'You were depressed.'

'Depressed . . . Well, I hadn't thought of that. I suppose I must have been. But it was more the way she chose of doing it. One day there, the next day gone – no sign, no trace. She was one of the Disappeared. Except that she wanted it. Even so, I was left not knowing. Not *knowing* . . . Suddenly, I felt that; I saw what it was like.' His eyes were closed. He felt her mouth on his eyelids, then his throat. 'What was it with Charlie? Anything that mattered?'

'Relationships were ideologically unsound. You remember.'

'Even so . . .'

She drew back to look at him, then gave him a light slap that opened his eyes. 'Are you having a problem—?'

'No, look—'

'I mean, I was really enjoying this, because—'

'It's not—'

'Until today—'

'I'm sorry, it wasn't—'

'I hadn't been fucked for damn nearly two years.'

He stared at her. She took his hand and laid it between her legs.

They could hear the sea from the bed. The afternoon light was strong; the fake waves on the walls washed in with each sound of cymbals from the shore. Sophie lay still, eyes shut, legs open, and suffered him to stroke her, his finger beckoning again and again as he drew her on.

She stopped him, then let him continue, then stopped him again. She seemed to have grown heady – unfocused. Her body carried a light dew. Suddenly, her hands were everywhere.

'What do you like?' she asked. 'Do anything you want.'

She was up on her hands and knees, the crown of her head resting against the wall, laughing softly. He knelt upright behind her. There came the light *slap-slap-slap* as he delved her, but she was laughing because the phone had begun to ring. He leaned across her to get it – cleaving her, going deep – then eased back and fitted it into the hollow of her waist, just where her spine dipped and her rump flared towards him. He continued – *slap-slap-slap* – as he lifted the receiver, and she reached back under her own body, touching him, touching herself, touching him. She was still laughing.

'It's a pleasant afternoon, Sam . . . A bit of a wind, but the sun's warm. Why stay shut up in there? Why not take Sophie out somewhere?'

He went away from her; she could have been in the room on her own.

'A stroll along the front, perhaps – down Dewer Street. A running sea, sunlight on the wavetops . . .'

Sophie sat with her back to the wall, knees drawn up, arms wrapped around her shins. Pascoe held the phone out and she listened to the hoarse, whispering voice that unwound in the space between them; at that remove, she could hear the tone but not what he was saying.

Pascoe nodded, as if to say: 'Take it. If you ever doubted, you'll believe me now.'

She shook her head – *I believe you* – but he didn't withdraw his arm. Syllable by syllable, she brought the voice to her ear.

'. . . and then, perhaps, call in at the bar for a drink. Why not? A cool beer after your walk . . .' A pause; whoever was speaking stopped for a moment suddenly attentive; perhaps he'd felt a change in the rhythm of listening. He said, 'Sophie? Is that you?'

And when she didn't reply, the voice confirmed it: '*Sophie* . . .' with all the warmth and fondness you might find when old friendship is renewed.

'What shall we do?' Sophie asked.

For the first time they felt naked. She walked awkwardly across the room, all tits and ass until she found something to put on.

'He suggested we go to the bar?'

'That's right.'

Pascoe said, 'Don't worry.'

'What does that mean?' She laughed briefly, and the laugh became a cough.

*   *   *

All passion had gone from the room, all pleasure, all ambition. Sophie sat on the lip of the bath while Pascoe took a shower. He heard her speaking, but couldn't tell what she said.

'His voice was like a worm going into my ear.'

They were two among fifty people enjoying the sun and the warm breeze off the sea. 'He was right,' Pascoe said, 'it's a nice day.' Sophie was setting the pace with a long stride. She had looped her arm through Pascoe's to keep him in step. As they reached the door of the bar, he asked: 'Was it Charlie?'

'I was waiting for that.' She detached her arm and he followed her inside.

The barman pretended not to see them for a while. It wasn't personal in any way: professionals have their tasks and their techniques. Eventually he came over with a letter and an enquiring smile. They had a round of drinks for the sake of appearance, then walked back out to Dewer Street and up on to the cliff path.

When Zeno had chased Nick Howard along that crest, he'd paused and listened, then seen a dim target for his knife. Nick had fallen, clutching his leg and tumbling downhill. Now Sophie sat down just at the point he'd fallen from, her back to the slope, feet pointing to the cliff-edge. She took up Pascoe's earlier question.

'I don't know. I don't know whether it was Charlie or not. You think because we were on-and-off lovers when I was barely out of my teens, I'll recognize that whisper, that pillow-talk voice? Wrong.' She looked at him. 'I wouldn't have recognized yours.'

He said, 'Yes, all right.' And after a moment, 'I'm sorry.'

She looked away, letting her vision swim in the dazzle off the sea. 'Open your letter. You might have won the car in a time-share raffle.'

The page was a pennant in the wind; he had to hold it

185

top and bottom like a town crier. 'I've been invited out to dinner.'

'Not for the first time.' She remembered something he'd said about his wife leaving: how he'd come back to find everything as if she'd only just left the room – like the *Marie Celeste*. Then there was another picture; Pascoe stepping into the bedroom of the empty house to see the table laid, the wine opened, the candles burning, as though someone had been there only a second before.

Life is a circle, she thought. We choose our images, and round and round they come.

'Different,' he told her, and held the letter out. 'There'll be people at other tables, a menu, a wine list, and a muzak version of *West Side Story*. I hope the service is better than last time.'

'Well,' she said, 'if you find a cassette-player on the table, only order half a bottle of wine.' The letter gave the name of a restaurant, a day, a time. The only other thing it said was *Come alone*. 'What's that about?' Sophie asked. 'Whoever he is, he knows I'm here. So why "Come alone?"'

Pascoe shrugged as if she ought to know. In case she didn't, he said: 'Unfinished business.'

Eighteen

The car stopped on the causeway in a sudden silence and the toll operator ducked out of sight. There was the kind of washy light you get on marsh-flats; a mild wind licked across the asphalt. When a second car drew up behind the first, there was still no noise, so maybe it had coasted the last few yards with its engine switched off. Men got out of the second car. At the same time, men were coming out of the toll office. They were all carrying automatic weapons.

The first car had only a driver. He looked round, startled, then he knew what was happening and he knew why and he knew who. He climbed out, but it was far too late. The men had already opened up, firing in long, rhythmic bursts, walking in behind the wall of noise. The car hopped; craters and gashes leaped along the body-work; the windows shivered and dissolved.

The driver was out of the car and a few feet from it. His body went this way and that as the bullets took him. He was hit so often, so fast, so relentlessly that he seemed to be pushed and pulled by invisible hands – thrown almost to the ground, kicked upright again, one minute teetering forward on his toes, the next knocked back on his heels. It looked as if they were hosing him down with blood.

The gunmen advanced on him, faces impassive, eyes on their target. You couldn't believe there was a breath of life left in him, but he was still upright, still moving, arms waving wildly, legs frantic in a mad dance. When they stopped firing, he dropped at once, hard, as much weight as a butcher's carcass. The silence that followed was unfathomable. As they turned away, one of them kicked the body and spat: Sicilian contempt for a dead enemy.

And there he lay. Sonny Corleone, dead on the causeway.

Charlie Singer kept the volume turned up. The noise of Sonny's murder had cancelled the sounds that came through the matchwood walls on either side. Singer had been in the hotel room for the best part of two weeks, going out from time to time to buy food, or to eat at a grimy café close to the railway station. Once or twice, when the noises were driving him crazy or the room had started to close on him like a fist, he'd gone to a movie and tried to feel safe in the dark; but he couldn't shake the feeling that they had followed him down the street and into the cinema – that one of them sat behind him, close enough to touch, that they'd be there waiting when he emerged on to the street.

Mostly, he went out at night. The girls were everywhere: at traffic lights, in side-streets, marking out the station concourse with heel-taps and cigarette-butts. He paid for his room in advance, but most of them seemed to rent by the hour. What he could hear through the walls – what he tried to drown with old movies and game shows and newscast violence – were men's voices laid over women's voices – grunts and howls, faked pleasure, real pain, faked desire, anger, indignation, urgency, bellows, sighs, outrage, laughter – all of it melding into the unmistakable, urgent rhythm of human coupling. The clients were mostly travellers – businessmen with meetings to make. The girls turned them round like assembly-line souvenirs.

Al Pacino hiked up a hill in Sicily, two minders with shotguns ambling along behind. Hills, dusty roads, stone walls – a lyrical moment, and quiet.

A girl's voice said, 'What do you like? You can do anything you want.' She was clear as a bell through the wall; you could hear fatigue under the wantonness, like grime.

188

Charlie Singer broke the seal on a bottle of Scotch. He thought, If I ever fuck again, it'll be too soon. He wanted to move on, but couldn't think of a better place to be.

Wallace Ellwood couldn't think of a better place either.

He sat in one of the restaurants across the street from the gym where Ronald Morton had died. It was a warm night, and the girl he was with had opted to take a table in the garden: it was a careful choice – at the back of the place and as far from the windows as you could get. At the centre of the garden was a single tree that had been tricked out with vivid electric twigs and leaves. When the girl bowed her head to look at the menu, a floss of pink neon tangled in her hair.

Annie Roland was Hilary Todd's PA. Ellwood had phoned her after listening to Todd's threats. A risk – he'd known it was; but he'd seen her with Hilary a few times, and he'd watched her carefully, as he watched everyone whose life might touch his own. What he'd seen was all efficiency, all discretion. Just a tad too much briskness, perhaps; an almost-imperceptible flare of aggression.

Annie ordered artichoke and a steak to follow, then lifted her wineglass. She had barely glanced at Ellwood since they'd sat down. Finally, she said: 'You're almost as deep in shit as you can get.'

'I know.' He'd ordered the wine to impress. When he took a sip, he impressed even himself.

'What do you want?'

'You know the answer to that.'

'Rough guess?'

'Rough guess will do.'

'You want me to give you something on Hilary Todd. You are carrying your own rock and being pushed towards a hard place, you know it, you don't like it, you see only one way out of it. Largely speaking, it's all a matter of time.'

'As bad as that?' Ellwood asked. His voice was light, but he wanted to know whatever she might know.

'It's not that the job you've been given is an easy one. It's known to be tough. And it's not just that everyone's getting train fever about the whole thing – although one or two of our people in Europe are beginning to feel cold winds and badly need to know if that means there's a storm on the way.'

'It's not those things . . . ?'

'No. Harold Piper is nuts; they know that. I suppose there might be some who would say that you should have taken faster action – riskier action, perhaps. But then there'd be others who would be against it, on the grounds that we'd show our hand and gamble everything. Mostly, they seem to be in favour of the line you've taken – doing things by stealth.'

'And so . . . ?' Ellwood knew the answer, but asked the question all the same. He needed to judge Annie's response.

'Hilary Todd dislikes you. It's as easy as that. I think it must be that you worry him in some way. I don't know why.'

I know, Ellwood thought. He knows things about me that frighten him. They frighten him because they attract him. He likes the things I like; he hears their music, he tastes their tastes. He has the appetite, but he doesn't have the capacity for risk. He's angry, but his anger's too green, too raw. Anger matures in the cask; it ferments in the heart. You have to nurture it, you have to let it take its time. You have to wait . . . Then, one day, you tap a little of it, and try it, and you've got what you waited for – *hatred*, a good vintage and ready to drink.

He said, 'Dislikes me. Yes. And what will that make him do?'

'It means he'll give you no leeway.' She smiled. 'I'm amused by your amusement – bringing me to this restaurant, to this street. The men you killed can't have mattered *that* much. Can they? You put yourself within Hilary's reach. Wasn't that careless?' She seemed genuinely intrigued. 'Why did you do it?'

'I wanted to.'

Although his hair was slicked back, it was dull; it kept the light. His face was a narrow triangle, the skin a shadowy grey. A faint smell came off him, sour and dark, like bad fruit.

'And now you want help.'

'Not really. Help is what people get from their friends. Help comes with all sorts of unpleasant attachments – generosity, gratitude, fondness. What I want is to find out whether you have anything I might want to buy.'

'Supposing I hadn't come tonight . . . ?'

'I was prepared to worry about that if I found myself sitting here alone, eating alone, enjoying this wine alone.'

'Would you have enjoyed it?'

'Not quite as much, perhaps.'

'I might be here only to make you feel safe. I might be loyal to Hilary. How do you know he didn't send me here? After I leave, I might report back: every word we've said.'

'No.'

'How can you be sure?'

'For one thing, it simply isn't Todd's style. If he thought I was trying to find a way to set him up, he wouldn't think of stealth – he's not that subtle and he's not that patient. He'd just target me and hit the button.'

'What else?'

'There's something in your face.'

'What is it?'

'Malice.'

Their food arrived. Ellwood had asked for prosciutto ham. He ate it quickly, then stared round at the people on other tables, leaving Annie to pick the leaves out of her artichoke like a heartsick girl . . . *loves me, loves me not* . . . then suck the buttery pulp. He smiled when she wasn't looking. She had chosen the wrong hors-d'œuvre for a power meal, no question about that. The mistake made Ellwood sure. Leaves piled up on her plate and toppled to the table. The water in her fingerbowl was scummed with grease.

She said, 'When you spoke on the phone, you said you knew it wouldn't come free.'

'How much do you want?'

'Ten billion sound all right?' She lit a cigarette while the waiter cleared her rubble.

'Yes, well, all things are relative,' Ellwood said. 'I take the point. But not all things have the same worth.'

'How do I know what it's worth – if I give you something you can use against Hilary; what's the proper cost?'

'It's not the value of the *thing*, you see . . .' Ellwood's eyes glittered dully, like tarnished metal. 'It's how you value yourself. What you might give – information, gossip, a scandal; it has no worth of its own.'

'It's worth something to you.'

'Maybe. I'm not talking about that. You've got something to sell, it's yours, so it's you who makes a profit. What do you hand over? Information – yes; but also deceit, betrayal, power. Parts of you. How much do they sell for? What will you charge for them?'

His hair smooth pewter; his skin ashy; his eyes full of dead light. His hand settled on hers and he took the cigarette, then put it to his lips, drawing until it dented and the coal glowed. He inhaled, and held his breath.

'Suppose you were a whore,' he said, 'what would you charge for that?'

She felt heat start in the pit of her stomach, then rise to her throat, a bitter column of bile and rancid butter. She closed her eyes a moment and the lashes were suddenly damp with sweat.

Ellwood put her cigarette down gently in the ashtray. One fingertip lay for a second on the back of her hand and the touch raced over her skin. He asked, 'What would you charge me for that?'

The leaves on the tree flickered a moment as if the power had dipped, and one or two people looked up for some sign of a storm. Without thinking, Annie lifted the cigarette to her mouth. It bore a sharp taste of tin, cold in her throat. The waiter put her food in front of her: steak, creamed potato, cauliflower florets, a little fan of mange-tout.

'Flat on your back with your legs in the air and my cock jammed into your womb,' Ellwood said. 'How much would you charge for that?' His voice was only just audible. 'Tied down with a spike up your ass and my sperm all over your face.'

The meal was a work of art: all the constituents in balance on the plate, a whorl of sauce round the centrepiece of meat.

'How much would you charge for that?'

Too late to go back, too late for second thoughts, too late for pretence and much too late for regret. Despite which she said, 'I'll think about it.' Her voice had grown hoarse; it cracked on the syllables.

'OK,' Ellwood said. He sounded oddly chipper. 'Don't take too long. I'm still willing to pay.'

She saw what had happened. The fact that she was with him was enough – was betrayal and commitment enough. Payment was only a way of sealing the bargain. He would give her time – a little – because it didn't matter.

'You walk up to a cage. Let's say it's getting dark. Inside, there's something you want. It could be anything: money, freedom, revenge, they're all the same. And you smell the heat of something sleeping in the straw.'

Taped to Ellwood's ribs, a little recorder saved every wise word, just as it had saved Annie's demands and then her silences.

'If you go into the cage and shut the door, and you hear the creature waking in the dark, there are certain things to remember that could save your life.' Annie watched shadows gathering in his face. 'Do nothing to startle the creature, nothing to alarm it. Don't make any sudden movements. Don't shout for help. Don't lose your nerve.

193

Act predictably. Take what you want. Leave something in return. Then you can go. Most important, of course, don't turn your back.'

The waiter took her meal away untouched. The pink tree glowed in the dark.

Nineteen

Sir Harold Piper liked to lie on his bed and look up through the square of window high on the wall of his room. He needed to see what the weather was doing. His calculations depended on that. He needed to be able to see clouds and birds.

Sir Harold was developing a lightning eye for bird identification. Some shape would pass the window, like a shadow across the glass, and he'd say, 'Black-backed gull', or 'Chough', or 'Herring gull', or 'Rook'. Life being what it is, ninety times in a hundred it was a herring gull, but Sir Harold lived in the expectation of surprises. From time to time, it had been a kestrel; twice, a buzzard. Rarity was crucial; you could make a calculation based on that.

Nights were often blank. Sometimes there were stars to be seen; sometimes not. You could take an angle of incidence from the stars, the window-frame, the desk, but it offered few variants. The best nights came with a full moon and wind-driven cumulus. Clouds covered the moon then passed. A certain time elapsed between each moment of obscurity. Crucial. The clouds were geometric, or had geometric tendencies. One would be more of a parallelogram, one more of a circle. An isosceles triangle might cruise across, its angles forged by a steely silver light. Every calculation was crucial. Sir Harold knew that by framing the world that way, he could best bring it to judgement. A geometric version of all love, all desire, all hatred, all sin, all loss. Murder, hunger, greed, corruption, kindness. All birth and death; all vice, all shining deeds. Alone among the inmates, he was allowed to sleep in darkness. He had explained to Dr Harris how important it was that he see the sky and apply his calculations.

Cloud-cover was utter darkness. The only thing to hear was the light sough of the wind and, from another room, an occasional shout like a seal-cough. He dozed for a minute. Then opened his eyes to a miracle.

In the dark vault of the ceiling fireflies were dancing. A hundred tiny white specks, each drawing a crooked trail of light as it moved. The lines intersected making angles and points of incidence, making rhomboids and shaky circles.

Sir Harold gasped, then held the indrawn breath as if the tiny creatures might fear a disturbance in the air. He began a series of calculations, his mind whirring like banks of flywheels. The violent little flight paths went this way and that, each line of light more mysterious than the last, each moment of randomness more thrilling, the whole pattern building like fault-lines in human lives.

Then the fireflies seemed to gather in a swarm. The bright lines converged; the points of light all drew together shedding a soft glow – a little lamp. Like a hermit receiving a vision, Sir Harold peered into that radiance. He saw the face of the clown.

They spoke in whispers. Piper's voice was throaty and urgent. 'Do you know who I am?'

'Who are you?'

'The Great Anarch. Alpha and Omega. I have come to judge the world.'

'What's the decision?'

'I'm gathering evidence. Thank you for bringing the fireflies.'

'They helped?'

'Enormously. It's such a vast project. So much to calculate. I started when I was a child; it's still not complete.'

'You made the calculations throughout your child-hood?'

'Always.'

'Did your parents know who you were?'

'Oh, no.'

'You made the calculations throughout your marriage?'

'Throughout.'

'Did your wife know who you were?'

'She never knew.'

'You made the calculations throughout the war?'

'The war was a most important time. It's obvious. Great destruction, great courage, great evil, great causes. All of them in the balance, all of them placed on one side or another of the scales. I made terrific advances then.'

'Did anyone know who you were?'

'No-one.'

'Did deceit go on to the scales?'

'All human emotion, all human endeavour, all human—'

'Did betrayal?'

The fireflies Piper had seen were neon spangles in three juggler's globes. Zeno had stepped up the power to one of them to get the glow that was half lighting the room. He held it up so that it hung above them like a dim lamp. *Did betrayal?* still circled in the gloom.

Piper said, 'I've come to judge the world.'

'Did anyone in MI6 know who you were? Did anyone in the war cabinet? Did any of your European colleagues know?' Zeno was reading Wallace Ellwood's script.

With infinite slowness, Piper raised a finger to his own face. 'If thine eye offend thee, pluck it out.' Zeno could see a glimmer of spittle on the old man's front teeth – a grin or a grimace, it wasn't easy to tell.

'Moloch. Alpha and Omega. Did anyone know?'

'How could I have judged them if they'd known me truly?' The grating whisper broke into a nursery sing-song. 'They'd all have been goody two-shoes, wouldn't they?' His finger brushed his eyelid once more. Very softly, he said: 'I didn't tell you I'm Moloch. I didn't say that.'

'If you're who you say you are, then you can do anything.'

'Can I?' The voice was foxy, now.

'You can do what you like. No-one could say it was wrong.'

A long silence followed. Piper turned to look at the wall, as if he might find some message waiting for him there. Zeno kept the globe aloft, arm aching.

Earlier that evening, he'd held Carla close, his lips next to her ear, and whispered her a promise. 'We'll go away soon.'

'It's OK . . . don't worry . . .' Love had shone out of her face. 'Whatever you want to do. You know that.'

This crazy old bastard was giving nothing more than the shit he gave to Harris. 'No matter what you did,' he prompted, 'it couldn't be betrayal. No matter what secrets you told, it couldn't be treachery. Could it? Surely everything was part of your purpose, wasn't it? Part of your design. Someone like you couldn't be restricted by petty ideas like country, like patriotism, like loyalty. How could you take sides?' He was conscious of having said too much, but offered another line of Ellwood's script. 'Tell me about Janus.'

Piper took the low chair and set it to face the wall. He sat down, as if the message had to be examined more closely. His lips moved in soundless shapes that meant: I didn't tell you I'm Moloch.

Zeno said, 'Tell me about geometry; I'd like to know about that.' It was too late. Piper said nothing. He stared at the wall. After five minutes, the glow in the room died and the door opened and closed with the least *snick* of the lock.

Piper sat in the dark. After a moment, working only by touch, he put out a finger and traced an invisible message on the wall.

Who is the clown?

Twenty

There were days when the weather changed hour to hour. Tom Carey had taken the path out to Meer's Point in sunlight that lit branches of gorse like brands. By the time he was ready for the first cast, the sky had lowered like a ceiling – a grey wash from horizon to horizon with darker tufts of grimy cumulus scudding underneath. He freed the brake on the reel, then hauled back on the big sea-rod, bringing both arms round in a fast curve. The weighted line paid out with a thin scream.

Carey was standing on the furthermost spit of the point, so that he could put the line along the wind. The ocean broke on a vast apron of black rocks either side of him, and the air was full of spray.

Carey reeled in to check his bait and cast again. He thought of the girl who had lain on Ellwood's bed. *Sleek things he'd fished*. He imagined a pull on the line and the girl coming in on the wash, pale in the wave-break, water as green as ice pouring off her shoulders as he gaffed her and brought her in. Stones in her eyes and her cunt full of pearls.

Carey had heard about Lori's death not long after it happened. No-one had missed her; she'd been in the house on her own. Her husband was away for a week – a trip back home to the States on USAF business.

Just about dawn. He'd parked by the phone box and found the track that went through the beech wood, parallel to the backs of the officers' houses. There had been barely enough light to see by. A songthrush had started up, then fell silent, waiting for other voices.

First, he'd seen her clothes where she had flung them – a sinister obscenity about that; her skirt seeming to hold its shape, her blouse torn off its buttons, the thin web of underwear caught up on some scrubby brushwood. Then he'd seen the pills scattered on the leaf-mould like the seed-pods of poisonous flowers. And finally he'd seen Lori, though not at first because all he'd been told was that she was dead – not how, not where.

She was hanging from the lower branch of a tree just a step or two away, head fallen forward, back bowed, as if she'd been frowning at some puzzle beneath her feet. Her arms were straight, like plumb-lines, fingers slack. All her weight had seemed to be aching for the ground.

Carey had looked up at her. She wasn't very high at all; his eye-line had run to about the crook of her knee.

He'd thought: As if the pills wouldn't make sure of her; as if it would take two deaths, at least, to settle all the fear and anguish in her.

There had been faint movements in the wood: creatures beginning to stir. A litter of birdsong had filtered down through the leaves. Around Lori, the stillness and silence hadn't changed. The light had been shades of grey, seeming to grow paler where she hung, herself a slender branch, her pubic hair a dark leaf, her breasts drooping like exotic fruit.

The wind brought little waterspouts in off the rock clitter. From the tip of the rod, the line bowed, then soon became invisible, but it sent tremors back along its length to hum in the hollow fibreglass pole. Carey felt the drag of the sea underneath his hand.

He hadn't come to Longrock because Ellwood had asked him to, nor for any payment Ellwood might devise. He had come to find the answer to an old mystery. This had only just occurred to him, but he recognized it as the truth. It was the mystery of his own cowardice and lost hope.

*   *   *

The sky cleared in less than half an hour and the wind dropped. Carey broke down the rod and loaded his tackle bag, then hiked back towards the town. Scents rose from the bracken on both sides of the path.

What am I, he thought, but a man whose faith lies dead. Dead in Poland, dead in Hungary, dead in East Berlin. And now dead at the heart – dead in Russia itself. What was it I believed in? Father, Son, and the Ghost that haunted Europe.

The smell of gorse on the wind has a tang, like brine.

He stowed the rod and the bag in his car and walked through the town. At first he couldn't have said where he was going; then it became clear.

The church was in a back-street close to the harbour; it was built plainly of plum-coloured brick, light oak for the porch and over the transom. The pews of light oak and the altar rail, too. A modern rose window was set above the altar, beneath it a triptych of windows linked by oak buttresses. The stained glass was the work of a modern craftsman – closely-worked reds and blues for the rose, blues and milky white for the triptych – nativity, passion, Christ in glory.

The sun struck through it, sending a river of colour along the nave. Carey sat close to the altar, dappled in blue and white light. Under his breath, as if it were really much too risky to say, he whispered, 'Forgive me, Father, for I have sinned.'

Dust motes sifted down through bands of light. The air in the church was like a drawn breath. Carey thought of the stillness that had surrounded Lori Cosgrove in the wood.

'Did you hear me? I said: Forgive me; I have sinned.' Carey's voice grew loud in the sunlit silence. He stood up, washed in light from the altar windows, and cupped his hands to his mouth, as if hailing someone a long way off. His bellow of anguish echoed out to the street.

'What's that? I didn't hear you. You'll have to speak up, you bastard!'

Blue light – love; white light – revelation.

'Speak up . . . You'll have to speak up, you bastard, you bastard, *you bastard*!'

Twenty-One

Pascoe said, 'Stay here, I'll be back as soon as I can.' He handed Sophie a piece of paper: Zeno's last letter. He'd added something to it. 'That's the number. Give me half an hour, then call. That way you can tell me you're all right, I can tell you I'm all right, and who knows: it might make the son of a bitch edgy.'

'If he wants to kill you, why would he arrange to see you in a restaurant with the whole world looking on?'

'Don't call too soon, in case he's intending to be fashionably late. I don't want to be on the phone when he arrives – it'll make him wary.'

'Edgy's good; wary's bad . . . I've got it.'

'What are you angry about?'

'I'm worried.'

'Does that make you angry?'

'You can see it fucking does. Now: what's the answer?'

'Why meet in a restaurant?'

'Yes.'

'If I knew what he wanted, I might be able to tell you.'

'He killed Nick.'

'Yes, he did. He must have.'

'And he tried to kill you.'

'But he didn't succeed. Perhaps that's why he wants to talk.'

'About Lori . . .'

'So it seems.'

'Don't go. Let's just . . . We could leave. We could pack and leave tonight.'

Pascoe went over to where she was sitting, perched like a nervous bride on the edge of the bed, and kissed her gently on the lips. He said, 'Unfinished business – remember?'

You could always hear the ocean in Dewer Street. Pascoe crossed over to walk beside the sea wall. It was something a stranger might do – someone who hadn't learned to take the view for granted. In truth, Pascoe wanted a clear sight of the other side of the street. Few people went to the seafront at night; a follower would be fairly easy to spot. He glanced to and fro as he walked back across the road, but no-one was there.

That's something Rob Thomas would probably do, he thought. I'm acting like a detective. He laughed out loud at the notion, and the laugh showed him that he was jumpy.

There was a sliver of moon, a white rind. The sea was a soft explosion in the dark. On his way to the restaurant he passed a man and a woman arm in arm, a man walking purposefully, as if late for an appointment, a woman standing next to her car and searching her bag for the key. He looked twice at the hurrying man, but decided that, like the others, he was what he seemed to be. He looked at the people drinking in the restaurant bar, and thought the same. One of them was an old man, sipping slowly at a beer.

A table had been booked in Pascoe's name. He ordered a Scotch, the only drink he would allow himself, he'd decided. The old man finished his beer and left. Shortly afterwards, a waiter came across to Pascoe with a note.

'What's happening?' Sophie had lifted the phone before the second ring.

'He didn't show. I've got a note instead.'

'Saying what?'

'Saying . . .' He paused; she could hear him shaking out the page. '"Lost my appetite. Come to forty-nine Dewer Street for drinks. Bring Sophie."'

'That's this street. The hotel's in Dewer Street.'

'Yes.'

'Are you going there?'

'Yes.'

'Look . . .' The phone was in the crook of her neck; she was wearing a scarab ring on her wedding finger and used the thumb and little finger of the same hand to twitch it back and forth across the knuckle. The other sign of nervousness was in her voice – breathy and rapid. 'I thought the idea was that you'd meet him in public. His idea, wasn't it? To make you feel safe. How good is that guarantee now? I also remember a specific instruction: come alone. What happened to that?'

'I know. I'm going anyway.'

'You want me to come?'

'It's what he wants. So let's pretend to be fitting in with that.'

'How pretend? Why are you whispering?'

'This phone's by the door – there are people at tables nearby, people coming and going. Listen: I want to flush him out. Go to that address. I'll already be there—'

'Sam—'

'No, it's OK. I'm not more than fifteen minutes' walk away. That puts me there at eight-thirty. I'll tell him I have to call you – it's what we've agreed. If I say, "Everything's fine, come round," that means stay away, I'm in trouble. If I say, "I'm in trouble," that means everything's OK.'

'What should I do – if it's bad news?'

'Don't come.'

'Jesus, I know that. What should I do about *you*?' She was sitting in an armchair, leaning forward, her eyes closed as if to concentrate better on what was being said. It was clear to her that something was wrong – something beyond what the voice was talking about. Then, in a moment of appalled recognition, she saw the lie for what it was.

The whisper continued. 'Don't do anything.'

'You're just going to walk in there?' she asked. 'On his

terms, no back-up, no weapon, no way of knowing what he's got planned?'

Sophie could hear the anger in his voice. 'Enough's enough,' he said. 'This bastard stuck a knife into me.'

A country saying goes: Bad luck if you see the new moon through glass. One of the waiters peered through the wall-sized window on to the street. Business was slow, so the tips would be poor: bad luck. He opened the door and smiled because a good-looking woman was arriving to keep a date.

Sophie sat down at Pascoe's table and said, 'I thought I'd find you here.'

He could see that something had happened. 'Where else would I be?'

'Forty-nine Dewer Street. I've just had a telephone conversation with the Great Zeno: magus, escapologist and clever bastard.'

'Go on . . .'

'Pretending to be you. He's calling again. I've worked out a way of stalling, but it won't hold him for ever. We've got about four minutes to get back to the hotel.'

They ran, but it took them six. In the room, Sophie worked on levelling her breathing. She was given a minute's grace, then the phone rang. She lifted it to silence. Looking at Pascoe, she said, 'Sam?' The silence extended. As if to reassure, Sophie added, 'I was in my room. *My* room. I thought you'd ask for my room. When you didn't call, I came back in here.' She waited to see whether she would be believed.

'I'm in trouble,' Zeno said, and hung up.

Sophie had given Pascoe the bare details as they ran back from the restaurant; now she told the rest. 'I'm supposed to go there. I'm supposed to think that you've just given me the OK.' She waited for a response, but Pascoe just nodded. 'A waiter brought you a note?'

'That's right,' he said.

'Did you ask who'd sent it?'

'Of course. It had been left on the bar: *Please give this to Mr Sam Pascoe.*'

'What did it say?'

He smiled. 'It said, "Delayed; sit tight." That's what I was doing.'

'You're at the restaurant. I'm on my way to forty-nine Dewer Street. He'll be expecting me.' She shivered. 'What shall we do?'

Pascoe said, 'That's what he thinks: me at the restaurant, you on your way. He expects to organize all the surprises – that's the way it's been until now.'

'You want me to go.'

'No. But it gives us an advantage. He thinks he's fooled us. This one time, he's off balance.'

'When they want to shoot a tiger,' Sophie told him, 'they tether a goat near a tree. A guy with a gun sits up the tree and waits. Eventually, the tiger arrives and tears the goat's throat out. That's when the man with the gun shoots the tiger.'

'No,' Pascoe said, 'you're right. I'll go alone.'

Sophie opened the door and walked to the lift. She got in and held the door-open button. Pascoe appeared in the hall, but he didn't get into the lift with her.

He said, 'I can probably handle it better on my own.'

Sophie laughed. 'Handle what? You sound as if it's all in a day's work. Get in.'

As they went down, he asked: 'When he called, how did you know it wasn't me?'

'He was clever – he whispered. You can't identify a voice from a whisper. But it made me think of the voice that sent us to the bar; he whispered then. Even so, I wasn't sure. He acted well. He made you sound worried and puzzled and angry all at the same time, and that was right for what was happening. I closed my eyes and concentrated on the voice, and I thought it wasn't you, but I didn't really know. So I asked him a question.'

'What did you say?'

'I said, "So you're going there with no back-up, no

weapon, no way of knowing what he'll do" – something like that.'

'He didn't respond to "no weapon".'

'That's right.'

Pascoe took her gun from his pocket. 'You'd better have it back now. For a moment or two you'll be in there on your own.'

Sophie shook her head. 'You've got it wrong,' she said. 'I'm the goat. You're the guy up the tree.'

First surprise was the boatyard. Sophie had been expecting a house, with a front door and a bell.

Second surprise was the music – a soft waltz coming to her through deep blue dusk, strings and woodwind, as if someone in a grand house up on the hill had just opened the door of the ballroom.

She stood just inside one of the big gates and started to act her role. 'Sam,' she called out. 'Sam?' As she stepped further into the boatyard, she thought: I hope you can hear me, Pascoe, and I hope you can see me clearly from the tree, because I can smell the tiger.

She said, 'Sam?'

The waltz was Strauss, a touch louder now. Just in front of her, enclosed by chocked-up hulls, was an open space big as a dance floor. The music went *pom-pom-pom*, three-four time, almost irresistible.

'Sam?'

Third surprise was the little table, suddenly under a spotlight, on it a top hat and a cane. A gentleman caller had arrived to take her to the ball. As she watched, the cane snapped and sprang, becoming flowers. Her corsage. Out of the hat came a dove – wings whirring – that flew up, circled once, and then was lost in the dark.

He tapped her on the shoulder – Excuse me – and when she turned he took her by the wrist and round the waist, holding her close, whisking her on to the floor. His tailcoat, his white tie, his dancing pumps, all impeccable. The white half-mask he wore made it seem as if the upper part of his face had been skinned. His lipstick was so thick that when he smiled at her, he showed teeth rimmed with red.

She was breathless, like a girl who had danced every dance. The arm wrapped round her back hugged her so tightly that her ribs threatened to crack. Shock did the rest. Her mouth was open, but she didn't make a sound as he whirled her into the darkness. His divided face looked down at her in disappointment. She wasn't dressed for the occasion: no gown, no satin slippers, no tiara. A girl should have something – a simple row of pearls, perhaps. A choker.

He spun her away, letting her go to arm's length as she twirled, but following closely. He stood behind her, his hands falling to her nape like someone about to fix the clasp of a necklace. She felt the cord fall on to her throat and tighten.

'*Sam!*'

In her voice there was terror and anger, summons and expectation. She was calling for someone she knew to be there. Zeno heard the difference and half turned as Pascoe stepped into the beam of the spotlight. His foot struck a cassette-player that skittered off into the darkness. The music stopped. He was holding the gun out like a target-shooter, everything wrong, and he didn't speak because he couldn't think of a thing to say.

Sophie grabbed the cord that encircled her throat, holding it out like a tight collar. When it came loose, she tossed it away. Already she had started to run. Her leg cracked against a trailer bar that sloped back to a set of wheels. She fell heels-up, almost making a somersault. Zeno and Pascoe faced each other, Pascoe circling to try to get advantage from the light. Eventually, he thought to say, 'If you move, I'll shoot.'

Sophie hurried towards the gates. All she wanted to do was get out of there. Her legs were almost too shaky to hold her up and she felt consciousness closing down. To stay on her feet, she talked, just gibberish – 'OK, I've got to go now, got to go, all right? I'd better go now, sorry about that, but I have to go, I'll find the gates and I'll leave, that OK? 'Cause I have to go now, no question about it, OK? I'm leaving, I'm going now . . .' – in a low voice, meant for no-one.

Zeno backed out of the light. 'If you move, I'll shoot.' Pascoe said it again, but all he did was point the gun. Zeno lifted a hand to say goodbye: a quick salute. Directly in front of the heeled-up dinghies, Pascoe ducked and lost his footing; he sat down hard, the breath squirting from his lungs, and fired a shot without knowing it had happened. Zeno's knife clattered away somewhere behind him. Another was already on the way, off-target because Zeno hadn't expected the gunshot. The blade sang in the polished boards by Pascoe's head, a thin note declining on the air. Pascoe scrambled up and found cover behind the light. He switched the barrel of the gun to and fro, looking for a target, but all he could see was the silk hat and the garish bunch of flowers, pink and green and orange, each with a button-centre like the mad eye of a moon-daisy.

The trick was to retreat towards the gates. If that was Zeno's move too, Pascoe might intercept him; if not, it would bottle him up in the boatyard. He started back, using the dinghies as cover. All he could hear was the sound of the sea and his own breath, dangerously loud.

The gunshot had immobilized Sophie. The gun was meant to give him control, she hadn't expected to hear it used. She would be bait, Zeno would be drawn, then Pascoe would appear with the gun and they'd be asking a few hard questions. That was the idea. Now someone might be dead.

She could see part of Dewer Street through the half-open gate and it seemed to be deserted. She stood in the gloom, not knowing whether to stay or run away. Twice, she opened her mouth to yell Pascoe's name, but reasoned that to call him wouldn't bring him any faster, and might well distract him. She switched her gaze from the street to the boatyard. The spotlight cast shadows that curled on the sculpted sides of the motor launches. She touched her throat where the garotte had lain and felt the flicker of her own pulse, like a flame in the wind.

Come on, Sam. Let's go. Let's go, OK? All right? It's time to go.

A new shadow sprang up on the hull, a dark wave, and then the light went out.

Pascoe froze. He stared towards the point where the light had been, wanting to see a darker shape on darkness. The absence of brightness made everything totally black. Then the pale spillage from streetlights seeped back again, barely enough to show him the gun when he pointed it.

He was angry with himself, and that made him reckless. He knew he should have fired when he had the chance; by leaving it too late, he'd lost the advantage. Now he was going cat-and-mouse round the yard, as much hunted as hunter. He'd fallen out of the tree and the tiger was close – somewhere just beyond the clearing.

He went deeper into the boatyard, treading like a man on a cliff-edge, and his hip struck the little table, toppling it.

Both Sophie and Zeno looked towards the sound.

As soon as he'd switched the light off, Zeno had taken the same route through the yard as Sophie had done a little earlier. Pascoe's original position, behind the dinghies, had cut off the route to the storage hut and that other means of getting to the street. The challenge of the light going off was: Come this way; come further in. Now Pascoe was doing just that and Zeno was between him and the gate.

Clever, he thought. Clever Sophie and clever Sam. And brave, to be used as bait. And unpredictable, to come with a gun. I hadn't thought of that – hadn't thought that you might fight back. I should have guessed, of course. Sophie was always reckless; and Sam had wanted to blow up a train.

He skirted the stern of the motor launch and looked to where the wash from the lights in Dewer Street fell through the gates.

Sophie tried to read meaning into the noise. The two men were fighting. Or Sam had found Zeno by the noise: he was captured. Or he was wounded and weak; he had fallen; Sam was standing over him. In a minute, she'd hear Sam speak. In a minute, she would dare draw breath again. She took a couple of steps into the yard as if Pascoe's voice were already summoning her.

The whisper stopped her heart. Just her name, '*Sophie*', spoken close to her ear, because no-one else deserved to share the moment. They had waltzed the last waltz together, now the evening was over. Her partner stooped to claim his goodnight kiss.

Pascoe heard her scream and scrambled across junk and debris in the darkness. He fell twice, going down the second time across a litter of boxes, and losing the gun. From somewhere in the darkness, Sophie made little, stricken noises, all on an indrawn breath.

She was sitting down by the gate, one hand on her neck, her head canted over at a fierce angle. Her knees were drawn up, like a child's. She said, 'Let's go, now – all right? Can we go? I think we'd better go now, is that OK? Sam . . . is that OK?'

He took her free hand and pulled her upright. The other hand stayed clamped to her neck. He said, 'I dropped the gun.'

'Let's just go.'

'I dropped the gun,' he said, 'and we'll have to go back and get it. I want those other things too.'

He tried to shift her arm in order to see the wound, but she turned away with a violent shrug. '*Don't*—' A yelp, high-pitched and full of anger; it meant: Don't touch, don't look, don't ask. Pascoe took his hand away as if it had been stung. His fingertips were wet.

★　　★　　★

The spotlight was a torch, tied to a stanchion. The table was bamboo and rattan. The cassette-player was pocket-sized and dented where Pascoe had trodden on it. The flowers were a cane in disguise. The hat was empty.

Pascoe walked the yard for another ten minutes, torch in hand, looking for traces of Zeno. Sophie was at his side, head bowed, but she wasn't looking.

He wrenched the knife back and forth to free it from the planking. The first one Zeno had thrown was lost completely.

He took a straight line towards the gates and found the gun at once.

'I've got to go now, Sam, OK?' Sophie wasn't looking at him. She stood quite still, her eyes on the ground, holding her neck. 'Let's go, OK? I've really got to go.'

She didn't make a move, so he took her free arm and led her out. There was no-one on Dewer Street to hear her cry.

Twenty-Two

The entrance lobby of the hotel was bright with neon. A phone rang in the office beyond the desk, but no-one answered it. Pascoe had abandoned the bamboo and rattan table. The cassette-recorder was in his pocket along with the knife. He carried the flowers and the hat in one hand like a rejected suitor whose props had let him down.

'You can shoot the tiger before it tears the goat's throat out, or you can do it afterwards.' Sophie took a long breath that came in torn fragments – the aftermath of weeping. 'But the trick is to shoot the fucking tiger at all costs.'

In Pascoe's room was a circular coffee table with a glass top. He laid everything on it and stood back to look, like someone in an art gallery sizing up a surrealist exhibit. There was bird shit in the hat. After a moment, he followed Sophie into the bathroom.

She stood sideways to look at herself, leaning towards the mirror, her palm still cupped by the place to trap what lay beneath. On the pale skin of her neck lay the red-and-purple butterfly of a love-bite. Blood-beads had seeped from tiny capillaries in the butterfly's wings. Circling it was a broken O of lipstick.

She looked at Pascoe's reflection with her own reflected face. 'He didn't have time to kill me, so he kissed me.'

'I shouldn't have let you go in there,' Pascoe said. 'I'm sorry.'

'He wanted me. He was expecting me.' She meant: Don't apologize – it can't make any difference. In truth, though, she wished that he had stopped her. She filled the wash-basin and soaped the lipstick off. The butterfly's dappled colours glistened and new points of blood started up, freshened by the water. Pascoe put out a hand to touch the place and she shied away, so he drew her in, pulling against her resistance and binding her arms with his.

He kissed her gently, expecting nothing back. 'It'll fade,' he said, 'it'll soon be gone,' and kissed her again before leaving her to herself. After he'd gone out, she continued to stand as she had when he'd kissed her – as she had when Zeno had kissed her.

Sophie . . .

Eyes closed, she called the moment back – his voice in her ear, his mouth on her neck, the way he dragged breath through his nose while he rooted at her. Pascoe had heard her scream and was coming across the boatyard, crashing and falling. Zeno's head shook with fury as he sucked her and bruised her. When Pascoe fell again, Sophie fell too. If her eyes had been open, she would have seen Zeno heading for the cliff path.

She ran the water out of the basin and held her wrists under the cold tap until they were numb. The Strauss waltz started up in the bedroom.

Pascoe was sitting on the floor by the coffee table, cassette-player in one hand, the knife balanced across one extended finger. He said, 'Whoever it is certainly likes to have fun. He's a performer – a showman.'

'Forgive me,' Sophie said, 'if I don't applaud.'

Pascoe fast-forwarded the tape, then pressed play, bringing the music back on the swell of a crescendo. 'Did he seem all right to you – when he kissed you?' She stared at him, not knowing what he could possibly mean. 'I shot at him, remember? I thought maybe I'd hit him.'

She shook her head. 'I don't think you could hit the ocean if you fired the gun from a boat.' The tape whinnied on as he pressed fast-forward again. 'Do you think he owns the boatyard?'

'Do you?'

'No.'

'No, but he might own a boat. We could look at that.' Pascoe chose another moment on the tape and the waltz seemed to be reaching a finale: all brass and basses. He thumbed the button.

'I'd better have a drink.' Sophie said it as if describing some tiresome duty. She poured Scotch for them both, then went towards the bathroom to add water. As she passed Pascoe he pressed play and a voice whispered '. . . *dead.*'

Pascoe said, 'Christ!' Sophie froze, a glass in either hand, her gaze fixed on the bathroom door, her lips parted in a silent cry. She didn't move when she heard Pascoe winding the tape back, nor did she look at him. There was a pause; he seemed to be waiting for her permission. She went into the bathroom and added water to the whisky, then came back out and handed him a glass. After she'd taken her first sip, she said: 'Play it – go ahead,' and sat on the bed to listen where she wouldn't have to meet his eye.

The waltz swayed to an end and died on a cymbal crash. Zeno's voice said, 'Goodbye, Sophie; you're dead.' It was the same husky voice that Pascoe had heard when he'd sat in the empty house at the table laid for one.

Zeno had recorded the waltz and second-guessed the scene: a dance, a dip, a twirl, the cord around her neck. *Goodbye, Sophie; you're dead.*

Pascoe would have been at the restaurant, waiting. Maybe Zeno had plans for him as well. He might have intended to arrive – late as his note had said – with some other surprise. He might have sat down with Pascoe and eaten the food and drunk the wine with her murder still at his fingertips. *Goodbye, Sophie; you're dead.*

Perhaps he'd timed it perfectly. Perhaps, if Pascoe hadn't arrived, she would have gone first to her knees, then sat down, her tongue out like dead meat, with Zeno kneeling up behind her using his hands like someone binding a bale. She would have felt her jaw cracking, her eyeballs filling with blood. Then he'd have rolled her aside and stood up, panting. Then the cymbal crash. Then, *Goodbye, Sophie; you're dead.*

Pascoe thought, only a real performer would bother

216

with a grace-note like that; only a real egotist. Sophie thought, *Goodbye, Sophie; you're dead*.

Pascoe stripped and got into bed. There was something bleak in his face, something unforgiving. He said, 'We can tempt him, or wait for him to tempt us, or leave. If we leave, it's a fair bet he'll come after us. Not certain, though.'

'Is that what you want to do?'

'I don't know. I don't think so, no. The idea of turning my back on him doesn't make me feel safe.'

Sophie was wearing jeans. She pushed them down and left them on the floor. Her sweater and T-shirt followed. 'How would you tempt him? If that was what you decided to do.'

'Basically, by staying here, but refusing to be drawn. No dinner-dates, no meetings. If we don't play his game, he'll have to be more direct.'

She took off her underclothes – bending, high-stepping – eyes on some distant thought. 'What else?'

'Take risks, I suppose. Go to lonely places and go there alone. Make it a pattern.'

'In the hope that he'll see the pattern and try to make use of it.'

'Yes.'

She got into bed beside him and closed her eyes, briefly. She could have been trying to picture the place where Zeno and she might meet; some barren scrap of land inside her head. She opened them when Pascoe leaned across, anxious to comfort her. He touched her cheek and she leaped, hot-wired, her hands all over him, almost ferocious.

'What is it?'

She was fighting to turn him, fighting to bring him on top of her. 'I don't know.' She sounded close to being afraid. 'I feel so horny I think I'll faint.' Her legs forked, greedily. 'For God's sake put it in me.'

In the same moment, she started to come, hips rising so

217

fast that she almost bucked him off. She yelled, as if touched by fire, and held on to the moment, her torso subsiding fraction by fraction.

She lay under him, loose-limbed, like someone who'd fallen, and raised both arms above her head to grasp the bedrails. 'Again,' she said.

Pascoe saw where it had come from, that excitement, that unstoppable hunger. It was the cord on her neck, the killer's hands there, his voice on the tape speaking her name out loud. He lay beside her as she slept, watching the slow fill and fall of her ribs, the tap of pulse in her temple, and felt as restless as a husband who suspects infidelity.

He switched out the light, but the darkness made his skin crawl so he switched it back on, then took Sophie's sweater from the floor and draped it over the lampshade. She spoke in her sleep, a little rill of syllables like someone imitating an instrument. Her warmth spread towards him when he got back into bed.

The noise like distant rain was the lift doors opening and closing. Pascoe got up and checked the lock on the door. He could hear himself breathing.

The Palings was an old building; it had stood full face to the sea and the prevailing wind for the best part of a hundred years. Pascoe lay still listening to beams settling, to pipes ticking. Sophie was like an engine that hadn't been switched off; he could sense the energy in her and feel the heat. She'd said, 'Again,' and stretched out, hands raised, and turned her face away. Pascoe felt a little rush of lust, as if her appetite had just caught up with him.

Her arm rose, then fell back on the bedclothes, and she flinched violently. Pascoe was almost asleep. He touched her hand and said, 'OK . . .' but it was a reflex; the bed was shelving under him.

When Pascoe woke, the room was a cave; the shrouded lamp cast a dull glow. It felt chilly and late. Street sounds filtered up to him. He opened the curtains on stark daylight, and a bright sea pouring in along the beach.

Sophie had gone. Her jeans were still on the floor, and last night's underwear, but she'd taken her make-up out of the bathroom cabinet and her toothbrush from the tumbler by the sink. He noticed that the cassette-player had been moved and saw that she'd removed the tape. As if it were a fair trade, she had left the gun on the coffee table next to the flowers.

There wasn't a note, but he knew she'd gone for good.

Twenty-Three

'Five thousand pounds. You can have fun with that. It won't buy the rest of your life, but it'll certainly fund a good time. Take a holiday. Go with a friend.'

Ellwood wondered where Annie Roland was calling from. A clear line in Hilary's office, he suspected. His little tape-recorder was attached to the earpiece of the phone with a rubber sucker. He was deep in an armchair, naked from the shower, heels lofted to rest on a mahogany writing desk. Room service had sent fruit for breakfast and Ellwood had skinned one half of a peach. He rolled the fleshy dome against his lips while he waited for Annie's reply. Take your time, he thought. You'll get there in the end.

'Why is five thousand right?'

'How do you quantify such things?' Ellwood asked. 'It's not the money – it's whether you want to do it. Would you kill someone for that money? I don't think so. But there are those who'll do it for pennies. They want to, you see. You'll do it or else you won't. Now, here you are, talking to me on the phone. So it's clear that you will. OK; the next issue is: how do we fix a price? Easy – five grand is what I'd pay if it wasn't you. It's what I'd pay anyone. It's the going rate – the market price, you understand? If you were someone the Department needed information from, I could put in an expenses slip for five thousand, and Hilary Todd would sign it.'

He felt buoyant. He always knew when things were going well. Snail tracks of peach juice ran from the heel of his hand, over his chest and down to the hollow of his belly.

'You'll know *how* to pay,' Annie said, 'if you know how *much* to pay.' She meant non-sequential notes; not new; middling denominations.

'You've done this before,' Ellwood said. He was grinning wryly, his voice sardonic; then, as he finished the remark, a little jolt of pleasure hit him and he saw that he was absolutely right: she had.

Annie said, 'Since you mention it, I *am* taking a holiday. I'll need the money tonight. I hope that's OK.' She sounded waspish and impatient.

'That's fine.'

Annie named a motel, a cabin number, a stretch of road between nowhere and nowhere. 'I'm your insurance, Ellwood. And you're mine.'

A bead of juice meandered into the crease of his thigh. 'Sure – that's how it works.' A silence developed, as if there were something left to say. Ellwood put the sucked peach into his groin and worked it up and down, clenching his fist to squeeze the sweetness out. Lust went through him like a sudden scorch.

'OK?' Annie said.

Ellwood tossed the peach aside and lowered his hand to the warm slick of juice and pulp, hardness and sweetness, hatred and desire. He moved the hand slowly, eyes closed, teeth clenched on a smile.

'OK?'

'Fine,' he said, 'yes, that's fine.' Another silence settled. And when she hung up, he kept the phone to his ear as if she were listening still.

Zeno's method for protecting Carla was lies and half-lies. Ellwood was the financial adviser – that was his story. Most often they would meet at Ellwood's hotel. If Ellwood went to the house, Zeno got him out of the place as fast as he could.

Carla made fun of Ellwood behind his back. She would return from her banishment to the kitchen as Ellwood drove away, imitating his spidery walk, asking: 'What did old Stoneface have to say?' Edgy, Zeno would turn away to laugh.

And Tom Carey? He was the priest who visited patients at the private hospital on the hill. That's how they'd met, he told her. Zeno said he liked the man well enough, but wouldn't want to make a close friend of him.

'Does he come too?' Carla had asked. 'When you put on a magic show for the people up there.'

'Sometimes.'

Carla had once met them as they were walking by the seafront. It wasn't intended; none of them had been paying any attention to the world round about: they'd all-but walked into one another. Carla had been carrying groceries to the car; she'd put the bags down on the sea wall to shake hands. Zeno had looked out to sea while a few words were exchanged, then laid a hand on Carey's arm, as if about to hurry him along.

'Fishing,' Carey had told her. 'I'm staying at the Windrush – along the coast.'

Carla had seen the tension in Zeno. His desire to be gone had been so strong – the desire for movement – that he'd seemed to be leaning into the wind.

'He might talk to you,' Carla said. 'He never talks to me – not about things that matter.' She was speaking from a phone-box near the sea wall.

'What's wrong?' Carey could tell she was anxious.

'Will you talk to him?'

'Yes, of course. But what's wrong?'

'I don't know what it is. I only know it's there.'

'Where is he?'

'At home. I made an excuse to come out. I'll walk for a couple of hours. It's a bright day.'

Carey left his room and went up to Ellwood's. 'I got a call from the girl,' he said. 'She seems to be worried about him.'

'Why?'

'Well, she didn't say that. He doesn't tell her things.

She's for adoration,' Carey said, 'not information.'

'You think he's in love with her?'

'I'm sure of it.'

'Really . . .' Ellwood smiled thoughtfully. 'That's good to know.'

'I'll talk to him. I'm going there now.'

'If something happened,' Ellwood said, 'I want to know what it was. There's someone I have to see. I'll be back tonight or tomorrow: talk to me then.'

Ellwood had answered the door wearing his bathrobe; now he shrugged it off and began to dress. Carey looked away. The other man's sinewy thinness, his smooth torso and the dull tone of his flesh, made Carey think of something bloodless and odourless; something skinned.

'I don't know how much time we've got with Piper, but I wouldn't have thought it was much.' Ellwood wasn't telling Carey how tight things were, or what methods might have to be used.

'He's changed,' Carey said. 'Had you noticed that?'

'We've all changed.'

'No, that's not true.' Carey glanced across. 'Grown older, perhaps.'

'What do you see in him now that you didn't see before?'

'Don't you know the answer to that, Wallace?'

Ellwood's clothes were so neutral in colour, so commonplace in style, that he seemed to fade as he dressed. 'Should I know it?'

'He's murdered two people.'

'Oh, that.' Ellwood smiled. 'You think he had to change before he could kill someone? It wasn't to do with change.'

'What then?'

'Evolution,' Ellwood said.

He picked up his car keys, his Raybans, his wallet. 'Father Tom,' he said, as if he were meeting Carey for the first time for a long time. The tone irritated Carey, and made him impatient.

'Look, Wallace, I was small fry. I was a very small link in an immensely long chain. I didn't go to Africa, I didn't go to Latin America, I didn't suffer for liberation theology. I didn't do anything *brave*. You recruited me when that wasn't difficult to do. A radical priest in a revolutionary decade. I did a few jobs for you – mostly, I listened to people and passed information along. Not very demanding. I allowed myself to think it was risky, and because of that, it felt right. Now here I am, doing it again; but this time, it *doesn't* feel right.'

Ellwood was waiting patiently. He resisted the impulse to glance at his watch. 'How *does* it feel?'

'Wicked,' Carey said.

For a moment, Ellwood looked vacant – a man hearing a word in a language he doesn't know. Then he laughed. '*Wicked*! Good Christ, where did you dig that up from?'

'The Berlin Wall's down, Eastern Europe's put on democracy like an old coat, Russia's bankrupt and we're all suckers, Wallace. Nobody won. Don't you think that's funny? And you're supposed to be down here finding out whether some crazy old man was a double. Now, I'm surprised to learn that you don't know the answer. After all, you were working the wrong side of the fence yourself, weren't you? A chain of information set up by you that ended somewhere in East Germany. I just passed on what I knew.' Carey gave a bark of laughter. 'And with every stolen syllable, the people's revolution came closer. That's what I was – a link in the chain. But you were something much grander than that. Much more glamorous. You were a traitor. But times change, Wallace, don't they? And here you are, a survivor, working for the winning side.'

Carey paused a moment, but Ellwood had decided to wait him out. 'You never chose sides, Wallace; you only chose yourself. I made myself believe we shared a cause. We didn't. And now I wonder whether I ever got the truth from you. I wonder what you really wanted. And I wonder why you're here at all.'

'I'm paid to be here,' Ellwood said. 'A more interesting question is you.'

'Families,' Carey said. 'I felt connected. I didn't come because you said I could have anything I wanted, I came because of the past.' It was something like the truth – as much as he would give to Ellwood. Unwisely, he added: 'I'm beginning to see that it isn't enough.'

Ellwood stepped forward slightly and lowered his voice, as if they weren't alone. For the first time, Carey felt menaced. 'I need to know about Piper,' he said, 'and I need you to help me find out. You're right to talk of the past. Here's why: the past can hurt everyone – you included. Perhaps you were true to your version of religion, who knows – who cares? But you betrayed your country. Remember that. Now, you've run a few errands for me since then, without enquiring too closely about their nature. Remember that, too. Our relationship doesn't have to do with a cause, *Father* Tom; it's based on fear and guilt and power – like all true relationships. You started out with a cause and wound up with a habit.' He put on his dark glasses and smiled with only his mouth. 'Do what I want you to do, then you can go. Remember the way it was? Just talk to him.' As if nothing else had been said, he added: 'I know he's unbalanced. Keep him level just long enough, OK? Keep him close to Piper. It's all he's for.'

Ellwood reached out with two stiffened fingers, the rest of his hand a loose fist, and made the sign of the cross close to Carey's face. 'Go with God,' he said.

Carey stood in the room alone. Fruit was piled up in a bowl; he took an apple and bit into it. *A few errands . . .* yes, he had; and without knowing, really, what they meant or who they were for. Maybe they had been for old times – the old times that had never really existed. First came belief, then involvement; after that – once you were part of the family – sides didn't matter.

Carey and Zeno had been on the same side once. Then they became part of the family – Ellwood as paterfamilias.

But now, Carey knew, it was every man for himself against the past.

I wish I could help him, Carey thought. I wish he could help himself. He realized he wished this for a man who had committed murder but, strangely, that seemed the least issue – not a family matter.

He feared for Zeno and, in fear, spoke as if Ellwood were still there to hear him.

'He's a killer, Wallace, but he talks like a suicide.'

Twenty-Four

Between nowhere and nowhere, Wallace Ellwood found the motel.

He had driven into London, then out again with a document case containing five thousand pounds. Another hour had taken him to a five-mile strip of dual carriageway cut through downland. Two lanes north and two lanes south – cars poured through in an unbroken line; container trucks, like cliffsides on the move, whammed into each other's slipstream. The noise was so constant and so intense that it fabricated silence.

The motel was built on a bank above the southbound road, and no more than fifty metres back. It was the only building: U-shaped, with two lines of cabins forming the outward arms, the base a restaurant. There was a metallic-grey VW Golf parked outside cabin fifteen. Ellwood drove past and parked close to the end of the row. A light, high tang of fuel lay on the air.

When you walk into one of those cabins, you would swear you'd just gone deaf. The triple-glazed windows block out every sound. Outside, endless engines and the boom of things at speed; inside, a vacuum. Annie had neither the television nor the radio on. When she closed the door after letting Ellwood in, her eyes went at once to the document case.

'That's right,' Ellwood told her. 'This is what you get. What do I get?'

'Show me.' Annie didn't seem to have unpacked. The room was untouched by her presence – no suitcase, no clothes lying about the place.

'I'm going to the bathroom,' Ellwood said. 'Look for yourself.'

In the bathroom he found no make-up, no toothpaste, no creams or shampoo.

Annie had emptied the document case, now she was filling it again. She worked fastidiously, squaring the little stacks of bills so that they alternated: first lengthwise, then breadthwise.

Ellwood returned. 'You're right to be careful,' he said. 'Trust is for household pets.'

Annie arranged the last of the money and closed the case. 'Here's the deal,' she said. 'I'm going to tell you something about Todd that will leave you safe. What leaves *me* safe is this – you killed four men in a gym in Chelsea. A few people know about that and it makes them angry – Todd's one of them – but they can't allow anything to happen to you. First, you're doing a job that's considered important; second, it wouldn't help the Department all that much. So, it remains an unsolved crime. Keep to our bargain and it'll stay unsolved. But try to implicate me in any way – or use me as a trade-off – and it'll be added to the police clear-up rate faster than the eye can follow. I know three or four investigative journalists who would do a front-page lead on a story like that – absolutely no question.'

Ellwood spread his arms. 'For Christ's sake . . .'

Annie looked at him for a moment, then turned away. 'Spare me that puzzled smile,' she said, 'I'm the person who had dinner with you, remember?'

. . . *a spike up your ass and my sperm all over your face.*

'So you've warned me.' Ellwood shrugged and swung up on to the bed, his shoulders against the headboard, his boots on the counterpane. 'Now pay me.'

'He fences drugs to a policeman, the policeman sells it on, Hilary takes half the money.'

'Drugs?'

'Heroin and cocaine.'

'Stash-for-cash,' Ellwood said.

'That's right.'

The Department often used narcotics as a means of pay-off, or bribery, or inducement. Drugs came without trace, without any kind of documentation. Illegal shipments siezed at customs went round like a kiss at a party – police, SAS, departments like the one Todd ran . . . then on to the people they'd been intended for in the first place – the syndicates who brought them down to street level, street prices.

'And Hilary's taking some off the top for himself . . .'

'A Drugs Squad copper called Tremayne. He offloads it and credits a John Doe account by London Wall.'

'Who else knows about this?'

'No-one. Todd, Tremayne, me.' She thought for a moment. 'Todd's broker, perhaps. I expect someone has to manage the account. I don't see Todd being content with deposit rates.'

'And how is it that *you* know about it?'

'Stash-for-cash is only one way of trading. All sorts of things are saleable. You have to work off what you can get. I can get information – every good PA can.'

'You've bugged his office.'

Annie laughed. 'Nothing so complicated: a tape-recorder. It's me they talk to first when there's going to be an office sweep. I simply take it out.'

'What else do you know?'

'Lots,' she told him. 'But your money's spent.'

'Terrific.' He swung his legs off the bed, grinning broadly, and started for the door. As he passed her, he gathered her hair in his hand, taking it at the nape of her neck and pulling tight. She was off-balance – nothing she could do to prevent herself from turning towards him as his grip pulled her in. She stumbled slightly, one knee buckling, her face close to his, and he kissed her, just a rapid peck, the tip of his tongue sizzling between her lips and running across her teeth.

The door closed behind him and Annie found herself sitting on the edge of the bed, her hands between her knees, her eyes on the floor. She wasn't sure how she'd got there: like someone who takes an electric shock from a kitchen implement and winds up on the other side of the room.

After a minute, she went into the bathroom and leaned over the basin and spat.

Ellwood walked to his car and got in like a man with a purpose accomplished. He drove a wide circle out of the car park towards the slip-road that would take him back to the dual carriageway. Each cabin had two curtained windows; the curtains on number fifteen were blind eyes. Out of sight of the cabins, Ellwood trod on the brake. He drove back and parked outside number three – at the top of the arm of the U that stood opposite Annie's cabin. Two or three other cars came in and parked; a couple left. Ellwood could have been anyone.

He climbed into the back seat and looked towards Annie's cabin, making little attempt to conceal himself or keep low. A piece of fundamental fieldwork: people don't look for the unexpected. A field of vision rarely extends beyond a table, a car door, the next patch of pavement.

As he watched, a young woman emerged from the restaurant and walked towards cabin fifteen. She was tall – long legs and a long waist – and was dressed in black. A wool dress sculpted her slender figure and ended at mid-thigh. She had blond hair that swung as she walked.

Ellwood smiled. He thought: Well, well . . .

Annie must have used the house-phone to have her paged at the restaurant. The girl was carrying a latchkey; she let herself into the cabin.

. . . who would have thought of that?

They were like one another. The difference was a matter of more-or-less. The same blond hair, except that Tessa Latham's was a little longer, had a little more curl. The same tilted nose, except that Annie's was just too snub. The same lithe figure, except that Tessa had a couple of inches advantage in height and a slightly fuller body.

230

People took them for sisters. In fact, they had known each other for only two years, and had been lovers for most of that time.

When they kissed, it seemed that Tessa had embraced a mirror image very slightly distorted by the glass. Annie held the kiss, both hands to her lover's cheeks, using her tongue until Tessa responded and washed Ellwood away.

'Is everything OK?' Annie had left the document case open on the bed, like a welcome-home present. Tessa walked over to it and lifted out a handful of the money.

'Fine,' Annie told her.

'He would have gone more than five thou.'

'No. He wouldn't. He might next time.'

'Who is he?' Tessa thought that putting the bite on people for fun-money was a terrific idea.

She flicked through a wad of bills without counting, then dropped them into the case and closed the lid. Ellwood hadn't seemed very exciting to her. 'I watched him in and I watched him leave. He looked like anyone to me. No-one. A grey suit.'

'He's poison,' Annie said. A slight shiver took her, like the onset of illness. 'Let's get out of this Christless dump.'

Ellwood watched them get into the VW and drive towards the slip-road. When they passed out of sight, he started his engine and backed out of the parking place.

'There's a lesson you have to learn . . .' He spoke pleasantly, as if passing on a gem of advice to a good friend.

Ellwood drove an Audi – fast but not flashy. He filtered on to the dual carriageway, overtaking a haulage truck and a couple of slow-moving cars, always going back to the nearside lane. The VW was in sight, staying in the overtaking lane, but hemmed-in. Ellwood settled down. He'd driven eight hours that day, but he was feeling good. Really good. He was feeling *fine*.

'The lesson is: don't threaten me.' His tone was still light. 'You dyke bitch.'

Zeno ran a coin across his knuckles, this way and that, a tiny acrobat, then flipped it; as it fell he clapped it to the back of his hand.

'Heads,' said Father Tom.

'Most people say heads. Most people choose seven or nine. We make our own illusions.' He lifted the palm of his hand; it was tails.

'Can you do that every time?'

'I didn't cheat.'

'I believe you,' Carey told him. 'What has Wallace asked you to do?'

'After I've finished the show, I go to the office and photograph the old man's records. Piper's. Then I give them to Wallace.'

'That's all he's asked?' Carey had been aware of the anxiety in Ellwood's voice when he spoke of Piper and deadlines.

'I went to see him.'

'Piper?'

'Yes.'

'When?'

'One night.' Zeno flipped the coin again. 'It's heads,' he said. 'You see – it's all a matter of luck.' He flipped once more, and when he raised his palm there were two coins on the back of his hand. He flipped a third time. Now there were three, all showing heads. 'Lucky,' Zeno said. 'Lucky, lucky, lucky.'

'Do you want to talk? Is there anything you need to talk about?'

Zeno crossed himself and bowed his head. 'Forgive me, Father, for I have sinned.' He laughed and the coin spun upwards, singing from the sting of his thumbnail, a silver disc on a silver spindle. He trapped it and showed his hand: now there were four. 'I told a lie: I always cheat. What will you give me? One Hail Mary for each coin?'

They had been together all morning, but little had been said. Zeno had smiled and prattled cocktail-party talk.

Carey had thought the whole performance eerie. After a couple of hours, Zeno had simply lain down on the floor and gone to sleep. He'd been asleep when Carla returned.

She had made them some food, then gone out again. She knew that Zeno wanted to preserve her from everything but himself. She'd invented some errands and left the two men alone.

Zeno said, 'Don't come here again. We can meet at your hotel. We can go down to the beach.'

'Yes, all right.'

'Pretty soon, I can go away. I'll take Carla away.' He was depressed by what had happened the previous night. Such a good show, such a good set-up – everything arranged for a fine performance.

I give a magic show . . .

First Marianne – a simple sleight of hand. Then Nick – a little playlet of magic and deceit.

. . . and someone dies.

Each time his performance had grown more elaborate: he wrote the script, set the stage, and took the lead. The moment when Pascoe had sat down and taken a sip of the wine! A triumph! When Sophie had joined him in a waltz . . .

They had to die to make the future safe. To keep the past secret.

But sometimes he only thought of the next performance.

'What did he say? Piper. When you went to see him.'

'He didn't want to talk, really. I made him an illusion. He liked that.'

'He said nothing?'

'I asked the questions Wallace wanted me to ask. He just talked gibberish. He's mad.'

'I know,' Carey said. 'Are you?'

A silence gathered and spread. Carey knew he'd gone too far, but didn't care. They sat in silence while the minutes passed, confessor and supplicant, knowing too much and too little. Finally, Zeno said: 'Listen. Sometimes I

233

don't know who I am. I can go to a shop and buy something. I can talk to people. I can ask the questions that Wallace wants me to ask. I can remember the past, and be afraid of it. I can imagine the future, and be afraid of not getting it. I know I'm not crazy like that old man, like Piper, because crazy is something else. Crazy is living in a fog and pissing your pants. I hate Wallace, and I think I hate you. I hate the past. I love Carla, but sometimes I frighten myself. I'm frightened now. Love and hate . . . and in between is me.'

'And you don't know who that is,' Carey said.

'I give a magic show and someone dies . . .'

'What?' Carey thought he'd misheard; a chill went through him.

'. . . Marianne and Nick, because *that's* who I am, *that's* who everyone sees, *that's* who Piper talks to, *that's* who steals notes from Harris's files, *that's* who Wallace needs . . .'

He thought of Sophie in his arms, the cord falling on to her neck. He'd marked her as he left, wanting to feel her fear. He'd been angry because Pascoe had rewritten his script. 'When I'm on-stage,' he said, 'I know who I am.'

'Who?'

He rolled the coin and flipped it. Five came down. 'The Great Zeno . . .'

Less than half an hour had taken them to the motorway; after that it was easy – they were heading north. Ellwood's technique was to let them stay about five vehicles ahead, but now and then he'd drop back and let them fall out of sight. He did it, though he knew it was a needless precaution. You can travel two hundred miles on those roads and realize that some of the cars you started out with have done the trip with you; but you wouldn't recognize the drivers. He always stayed close when they were approaching a service station, because he knew that sooner or later, they'd have to stop for fuel.

His plan for that was to go into the restaurant car park

and allow enough time for the other car to clear the fuel service area, then fill his own tank and give chase. When the moment came, it happened the other way round. Annie and Tessa went to get coffee and a sandwich. Ellwood filled up and parked off the forecourt behind some store-rooms. The VW drew up at the pumps about twenty minutes later.

They had a routine for it, as most couples do – Annie put the fuel in, Tessa took some paper towels from the dispenser and cleaned the windscreen; then Tessa went to the pay-window and handed over a credit card as soon as Annie put the pump nozzle back into position.

Oh yes, Ellwood thought, and I'll bet you fit each other just like a finger in a glove.

He gave the women a thirty-second start and picked them up on the northbound carriageway with ease. The first, slight sign of tiredness came on him – a moment of dizziness and a thin line of pain from the tension in his shoulders.

If you're taking a holiday more than a three-hour drive from here, he thought, I'll have to find a different way of doing this.

'What's making you unhappy?' Carey asked. 'What's making you depressed? Is everything all right – with Carla?'

At the mention of her name Zeno grew alert. He swung his head like an animal that suddenly intuits a reason for fear. 'Where is she?' he asked. 'Where's Carla? She ought to be here.'

'She had some things to do: that's what she said.'

'It's getting late.' Zeno's head was lifted as if to search for scents on the air. 'You'd better go now. She'll come back when you go.'

'Has Wallace given you any new instructions about Piper? Has he asked you to do more than just bring film of Piper's records?'

'You'd better go now.'

'I can see that you've been made upset. All I want to do

is help. Like I used to.' Carey felt old and grimy, worn threadbare. 'Forgive me, Father . . .' he prompted.

Zeno ran at him – a sudden rush, murderous fury out of nowhere. He swung a fist clamped round five coins – the punching power of a sap-glove. Carey went back on his heels, his head snapping to and fro like something spring-loaded, and a little fan of bloody spray rose from his face. Zeno stood in front of the priest, arms hanging down, his face sallow and lean with rage. His blow had taken Carey on the eyebrow and split it, a long gash that extended to the other brow. As they stood there, less than an arm's length apart, five lines of blood started across Carey's face, like beads of rain chasing each other on a window pane. He put his hand up to his cheek and collected the drops.

'It's all right,' he said, and held out the bloody hand as if refusing a favour. 'Don't worry.'

The anger subsided in Zeno. He took a step back, dizzy and breathless, then found himself sitting on the floor, back to the wall. He thought the door closing might be Carey leaving, but it was Carla arriving. He wondered whether he'd been asleep for a while, or just deep in thought.

He clambered up and intercepted her at the kitchen door, enfolding her and drawing her in to his body so that his warmth flowed through to her, just as he had that day when he'd found her on the beach, lost and afraid; like him, a victim of the past.

'I was thinking about you,' he said. 'I was worried about you. I didn't know where you were.'

She couldn't reply, he was holding her so tightly; and, in any case, there was nothing she wanted to say. She clung to him, arms round his neck, her face hidden in his shoulder, like a child afraid of a storm.

She was everything he wanted – all ambition, all love, all comfort, all need, all passion embodied in Carla. She murmured something to him, some affirmation of love, and he felt the vibration of her voice strike through him. She eased back and kissed him, then walked on into the kitchen, her limp dictating the tiny sway of her hips. She had brought things to make their evening meal and she emptied them on to the work-counter: wine, cheese, spinach, onions, bread, the pink-white tines of a rack of lamb, as if all the promise of their future lay in the guarantee of such ordinariness being possible.

I give a magic show and someone dies . . . When this is over and we are far away from here, and living quietly and happily and safely, Zeno will have to die too. Like stepping out of your skin, like changing your face.

He followed Carla into the kitchen and produced the coins for her to see, then started to flip them one by one. She smiled and said, 'Heads.'

One by one they came down. As he caught them, he placed them on the counter in front of her, all in a row, all of them heads. Carla smiled and kissed him. 'Lucky,' she said.

He smiled back. 'It's just a magic show,' he said. 'It isn't real.'

The drive was a little over two hours – due north, then north-west into the southern part of the Lakes. When Annie signalled to take the motorway exit just below Kendal, Ellwood had pushed forward a little, leaving only three vehicles between them at the intersection. After that, things had become more difficult. Annie must have been tired, but she drove quickly and cleverly, overtaking on the narrow road when she could and leaving Ellwood stranded. Twice he'd lost sight of them and been obliged to put on speed or else run the risk of failing to see them as they took some minor road or turn-off.

The first time, he'd been virtually on their tail as he'd rounded a bend. Desperate not to have to overtake, he'd braked hard and had felt the car shimmy dangerously. The second time, travelling fast to find them, he'd passed a junction just in time to see the VW rounding a bend on the other road. He had overshot by fifty yards but, since there was no room to turn, he'd backed up to the junction in a rapid, snaky line, and picked them up again after ten minutes of anxious-cautious driving – fast on the straights, slow on the bends.

Although the traffic wasn't heavy, there was a string of other cars on the road. Ellwood reasoned that the women would only have felt curious if Annie was driving on the mirror: clearly, she wasn't. The VW kept a more or less constant speed – no avoiding action, no tricky moves.

After another mile or so, Ellwood saw them pull off into the gated driveway of a hotel. He drove past until he found a rest area: just a track behind trees and a few picnic tables. He locked his doors, cranked the seat back, and set the alarm on his wrist-watch.

When he closed his eyes, fatigue swam up at him in a mazy spiral, making his head spin as if he were drunk. A moment later, he was asleep.

Improvisation is the secret of success.

Wallace Ellwood's plan had been a loose one: find out how great a risk Annie Roland might be and act accordingly. He'd been pretty sure that Annie would prove potentially harmful. For one thing, he'd made her fear him; in addition to that, she'd threatened him too readily. The threat could be used as a safeguard, sure; but it could also be used to turn a further profit. It didn't take a psychic to see that Annie had worked that out for herself.

Improvisation means work with what you've got.

During the drive, Ellwood had turned a number of ideas and opportunities over in his mind. The trick was to get this bitch out of his life as soon as possible. Ellwood didn't want her back in Hilary Todd's office and close to people who posed a threat to him. Her life in London would be full of secrets and safeguards; full of routines and regular habits. It made her less vulnerable. And the fact that she was taking time off with her dyke lover offered more flexibility, more opportunities for invention.

Improvisation means take your chances *while* you can, *where* you can; it means ride your luck.

The watch-alarm woke him at midnight. He got out of the car and went up and down on his haunches a few times to ease some of the stiffness from his legs, then started to walk the mile or so back to the hotel gates. The night air was cool and sweet, the country dark limitless; he picked his way along the road almost by instinct, except when a quarter moon found a space between clouds. Ellwood hated it. He wanted toxins in the air.

The hotel was a converted manor house. Between the gates and the big double doors was half an acre of lawn; the driveway was lined by poplars. Ellwood walked down the row of trees, then circled the house, staying well back from the lighted windows. The dining room was empty apart from a couple of staff members who were laying tables for breakfast. At the rear of the house, the bar had its french windows open to the lawn; a man and a woman were drinking a nightcap, each cradling a brandy balloon. The lawn was scrubbier there; a small apple orchard bordered a kitchen garden.

Ellwood stood close to the bole of an apple tree and watched the bar. After ten minutes or so, the couple finished their drinks and left. The barman pulled the knot on his bow tie, gave himself a shot of booze, drank it, then gave himself another and carried it out into the garden, strolling away from the orchard and the tufty grass. Ellwood smiled.

Improvisation means if it looks like a gift, it probably *is* a gift.

He went through the bar and into a corridor: the corridor led to the narrow entrance lobby with a sofa covered in chintz, a row of sporting prints on the wall, lights on a dimmer switch turned low. The office behind the reception desk was dark. Ellwood flicked through the register and found Annie and Tessa immediately. Names, car registration, room number. He took the dupe key from a hook behind the desk, then went upstairs, moving casually, easily, like any guest returning late.

He unlocked the door and stepped inside. When he

closed it, there was a gun in his hand: a short-barrelled ·38 made awkward by its silencer.

The room was in darkness. Ellwood stood very still, the gun held just in front of his chest and slightly to the side. After a few seconds, he heard them breathing – one breath long and light, the other slightly shorter and huskier. He imagined them lying close, arms round one another, Annie, perhaps, with her leg drawn up over the other girl's haunch, and breathing softly on to one another's faces.

When he switched the light on and dragged the bedclothes back, he saw that his image of them had been perfect. He thought that it would be Tessa who'd yell, so he'd already put a hand across her mouth. And he let them see the gun.

Annie said, 'Oh, shit.' Then she added, 'You won't kill us here, Ellwood.'

Ellwood's voice was little more than a whisper. 'I'd sooner not, but I will if you raise your voice. The only danger to me is someone hearing us in here, getting alarmed, calling the police, maybe. But listen – that's also the danger to you. If it happens, you're dead and I'll get out as best I can. Otherwise, you're not in too much trouble. I don't want to kill you. I want my money back: that's all.' He took his hand from Tessa's mouth and smiled at her. 'Nice tits, sweetheart.'

Annie looked at him in amazement. 'You can't imagine it's worth the risk,' she said. 'I've told you what I'll do.'

'You've told me. I don't believe it. Why? Because it cuts both ways. It's a Cold War equation – it depends on mutual destruction. But if I take my five grand back: what difference? None. The balance of power doesn't change.'

Tessa had crossed her legs, leaving only the tiniest triangle of coppery hair visible; she had put a pillow across her breasts. Annie was behaving as if she were fully dressed.

She said, 'Yes. But it is mutual. And it is destruction. And in any case, I might just come out of it OK. You're forgetting that it's Hilary you would have to turn to if you

240

want me taken out. But if you use the information, Hilary's dead. And if you don't use the information, then *I* can – and he's still dead.'

Ellwood shook his head. 'There are people you answer to other than Hilary Todd.'

Annie shrugged. 'I don't get it. All this trouble for your five thousand. Why not just pay for the information like anyone else? Who knows – we could do business again.'

'I don't think so. You threatened me. I don't like that. I'm teaching you a lesson and taking your profit away. Call it pride; call it spite. Call it what the fuck you like. You lose, that's the important thing to me. I know you don't like me. You're prepared to let it show. Bad move. Bad business practice. It makes me resentful. That's why I'm here taking my money away.'

Ellwood could see that she almost believed him. Turning slightly, he stabbed the gun barrel with its fat, cylindrical silencer into the crack between Tessa's thighs; she could have only moved away by uncrossing her legs. She froze, her breathing stalled.

He said, 'Now, I'm sure you can see that there's no future in all of us being found here.' He didn't bother to look at Tessa. 'You can scarcely pretend that I'm a prowler or whatever: someone you've never met. But I don't want you to fly off the handle,' he smiled at Annie as if he knew her temperament of old, 'or do anything rash. I think you should talk it all over with Miss Nice Tits, here. But I can see how you might think you could gain an advantage – me having problems with the local police while you work out a way to come up smelling sweet. So I'm going to tie you up while I leave. I'll make a good job of it; enough to put me a county or two away.' He switched his attention to Tessa and waggled the gun. 'So take your ass over to that chair.'

She walked clumsily, not sure where to put her hands, as if movement made her more naked than before. The chair was a rush-seated ladderback; one of the girls had draped her clothes over it.

'Sit down, Nice Tits.'

241

He opened a few drawers in the dresser until he saw what he'd expected to find – half a dozen packets of tights. He used three of them for Tessa, the legs of one pair tying her ankles to the chair legs, her hands pulled behind and tied together with the second pair. He used the third to make a cinch between her hands and the chair's bottom rail. He lifted a sock from the floor and pushed it into her mouth, then held a silk blouse out by its cuffs and spun it until it became a rope to hold the gag secure. All the time, the gun was in his hand or close by on the floor.

Once or twice, Annie glanced towards the door; each time Ellwood tracked the line of her gaze with his own, then smiled. The smile meant: No chance.

He worked as if he were roping a piece of luggage, barely looking at Tessa, not touching her unless he had to. When the gag went in, her eyes widened and her shoulders braced as she pulled in air through her nose.

Annie said, 'You don't have to do that.'

'It makes me feel happier.'

'Just go away, all right? Take the money and go.' There seemed to be a hint of alarm in her voice.

Ellwood shook his head, seeming to suggest that Annie hadn't understood the point. 'I don't want you to act hastily. I'll be gone – you'll have had time to think things through and come to the right decision.' He was standing close to her. 'Put your arms up – reach out to either side.' It was a brass bed with rails top and bottom. He used tights to tie Annie's hands in a cruciform; then he gagged her.

He seemed about to leave – walked to the door, in any case – but when he reached the foot of the bed, he took hold of the brass upright and pulled the bed out into the room; then he carried a second ladderback chair to the head of the bed and sat down behind Annie. She struggled to look over her shoulder at him, but her arms were tied too tightly for that so she lifted her shoulders and thrust her chin up, like someone attempting a headstand. She saw his face upside down, and saw that he was smiling.

The final pair of tights went round her neck, then round two brass rails. Ellwood yanked, and the back of her skull slammed up against the bedhead. He twisted the garotte until it was a hard torc, leaning forward in the chair to get leverage, busy at his task, absorbed, like any technician.

Annie's legs drummed on the bed; her body was leaping and bucking, like a big fish barrelling upstream. Ellwood hauled her in. He leaned the chair back on two legs and put the sole of one shoe against the bedrails, then pulled on the rope of nylon until his biceps began to crack. Annie's face was purple-black. She could detect only agony: her eardrums rupturing under the pressure; something cracking and tearing free, deep in her chest.

Ellwood shifted the sole of his foot to put it directly behind Annie's head, knee bent. He took the strain like the anchor-man on a rope, pushing hard against his own backward pull – all the power in his leg and all the power in his arms – his face a rictus of effort, his lips drawn back like someone enduring pain. Over Annie's shoulder he could see Tessa watching in a nightmare of dumbness, a silent scream of terror belling from every line in her face, from her wide eyes, from her rigid limbs.

A quietness came into Annie's body. Her legs were still; her shoulders dropped; her torso folded into itself. Despite the ligature, her head tilted forward an inch. It was as if a fall lay within her that she wasn't able to make.

Ellwood continued to strangle her even when she was dead. Something in her throat cracked. Her eyes were as dark as a rotten egg, and a tear of blood ran down alongside her nose to the corner of her mouth like a symptom of regret.

Finally he let go, falling against the bedhead, elbows on knees, panting like a runner after a close finish. Their heads were together: friends sharing a secret. After a moment, he looked up and smiled at Tessa through the rails.

'Now – what shall we do with you?'

He picked up the gun and walked towards her, enjoying

the effect that had. As he came close she started to urinate, the stream trickling through the rush seating and darkening the carpet.

He untied the silk blouse very slowly, to let her know what he was doing. He put a finger to his lips: *Shusssshhh* . . . then removed the sock from her mouth. She made sounds, but she didn't speak.

Ellwood crouched down in front of her, putting their faces close together. He said, 'Now . . . you've got a terrible problem, here. It's not the problem you think it is – I'm not going to kill you. You're much more use alive. Know why . . . ?' He paused, then gave a pleasant little laugh. 'I've forgotten your name; how rude of me.'

She opened her mouth, then closed it, but nothing happened. Ellwood waited. Finally, she whispered: 'Tessa.'

'Of course it is; I saw it in the register. So forgetful these days . . .' He was down on his haunches, looking comfortable and wearing a slight smile, the gun held loosely in his right hand. 'Well, Tessa, your problem is this – you don't have the kind of cover she had. I don't know you, so I'm certain you're not with the Department; in their parlance, you're a stranger. That makes you dispensable. All strangers are dispensable. Department business is sacrosanct – protected at all costs. Annie was foolish to involve you. I expect she thought it would be more exciting to share, to have an accomplice.' He made the notion sound endearingly old-fashioned. 'But she put you at risk. Now here you are with your lover's body and a terrible story that you simply can't tell. What would you say? That I killed her because you were blackmailing me? That you possess all sorts of incriminating information about a department head?' He glanced back at the dead girl and smiled, as if to chide her gently for her folly. 'You're a stranger . . . Guess what would happen next.'

Tessa shook her head – not disagreement, but a gesture of hopelessness. 'It's a mess, isn't it?' Ellwood asked. 'But it's perfect for me . . . Annie found naked and strangled, her girlfriend – what? – mysteriously disappeared, I expect. Who knows what funny sex-games? Who knows what jealousies? Someone else involved? A lover of yours, maybe. A man . . .' Ellwood shrugged, grinning, as if he himself might fill the role. 'So you'll need to make yourself scarce for a time, won't you?' He went to the document case and took out a fistful of money, pretending to weigh it in his hand. 'Feels like a thousand pounds. That'll buy you some time. Go to Scotland. The car's pointing in the right direction.' He tossed the money towards the bed. The bundles of notes landed in Annie's lap. 'Does anyone know about the two of you? Friends of hers? Friends of yours?'

Tessa's breathing had grown shallow. She couldn't find a way past the fear. Somehow she managed to whisper: 'No friends, no . . . Just me and Annie.' Speaking her lover's name was almost too much for her. Ellwood saw her eyes roll up to show the whites. He slapped her hard to bring her back. A blush spread on her cheek, thickened by his fingermarks.

'Good. You see? You're in luck already. The police won't know who they're looking for. Just a description they'll get from the people who run this place. A change of make-up, have your hair cut short and change the colour, dowdy clothes . . . It's easy for a woman.'

He touched her breasts, briefly, as if her nakedness confirmed her as the victim.

'Get clear, go to ground, stay there. Ditch the car and take a train. No problem. Two days for the papers and TV to forget; three days maximum. After that you're clear.'

Tessa was looking past him at Annie's body. Her mouth was open and she was making little wet gulping noises – horror ladled over grief.

'I'll untie your hands,' Ellwood told her, 'but not your legs. It won't take you long. Then you're on your own.' He was standing directly in front of her, smiling down. His smile was ovens and chains and darkness.

Twenty-Five

A sheen of seawater sluiced the cat's back. Foam boiled up round the seal's flank, then fell away with a soft, diminishing hiss.

Here I am, Pascoe thought. Can't I tempt you? Come and get me, you bastard.

Rob Thomas still had Sophie's address from the junk-mail source on Alex's computer. Pascoe had obtained the number from directory enquiries and listened to her answerphone message a dozen times or more. Sophie had thrown up a wall. Pascoe tried out several emotions for that, coming closer to the real thing each time – impatience, irritation, concern, anxiety . . . Finally, he realized that what he really felt was fear: not for her safety, but fear that she might have gone out of his life.

I'm alone, Zeno, he thought. No-one's here with me. Come on . . .

Once is bad luck, twice is a pattern. He remembered Karen's absence like a silhouette cut from each scene in the house; he remembered Sophie's jeans and her under-wear still on the floor.

Here's what I'll do. I'll go back to London, I'll move to a new district, I'll start seeing Sophie on a regular basis, I'll do my job as if I were any competent lawyer, and I've come here alone, you bastard, so why don't you do whatever you've got in mind?

Sophie's gun was making a bag of his pocket. He thought: And why did you *have* a gun for Christ's sake? Did I ask you that? Did I ask you anything? We talked about the past, but only the past we once shared. What happened to you since then? I want to know.

The tide was ebbing. The arched spine of the cat's back began to dry out, changing from sleek plum to a dull lilac. Veins of crystal ran through it, glittering in the sun.

Don't you know what I've come here for? That's right. To meet you again. I'm expecting you. Zeno . . .

Clouds going like banners across the sky, gulls drifting and screaming, great gouts of brilliant light riding like spillage on the surface of the sea.

Zeno . . . It's the logical thing to do, now; it's what I *ought* to do. Back to London, pick up where I left off, more crimes and misdemeanours, more Anthony Stewarts and the commonplace killings that proceed from a lifetime of domestic loathing, or lust, or rivalry, or greed. Find Sophie again, and agree to forget the past.

But I know I won't. You killed Nick. Maybe you killed Marianne. You tried to kill me. You tried to kill Sophie. Will you let it drop if I will? No, I didn't think so.

Here am I – where are you?

. . . Find Sophie again, because something was happening there that hasn't happened to me in a hell of a long time. Maybe it was the power of the past, maybe it had to do with bonds of fear and guilt. I don't know; but I'd like the chance to find out.

I'm here, I'm alone, I'm waiting, but you don't seem to want to join me. OK. So far, it's all been on your terms. Letters and invitations, lies and illusions. I'm changing that. If you won't come to me, you bastard, I'll come to you. Not at your request. Not for one of your stagey trick-or-treats. My turn now. *I'm* coming after *you*.

The sea was drawing off across the foreshore – leaving acre after acre of rocks – with a long series of hollow roars, diminishing, diminuendo on diminuendo. Soon the cat's back and the seal would be high and dry. Fronds of bladderwrack began to stiffen and blanch in the sun.

He sat still for another half-hour or so, then got up and walked slowly out to the water's edge. Anyone out for a morning walk on the cliff path would have seen him, a single figure in a wilderness of sea and stone.

Twenty-Six

Families feud, but always protect their own. When Wallace Ellwood was summoned to Hilary Todd's office, no mention was made of Annie Roland's death.

Ellwood wondered how the search for Tessa was going and how long it had taken the Department to close the story down. He smiled a winning smile. It was on the tip of his tongue to ask after Annie: was she ill, perhaps, or taking a holiday? He suppressed the temptation, but the idea made his smile grow broader.

'What in God's name are you grinning at?' Todd appeared bringing coffee for himself; none for Ellwood.

'It's a nice day, Hilary. The river looks lovely.' The Thames sluiced by the window, sluggish and brown. When the tide fell, you could see oil drums and supermarket trolleys in the shallow reaches.

'We're in trouble,' Todd spoke sharply, like a businessman on an impossible schedule. 'Which means you're in trouble.' He cast a quick glance at Ellwood to make sure he'd registered the threat. 'An insider . . . A man at the centre of a stay-behind group in France has been killed in a Brittany sailing resort. There wasn't even much attempt to make it look like a mugging; he still had his wallet. You might even think we were supposed to find the death notable.'

'They were advertising . . .'

'A warning, an example, a statement of intent: maybe all three.'

'Piper,' Ellwood said. 'Don't worry, I've got—'

Todd cut across him. 'You may or may not have guessed this, Wallace, but I don't like you. Not a bit. Not at all. I

248

argued *very* hard to have you thrown to the wolves after the police found four low-lifes strewn around the locker room of that gym. The only thing that's keeping your neck out of a noose is that little set-up you've got going in Longrock. We think Piper can tell us who knows about the insiders; then we'll know what to do. We might get that information through you. Now, as things stand, that knowledge is still useful to us. In fact, it's crucial. But there might come a time when it no longer matters. If we lose our grip on this, if it gets away from us, we'll be very unhappy, very embarrassed, and very much in debt to all sorts of people we prefer to control rather than be controlled by. We need to work hard to avoid that.

'But if we don't – well, some might think it your fault, Wallace. Some might say that you'd been given a job and failed to do it. And whether that was said or not, Wallace, the bald fact is that we wouldn't really need you any longer, would we? You wouldn't be at all important to us. We could – how shall I put it? – dispense with you quite happily.' Todd paused. 'Well,' he added, 'I know *I* could.'

The smile came back to Ellwood's face. One of the things that particularly amused him was that Hilary had pushed a red handkerchief into his sleeve as if it were a sign of breeding and distinction. He thought: You're going to be so sorry you ever said that, you ridiculous fop, you silly tart, you piece of shit.

As if Todd had never interrupted him, he continued with his original remark: 'Don't worry, Hilary. I've got someone close to him.'

If you travel across the city, you move from numbered zone to numbered zone. The centre is One, the outer fringe is Six; zones where there used to be neighbourhoods.

Buffer zones and war zones.

On the cusp of the second zone, close to the mainline station – the place where he always went – Ellwood picked up a girl and took her home. He shut the door of his apartment and turned to her at once, putting her shoulders against the wall, knocking her legs apart with his knee. Although their faces were inches apart, he seemed not to see her. His eyes were dull like slate, grey like slate. She raised one leg to make things easier, and he caught her thigh in the crook of his elbow, hoisting it up. Backed-up and hog-tied. She noticed how his slicked-back hair carried the faint, sweet scent of gel.

After that, there was more time. He stripped, slowly, and pulled his belt through the loops, then stood naked by a chair, gripping its back.

Hilary Todd's contempt was still stinging him; he wanted to cover it with pain he really owned.

He threw the belt to the girl and said, 'Hit me.' She'd heard that before and knew they didn't mean it. The belt licked his shoulders – a loose slap. 'No,' Ellwood said, 'do it. Hit me.'

She tried again, unconvinced and so pulling the blow. He turned his head towards her, eyes suddenly burning, lips tight. 'Do it to me,' he said, 'or else I'll do it to you.'

She looked at the look in his eyes and swung the belt like an axe.

Zeno said, 'I'm sorry I hit you.'

Tom Carey put a hand to the place, lumpy and healing over, but tender still. He thought he could detect something odd in the other man's voice – a faint sing-song tone; a little, obsessive rhythm, lilting and mad. He said, 'It's OK; it doesn't matter.'

Down there in the dunes, they were out of the offshore breeze and out of the sun. Zeno had turned his face away, like a penitent at prayer.

'All I want to do,' he said, 'is cut off the past.' Carey knew that he wasn't talking about forgetting. He meant amputate, as you would a diseased limb. It was how Zeno saw those memories, those people – gangrenous things, putrid flesh to be flensed away.

'Carla . . .' Zeno spoke the name to himself; a little

fluting sound. To Carey he said, 'Is that too much to ask . . . ?'

Ellwood made the distance in under five hours, overtaking on the inside, riding the rear bumpers of faint-hearts in the fast lane. He arrived in a violet twilight; a sickle moon standing in a hoop of its own light, birds making dark arrows just above the wavetops. He stood at the lit window of his hotel room and saw his own reflection, and beyond it the room, and in that ghost-world the image of Tom Carey walking to and fro, a glassy shadow.

Carey shrugged, answering a question. 'He's under pressure, he wants out, a safe future – secure, you know – himself and the woman – Carla – that's all he can see. He has his own ideas about how to get it. The ideas include killing people. He's doing a job for you, just like he has before; but something's different. For the first time, he wants something for himself. He's got something to lose.'

'That's not what I asked you,' Ellwood said. 'I don't care about that crap. What I want to know is: how long will he last? How long is he good for?'

Carey shrugged. 'God knows.'

Ellwood continued to look at his reflection in the glass. If he stared long enough at his own face, he began to see another creature there, himself but not himself.

'Does he? Then you're just the man to ask.'

Twenty-Seven

'Pascoe?'

Your dreams will dance you through doorways.

'Pascoe?'

He had lifted the phone and put it to his ear without ever coming properly awake. He might even have said, 'Hullo.' Then Rob Thomas spoke his name a third time and he was back in the world.

He pulled the pillow over from Sophie's side of the bed and propped himself up.

'Rob . . .'

'Were you asleep, or what?'

'Asleep, yes.'

'I'm sorry.'

'It doesn't matter. What have you got?'

'Sam – you're sure it's OK to bill your office for this? You know: I have to make a charge, but you're not *there*, are you?'

'Why are you asking?'

'I spoke to George Roxborough . . .'

'He queried your bill?'

'Not really. He sort of behaved as if you didn't work there any more.'

'I'm a lawyer, not a store assistant. They can't fire me like that. Don't worry, Rob. What else did George say?'

'There's a message. I'll get to it in a minute. Listen, I've got Charles Singer for you.' The phone line buzzed like a tiny, expectant crowd. 'Sam?'

'How?'

'Holland, Carlton and Shakespeare, remember?'

'Yes.'

'It's the Shakespeare: a hotel. Tough to see the connection, unless someone was thinking of the body count in *Hamlet*.'

Pascoe smiled. 'When did *you* see *Hamlet*?'

Thomas sounded indignant. 'I'm a dedicated movie-goer.'

'What's he doing there?'

'Lying low. Very low. Almost invisibly low. Goes out to eat at night, or brings food back to his room. Stays banged-up. I'd guess he's trying to decide what to do next, but the decision's eluding him.'

'You're sure you've got the right guy?'

'The Holland and the Carlton are hotels too. I suppose he must have been choosing between them. He sure as hell found the right one if anonymity is what he's after. It's Apache country. Attack dogs go round in pairs.'

'But it's him?' Pascoe persisted.

'I nipped in for a look. His passport's there. An Amex gold card that I suspect he can't use. One or two other personal bits and pieces. He probably didn't take them out with him because he was afraid of being mugged. So he leaves them in a room where the locks open if you give them a threatening look.' Thomas sighed; he sounded genuinely sorry for Singer. 'People don't know how to truly disappear; or they can't bear to. Always hang on to something that tells them who they are – and tells me, too, in this case. I'm sorry it took so long – there were the other two hotels to check. Also your description isn't that accurate any more.'

'How has he changed?' Pascoe asked.

'Booze. Also he's on the run and he's scared and he looks like hell.'

'On the run—'

'Who knows? Taxman, bogeyman . . .' Pascoe could hear the shrug. 'Listen: I don't know what name he's using. I mean – no surprise, but he's not registered as Charles Singer.'

'Where is this place, Rob?' Pascoe looked round

hopelessly for a pen and paper, then memorized the information Thomas gave him – a room number and an address close to the edge of Zone Two.

'The other thing,' Thomas said, 'the reason I was talking to George Roxborough – well, he called me. He's been trying to get you. A woman's been phoning your office every day: wants to speak to you. George wouldn't give me her number. He says he needs to talk to you first. He might try you again, but I said I'd pass the message along. So I have.'

'What's her name?' Sophie, Pascoe thought – phoning when I was out at the cove trying to tempt that bastard out of hiding. Sophie, worried about me, and wanting to talk.

'Susan Larkin?'

Almost a sense of loss; a tiny death. 'Don't know her,' Pascoe said.

'She used to be Susan Hart: that help at all?'

Pascoe felt a trickle of shock like electrodes on the temples. 'Yes,' he said, 'that means something. Thanks, Rob.'

Pascoe's recognition stirred a faint memory in Thomas, too. 'Wasn't she on the list you gave me? Hart?'

'She was.'

'That's the problem. Men remain themselves if they stay honest. An honest woman changes her name: she marries. Go to the computer for Hart: she's not there. You're still Pascoe – and that'll be how she found you – phone book, nothing simpler. Pity she wasn't a feminist – we'd have got to her easily enough.'

'George wouldn't give you her number.'

'That's right.'

'Why not? Did he say?'

'No. He sounded a little jumpy, you know? Harassed.'

'Who signed your last cheque, Rob?'

'He did. Roxborough.'

'Keep sending the bills.'

'There's more you want me to do?'

'There might be,' Pascoe said. 'You're on retainer.'

'Listen, Sam, are you going to see Singer? Confront him, or whatever.'

Pascoe hadn't had time to think it through, but he knew he would. He said, 'Yes.'

'Take it easy.'

'I will.'

'I could . . .' Thomas paused, as if having second thoughts, then said, 'I don't know what the fuck you're doing down there, I don't know what's going on, and I don't really know why I'm offering this, but I could probably get you a gun, if you'd feel – I don't know – *safer*, or whatever.'

'Thanks, Rob. I've got one.'

'You have?'

'That's right.'

There was a pause on the line long enough for Pascoe to have taken a nap. Thomas said, 'I don't know about that. I didn't hear you say that.'

Pascoe laughed. 'You just offered to *get* me one.'

'It would have been the same if I had . . .'

'Hear no weapon,' Pascoe guessed, 'see no weapon—'

'Speak of no weapon – right.' Thomas cleared his throat, as if dislodging an embarrassment. 'You tried calling her – your friend Sophie?' Pascoe had got her address from Rob Thomas; at the same time, he'd added a quick surveillance job to Thomas's bill.

'I tried, yes.'

'She's there,' Thomas told him. 'She's just keeping the answerphone on full time.'

'OK,' Pascoe had expected it.

'Sam . . . Some guy called on a couple of occasions. Spent some time with her.'

'Yes?' Pascoe could hear the residue in Thomas's voice and didn't want to know what was left to tell.

'In fact, he spent the night there.'

Pascoe nodded, as if Thomas could see him. 'OK, Rob, thanks.'

'Do you want me to take another look?'

'I don't think so.' Pascoe closed himself off from the knowledge, like someone turning to face a wall. He said, 'Tell me about the hotel.'

'A few itinerants. Some labourers from the sticks living cheap while they get the job finished. One or two people who'll be sleeping rough if they can't beg the room rate. The streets round about are a meat market; couples rent by the half-hour – I don't think many of them are man and wife.'

'OK, Rob. Thanks.'

'Take your rabbit's foot,' Thomas said. He sounded sincere.

Pascoe stood in the shower for twenty minutes, but still felt sluggish with sleep.

When the shower finally ran cold, he continued to stand under the jets for a while, then stepped out and put a towel round his waist and another over his shoulders. He sat on the edge of the bed and dialled his office number. The girl who sat in the reception area and answered the switchboard was called Lucinda. She told him that Mr Roxborough wasn't in the office and could his secretary help? It was with a little fillip of surprise that Pascoe realized she hadn't recognized his voice. Surprise and a strange excitement; in some odd way, the incident seemed to mark a life-change.

He dialled George's home number and got no reply. As soon as he hung up the phone, he started to pack a few things. He would hold his room at the Palings while he went back to London. He'd more or less stopped thinking about money; he'd stopped thinking about ordinary living. Like a stranger in a strange land, he travelled with his other life in abeyance.

He would talk to Roxborough when he reached London. He would talk to Charlie Singer.

Twenty-Eight

They sat on high stools by the window of a pub, enduring the after-work rush. Someone nudged Pascoe twice, the second time more violently. When he turned, he saw that he was backed up to a young man with crinkly hair and a baggy silk suit, sleeves turned back to mid-forearm. He was standing with three friends and telling a tale in which he'd conned some adversary into covering a dubious investment. The young man was the star of his own story. In telling it, he cackled like a corncrake and waved his arms about.

An elbow came back and took Pascoe beside the ribs. He shifted his stool a little closer to Roxborough's; at the same time, he organized a few ounces of beer into the young man's jacket pocket.

'I don't know what's happening in your life, Sam. I'm not sure I want to know.' Roxborough watched the stain spread on the pocket and start to travel along the jacket's hem. He smiled. 'You might find it difficult to keep your place. We can't get along being under-strength for ever.'

Pascoe shrugged. 'I wish I could say I was worried by the thought. Someone called me. Susan Hart, yes? Susan Larkin.'

'She did. I've been writing cheques to Rob Thomas. Meeting his bills. Which is odd, since he hasn't been doing any work for me.'

Pascoe snorted. 'Don't tell me you care . . . This *is* George Roxborough of expense account fame I'm talking to? Your annual lunch bill is twice a teacher's salary.'

'Just letting you know.'

'I can hear you letting me know. What do you want?'

'Anthony Stewart comes to trial in just over a week's time.'

'There's a problem . . .'

'Yes and no. I'm worried. I wanted the chance to talk.' Pascoe spread his hands, inviting Roxborough in. 'Nothing's changed. Nothing significant. He and the mother are still telling the same story. They're word perfect – in fact, that's a trifle worrying in itself.'

'But it's not that.'

'No. I feel secure with Stewart; he's not a problem. The prosecution will take him through it all a thousand times, but they've got sod-all evidence, and they know it. With his mother to back him, I don't see what the opposition can do. And that's where I feel edgy. She tells their story well enough; she doesn't seem shaky at all. But she's hostile. She doesn't like me. And it shows. It might show in court. I don't feel I can predict what she'll do.'

Pascoe said, 'She doesn't like anyone. You have to earn it. Bribes. She's been expecting them – you haven't delivered.'

'What bribes?'

'You take her chocolates,' Pascoe said. 'And flowers. She likes roses. And she likes liqueur centres.'

Roxborough looked at him, mouth slightly open. He held the look so long that Pascoe laughed.

'That's *it*?' Roxborough asked. 'The whole trial could hang on whether or not I'd thought to take that stupid, self-centered, mad old woman flowers?'

'And chocolates,' Pascoe said. 'The trouble is, George, you're a good lawyer, but you forget about the people. They're odd; they have foibles; they rob banks or steal cars or kill people, but otherwise most of them have normal lives.' As he said it, he felt the hairs rise on his arms.

Zeno . . . Otherwise, they have normal lives.

'Take her flowers and chocolates; she'll say what she's supposed to say, the jury will believe her, and you're a star. OK? Now, keep signing Rob's cheques and let me have Susan Hart's phone number.'

Roxborough handed Pascoe a slip of paper. 'I'd've given it to you; I wasn't holding out. Just needed some advice.' He sniffed his whisky as if someone might have doctored it, then took a gulp. 'She said to phone only in the evening.'

'Why?'

Roxborough raised his eyebrows as if the answer were ludicrously obvious. 'I imagine she's not there during the day.'

Pascoe looked at the figures, but the dialling code meant nothing to him. 'How did she sound?'

'Sound?'

'Susan Hart – Larkin? She didn't leave a message at all?'

'Just to call.' Roxborough finished his drink and got down from his stool, then collected Pascoe's beer mug and prepared to dive into the crush at the bar. 'Is she a professional woman? You know – futures, perhaps; something fast and financial?'

'I don't know. Why?'

'She sounded tough,' Roxborough said. 'She sounded like a ball-breaker to me.'

Pascoe left as soon as he could. Roxborough was a colleague not a friend; and, in any case, Pascoe wanted no-one's company but his own. He went to his flat and kicked through the residue of ordinary living that lay behind his front door: letters, bills, journals. As if that kind of world were possible or real, he sat down at his desk and wrote cheques for the bills.

Down on the southern edge of Zone One, you can hear sirens most of the time; you could imagine that wild animals roamed the park outside Pascoe's window, the constant *whoop-screech-whoop* their cries. He walked round the cold rooms and looked at the place with a stranger's eyes.

All these odd trappings of a salvaged life, he thought. All these bits and pieces washed ashore. After Karen left, I

259

lightened my life – threw things overboard. What did I keep? Some things of hers; some things of mine. It wasn't what I planned. The idea had been to keep only what was mine, but I found there were things I couldn't bear to part with. Perhaps I was trying to make an amalgam of what was best in both of us. In which case . . . He smiled at himself in one of Karen's mirrors. In which case, there ought to be more of her things here than mine.

Each room dusty and unlived-in. A faint, stale aroma like the residue of sweat – the city's stench seeping in. He roamed around like a visitor who's been left to his own devices, curious and oddly furtive, opening drawers, reading a letter or two, shuffling through a deck of photographs.

So this is how I used to live . . .

Pascoe drove to the Shakespeare hotel and passed it, then turned round and passed it again. The girls on the roadside looked like crippled birds – bright plumage, hobbled feet. He parked the car a street away and walked back through a gauntlet of whispers and stony smiles.

He watched from a nearby bus-shelter. Maybe not tonight, he thought. Maybe he's eaten, isn't hungry, got drunk. He let five buses go by and the girls kept at him, sure that they knew what he wanted. He just said, 'Later, later . . .' They laughed, wondering how long he'd take to change his mind. Charlie Singer appeared in front of the hotel and went towards the railway station, moving fast as if it had suddenly started to rain.

Nimble Charlie; nervy Charlie. A private man; a man with secrets. 'Just the type to bring a rabbit out of a hat,' Sophie had said.

But Pascoe had come to this broken-down hotel in these bleak streets already guessing that Charlie probably wasn't Zeno. For one thing, Longrock was three hundred miles from London – a long way for a bolt-hole. And Rob Thomas's description of the man made him seem a fugitive, not a killer.

Then, when Pascoe saw Singer leave the hotel, he knew for sure. He recognized the man only because he was looking for him. Charlie was older, of course, but it wasn't only age that had changed him. His features were smudged by drink and fear, fleshy and haggard. Pascoe saw a face he knew locked up in the face of a stranger.

We'd better talk, Pascoe thought. You and I, Charlie – we'd better see what there is to be said and what there is to know. I'd like to hear why you're on the run. I wonder – was it because someone sent you a letter?

The girl who picked Pascoe up was a tall redhead in a glove-leather halter top and a skirt no bigger than a broad belt. As they walked towards the hotel, she gave him the rates on an ascending scale and spat her gum into the kerbside as if she had already decided what his preference would be. The sexual act, it seemed, was low on the list of priorities and was on offer at bargain prices; then, as you toured the body's locations, the cost increased. Pain was the most expensive thing you could buy.

The redhead was leggy and had a terrific figure. Pascoe thought of the things she did, hour in, hour out – the things that were done to her. Each time a different man, each time the same things. As they went into the hotel lobby, he noticed that her make-up was a mask, crimson lips and fake tan and eyes dark as a domino. For a moment he saw Zeno, and his head sang.

'Sign anything,' she said. A fat man in a bow tie tapped the register. The girl nodded. 'Anything – you know.' He signed *Samuel Pascoe, Esq*, collected a key to room 308 and followed the girl to the lift. She slammed the gate across – surprisingly lithe, her bicep bunching – and hit the button for the third floor. They travelled upwards slower than grass grows.

Pascoe fished some money out of his wallet and handed it over. 'That buys me a blow-job, doesn't it?' The girl gave a tight grin, amused that she'd been right. 'I'm buying it, but you can save it for the next guy. Do you know a way out of here that isn't past the desk?'

'Are you kidding? I know six ways out of here that aren't past the desk.'

'Good. Take one of them.'

'OK.' Her shrug meant, I don't know, I don't *want* to know, and, anyway, I couldn't give a fuck. When the lift stopped she yanked the gate back and stepped out like someone in a hurry. 'Was it good for you, honey?' There was a good-natured lilt to her voice. 'It was *perfect* for me . . .' She started down the hallway with long-legged strides: anxious for the street where time is money.

Pascoe took the lift back down a floor. According to Rob Thomas, Singer was in room 215. Pascoe walked down the hallway, still feeling a little light-headed. Along its length were neon strips that fluttered and buzzed. The noises that came from the rooms on either side seemed like the sound-track of a film that everyone in the hotel was playing, a film in which various people were constantly ambushed, or tortured, or – in joy – found God.

A man and woman were walking ahead of him, so he slowed his pace until the woman opened the door to room 214 and went in without bothering to look at her partner. Pascoe went past as the key clicked in the lock. At the end of the hallway he turned a corner and saw that he was facing a dead end, doorless apart from a fire exit, the walls dappled with scabs of paint and sick yellow neon light. He stood just out of sight and listened for the lift.

People arrived in couples, but the men were the first to leave. The hotel was a factory where itinerant shift-workers put the finishing touches to pleasure and pain. Pascoe heard the mechanics working hard in rooms close by.

And then he heard the lift. Footsteps approached, shuffling, and stopped. When Pascoe looked into the hallway, he saw Singer leaning against the door of his room, his back half-turned. He seemed to be either massively weary, or massively drunk. Eventually, he got his key into the lock and nudged the door open with his knee. He was carrying a brown bag, blotched with grease stains.

Pascoe walked up behind Singer as he opened the door and then simply followed him into the room. Singer sensed a presence and turned, swinging a punch as if instinct or fear dictated it. Pascoe side-stepped and Singer fell, towed by the trajectory of his own fist. He lost his hold on the bag and a slew of rice and chicken and ochre sauce splashed on to the carpet. Singer was up surprisingly quickly. He got on to his knees, then rose in a crouch and hit Pascoe full on the chest with a tight fist. It was a lucky punch, but Pascoe stepped back from it gulping after breath, and Singer followed, swinging his arms in the hope of connecting again. His hand rapped the door frame and he gave a chirrup of pain. Pascoe threw a punch and missed, then threw another and felt the connection travel to the point of his elbow.

As Singer went back, he grabbed Pascoe's lapel, dragging him on, and they both fell. Singer's face was flushed as if he'd just got out of a hot bath. As they lay on the floor, he went at Pascoe with knees and elbows, everything uncoordinated, getting a blow in to the cheekbone and then a knee close enough to the groin to make Pascoe panic. A chair went over and Singer rolled through the mush of food, trying to gain his feet. Pascoe got on to his knees like a man at prayer, and hauled Singer towards him by his hair, punching twice, hard, as he pulled the man in.

There was a sudden pause. Singer put both hands up before his face, arms outstretched; he was begging. Blood was running freely from his nose and dripping in rapid little jots from the point of his chin.

Pascoe said, 'You needn't have done that, Charlie.' He was so out of breath that he had to swallow a couple of words to get air.

Singer peered, as if through a fog. He said, 'Sam Pascoe?' If there had been any last doubts in Pascoe's mind about whether Charlie Singer might be Zeno, Singer's tone of voice would have dispelled them. The surprise and confusion couldn't have been faked.

Pascoe dropped his hands. He said, 'I've been looking for you, Charlie.'

Singer tucked a leg underneath, put a hand to the floor, and pushed himself into a squat. He stayed that way for a moment waiting for a sudden onslaught of dizziness to pass; three or four times, he shook his head and bloodbeads flicked across the room. When he'd recovered, he went to a suitcase in a corner of the room and took out a T-shirt to use as a swab.

'Looking for me . . .' Singer draped the T-shirt over his head, but his laughter was evident in the way his shoulders shook. After a moment, he pulled the T-shirt away; his face was streaked red and his mouth was wide open in a silent howl of laughter. Pascoe waited him out. Finally, Singer sat on the edge of the bed, laughter spent, his face now peculiarly solemn. 'Yes, well, you're not alone in that.' He looked at Pascoe in astonishment and shook his head. 'What in fuck's name do you want, Sam? Planning to blow up a train and need some help?'

'What are you doing here?' Pascoe asked. 'What's wrong?'

'I asked you a question, you asked me a question, but I didn't leap out of nowhere and start a fight, did I? You go first.'

'I had a letter,' Pascoe said, 'about Lori. I don't know who sent it and I want to find out.'

'Lori . . .' Singer looked incredulous. 'Jesus Christ, about *Lori*?' He felt a trickle of blood touch his lip and wiped it away. 'A threatening letter?'

'Well,' Pascoe said, 'it wasn't a *news* letter.'

'Blackmail.' Singer started to laugh again. 'Well, I'm not at my home address, as you see, so if there's a letter for me, I haven't got it. And even if I had, I don't think I'd've paid it much attention. Someone's bringing his bucket to a dry well.' He paused, realizing what Pascoe had meant. 'Looking for *me*. You thought it might be me.'

'It's someone who knows.'

'Jesus, *anyone* could know.'

'Have you told anyone?'

Singer shook his head, allowing the point. 'No.' Then he added, 'It's not me.'

I can see that, Pascoe thought. He was giving Singer the bare minimum – nothing about Nick's death or Marianne's disappearance, nothing about Sophie or Zeno. He said, 'Now you—'

'I owe some people some money.'

'Much money?' Pascoe didn't ask about the people, but he guessed that they had grown angry waiting for the debt to be paid.

Singer grinned like someone about to reveal an amazing piece of gossip. 'More than a quarter of a million.'

'They want your hide.'

Singer's grin didn't fade; if anything, it grew broader. 'Oh, I'm dead. No question: dead. You're talking to a dead man.'

Someone came into 214. They heard the door open and close. The man's voice was a soft bass, the syllables blurred. The woman's higher voice was dampened by the wall, but clear, like all the women's voices from all the rooms.

'*Listen – you can get your hands round that when I've seen some cash . . .*' She managed to sound both coquettish and businesslike, though what really lay in the voice was endless anger.

'What are you going to do?' Pascoe realized he'd spoken in a whisper.

Singer gave a half-laugh. 'I don't think they're listening to us.' Even so, he dropped his voice. 'I'm becoming anonymous. The theory is that if I stay among the faceless long enough, I become faceless myself.'

In 214, the bed creaked like a rack. The man's low voice rumbled an instruction: '*Do this, do that.*' It never changed.

'How long will your money hold out?'

'About another three months,' Singer said. 'The thing about betting the horses – sometimes you win.'

'But mostly you lose,' Pascoe observed. 'You lose two hundred and fifty thousand or more.'

'I'll wait for a month or so: here, some other place, I don't know. Then I'll try to get to France. It's moving that's the problem. And the passport. It gives you an identity. Having no identity at all – that's the trick. Becoming someone else; becoming someone new.'

'*Is that what you like?*' the woman asked. '*Is that what you want to do?*'

'What happened?' Pascoe asked. He thought back to the moment when he and Sophie were inside Singer's flat: the bed littered with clothes hangers, the dim light, the stale air.

'The same as always happens,' Singer told him. 'There's nothing original about a mess like this. I made some bets and they came good. I made some more – the same. What was that about? Clear as day – I was on a winning streak, I'd hit a seam. Made some more bets that didn't quite work out, but I could still see the pattern – a good one, too. More bets; I started to lose. Well, that couldn't last, because I'd found my touch, right? So: more bets, then more, then more again. Woke up one morning and I was in for twenty thousand. There was a pattern all right; problem was I'd misread it.'

From beyond the wall came: '*You want to do that?*' Then the man's voice, rumbling a response. She said, '*OK*,' and laughed. '*You're going to need an entry fee.*'

'There's a gambler's remedy,' Singer said, 'the equivalent of hair of the dog. It's called bet your debt.'

'That's what you did?'

'That's what I did. Twenty grand spread on straight bets and accumulators.' Singer laughed. 'God was not good and I was broke. So I did the logical thing – for a gambler, that is. I went after the money with money – borrowed from legit sources so far as I could: you know, against property, against insurance policies. By the time that had gone I was close to fifty thousand out. There was only one place left to go.' Singer shrugged: 'Well, *places,*

266

really. Soho, Chinatown . . .' he laughed, 'Mayfair . . . You don't pick up a quarter of a million all in one place.'

The woman said, '*That hurts.*' Then, again, '*That hurts, Goddammit.*' The man seemed not to be listening; he was cursing her – a growing crescendo of long-hoarded hatred and fear.

Lines of blood had dried on Singer's face, a little map of pain. He sat on the bed, shoulders down, face averted, like a refugee. 'You couldn't lend me some money, Sam?' Pascoe handed over almost all he had and Singer took the cash without looking at it. 'Lori . . . Who in God's name would write to you about Lori?'

Pascoe said, 'Someone troubled by the past.' Then, remembering Singer's remark about blackmail, added: 'Someone who needs money.'

'I need money,' Singer confirmed. 'It isn't—'

'It isn't you; I know. I can see that.'

Nimble Charlie, Charlie light on his feet, skinny and quick and deft. Charlie once-upon-a-time . . . Now the face was lost in flesh and a paunch hung on him like a soft bell. Pascoe thought of Sophie and felt no jealousy. He felt sadness.

The woman in the next room gave a brief shriek of outrage and damage; then came a silence so long that it was almost eerie.

Pascoe looked around the room as though he were checking to see whether he'd left anything behind. He said, 'Lots of luck, Charlie.'

'Lori . . .' The way Singer spoke the word seemed to endow it with some great mystery. 'I'd forgotten she ever existed.'

Pascoe could tell a good lie from a bad. He said, 'Sure . . .'

'*Did you have fun, Darling?*' the woman asked. There was strain in her voice plain to hear. '*So tell your friends, OK?*'

There were fires burning in the park. You could imagine

you were prospecting some dark land and seeing camp fires, or signal fires, or fires that were the only known evidence of a hidden tribe.

The flames ran in red-gold points of reflection on Pascoe's window. He looked out, only half-focusing, until it seemed the fires were burning in his room, or else his reflection had stepped out through the window to roam the park like a ghost.

There was a rough, unshiftable pain where Charlie Singer had landed his punch, and Pascoe was drinking whisky to take the edge off it.

He called Sophie and listened while her voice ran through the little script that people write for answer-phones, then doubled his double Scotch and went back to the window.

Dear God, I'm tired . . . As the thought struck him he felt a sudden wild dizziness, and fatigue ran through him like an electrical surge. He went to sleep as he stood there, clutching his glass, his forehead resting on the window-pane.

His breathing fetched a tiny, circular patch of dew to the glass, that faded and swelled to the rhythm of his sleep.

An image of distant fire danced on his brow.

He woke next morning without remembering that moment of sudden sleep. He was in bed, fully clothed, feeling a hangover latch on hook by hook. He emerged swearing softly at himself and swaying slightly. The discomfort in his chest had settled to a hoarseness as the bruise blossomed, but his stomach churned on the lees of booze and bile. One or two deaths from old age had taken place in the fridge. He rooted around for survivors but there were none. In the store cupboard, he found a can of beef stew and dumped it in a saucepan to heat. He ate it with some biscuits, getting it down fast, his face close to the plate, his fork-hand hooking round to beat illness to the punch.

He made coffee, then found the piece of paper Roxborough had given him and took it to the phone. He had almost decided to hang up when a man's voice came on the line, sounding muzzy and oddly worried.

'Is Susan Hart there?' Pascoe corrected the mistake. 'Larkin.'

'Who do you want?' The voice seemed tremulous with age.

'Susan Larkin.' Pascoe glanced down at the paper to check the number.

'I know who you are.'

The remark was so puzzling Pascoe continued as if it hadn't been spoken. 'My name's Sam Pascoe. We used to know one another.'

A silence came in, inexplicable and laden with unease. Pascoe heard a woman's voice, growing in volume as she approached. There was a clatter as the phone was put down. Out of the jabber of syllables – the man's and the woman's – came her question. 'Who is it?'

'Who is it?' The man gave a little squawk of indignation. Of fear. 'Your lover,' he said.

The woman lifted the phone and said, 'Wait, please.' Pascoe guessed that she must have put her hand over the mouthpiece. Her voice grew muffled, though her words remained clear enough. 'Go back to bed, all right? What are you doing down here?'

'Intercepting your secret phone calls.' Now he was angry, the man suddenly seemed younger.

'Go back to bed.' Pascoe pictured the woman watching the man out of sight before she turned back to the phone. 'Yes?'

'Sue?' he asked. 'It's Sam Pascoe.'

Her voice was like flint. 'When I left my number at your office, I said that you weren't to call me during the day. Didn't they tell you that?'

'I forgot. I'm sorry.' It seemed such a bizarre exchange after two decades of silence that he repeated her name – 'Sue?' – as if it might turn out not to be her after all.

'What's your address, Sam? Where are you?' He told her. 'OK,' she said, 'give me an hour.'

'Sue—'

'An hour,' she told him. Then the phone went down.

Twenty-Nine

Zeno's house was in woodland, half a mile from Long-rock and in sight of the sea. You could drive to a track where there was a parking circle and from there walk fifty yards uphill to a gate, a garden, a cottage built of granite and constantine. Its virtue was that it had no neighbours and it had been picked out for just that reason: no-one to ask questions, no-one expecting to start up a friendship. As you walked from the house to the sea, the sound of the wind in the trees became the sound of waves on the rocks.

Because Zeno was edgy, Carla was telling him a story. It was a story that began in sadness, but came out well – the story of herself. They were sitting in front of the house and looking at the ocean.

'Once upon a time,' Carla said, then stopped. She was picking at a leaf – taking the green out to leave a filigree of veins. 'Except it can't begin like that, since I don't remember specific times. All I see are snapshots. Each snapshot has a feeling that goes with it: mostly sadness, sometimes fear, once or twice happiness. That's all the past is: snapshots and feelings.'

Zeno's snapshot was Lori in the instant that she leaped from the low branch. Her arms and legs were spread like a flayed hide; her face was a gargoyle's grimace.

Carla said, 'One moment is with my father. We're standing on a hill. I'm wearing a red dress. I suppose I was about five years old; maybe four. It's the only moment with him, there weren't any others.'

Lori as she leaped from the low branch . . .

*   *   *

271

When Pascoe opened the door to Susan Hart, he recognized her at once; then the recognition fled. Before his eyes, the person he'd known did a slow dissolve into the person she'd become: the face sharper and sterner, the hair short and severe, the body lean as a toothpick on salads and work-outs. The make-up did a terrific job, but couldn't get rid of the two deep creases that ran from the corners of her mouth to her jawline, or the network of lines on her brow.

'You look great,' he told her.

'I look like hell; if it comes to that, so do you.'

'I'm sorry about the phone call. I got the instruction but I didn't really take it in.' Pascoe was still shaky, the hangover circling like a storm amid mountains. He made coffee for Susan, but decided not to risk a cup himself.

'I got a letter,' she said.

'About Lori.'

She didn't seem surprised. 'Yes.'

'I got one too.'

'I thought you must have done.'

'Did you?' Pascoe felt a little rush of nausea, as if someone had pulled a spigot in his gut. 'Why?'

'The only person I stayed in touch with – after Lori – was Marianne Novaks. Not for long – I mean, we hadn't seen each other for years. But I knew where her father lived. I called. He told me that you and Sophie had been there; he also told me that Marianne had disappeared. I didn't think you were down there renewing an old acquaintance. How is Sophie?'

Pascoe shrugged. 'Fine. She had a letter as well.'

'I couldn't find her. I expect she married and changed her name. But you were easy enough – your name was all over the papers recently.' Pascoe looked at her as if he couldn't make the connection. 'You're defending Anthony Stewart.'

'No, I'm not,' he said. 'But I was.'

Susan was dressed in businesswoman's black. 'Here we sit,' she said. 'The great revolutionaries. You a lawyer,

272

me—' and she spread her hands, inviting Pascoe to guess. He shook his head, though he was thinking what George Roxborough had thought: broker, investment banker. 'Kept woman,' Susan said. 'I married for money, and I got just what I wanted. A rich man, devoted to me.'

'Lucky you,' Pascoe said. He thought: Just like Sophie – the same journey, the same cash contract. In Charlie's loft, they had talked through the night about the sickness money brings, the violence and fear that money brings, the corruption money brings, and all along the real subject was not fear or corruption or violence, but money.

Pascoe changed his mind about the coffee; anything to distract his body from what was happening to it.

Susan laughed. 'Lucky . . . Maybe then; not now.' Pascoe didn't ask her what she meant. 'What about the letter?' she asked.

Pascoe told her what had happened: everything; about Nick Howard's body being found in the cove, about dining and dancing with death, about magic. He saw knowledge and pain in her eyes long before he'd finished, but he told her the rest anyway.

She said, 'It's Luke.'

Except he hadn't told her about finding Charlie Singer. 'It could be Charlie,' he said. 'What makes you sure?'

'It's Luke.'

Lori in bed beside him saying, 'Never leave me.'

'Another snapshot,' Carla said, 'is my mother waving goodbye. I don't remember what the occasion was – maybe it was my first day at school, or maybe I was staying with my aunt for a few days . . .' She pondered, seeming anxious to trap the moment, then gave up. 'No: I can't remember. But it was seeing her waving – standing there and seeming to wave for ever as she backed away from me. I think it must have been out of doors, because what I recall most is the way she seemed to dwindle on planes of blue.'

They had begun to walk through the woods towards the

sea; two lovers out for a stroll, telling each other everything. Because they were walking downhill her limp was making her awkward and she linked arms with him to keep her balance.

Lori wrapped up in him, her face a love-mask.

'You know that Luke and I were lovers?' Susan asked.

'Ah . . .' Pascoe was thrown by her bluntness. 'I thought it was on and off.'

'Everything was on and off in those days. Permanence was a *drag*, man. *Change* – that was the issue.' Susan held her cup out for more coffee. 'No, we were having a relationship, such as it was. After the Group split up, we got married.'

There was an extravagant pause. Finally, Pascoe said: 'Married?'

'It was Luke's gift to me,' she said. 'He handed it over in return for disappointments and betrayals. Though, of course, betrayal wasn't a word you were allowed to use either.'

'What happened?'

'They were heady days, weren't they, Sam? Luke wanted to blow up the world and start again. He used to use the word "bloodbath" as if it were a form of baptism.'

'Did you want that?' Pascoe asked.

'He used to make hit lists – you know? Members of the Cabinet, right-wing back-benchers, policemen, soldiers . . .' She paused. 'Did I want it? I wanted whatever he wanted.'

'If you're right – if it's Luke – why? Why is he doing it?'

'The marriage lasted a year, almost to the day. Lori . . .' She glanced at Pascoe quickly, then looked away again. 'That was tough for everyone. Tougher for me, though, since I knew Luke was sleeping with her. "For the cause," he said.'

Pascoe looked at her blankly. 'He was sleeping with her, yes. What do you mean: for the cause? What did *he* mean?'

'You thought it was just a gag,' Susan said. 'Luke

Mallen, revolutionary and acid-head, bangs the wife of a USAF colonel. Poor Lori. After I'd finished hating her, I began to feel sorry for her. Then we killed her, and I felt frightened of her. As it happened, I was right to feel that.'

'Some people would say she killed herself.'

Susan's gaze was bleak with knowledge. 'We harassed her. We made anonymous phone calls. And we knew how frightened she was, how disturbed, because Luke told us that – told us fresh from her bed and hardly able to speak for laughter.'

'For the *cause* . . . ?'

'There was a man called Wallace Ellwood. He knew about Luke and Lori: God knows how. He was—' Susan threw her hands up as if inviting Pascoe's disbelief. 'He worked for British Intelligence, but he was a double agent. Or said he was: told Luke that. He was stationed at the Base in some sort of fake capacity. The British keeping an eye on the Yanks was the idea. Except Ellwood was keeping an eye on everyone and seeing to it that East Germany got the news. He recruited Luke – not that Luke needed to be persuaded. He thought it was terrific – you know? – the real thing, *professional* stuff.'

'How did you know this – about Ellwood?'

'Luke told me. It worked well: Luke slept with Lori. Lori gave him bits and pieces of information gleaned from her husband. Luke passed them on.'

'To Ellwood.'

'No: to a priest called Carey. Luke used to go to confession.' Her smile was almost a grimace. 'Confession . . . Carey was part of a chain. Ellwood didn't want the limelight; he had a cover to preserve at the Base. He saw Luke now and then: just to stay in touch. The chain was the Colonel – unwittingly – then Lori, Luke, Carey, after that . . . wherever.'

'What was it about Ellwood?' Pascoe had seen how the name filled her face with darkness.

'It seemed like a joke, didn't it? "*We know all about you* . . ." A cruel joke, but then it was supposed to be that.

But when we phoned her, when we made those calls saying, "We know," it wasn't just the infidelity that Lori worried about. It was all the things she told Luke. It was spying, giving away secrets, pillow talk . . . Luke knew how desperate she was. She never told him about the phone calls: I think perhaps she thought that might drive him away. And the truth was – the bald truth was – Lori was crazy about him. He could see how hopeless it was for her. She was twenty years older than Luke. Too late to change. And, anyway, she wasn't so deluded that she thought they might make a life together. But she was so much in love with him it was witchcraft – he had her in thrall.'

Susan stopped speaking. Her face was turned away, as if she had seen something out of the corner of her eye. Pascoe was like a man watching from the shore, too far off to give help, while a swimmer fought to stay afloat.

Finally, Susan said: 'Me too.'

'All I really remember,' Pascoe said, 'is that Luke was screwing the Colonel's wife. I remember we laughed about it. He'd give us funny stories – the Colonel coming in the front door while Luke left through the back. The phone calls were just . . . they were stupid . . . we were mostly out of our minds, for Christ's sake.'

'Lori was out of hers. We didn't know that. We didn't think of that.'

'You knew,' Pascoe said suddenly.

Susan nodded, slowly. 'She was my rival. She loved Luke as much as I did. You think I cared what happened to her?'

And here's a group shot: everyone standing under the tree, Lori's face among the branches, dark like bruised fruit. Everything still. Then a woman, crying. The acid trip came and went like an image on a screen, sometimes faint, sometimes strong – music among the trees, Lori's dark head singing, colours among the undergrowth, curling like lurid fog, light crowning the treetops, Lori seeming to move in a stately dance. And a woman crying.

Carla said, 'In hospital, everything was white or black.' The memory seemed to worsen her limp; her hip knocked his as they walked. 'I was there for a long time, but I can't remember anyone visiting me. My hospital snapshot is a doorway where people came and went. I could see into the hallway. Ordinary life was going on outside.'

They had reached the foreshore. Carla took her shoes off and loosed his arm so that she could walk through the lip of foam.

The shutter went click. Lori climbed the tree: click. She fixed the rope: click. She jumped: click. Everyone there . . . Look at the camera – smile – click!

Pascoe realized that he'd been asking questions that Susan hadn't answered. He tried again. 'How do you know it's Luke?'

'A year to the day it lasted. God knows how. We spent most of the time on the planet acid: the best place for us to be. Luke would rave on about change. Changed states, changed lives. Everything had to change . . .' She smiled, then picked up on his question. 'From the letter itself – that's how I knew it was Luke. I was in love with him; I was his wife. The tone of the letter, the way it spoke of Lori; I was sure Luke had written it.'

'Were you?' A thought occurred to Pascoe. 'I'd assumed the letter was identical in each case. Maybe not . . .'

Susan shrugged. 'It was meant to threaten and compel, it was anonymous, it suggested a meeting. I expect they were all much the same. The difference lay in the reader.'

'If you knew . . .'

'Knew what? I knew it was Luke. I didn't know he was likely to kill anyone. Blackmail was what I assumed. I thought: If he tells someone, my life will change. It seemed like a good option – a chance for chaos. I wanted that. When nothing happened, I was almost disappointed.'

'Still, it's only guesswork,' Pascoe was being the lawyer – asking for better and more secure evidence.

Susan shook her head. 'Maybe . . . before this moment. Not now.' Pascoe looked at her, asking for the proof. 'We were on a beach in Greece,' Susan said. 'There was a guy doing tricks: you know, magic, conjuring, juggling . . . Luke was like someone who'd seen a vision of the Holy Grail – completely obsessed.' She smiled ruefully. 'Obsession is in his nature. I've been his obsession, and I know. It's quite a responsibility.' The smile went away. 'It turned out that the guy was a pro; he gave performances here and there, novelty turns, you know. Louis Maddox: but his stage name was Orso. Luke started going to all his shows. Made a friend of him. Eventually wound up taking lessons from him. And Luke was good. They did a switch on stage one night – Maddox got into a trunk tied hand and foot, but it was Luke who emerged. He finished the show pretending to be Maddox, and no-one knew.' She picked up another question Pascoe had asked. 'It's Luke,' she said, 'but I don't know why he's doing it.'

She jumped and came up short as the rope went taut. The shock seemed to travel through the entire tree, as if that drop, that weight, that terrible dry snap became a tremor in the tap root, as if it bled into the sap.

When they reached the dunes, Carla sat down close to where Tom Carey normally sat. She said, 'Now I've found you, those old photos don't matter any more.' Her pale, plain face was turned to him as a flower turns to the sun. She lifted the hem of her skirt back to her waist, and smiled, and touched herself briefly between the legs.

'Come on,' she said.

'Revolutionaries – were we?' Susan laughed. 'Little acts of sabotage, little deeds of spite; that was us. And what have we become?' She extended a hand to Pascoe, as if introducing him to strangers. 'A lawyer, defending seedy killers,' – the hand returned to herself – 'an opportunist trapped by her own greed.'

'Is that who you are?' Pascoe asked.

'My husband has cancer. He's dying. He's convinced that my lover and I are waiting eagerly for that event, so he's written a will that leaves me destitute. The most amusing part of all this is that I don't have a lover.'

Pascoe realized that what he'd heard in the voice on the phone hadn't been age, but sickness.

'I only ever loved Luke,' Susan said. 'I don't know what happened to us. He took a lot of acid; he practised all day and all night – magic, tricks, illusions. He became secretive and distant. I know he saw Wallace Ellwood sometimes, but I don't know why.'

She stood up and Pascoe stood too, oddly formal. He felt weak, like someone who has endured months of broken nights. He said, 'Now that you know that it's Luke, that he sent you the letter, what are you going to do?' Even as he spoke, he saw that it was a dead issue for Susan.

'Go home to my husband,' she said. 'He's dying, and he's afraid.'

Carla stretched out, feeling the rub of sand against her thighs. She pulled her dress up over her face and looked at the sun as it washed into the cotton. He lowered himself and kissed her through the weave.

'The best . . . The best ever . . .' Her voice was muffled and indistinct. She lifted her legs and scissored them on his back. Seen through the sunlit material, he was nameless and faceless, a pleasure device.

Lori strung up like meat in the windless wood, everyone standing there, and someone . . .

Susan had her hand on the door. Pascoe asked, 'Ellwood? What was it about Ellwood?'

He thought she wouldn't reply, then she shrugged and tried to laugh, but couldn't bring it off. The failure chilled him. She said, 'Wallace Ellwood is the most evil person I've ever met,' then wiped a hand across her face as if his name had fouled her mouth.

*   *   *

. . . and someone crying. Susan, crying.

The dress slid from Carla's face to show her eyes wide with desire, wide with love. A great flush spread on her throat and she drove her heels into the sand and arched her back, whispering his own name to him like a fierce incantation.

'Luke, Luke, Luke, Luke, Luke . . .'

Thirty

As an invalid might, or a child, Wallace Ellwood sat in a chair by the window of his apartment and watched the traffic go by. The phone was wedged under his chin. He was eating nacho chips and drinking beer from the bottle and listening as Hilary Todd told him to forget about Piper, to stay in London, to wait for further instructions. Ellwood's ear was tuned to the glee in every word, a little bugle call that meant, 'No quarter'.

Two more men had died – another in France and one in Italy, both of them Insiders.

'The chance has gone,' Todd said. 'Your chance.'

Ellwood could have been talking to a simpleton. 'You'll have to give me more time down there, Hilary. I'm inclined to finish the job, now it's begun. I think I'd prefer that. But I'll need a little more time.'

Todd laughed. 'No-one could accuse you of unnecessary panic, Wallace. But let me give you a tip – panic. Do it now. Look down: you'll see your balls in my hand.'

'Now you can find a way, Hilary, I'm sure of it. I can see that we're going to have to speed things up: I'll give you that.' Ellwood was having fun. His voice was just a hint more than a whisper.

'You're a headless chicken, Wallace. Still in motion, but dead meat.'

Ellwood's timing was perfect. He could see Todd's smile, could feel the gesture forming as the other man leaned forward very slightly and prepared to put the phone down. He said, 'Poor Annie . . .'

A silence grew on the line, a vacuum that drew loathing and dread towards it in a soundless rush.

'Poor Annie,' Ellwood continued, 'gone, now, and out of harm's way, but so curious, Hilary, and so indiscreet. She seemed to know an awful lot about you. I'm sure she didn't tell me everything. But she mentioned the stash-for-cash deals, and she kept a little record, and she named names. We had dinner one evening and although she didn't know it, I was recording everything she said. Because I like to keep a little record myself. I've had a few copies made to be on the safe side: solicitors, banks . . . you know. If I come to grief, Hilary, then so will you.'

Ellwood waited, happy to hear the line humming between them. He took a swallow of beer and watched a red Lotus Elan convertible cutting an aggressive, jagged line between trucks and lazily driven cars. A woman was driving, her straight, dark hair streaming like a banner, her skirt hiked up over lean thighs, her arms held straight from shoulder to wheel. She cut in on a station wagon, forcing the driver to brake heavily, then made fifty yards on the hard shoulder. Even after he'd lost sight of her, Ellwood retained the image of power.

'Now I can see that things are growing difficult for you, Hilary, with people dying in foreign countries. I'm sure you're under pressure. I don't expect you to be able to give me all the time in the world: that would be unreasonable.'

Todd hadn't spoken in over a minute, but there was a harshness on the line that Ellwood knew to be his breathing, and a thin, reedy, barely audible sound behind that, which resembled nothing so much as a cry that had been buried alive.

'So I'm asking for another week, Hilary. A week or *so*. Because I'm going to take some measures to . . . speed things up. And after that, a little holiday. And after that, you can find me another nice job to do.' He put a nacho chip in his mouth and soaked it with beer. 'Life's deceptive, Hilary. Life is a hall of mirrors. You think those are *my* balls in *your* hand? Nah . . . Look again. You see? It's a mirror. And have you noticed what's in my other hand? That's right, Hilary; a knife.'

* * *

Less than ten minutes later, Ellwood was driving west on the elevated section, carving a path through the laggards and deadheads. He hoped he might encounter the girl in the Lotus Elan making the return trip. Still, he reflected, you can't have everything you want.

Thirty-One

Pascoe watched a globe as it glowed in the darkness, then rose and fell in a sizzling arc. Another joined it, then a third. All three hung in the air, moving and looping, until they were joined by a fourth: white, green, red, blue.

Out of the blackness a voice said, 'Spectacular, isn't it?' Louis Maddox kept the globes suspended for a little longer, then caught them in turn, letting their brilliance fade. When he drew the curtain back from the windows, he was smiling. 'Everyone likes that trick. Look—' he held one of the globes out to Pascoe. 'It's a neon circuit, with a damper switch in the perspex, right here.' Pascoe could see a tiny, colourless button in the seam where the two halves of the globe were joined. Maddox pressed it and the little circuit hummed with white light. 'Makes simple juggling into a magic show.' He stowed the globes in a styrofoam case like an over-sized egg box. 'How is Susan?'

'Fine.'

'It's a long time,' Maddox said. 'And I'm not sure what it is you want to know.'

Pascoe had found Maddox easily: he was listed with several theatrical booking agencies. Deciding what to tell the man wasn't so simple.

'Neither am I.' Pascoe was busking. 'I'm a lawyer. Susan and Luke and I were friends years ago: we lost touch not long before you and Luke came to know one another.'

'They're still together?' Maddox said it as if even this world could deliver miracles.

284

'No. Luke's been in touch with her, though; and with me. It's possible he's in trouble. We want to find him.'

'And you're a lawyer . . . ?'

'I'm also Luke's friend.'

'So why come to me? I haven't seen Luke in years.'

'I don't expect you to know where he is,' Pascoe said. 'I just want to talk to you about him. It's called background.' When Maddox shrugged, Pascoe lifted a store bag he'd brought with him and took out some fake flowers and a top hat. He passed them to Maddox. The top hat had bird shit in it.

'What's this?' Maddox asked. 'Left at the scene of the crime?'

'Something like that.'

'You're not going to tell me, are you?'

'I will if you say I must.'

'Forget it,' Maddox told him. 'I'm guessing that I wouldn't want to know.' He made the flowers a cane and twirled it like a drum majorette. As Pascoe watched, it exploded in Maddox's hand to become a bunch of flowers again. 'Tricks are OK,' Maddox said, 'tricks are fine.' He tossed the flowers aside. 'They're a warm-up device: nothing wrong with that, but it's not magic. Magic is illusion and belief.'

'Was Luke good at that?'

Maddox was tall and slender, like a wand. He must have been sixty or so, but you had to get close to see it and if his hair was grey, someone had made a good job of disguising the fact. Pascoe noticed how nimble his hands were: long fingers, a delicate touch.

A slow smile, almost sad. Maddox said, 'Luke was the best natural talent I ever saw.'

'You taught him . . .'

'Well . . . I showed him what to do. And he had tremendous flair. But remember I said illusion and belief. There are good mechanics who can produce a series of illusions flawlessly. It's a job, to them; a technique. They can show you magic, but not a *magic show*. A magic show is a story. You can be a performer, or else you can be the hero of the story.'

'And Luke knew how to be that,' Pascoe suggested.

'Luke knew how to be that.' Maddox shook a cigarette from a packet and drew it back and forth through pursed fingertips. 'You have to construct a story, of course, sentence by sentence, trick by trick.' The cigarette slid back into his hand, then popped up again, a sly temptation. 'I'm trying not to light it.'

'Will you succeed?'

'It's tricky,' Maddox said.

'What was Luke's speciality? Did he have one?'

'He was good at everything.'

'Escapology,' Pascoe wondered.

'You've seen him work,' Maddox was sure of it.

There wasn't a trace of the sardonic about Pascoe's smile. 'In a manner of speaking – yes.'

'It fascinated him more than anything else. He loved it. He used to liken it to confession – you go in a sinner, laden with chains, bound by evil deeds, then, *whoof*, the sinner emerges, unfettered and free.' Maddox was fighting an uneven battle. He lit the cigarette and waved an apologetic hand through the smoke. 'He could always see the illusion from the point of view of the audience. I mean, he was able to put himself among the duped. Which was particular and odd, since all magic is to do with knowledge versus ignorance. A key hidden in your mouth or under your scrotum, a button to press, a collapsible blade . . .

'Would you like something to drink?' He moved with a lithe grace; only the lines on his face gave him away, the little scrawny pouch under his chin. He went through to his kitchen, then returned with a bottle of claret and two glasses. 'Just wine and beer now,' he said, as if that told Pascoe all he needed to know about Maddox's state of health. 'And, in theory, no cigarettes.' He poured the wine and said, 'It should have had longer . . .' Then: 'Why are you looking for him?'

'I thought you didn't want to know.'

'You're right; I don't.'

'What else could Luke do?'

'He was good at make-up – disguise. He used to do a show for me sometimes. Never went pro, but I used to put him on as part of my act. He'd do a standard trunk escape, but come on as a clown to test the chains. It was a good ruse. He'd palm a key and undo the locks that way.' Maddox held his wine to the light, then sipped. 'Everything – close work, cards, juggling, knife-throwing.' His head lifted sharply as if an idea had struck him.

'Don't think about it,' Pascoe said.

Maddox took another cigarette from the packet and lit it straight away. 'I knew it must have been something like that.'

'Don't worry, you never saw me. I was never here.'

Maddox didn't seem worried, he seemed curious. 'What did you hope to get from me?'

'Confirmation,' Pascoe told him, 'and I got it.'

Maddox nodded and poured more wine for himself. Pascoe's glass was untouched. He said, 'If you find Luke, what will you do?'

'Don't know.' Pascoe got up, leaving the flowers and the hat where they lay.

'From the moment you arrived,' Maddox said, 'I knew it was something like that.'

Luke Mallen walked out along the strip of headland that led to Meer's Point and stood with Tom Carey as he fished. It was early evening. A layer of cloud had drifted in to take the warmth out of what remained of the day; the wind tore it occasionally, leaving rags of blue. Carey's reel clicked slowly, then stopped. The two men stood side by side in silence. Carey re-baited his hook with fish-scrap and cast again.

'What would you have done? Marianne said she wanted to . . .' Luke stumbled on the word, '. . . confess. I thought: She'll have to die. It's obvious: they'll all have to die. Then Carla and I can be safe.'

The line payed out, making the ratchet sing. Carey checked it, then dragged back on the rod and took up the slack, working that way for five minutes or so before he beached the fish. It was pale and hammer-headed, with thick, fleshy lumps on the brow like some awful growth.

'All of them,' Luke said, 'because they know about Lori.'

Carey fixed the rod into its vee and stooped to the fish. Luke squatted alongside, like a child anxious to keep the priest's attention. Carey took out a disgorger and removed the hook. The gills were crisp and sharp as paper, and bright with blood. From the lip trailed two white mandarin moustaches like pulpy tubers.

Carey stood up, the fish held in the crook of his arm, as you would hold an infant. He could only think of the confessional's stock-in-trade: 'Did you find pleasure in it, Luke?'

The fish made little leaps and flips, as if it could feel the sea along its flank, its mouth wide open in a frantic dumb-show of breathing; all the time, its eyes were growing dull and yellowed as old tinfoil.

Luke scooped the fish up from Carey's arms and threw it into the shallows. He smiled at the ease of it; one minute the fish was dying, the next it was in its element. *With one bound – the Great Zeno, escapologist.*

'Pleasure,' he said. 'I don't know about that. It was magic – you understand? It was a magic show.'

It was almost a habit with Pascoe: every time he passed the phone he called Sophie; and every time he got a machine with a message. It had become so much a matter of routine that when she answered he came close to putting the phone down before he realized that all he'd heard was, 'Hello.'

'Don't hang up.'

'No. OK.' Then she said, 'I wasn't going to.'

'I want to see you.'

'Where are you?'

'London.'

She said, 'Oh . . .' It wasn't what she'd expected to hear. 'Are you planning to go back?'

'I don't know,' Pascoe told her. It was a lie; they both heard it ring like a dud coin. 'I woke up and you were gone; why did you leave?'

'Well, this might come as a surprise to you, but I felt safer here than down there. It was down there that someone tried to kill me.'

'Luke,' Pascoe said.

Sophie sighed, as if the news were too sad for words. 'Was it? You're sure?'

'I came back because Rob Thomas found Charlie Singer for me. Also because Susan Hart had been trying to reach me through my office. I saw Charlie – he's holed up in a cess-pit hoping that the stench will cover his scent. He owes money to some very rough people. He's not Zeno.'

'Luke is . . . ?' Sophie was asking for better proof.

'Susan came here to see me. As soon as I told her about the things that had happened, she knew. She and Luke used to be lovers, do you remember that? And—'

'Yes, I remember; but so what? It wasn't—'

'And they were married.'

He waited a long time for her response. 'I can be pretty sure you'll have enough to drink, but is there anything in your fridge?'

'Botulism.'

Thirty-Two

The past is moments half-forgotten; it's the ghosts of joy and misery; it's places and faces. Pascoe expected to open his door to the present, and found, instead, a face from the past.

Karen read his look faster than he could recover it and smiled as she asked, 'What's her name, Sam?'

Pascoe said, 'If it comes to that, what's *your* name?'

He leaned against the door jamb, hands in pockets; it looked casual enough, but in truth it was a method of recovery. After a moment, the tremor left his legs and he stood aside to let her in. She walked round the room, looking at the fragments he'd preserved from their life together. Pascoe felt as though he were seeing a moment from his future but couldn't guess what he would feel when the moment arrived.

Karen ended her tour at the window. 'When George Roxborough said you were living down here I didn't believe him.'

'Where did you expect to find me? This city used to be villages; now it's castles under siege. It doesn't matter much which drawbridge you raise.' Neither of them spoke for a while. Pascoe watched her as she peered out at the lowlife in the streets. She was still slim, but her figure seemed to have wasted slightly; she was still pretty, but her features were more sharply etched.

He said, 'Where have you been?'

Karen laughed. 'You sound as if I'd been gone for a few hours and forgot to leave you a note.'

'Well, you forgot to leave a note; go back to that and start again.'

'I let it be known that I wasn't dead; that I was safe.'

'Let it be known . . . There's not a lot of heart in that, is there?'

'There wasn't a lot of heart in our marriage, Sam.'

'You might have told me that.'

'Well,' Karen put her back to the window, leaning against it, and folded her arms. 'It was the fact that you needed to be told that made telling you impossible.'

Pascoe said, 'I'm going to have a drink.' He collected a bottle and glasses from a low table.

'Of course you are.' Although she was facing into the room, Karen said, 'You don't drive a green Merc, do you, Sam?'

He shook his head. 'No.'

'Just that a couple of guys are taking the sound system out through the window.'

Pascoe walked over, bottle and glasses in hand. He hadn't registered the two-tone scream of the car-alarm; in much the same way, a countryman might be deaf to the cry of a rooster. There was a clutter of glass in the road and two men were working unhurriedly, anxious not to bruise the equipment. 'London life,' Pascoe said, 'you'll never die of boredom.' He poured two drinks. After a moment's consideration, Karen took the glass he was offering, then moved away from him.

'Italy,' she said. 'Italy is where I've been. Perugia: it's near Florence.'

'How long have you been there?'

'Since I left. I mean, for the last ten years. It's where I live.'

Pascoe thought about it; he was looking for the clue he knew he must have missed. 'I came home one day, ten years or so ago, expecting to find you there. The house was just as I'd left it – just as *you'd* left it. It was some while – I mean, a day or so – before I realized just what "left it" really meant. I didn't know you were going to do it, and after it had happened, I didn't know why. No note, no phone call. You might have been dead. It was one of the

291

possibilities that the police finally considered – until you "let it be known" that you were OK. In the meantime, I went through all sorts of misery, puzzlement, desperation, confusion, fuck knows what. Do you know how lousy I felt, how . . .' He struggled to find some simple way of saying: lost, drunk, frightened, lonely, filled with self-loathing. In the end, he simply stared at her, shaking his head as if she had been the one to ask the question.

'It seemed sudden to you?' Karen asked. 'Me too. I'd been out to meet someone, I was on my way home, I realized I didn't want to be going there. Before I got back, I said enough is enough. I turned around; I never got home. That's why I hadn't taken anything with me.'

'Enough is enough . . .' Pascoe took a swallow of Scotch; it made his head swim.

'Enough of nothing,' Karen said. 'Nothing was what I seemed to get most of.'

The clue remained hidden. Pascoe said, 'Why Italy? I don't understand what took you there.'

'You think it was the climate?'

'Climate, wine, art galleries; I don't know. Surprise me.'

'An Italian. An Italian took me there.'

Very slowly, Pascoe unscrewed the cap of the whisky bottle and topped up his drink – just a dribble, just a tot, just something to do. Karen smiled and raised her eyebrows: *Check that!*

Finally, he said, 'Well, you surprised me . . .' The memory was only a couple of minutes old, but he felt that scrap of the past unravel to bring him back to the moment when she said, 'I'd been out to meet someone. I was on my way home . . .' And there it was: the clue.

'What's his name?' He asked the question just as Karen had asked it of him when he'd opened the door. The difference was, she hadn't really cared.

'What's his name? Where did we meet? How long had it been going on? All those questions are ten years old, Sam. I loved him, I'd stopped loving you. The really interesting

292

thing – really staggering – is that you never came close to noticing.' She swallowed her whisky in one, as if about to leave. 'What an ego.'

'Was that it?'

'Egotism, indifference – opposite sides of the same coin.' Then she said, 'Eduardo,' because it didn't matter much whether he knew or not.

'You live there now?'

'Yes. We've moved a couple of times, but still the same area. Just outside Perugia now. A farmhouse; we even have a small vineyard.'

Pascoe closed his eyes on the image for a moment. A hillside under a blue sky, terraced vines, the building itself pale stone with a roof of big, weathered terracotta tiles. Outside on the terrace, Karen and Eduardo drank wine and took the last of the day's sun.

He said, 'It sounds idyllic.'

'It suits us.' She sounded deliberately modest.

Pascoe wanted to say: I was desperate, I was frightened, I wanted you back but I didn't know where you were. I tried to make choices, but wound up with empty gestures. I went to Argentina and sat in a cell and waited for the torturers to come in.

He said none of it. He could see that his life wasn't at issue; she hadn't come to hear about that. 'Well, Karen,' he smiled at her as if she were an acquaintance he'd just spotted in a crowd. 'I think you haven't made the journey to say sorry.'

'We've decided to get married,' she said. 'I'm here to ask for a divorce. I didn't want to say that to you in a letter or over the phone.'

'Why not? You left without seeing me; you haven't seen me since.'

'That's true,' Karen said. 'The difference is, it doesn't matter any more. At first, I was angry; then I was living a new life – other things to think about, other people to consider. But the past was always there, like a whisper in a room of other voices.'

'But not now.'

She confirmed it: 'Not now.'

A silence grew between them. Pascoe was walking through their house, ten years before, going from room to room, first puzzled, then anxious, then searching for something that would explain her absence. The moment came back to him, flush with scents and sounds. The cello concerto swelling through the house, the briny tang of the scallops in their marinade, doors opening and closing as he searched for the missing clue.

The memory was so strong that he lost himself in it. When he emerged, Karen was sitting in an armchair opposite, clearly amused. She half turned to look over her shoulder; when he followed her gaze, he saw that Sophie was standing in the doorway.

'The door was open,' Sophie looked at them in turn, 'bad security in this district, no?'

Pascoe said, 'I didn't . . .' and 'How could . . . ?' and 'She's—'

'I can see who she is, that's why I'm about to leave. You'll have things to talk about.'

'Not many things,' Karen said.

'More than I want to hear.'

Pascoe said, 'For Christ's sake, don't go.' All he could see was loss.

Before she closed the door, Sophie asked, 'What would you suggest I do instead? Stay and counsel you both?'

Karen spread her hands. 'I'm sorry, Sam. Lousy timing. I couldn't have known.'

'Speak to George Roxborough about the divorce. It'll be trouble free: mutual consent.'

'No money,' she said. 'There won't be any settlement involved.'

He nodded, 'OK.' Then: 'How do you . . . ? How has it been?'

'My life?'

'Your life, yes.'

'The house is beautiful; it's falling down, bits of it, you know. It's very old. But the roof's secure and the summers are hot, and there are wood-burning stoves for the winter. We have seasons that seem to revolve round the grape harvest. It's a tiny vineyard – we just drink the wine ourselves, but we follow the old festivals. Friends come in to help us gather the crop and press the grapes. I live there with a man I love. We have just about enough money.' It wasn't coming out in any special order, though Pascoe suspected that something was being saved until the end. 'I teach English sometimes. I go to the local market once a week. I keep a journal that seems to be turning into a sort of year-book of the area, a little account of the way the seasons turn. I'm sorry, Sam; I can see that I'm either too early or too late with this, but the time is right for us. Eduardo and me. What else . . . ?' She seemed to be completing the check list. 'My life's slow; I can see the moments passing; I like that. There are two children, both girls – seven and four.'

Pascoe laughed – too loudly, too lengthily. He said, 'Well, I asked about your life. You told me.'

As she was leaving, Karen said, 'I'm sorry . . .' She made it sound as if she were saying it for the first time.

Pascoe drank some more whisky; then he drank a little more than that. He thought about the house in Tuscany, the perfect life. He suddenly wished, with an almost desperate fervour, that he'd asked the names of Karen's daughters.

Little electric pulses of tiredness buzzed behind his eyes. He thought, I know what this is: sleep as self-defence. The admission was enough to make him doze.

It seemed that Sophie was best at turning up when his guard was down. He felt the glass being tweaked from his fingers and opened his eyes to see her disappearing into the kitchen. Her voice floated back to him.

'Bad security, I told you that. I've double locked it. There's a boozer down the road; I watched your front door from there. I have to tell you, Pascoe, you're living in the dead zone. You know? Zone of the fucking dead. During the time it took to drink three glasses of unspeakable piss masquerading as wine, I had close to twenty offers: straight sex, not so straight sex, definitely warped sex, threesomes, foursomes, orgies, photos, videos.' She returned and stood in front of him. 'I'm definitely not coming down here again. You'll have to move.'

He said, 'She was asking for a divorce.'

'Did she ask nicely?'

Pascoe laughed. He felt weak and the laughter sounded shrill. 'She did, yes.'

'Good. I've put some coffee on; there are things I want to say to you later.' She held out a hand and, when he took it, heaved him upright and pulled him towards the bedroom. 'I tried not to listen to all that dirty talk, but the truth is a couple of suggestions left me wondering . . .'

Carey said, 'You're not thinking, Wallace. If he's not in control, you're not in control. And he's not in control. He seems to be, but . . .'

'I've spoken to him. I saw him an hour or so ago.'

'You went to the house?'

'That's right. New instructions: you know? We're running out of time.'

'He doesn't like people going to the house – because of Carla.'

'Fuck what he likes.' They were sitting in the restaurant at the Windrush. Ellwood had ordered lamb cutlets, French beans and button mushrooms; he was using his fingers to eat. 'Fuck what he likes, and fuck him.'

'I've had enough of this, Wallace. More than enough.'

Ellwood balanced a cutlet between fingertip and fingertip and took half the meat off in a single bite. He chewed and smiled and cuffed a little run of juice off his chin with the heel of one hand. 'Well, Tom . . .' He took the second bite. 'I think it won't take long now. Just hang in. He needs someone to talk to.'

'You don't understand, Wallace. It isn't that. I'm not frightened or bored or weary. I've had *enough*. I don't want to be part of this. I don't owe you. I don't owe anyone except, perhaps, myself. You're trading off loyalties, off ambition, off belief . . . it all died years ago. *Years* ago, Wallace. I felt responsible; I felt an affinity with him – God knows, even with you. That's why I came. But what's happening here has nothing to do with loyalty or belief.'

'No kidding.' Ellwood pursed his lips round a bean and sucked it in like spaghetti, then touched his mouth and hands with his napkin before taking a sip from a full glass of red wine. 'This is very nice, you know. Rasteau – very round, very fruity.'

'Don't make fun of me, Wallace.'

Ellwood smiled; the smile became a chuckle; the chuckle grew into a brief laugh. When he spoke, it was in a low whisper, ragged as a band saw, his mouth barely moving. 'I can't have this conversation with you, Tom; Father Tom; Holy Holy Father Tom. I can't hear all this. There are things I have to do; things I have to think about, Holy Father, Father Tom, things that are occupying my mind and I can't give you time for these things, these words, Father Tom, Your Holiness.'

Carey could feel a vast energy of violence and savage anger coming off the man. The words seemed to clog in his throat, then come free in little gouts and spurts. He was looking down at his plate and there was a tremor in his jaw as if each syllable was finding a nerve in a broken tooth.

'So you'll see, I'm sure you'll see, that I can't listen to you, Holy Father Tom, can't hear you, can't, not for a minute, so you'll have to do as you're told, have to do what I want, Father Tom, because there's no time for this, no time, no time for these words of yours, you fuck, Your fucking Holy Holiness, only time for what I want, time for words of mine, time for what I want to say, nothing else, Father Tom, you fuck, Your fucking Holiness, you see, for my words, nothing else, nothing Holy Father, nothing else, just me, just mine, only time for that.'

Ellwood kept his head bowed. His eyes were fixed, like someone watching a flow of water across a weir.

Carey said, 'Whatever you—' It was as far as he got. Ellwood snatched up his wine glass and clapped it to his mouth, driving the rim past his teeth. He yanked down with his hand and lifted his head, biting a chunk out of the glass, then turned the rim and bit again, splintering the glass almost to its stem. He half rose, leaning towards Carey, and spewed the fragments at him, shaking his head with rage, spraying glass and wine and blood. People at other tables turned to the commotion. A waiter came hurrying across.

Carey's face and his shirtfront were speckled with wine and glass; he was shaking. Ellwood sat still, a filigree of wine and blood and saliva strung across his jowls. After a moment, he picked up his water goblet and rinsed his mouth, then spat the rinse back into the glass.

To the waiter, he said: 'My friend's had an accident.' He offered a winning smile, grouted in red. 'I'm sorry. He's always been accident prone.'

They had made love then fallen asleep, so the curtains were drawn back. A spillage of lurid neon light, yellow and orange, dribbled from the windowsill to the floor. Although it was after three in the morning, Sophie could hear the low, penetrating *drub-drub-drub* of a bass-line and a siren somewhere wailing in counterpoint.

She got up on an elbow. With an outstretched finger, she traced the lines of Pascoe's sleeping face. His handsomeness was a little battered now, but he still had the wolfish look she remembered from years ago – long face, strong jaw, broad brow; his mouth was full and slightly lopsided, which gave him a crooked grin.

Every time he touched her, now, she could remember the screen and the butterfly shawl, and the long, looping rhythms of their lovemaking – a single, endless, fluctuating note.

He stirred under her touch and turned towards her,

his head rooting for her shoulder, like a child's.

Her whisper was almost too faint to be heard. 'You don't know this, Pascoe, but we're in trouble.'

Drub-drub-drub-drub-drub . . . The bass was a word of warning from the dead zone.

She kissed the corner of his mouth. 'We're in real trouble, you and I.'

Thirty-Three

Out of the room and into the hallway, along the hallway and up to the door, out of the door and down the driveway . . . The clown and the Man with the Big Bow Tie were out for a walk.

The drive was tree-lined, so they went down the farther side, only visible now and then. Piper toddled along, holding the clown's hand.

He thought: *I like this clown*.

Past the trees and down towards the gate, out of the gate and into the clown's car, through the town and then beside the ocean . . .

Piper sat bolt upright in the passenger seat, smiling a fat smile, his hands clasping and unclasping in his lap. He leaned out of the window and waved at passers-by.

The clown said, 'Don't do that.' When Piper turned, he saw that the big, red, down-turned mouth had gone, the spots of colour on the cheeks had gone, the arched eyebrows had gone. The hair was no longer an orange porcupine; the nose had lost its red blob.

He said, 'Where's that clown?'

Under Luke Mallen's feet lay a wad of tissues clotted with cold cream and make-up. 'It's me,' he said, 'I'm the fucking clown.'

Ellwood said, 'Where does Carla go when you send her out?'

'She usually walks. She likes to walk by the sea. Don't worry, she won't be back for a while.'

They were in the house that Luke and Carla shared. Piper walked round, inspecting things. The main room had low ceiling beams; a rough oak pillar, square-sectioned and glossy with age, went from floor to cross-beam, partitioning the space. On the other side, Piper found Tom Carey sitting in an armchair.

'You're the priest,' he said. Carey looked at him, but didn't reply. 'I'm the Great Anarch,' Piper said conversationally, 'I order the spheres as they dance in the vault of space.'

Ellwood tapped the barrel of a syringe and pumped a little jet of sodium pentothal into the air. Almost inaudibly, he said, 'For my money, you're the Great Pain in the Ass.'

Carey led Piper back into the other half of the room, but the old man seemed to have other things to do. He pulled away and began to wander towards the stairs. When Carey grabbed his arm, Piper wrenched it away. Luke went over. Between them, they trapped Piper's arms and brought him back to where Ellwood was standing close to a couch.

Luke pulled the collar of Piper's jacket down, trying to free the old man's arms of the sleeves, but he shrugged it back into place. Carey was pulling at the lapels. Piper squirmed between them for a moment, fighting to get free, then went limp. Carey stumbled, suddenly having to take half Piper's weight, and he fell on to the couch taking Piper with him. Luke wrestled one arm out of a sleeve and went after the cuff button. Piper wagged his hand up and down like a broken automaton.

Ellwood handed the syringe to Luke. He leaned down and took Piper by the shirtfront, hauling him upright then turning the man and running him backwards across the room. Piper slammed into the oak pillar; in the same moment, Ellwood hit him backhanded. Piper screamed, then he began to cry. Still holding the old man's shirtfront, Ellwood yanked him back to the couch and threw him full length. Piper lay there; he was sobbing and his eyes were full of fear. Ellwood unfastened the shirtsleeve button and laid Piper's arm bare for the needle.

He picked up the syringe and tested it again, speaking softly, gently almost, head turned away, his concentration reserved for the task in hand: '. . . fuck with *this* old creep. Forget it.'

Ellwood asked a lot of questions; Piper told him a great deal about how the universe was ordered by the laws of music.

'You've got about another fifteen minutes,' Luke said. 'After that, they might start to wonder where he is.'

Tom Carey found some brandy and gave himself a double. There was a coldness about the house that showed it for what it was – a rental for two people whose life together had hardly begun. He noticed how bare the room was of the bits and pieces that usually make two lives one life; but Carla had tried to compensate for that with a beachcomber's finds: little groups of pebbles and shells on the windowsills, a fan of dried marram in a vase, a gnarled limb of driftwood that she had smoothed and varnished. It made him unspeakably sad.

Ellwood and Luke were crouched over Piper as he told them about the slow, magical dance of the cosmos.

'Jesus *fuck*,' Ellwood said. 'You'd better take the old bastard back.' His eyes were glittering with anger and he seemed to be about to throw a punch.

Piper allowed himself to be threaded back into his jacket. He said, 'Janus was the guardian of doorways. Janus was double-faced. The doors of his temple were open in times of war, closed in times of peace. A pretty good pun, we thought, to call it Janus. Three men in each country, the classic triangle: one visible agent, one in support, one underground. Three Insiders, each of them double-faced, each looking both ways.'

Ellwood said, 'And what about you? Were you double-faced? Did you betray them? Did you – years ago? What were their names?'

Piper looked at Luke for a long time as if trying to find a face behind the face.

Ellwood put his mouth close to the old man's ear and whispered, showing his teeth. 'What were their names?'

'Where's that clown?' Piper asked. His face had closed down; it was the only thing he would say.

Piper sat in his room and counted birds as they passed the high window. They all seemed to be choughs, black smudges against a dappled sky; bad omens.

You don't know who I am. You don't know what I know.

He felt sick: the after-effect of the drug, and his face throbbed where Ellwood had hit him.

Janus guarded the doors. Sometimes the doors were open, sometimes they were locked.

Dr Harris arrived for an afternoon session and found his patient strangely silent. He sat with Sir Harold for a while, but they exchanged few words.

Janus was double-faced.

Dr Harris said, 'I'll call in to see you tomorrow, OK?' He added, 'Have you been looking at birds? Did that tell you anything? Have you been looking at cloud-shapes?'

Sir Harold sat still, his eyes turned away from the window, his head full of old dreams. Dr Harris left, closing the door softly as if anxious not to wake a sleeping child.

Piper saw more choughs and, later, a skein of crows; only black birds. He saw a cloud shaped like a man's fist. A tear sprang up in his eye and meandered across his cheek.

He said, 'I don't like that clown.'

It was warm in the city, but you couldn't see the sun; it hung somewhere behind a sky pale as a cataract.

Sophie said, 'I'm fucked out, Pascoe. I've fucked all I can; I can't fuck any more.'

He was coming into the bedroom with mugs of coffee. They hadn't bothered to get up to eat. The things they had grazed on lay around the bed – the remnants of a baguette, some salami, tomatoes, a pot of cottage cheese, a big wooden bowl of fruit. Sophie had brought them with her the previous night. An empty bottle of wine and a bottle half full of mineral water stood on a cabinet.

There were grapes crushed into the sheet, some rolling loose; another popped as Sophie rolled over in a parody of sexual refusal. When she turned back, the crushed grape was stuck to her belly and sending a thread of juice into the crease of her thigh. Pascoe leaned forward and tongued the grape up.

'I've told you,' she said, 'I'm out of fucks. This is a fuck-free zone.'

He grinned: 'Thank God for that.'

She took her coffee from him and shifted across the bed to give him room to lie down. 'Now you know it's Luke, what will you do?'

'Not sure.' He sipped his coffee and hissed because it scalded his lip.

'If you go back,' she said, 'you go without me.'

Pascoe nodded. 'OK.' Then: 'Will you be here when I get back? If I go . . .'

'It looks that way, doesn't it?'

Pascoe wanted to ask questions about the man Rob Thomas had seen visiting her. The man who'd stayed the night.

'Luke and Lori . . .' Sophie's eyes were half closed as she sought the memory. 'Was he more to blame than the rest of us, do you think?'

'No.'

'No, I'm sure you're right.'

Luke screwing the Colonel's wife; what a joke, what a jape. And then the phone calls; what a ruse. They had passed the phone from hand to hand, listening to Lori's terrified silence; and they would take it in turn to say, *'We know everything; we know all about you.'*

On a few occasions, they had driven to the lane, made the call on the public phone, then hurried through the wood to watch the house. Sometimes they'd seen her, other times not, but it was always more exciting to be that close.

Sophie's eyes were tight shut. She saw the call-box and the members of the group crowding in, the phone going round. The colours were bright, the sounds distant and oddly distorted. The drug wafted round her and the airwaves brushed against her like a cat. Time telescoped strangely – they were in the lane, in the wood, opposite the house. Sophie was in the branches of a tree eating an apple while she watched Lori going from window to window like someone trying to escape from a fire.

Sophie concentrated on the sweetness of the apple and by the time she had gathered drops of juice along her tongue, Lori was below her, lying on the turf and crying because she had fallen in the near-dark. She sat up and put her hand to her mouth: the gesture of someone gobbling peanuts. A few of the pills slipped from her palm to the ground.

She stood up, cheeks bulging, and started to tear off her clothes, walking in a ragged circle as if invoking the spirits of the place.

It was when she was fully naked that Sophie saw the line round her neck, just a piece of thin cord. When she looked down again, Lori was climbing the tree.

Pascoe tried to keep his voice light. 'I couldn't get in touch with you; always your answerphone . . . So I put Rob Thomas on the case. He let me know you were all right. He saw your visitor.'

Sophie didn't respond. She had turned away from him and he wondered whether she might have dozed off.

'Someone who stayed the night. Or so Rob said. I guess he must have seen him go in sometime late, and come out the next morning.' Pascoe tried a laugh. 'Rob's nothing if not thorough.'

He leaned over, bridging her body with an arm, wondering whether she was asleep, and saw that tears were sluicing her face.

Although Lori was climbing, acid tricked the moment and Sophie imagined that she could see the other woman floating slowly towards her. She expected to find Lori's head swimming into focus, close to her own, like a pale balloon and looked away in order to avoid that confrontation. When she looked back, Lori was standing on a thick branch nearby, the line tied off near her feet, the noose dark against her skin like a piece of primitive jewellery. She was making a tiny, repetitive sound, a little *mew*, as if in response to a lover's touch.

When she jumped, the leaves on the branch rustled and shook. Sophie looked down and saw Lori swing out, then back, then into view again. Her legs were pumping and her fingers were wild at her throat.

Pascoe said, 'It doesn't matter. Don't tell me about it. I don't need to know.' He put his arms round Sophie in the hope that she would turn to him.

She said, 'It isn't that,' but the words were muffled and all he caught was her tone of voice, thick with distress and remorse.

The curtain stirred and a smell of the city slipped in past the half-open window – acrid, high-octane, with a touch of rot.

They stood round in a ring long after she'd come to rest, after her legs had stopped wagging, after her fingers had stopped tugging. She hung still, a totem at the centre of their circle, suddenly powerful in death.

The drug cleared from Sophie's head like a dream dispersing. She backed off, then turned and ran through the wood. Someone called her name. Was it Pascoe? Then she heard all of them, crashing through brush and low branches as they followed her towards the road.

She turned and put an arm round Pascoe's neck, as if he

might be in need of comfort. 'Not that,' she said, 'I was thinking about Lori.'

'It's time to stop,' Pascoe said. 'We didn't mean it to happen.'

She nodded, as if she knew he was right but doubted whether forgiveness was possible. After a moment, she sat up in the cluttered bed and regarded him in mock-annoyance. 'You had me watched; your *dick* followed me around.'

'He watched the house. I was worried about you, I wanted to be sure you were all right.'

'It was my husband. We talked a bit; it got late so he slept in the house. But not with me. Next morning he went away.'

'What did he want?'

'His gun.'

Pascoe said, 'I wondered where you got it.'

'That's where.' She smiled, leaving him guessing for a moment, then added: 'He's a politician: Northern Ireland Office.'

'House-sweeps on a regular basis, mirrors under the car each morning, a discreet bodyguard and,' Pascoe added, 'a gun.'

'He's on their list; not high, but he's there.'

'How did you get it?'

'I went to see him one evening and asked to borrow it.'

'He handed it over?'

'Yes.'

'Why would he do that?'

'We're divorcing. I'm being nice about it. Apart from other things, I'm not bringing into court the fact that he liked to beat me. One time, he cut me.' Pascoe saw her hand go towards the puckered scar on the underside of her breast. 'I told him I needed the gun to feel safe – just the same reason he needs it.'

Pascoe watched her as she went through to the bathroom. When the phone rang, he answered it but kept his eyes on Sophie.

'Sam?' It was Roxborough, drunk and elated.

Sophie stepped into the shower through a billow of steam, her body a blur that trickled across the frosted glass.

'Sam, listen Sam, we won.' Roxborough's words clattered against one another. 'That old woman did the business, word-perfect, she was *perfect*, the jury took one look at that little old lady and he was off the hook, she never made a slip. Oh Jesus, Sam, she was everybody's Aunt Jemima, if she'd turned up with her hair in a bun and flour on her apron she couldn't have made them love her more, Jesus, Sam, we're not guilty. We're not guilty, Sam.'

'That's great, George.' Pascoe lowered the phone on Roxborough's jubilation and set it gently back on to its cradle. Very quietly, he said: 'That's great.' He went and stood by the shower and watched Sophie in soft-focus shampooing her hair then turning her face to the shower-head.

He said, 'I'll have to go back.' The foggy shape behind the glass stood still and didn't speak. 'To Longrock . . .' Pascoe raised his voice. 'I'll go in the morning.'

The shower door slid back and Sophie's head emerged. 'I thought you would.' Her arm appeared, fist clenched, as she offered some hidden trophy. 'I just found this,' she said. 'Buried treasure; and I think I know how it got there.'

He opened his palm and she let the object go. A grape.

Thirty-Four

Next afternoon, they drove across two zones and parked close to the river. Sophie said, 'I thought you'd go this morning. I thought you might be gone when I woke up.'

'Tomorrow,' he said, 'maybe the day after.'

'What are you waiting for?'

'I don't know.' They crossed a bridge and came down steps to the water's edge. 'Yes I do – I want more of us.'

She had kissed the corner of his mouth while he slept. She'd whispered, 'We're in real trouble . . .'

There was dust on the leaves of the riverside bushes. Their toecaps turned little scoops of dust as they walked.

There's only one way to do this, Sophie thought. She waited for a pleasure-craft to go by, so there was no chance that its engines would drown her voice.

'We're in trouble,' she said, 'I'm pregnant.'

Beside the ocean, then climbing a narrow road towards woods – the clown and the Man with the Big Bow Tie were out for a drive. Luke Mallen brought the car to a ragged stop in the parking circle, then wrestled Piper out of the passenger door. They went up the track with Piper dragging his heels like a recalcitrant child.

In the house, Ellwood took the old man by the shirtfront and pulled him round in a circle, then round again, as if they were playing a manic version of Ring o' Roses. Piper leaned backwards, staggering, and watched the room revolve until his brain seemed to hum with the motion. Ellwood spun him a dozen more times, then released him on to the sofa. He lay there inert, as the room whirled past and Ellwood slipped the needle into his arm.

Ellwood said, 'I know about Janus. I know how that worked. What I want to know is: who did you tell? Who were you working for? Who did you speak to?'

'Janus,' Piper said. 'Janus was the guardian of doorways. Janus was two-faced.'

Tom Carey turned away. Under his breath he said, 'I've had enough of this.' He went through to the kitchen to look for the brandy bottle. 'I've had more of this than I can take.'

Pascoe was laughing, or else he was crying. He had walked away from Sophie and now she lengthened her stride to catch him up. He turned to face her, shaking his head, and she still wasn't sure what his expression meant. He put a hand to his mouth. 'I don't know what to say.'

'Try the stock responses: Are you sure? Is it mine? How could you be so stupid? That's generally how it goes.'

'You've done this before.'

'But I've never had a child.' A cargo boat went past, sending lick after lick of backwash against the bank. 'I couldn't see what that was – tears or laughter.'

'Both,' he said. 'Didn't it seem that way to you?'

'What do you want to do?'

'Christ knows,' Pascoe said. 'What's your plan?'

They walked on in silence for a while. She said, 'I'm not making any plans.'

Dr Harris sat and watched while Sir Harold Piper rocked slowly to and fro. There were tears on the old man's face and his mouth was drawn up in a silent parody of a grin. Harris knew that something had happened but he couldn't for the life of him think what it might be.

'Janus . . .' In Piper's mouth the words distorted so much that Harris could understand no more than one in five. 'Janus is the guardian of doorways. Janus is two-faced.' He rocked and rocked, arms wrapped round, head bowed. 'I told no-one; I didn't tell anyone anything. Leave me alone.'

Harris understood that. He said, 'I'm here to help. What can I do to help?'

Piper said, 'Keep that clown away.' His voice was a thin whine, like a broken engine. Harris struggled to separate the words, but all he could hear was Piper's anguished keening. 'Keep that clown away. Away from me. Keep him away. *I don't like that clown.*'

Pascoe peered at the drink before putting the glass to his lips, as if drinking it at all was a risky thing. It was a single malt whisky: nutty and rich, but with a sharp tang underneath.

'Drink it,' Sophie said. 'Get drunk. Do the bottle.'

'I've thought of that.'

'I'm sorry . . .' She smiled: 'I hadn't said sorry yet, had I?'

Pascoe squinted through the faceted glass and warm amber lights flooded his eye.

'What can you see?' Sophie asked. 'In your crystal ball?'

'The past.'

'What does it look like?'

'It's a great crowd of people,' he said, 'all saying sorry, sorry, sorry . . .'

Thirty-Five

When Susan Hart arrived in Longrock, the first person she saw was Luke Mallen. She had given herself two days, no more, and it was as if her urgency had crowded the place with chances.

The agency nurse had folded her arms and smiled the smile of someone competent and in control. Susan's husband had stared at her bleakly from the bed, already certain of her betrayal.

'What's his name?'

Susan had been taking a few items of clothing from a chest of drawers to a suitcase open on the bed. She said, 'There's no-one. It's business. I've told you that.'

'I'll be dead in less than a year. You could wait till then.'

'It's business. There's no-one else.'

There had been a terrible fragrance in the air that she'd noticed before, as if the mad cells in his lungs were blossoming, scarlet and fleshy, like poisonous hothouse orchids.

'There's no-one . . .' When she'd closed the case he had sunk back on the pillow, a thin smile on his face, his lips tinged with yellow. He had seen the lie, but was nowhere near the truth.

Two days – she would give herself that long to see him again. *I only ever loved Luke.* When she'd said that to Pascoe she'd realized it was true. Nick Howard dead; Marianne, too, if Sam Pascoe's guess was right. Luke was drawing them all in, drawing them back, drawing her . . . Unfinished business.

And then, when she looked out from the window of her room in the Palings Hotel, there he was, a star performer

312

modest amid the crowd, the Great Zeno, walking past with his twin, Luke Mallen. He was wearing a navy sweater and a light-coloured shirt and blue jeans, and her heart lurched because time shrank to the moment when she had finally walked away from him, one autumn morning, early, with their love already an awful deadweight in her memory.

She ran downstairs, circling the lift-shaft, certain that he'd be gone, but when she emerged into the street, he seemed to have moved only a few yards, walking slowly, his head bowed. There was a moment when she almost called to him, but instead she dropped back and followed. He didn't go far; his car was parked outside the double gates of a boatyard. Susan thought: Now I've lost him; but he sat behind the wheel without starting the engine. He might have been waiting for someone. She walked rapidly back to the hotel and collected her car from the parking area, then drove back and parked a few cars' lengths from the boatyard. She could see that Luke was still motionless in the driver's seat.

The sky was slate-grey and a cool breeze came off the sea. A perfect day for fishing, but Luke hadn't been able to find Tom Carey at the usual places. It made him edgy. Everyone had gone missing: Carey, Sam Pascoe, Sophie Lanner. He felt that things were loosening and slipping from his grasp.

He had seen the fear and disgust in Carey's eyes when Ellwood roughed-up the old man, when he pushed the needle in. By the time Ellwood had done with Piper, got as much as he could in the time they dared allow, Carey had gone. They found a brandy glass in the kitchen and the door open. Luke wanted to find the priest and say, 'Don't do anything risky, don't fuck up. It's not just your life, it's not just your future.'

When he started the car, Susan eased out to follow. They went up on to the cliff road, then turned inland, driving between wooded banks. She was anxious to keep a distance between them, though there was no reason why

Luke should guess he was being followed, much less who was following. When he turned off at a small junction taking a no-through road, she stopped and watched him out of sight. She let five minutes pass, then followed slowly.

His car was in the turning circle. Immediately, she backed up until she got to the junction and found a gateway to park in, then returned to his car on foot. The track was the only option.

It was like watching a clumsy remake of an old movie. Susan stood among tree-cover and watched a woman go from window to window – she was taking Lori's role. Susan clasped her hands because she was trembling, but the tension in her locked fingers only made her shake the more. Luke came into view and put his arms round the woman; he smoothed her hair with one hand, then gave it a little tug – reassurance, a reminder: *I love you*. Susan felt the gesture as if it had barely lapsed – felt his hand on the nape of her neck, the gentle pull that turned her face up to his – and she cried out, almost as if she hoped to be heard.

He said, 'I have to go out again. I'm sorry; I won't be long.'

'It's OK.' Carla smiled in a way that meant: I don't ask about your affairs, I don't need to know. I trust you. Make me safe.

He was taking risks with Piper. He had lost Pascoe and Sophie. He couldn't find Tom Carey. Only Marianne and Nick were safely out of his life. He pulled Carla into his arms and closed his eyes, feeling a vast, directionless violence, as if his task were to kill everyone in the world and the problem was how to start.

Susan saw him come out of the door and start back down the track, anger and anxiety making him push his pace. It was impossible to follow on the track without being noticed. She heard his car start up and drive away. When she looked back towards the house, Carla's face was

314

at the window, peering out like a sailor's wife watching for masts at the quayside.

Luke drove to the Windrush and went to Ellwood's room. He sat on the edge of a chair, eager to be away. 'I looked in the likely places; he could be anywhere.'

'The headland where he goes to fish?'

'Yes.'

'The church?'

'Yes, of course.'

'Well,' Ellwood said, 'he hasn't checked out. He hasn't left without saying goodbye.'

'He could have just taken off.'

'I don't think so. Unpaid bills make trouble.'

Luke said, 'I'm going too. I can't stay here much longer.'

'Yes you can. You can stay as long as I like.'

'No,' Luke shook his head, 'you don't understand. I have to go soon.' He spoke almost offhandedly, making it clear that Ellwood had little or no say in the matter. It was a private thing.

Ellwood walked over to where Luke was sitting and crouched down in front of the chair. He smiled – preparing to explain a simple fact to an even simpler person. 'There's a job to be done,' he said. 'It's almost over. We're behind schedule, but we're getting there. You're a part of that – part of the solution to a problem I badly need to solve, and I need you, and you're going to stay here until we're finished, and you're going to do what I tell you to do. Now,' – Ellwood shifted slightly on his heels, finding a more comfortable position – 'let me tell you why. Because I know a great deal about you and about your past. I know about Lori; I know about a lot of other things. I know that you killed two people. I know that you're in love with someone and I know exactly how to fuck all that up. Yes? Fuck it *up*. And I will. That's just what I'll do. You think you can be safe by getting rid of a few hippy revolutionaries you used to know? You stupid bastard. There's me. *Me*. And there's all the people I

315

know, the people I work for, the people who work for me. I'll throw you to the fucking wolves – are you listening, you stupid fuck? – and there'll be nothing left of you but a pile of shit and a hank of hair. And if I feel like it, I won't just screw up your life with that stupid, lame bitch, I'll make her part of the deal. How would that be? You in jail, Carla in jail, you think I can't do this? I can. It's easy. Or how about kill you, and leave her stranded? Or kill her and let you go? I don't care; any will do. I'll make my mind up at the time.'

Ellwood straightened up and backed off. Luke seemed not to be breathing; he didn't blink. Ellwood said, 'So just stick around for a little longer, yeah? That would be nice. I'd like that. OK? I think that would be best.'

Luke stood outside his own front door and read the note that Susan had left under the door-knocker, telling him that she was staying at the Palings Hotel. At the end of the note, she had written: *Don't be afraid.*

He imagined the moment and fear overwhelmed him – Carla on one side of the door, Susan on the other. Suddenly, everything Ellwood had said stood on the threshold.

Thirty-Six

Wallace Ellwood sat on a lip of rock above the path that led to Meer's Point and waited for Tom Carey to appear. First a drive, he thought, headed anywhere, fooling himself into thinking he might simply keep going. Then he'll turn round. Then he'll come here.

A great flood of anger washed through Ellwood. He half closed his eyes, deliberately losing focus until the sea was a vast grey void. He needed to solve the puzzle that was Harold Piper. He needed success, a clean slate, because that would give him freedom to do much as he chose; and that freedom was everything in life to Wallace Ellwood. It put him in the forefront at the Department. Given time, it would put him in line for Hilary Todd's job. Most important of all, it put him beyond the law.

Above all else, Ellwood hated weakness. He exploited it where he found it; he fed off it like a predator. Love was weakness, compassion was weakness, attachments were weakness; forgiveness, guilt, generosity, mercy – all weakness. He thought of Carey and fury bubbled up in him again like black lava.

As if summoned by that anger, Tom Carey rounded a bend in the path, rod in hand. He passed under the rock where Ellwood was sitting and went down to the narrow spit where he always stood to fish. Ellwood stayed still for a while, letting the priest set up his tackle and make a couple of casts, then he slithered down to the path.

The light was going and the sea was calm. The surface of the water had a slick, glassy look about it and Carey's cast disappeared with barely a splash.

Without looking round, he said: 'It's the end for me,

Wallace. Twenty years late, or more; but now it's the end.'

Ellwood felt light-headed with tension; his anger ramrodded each limb with a wild energy. 'Just behave, Father Tom,' he said, 'just be good.' His face was rigid, his mouth partly open, lips stiff. Carey couldn't tell what had been said; the words were spoken far back in Ellwood's throat and seemed to gush from his mouth and nose like a great gulp of water swallowed too hastily. He turned and saw Ellwood's face gnarled and dark with rage.

'What will you threaten me with, Wallace? What can you blackmail me with – now that I don't care?' He reeled in and prepared for another cast, seeming absorbed by his task.

For a moment, Ellwood was half blind. He shouted something, though he couldn't tell what it was. Carey swung the rod out for a cast, and Ellwood tore it from his grip, then stepped back and lashed at the priest, holding the rod two-handed, bellowing with outrage. The carbon pole cracked across Carey's brow, opening a gash. Twelve inches of weighted line hung from the tip, ready to feed the cast; it wrapped round his face like a bolus, sending the big hook shank-deep under his cheek-bone, close to the nose. He turned away, dancing with pain, both hands to his face. Ellwood yanked the rod back for another blow and the barb tore a strip of meat out of Carey's face from nose to eye.

Ellwood couldn't tell what damage he was doing, and couldn't stop doing it. Carey had covered his face, but blood was pouring through his closed fingers. The rod lashed him repeatedly, cutting his neck, his scalp, his jaw. He lost his footing as he backed away and went down heavily. Instinct caused him to put out both hands in an attempt to break the fall, and Ellwood was on him, the rod flailing, blood rising from Carey's face in a thick mist of spray, the hook going into his flesh wherever it landed and ripping out again as Ellwood's arms rose and fell, rose and fell.

'Holy Father, Father Tom, you fuck, you fucking Holy

fuck . . .' Ellwood's voice was a klaxon, one note, hoarse and maniacal. His arms flailed faster and faster, like some crazed woodsman trying to fell every tree in the forest.

Carey's face gouted blood, shredding in strips as the rod came at him again and again, the hook trailing and tearing. After a while he simply lay there, numb, half conscious, his hands making hopeless little passes in the air, until Ellwood stopped, suddenly, his arms raised, as if a connection had been broken in some terrible machine. He let the rod drop and stood there breathing hard, Carey between his feet.

The sea came in with a weightless rush and trickled between dry rocks.

That sound, *plashy* . . . And over it another sound that was Carey's breathing. His face was a red mush.

The hook had ripped a great tuft of flesh from his throat. Air sawed in and out with a curious, inhuman noise like a faulty ratchet.

His shoulders moved and bubbles rose from his face. The words were a faint gargle, unknowable.

He was saying, 'I knew you'd think of something I really wanted.'

His head was a wellspring. His eye-sockets were cups, full to the brim.

Ellwood said, 'You fuck. You stupid *fuck*.'

A flight of cormorant went past the tip of the headland, low to the water but sharply silhouetted in the last, lucid moment before true dusk.

Ellwood crouched down alongside the priest and looked this way and that, as if he might be given some notion of what to do next. After a moment, he straightened up and began to strip.

'You stupid *fuck*.'

He wedged his clothes into a gap between boulders above the waterline, then grabbed Carey's feet and pulled him towards the edge. Looking over his shoulder for a second to be sure of his footing, he backed into the water, dragging Carey after him. A dark cloud rose from Carey's head and was swatted away by a wave; it made a little slick that thinned and trailed out to sea. Ellwood stood waist-high in the water as Carey floated free. Wave-motion knocked the slack limbs this way and that. As an afterthought, Ellwood emptied the priest's pockets, then scrambled back on to the rock and pushed Carey's belongings in between the boulders along with his own clothing.

When he returned, he was carrying four good-sized rocks in the crook of his arm. He loaded them into Carey's shirtfront, filling it like a sack. The priest turned turtle and dipped in the water. Just above the spot where Carey had stood to fish was a spread of broom, so close to the edge that it seemed to be rooted in granite. Ellwood made it his landmark. He kicked off, towing his burden like a lifesaver. He knew he wouldn't get far, but hoped to find deep water. Carey bobbed like jetsam, always awkward even though Ellwood was swimming with the tide.

Now there would only be days to finish things. When Carey's body was found, there would be more trouble, more disruption. Apart from anything else, it would be necessary to keep Hilary Todd on a tight rein.

The landline darkened. He kicked hard, clutching Carey's destroyed head, pulp under his hand, the hair wagging like weed. In a farther reach of the bay, the seafront lights came on.

A shearwater skipped the surface almost under his nose and skittered off with a *whip-whip-whip* of wings. The light was so poor, now, that the land and the sea seemed to meld under the blue-black sky. He trod water and realized at once how cold he was. A wave swamped his face and he turned his head away. When he looked back, his landmark had gone.

He turned in the water, panicking for an instant, and Carey's body got away from him. It bobbed off, listing clumsily, then started to sink.

Not yet, Ellwood thought. His arms were stiff from

holding Carey up and his legs were tired. He turned and made a few fast strokes in pursuit, and swam into a current of colder water that snaked across the bay and washed round him.

He felt the cramp come on like iron bars bending in his limbs.

Thirty-Seven

On the table was a light supper, white wine in a cooler, candles in silver candlesticks. Apart from the table and two chairs, the room was bare. Susan Hart stood in the doorway, a hesitant guest.

She said, 'This house is empty; no-one lives here.'

Luke was pouring the wine.

He said, 'A stage is empty: it's just a space, nothing there. Then someone decides on a set to suit the play – someone brings the props and suddenly, there it is' – he waved a hand – 'dinner for two; it's magic.'

Pouring the wine, just as he'd done for Marianne Novaks.

'Is that what this is? A play?' Susan walked into the room but didn't sit down.

'It's a scene from a play. A very long-running play.'

'I got a letter from you,' she said, 'then I talked to Sam Pascoe . . .'

'What do you see when you think about the past? Sit down . . . You might as well sit down, now that you're here.'

Susan sat opposite to him. She took a sip of wine before she'd had time to wonder whether that might be wise. He clapped his hands, delighted by her boldness.

'When I think of the past,' she said, 'I see what I want to see.'

'Is that possible?' He looked at her in wonder. 'Surely that isn't possible.'

Susan felt light, unsubstantial. She said, 'My life is so full of failure, Luke. What does the past matter?' Her words set up a faint echo among the room's bare boards,

322

its scabby walls, its uncovered windows. 'Did you kill Nick and Marianne? Why did you kill them?'

'What I see when I think about the past . . .' He paused; the words were an introduction, a title. He poured more wine; he gestured towards the food like a concerned host. 'I see scenes from a play; I see myself . . .' He put his hands together, palm to palm, then drew them slowly apart. 'Look,' he said.

Something glittered in his hand. Susan bent forward slightly for a better view and saw what it was. Luke clapped his hands again and it disappeared. He reached out and drew the object from Susan's ear, then dropped it on to her plate. A wedding band. It rang on the china briefly, then came to rest.

'When I think about the past,' he said, 'I see us. You and me, and all the rest of us. Nick and Marianne and Sam; Charlie and Sophie.'

'Lori,' Susan said.

The wine was making her heady, but she let him refill her glass. She thought: I must be here because it doesn't matter to me much whether I live or die.

'Why did you come?' He might have been reading her mind.

She answered with a question. 'Why are you here?'

He said, 'One place is as good as another. The past is everywhere; it makes no difference.'

'I came because of the past,' Susan told him. 'You're right.'

Luke steepled his hands again. 'Marianne talked about Lori. It was something she couldn't forgive – couldn't forgive herself. There's a way the past can become the present, you know? A way it can spoil the future. That's what Marianne wanted. She wanted to tell about everything. She said she had bad dreams all the time.' He parted his hands an inch or so, and another glittering thing was there. A lockpick, his own invention, something that could be easily concealed during an escape routine; it telescoped – a little spring-loaded spike.

Susan watched the steel as it unfurled between his hands. 'And are you going to kill me, Luke?' She raised her glass and sipped, as if that were an act so casual, so ordinary, that death couldn't possibly accompany it.

'I don't know,' he said. 'I ought to.'

The last of the light was flowing into the horizon. Wallace Ellwood was out to sea, drifting like a rudderless boat. He had turned on to his back and was sculling slowly with his forearms, face-up to the evening sky, the chill spreading in his limbs, spreading up under his ribcage, spreading behind his eyes. He had been making progress that way for almost an hour. The faint glow on the skyline gave him some guidance, but apart from that, he couldn't tell whether he was moving towards the shore, or across the bay, or just circling endlessly.

It never once occurred to him that he might die.

He thought: It's win or lose, now; unravel things – move swiftly – a straight line.

A tiny wave broke on the crown of his head and swamped his face.

Get the truth from Piper, make the best use of it, then unload a few unnecessary encumbrances.

He kept pedalling his legs, bending them at the knee then pushing away; he kept scooping water with his arms. The coldness was creeping through him, atom by atom, like frost forming on stone.

He bore a line of cramp across his shoulders, thick as a yoke.

Susan watched her wineglass as Luke filled it. She seemed to see the splash and curl of the liquid as an image of whirlpools. Behind the glass as it filled was Luke's magnified smile.

She said, 'There's something wrong with the wine.'

'What?' He handed her the glass and she drank.

'Something wrong – something in it.'

324

'There's nothing wrong with the wine,' he told her. 'You're doing that yourself.'

'Am I?'

'It's tension,' he said. 'Tension and fear.'

Susan picked up the wedding ring – Luke's ring – and slipped it on to her finger. 'When we were together, when we were married, I used to dream of an ordinary life.'

'What was it like?' He had retracted the lockpick, but held it still in his hand.

'Ordinary; day to day; uneventful. Nothing strange happened, nothing risky, nothing to make me unhappy or break my sleep.'

'Is that how you live now?'

'I thought I could. I married someone to get that life. It was like putting together a jigsaw.' For a moment, she wasn't sure of what she'd just said. It seemed to Susan that she must be terribly drunk or terribly tired. She asked, 'What was that?' as if she'd just failed to catch some remark that Luke had made.

'Jigsaw . . .'

'Yes . . . all the pieces in place, one by one by one. A house not in the city but not quite in the country either – safe, you see. Safe things going on in my life. That was the idea.' She drank some more wine; the food sat on their plates untouched. 'But there isn't a life like that; it doesn't exist. All those domestic things, those ordinary things, they're strangest of all – more dangerous. And one day – it's an ordinary day – he comes home in the usual way and says, "I'm dying; I'll be dead in a year or so." And you think . . .' Susan paused, as if the moment had happened only yesterday and she was still finding out how she felt, '. . . you think: How strange, how commonplace, how dangerous. You think: I wish I could care. You think: Does anyone know who I am?'

She found a little space on the table and rested her head.

He seemed to have come to the deep, still centre of the sea: a place where you felt nothing, where you saw nothing except the coal-black atoms that danced before your face and knitted up the dark.

A wave slapped the back of his neck, first throwing him upwards then drawing him down, and he slid beneath the surface like a waterlogged spar. Ellwood gritted his teeth against the weight of water, trying furiously to work his arms and legs against the deadlock of cramp. He surfaced, briefly, but the swell rolled him over and drove him down again before he'd even had time to draw breath. He turned in the current, head singing, a knot of fire flaring in his chest. He felt as if he were being fished.

'You were right,' Luke said, 'there's something in the wine.'

Susan didn't hear him. She slept like a drunk, head on the table, one arm alongside her face, the other hanging straight from the shoulder. Each indrawn breath was a little throaty snore.

Luke got up and walked round the table. He put out a hand and drew Susan's hair away from the side of her face. Her cheek bore a faint blush.

'The others were different,' he said. 'I couldn't look at you and kill you' – he clapped his hands – 'just like that.'

Ellwood surfaced and sank, surfaced and sank. Below the water was silence and blindness; above was all frenzy and wild, all effort. He had managed one gulp of air, no more. Now his mouth was stretched in a mad parody of a cartoon character's grin – lips wide, teeth clamped – as he fought against the terrible urge to breathe.

He rolled and rolled, not knowing which way was up. The ocean was a vast black room, no floor, no rafters, nothing beyond. Then his shoulders rapped against granite, scoring the flesh, and he was bounced upright. The jolt rattled his ribs and he breathed in at the same moment as his head crashed through the surface, like a seal in the surf.

He roared and roared, waist-high in the shallows,

pushed this way and that by the breakers, his head lofted, air piling into his lungs, as he fought his way towards the granite rockpile.

He found it and clung there for a while, then pushed clear and knelt among the waves, head lowered. After a moment, he waded ashore and sat down. He was on the southern side of the narrow spit of Meer's Point, no more than a hundred yards from the place where he'd killed Tom Carey.

The table was bare again, as if there had never been good food and wine. The room was silent, as if there had never been conversation between old friends. The window was dark, as if there had never been candle-light.

Susan's head lay where she had rested it, one arm curled round, the other hanging so that her fingertips brushed the floorboards.

Carla heard Luke come into the house, and went to meet him, just as she always did.

He folded her into his arms; she could feel the tension singing inside him, as iron sings when it's brought to a white heat. He said, 'A couple of days, that's all. One way or another, a couple of days. Then we're gone; then we're out of here.'

Carla put her arms round his waist, one hand lifted to clap his back, as a mother does to a child; and held him so closely that the deep tremor of his sobbing ran through them both.

Once he had found his clothes and put them on, Ellwood stood up to massage his arms and legs, rubbing and slapping to get the feeling back and loosen the knotted muscles. He stuffed Carey's belongings inside his shirt. His fingers were numb and he had trouble fastening the buttons. He wagged his hands like flippers, feeling a fire of sensation stealing back; it hurt like hell, but he kept going – kneading, chafing, running on the spot.

Only now that he was safe did he feel a little black jet of fear rising in his chest, a gobbet of bile that filled his mouth, washing his teeth in acid. He turned his head and spat, then buckled and retched up a thin stream of vomit.

'Father Tom,' he said, 'Father fucking Tom, you fuck, you Holy *fuck*.'

He put out a hand and leaned against an outcrop of rock, head bowed, his torso thrust forward, and let go two more jets of puke.

'I wish you weren't dead, Father Tom, you fuck, I wish you were still alive, because I'd like to kill you again, you fuck, I'd like to be starting now, starting to kill you *now*, starting *now*, holy Father Tom, you *fuck*, I'd like to be killing you *now*.'

Steel-grey light at the windows, opaque at first, then each pane slowly clarifying as if the dawn were melting frost from the glass.

The light got into corners, casting shadows on the bare boards.

Susan's arm lay close to her head. Luke's wedding ring was on the table, close to her hand, and her eyes were wide open, like the eyes of someone who has just woken up.

'Thank you,' she said. Her fist closed round the ring. 'Thank you.'

When she got to her feet there was no strength in her legs to hold her. She grabbed the chairback, her head thick with drugged sleep, then lowered herself to the floor and sat there cross-legged.

In one corner, a pine cabinet. Dust motes climbing and falling, now, in sudden shafts of sunlight. By the door, dark stains on the wall and the floor.

She wondered who would buy this house, moving in with their everyday things, their everyday lives.

Whoever you are, she thought, we'll be your ghosts: old loves, old crimes; we'll never go away.

Thirty-Eight

She checked out of the Palings and drove away from Longrock with the windows open and the early morning sun strong on her face. After a hundred miles or so, she came off the motorway to pick up fuel and drink a cup of coffee. She phoned Pascoe from there.

'The house is up in the woods. Come out of the town on the coast road, then find a no-through road on the right that ends in a turning circle. From there, a track.'

'What did he say?' Pascoe asked.

'He talked about the past. Listen, Sam, that's all. I went there to lay a ghost. It didn't work. That's all from me.'

She told Pascoe about the house and the woman she had seen there; she told a little of her meeting with Luke; the rest she kept for herself. Then she went back to her car and sat there for a while. She wound the window down and watched her own reflection disappear. It reminded her again of the woman who had drifted from window to window waiting for Luke – her unadorned face, the limp that made one shoulder dip as she hurried to meet him.

Susan thought, Maybe you love him, whoever you are. Who knows? Maybe you're lucky.

Pascoe said, 'You won't wait here?'

'You're kidding.' Sophie was already getting her things together.

'But you will wait . . .'

'I'll go back to my own place. It's closer to the DMZ – I can go out during the day and sustain only flesh wounds.'

'But you will be waiting.'

'Anxious?' she asked. 'You sound really anxious.'

329

'I just need to know. Nothing more than that. My life won't support any more uncertainties.'

'I'll be there.' She found an envelope in her bag and wrote something on the back, then handed it over.

'What's this?'

'Mobile phone – no answering machine on this.'

'OK. How's baby this morning?'

'Don't be coy,' she said, 'it doesn't suit you.' But she put an involuntary hand to her belly, as if checking for signs of life.

'Not coy,' he told her. 'I've never done it before; I don't know the vocabulary. The child; the foetus; the little visitor . . .'

She laughed. 'It's not important.' After a moment, she said: 'Take care of yourself.' She went to the window and watched him into the street, then into his car, then out of sight. A taxi was on its way to take her home.

The sky was grey and came all the way down to the ground. Although it was only ten in the morning, the temperature sat in the high seventies. Sophie shook the collar of her blouse to make a little breeze, but didn't think of opening the window. Four boys, drunk to the wide, started a mock fight down by the park railings. A woman went by pushing a child in a buggy and they yelled at her, grabbing their crotches and grinding their hips. As an afterthought, one of them threw a beercan at the buggy.

Sophie went into the bedroom. Earlier that morning, she had piled the bedsheets in a corner of the room; a sweet aroma of grapes still clung to them. Street-noise wafted through to her. This is a two-note city, she thought. All you ever hear are bass-lines and sirens, sirens and bass-lines.

It occurred to her that what Pascoe had said earlier wasn't at all coy; in fact, the more she thought about it, the more carefully judged it seemed to be.

How's baby?

Not your baby, not our baby, certainly not my baby. Just baby.

Pascoe arrived in Longrock at four in the afternoon. He took Susan Hart's directions and found the no-through road and the turning circle and the track. He thought what Susan had thought: *The parking place close to Lori's house. The track through the woods.* He watched the house for ten minutes or more, but saw no sign of movement so he simply went to the door and knocked. No-one was there. He circled the house, looking in, and saw nothing but the bits and pieces of ordinary living.

Dishes stacked in the sink. Coats on hooks in the hallway. In the living room, a forgotten glass half-full of wine. Someone had arranged a scatter of sea-shore pebbles on a low trunk, trying for a random pattern to make it look as though they had been cast like dice. Each room lay in stillness, the air unstirred by breathing. A terrible pause, he thought; the moment before the accident.

Going from window to window, he could see traces of the woman Susan had told him about, but Luke Mallen was a ghost in the place – nothing of him to be found; except, in all that stillness, a sense of violence.

Thirty-Nine

He showed an empty hand, then made a fist. Out of the fist he drew two silk scarves, a red one followed by a blue. He threw the scarves up and clapped his hands. A dove sat on his wrist. From the trunk he took a small lacquered box and removed a sliding panel at the front to show that it was empty.

Sir Harold Piper watched warily. *So long as that clown doesn't come on. I don't like that clown.*

The dove went into the box; the little panel slid shut. Zeno took six daggers from the trunk and threw them one by one at a target board to show that they weren't fakes. The lacquered box had slots in the left side and the right.

There was an air of tension in the room, as if Piper's fear was contagious. Mac the Cough went *hek-hek-hek*; Dog Face blotted her lipstick on her sleeve, leaving tiny kisses there. Birdie gave an owlet's screech; he could hear the dove's wings flickering on the lacquer.

Zeno drove the daggers through one by one. Part of the trick was a glassine bulb of cochineal, palmed then crushed against the bottom of the box. When they saw the redness trickling off the heel of his hand, little screams and cries welled· up in the audience. One of the nurses looked at Zeno, trying to catch his eye. The whole room stirred.

Zeno yanked the daggers out, then slapped the sides of the box to make it collapse – six sides, flat in a pile. He threw them into the air and they fell as a glittering cloud, silver and gold, with the dove erupting from it like a sudden shout.

*　　*　　*

Carla could raise her head, but that was about all. Her arms were spread and tied to each side of the bedrail. With her legs held close together, she made the letter Y. Wallace Ellwood was amused by the way she had clamped her thighs together. He stood close to the end of the bed, undressing himself slowly; he might have been thinking of something else entirely. Carla was still wearing jeans and a shirt, though Ellwood had pulled off her sneakers and her socks, as if anxious not to soil the bedcover.

He removed his shirt and draped it over a chair. 'I'm glad you decided to come and see me,' he said. 'All in all, I've had a lousy couple of days – disloyalty in a colleague, plans going awry . . . It sounds like an unfavourable horoscope, doesn't it? And I'm feeling badly in need of a little relaxation. It's something we find in our lives all too infrequently, don't you think? *Relaxation*. And the whores in this place are pretty dull, to be frank. Country whores – all lusty and gleeful and flat on their backs in an instant. A kind of innocence, really. They seem to think sex is about *coupling*.'

He was making it up as he went along, enjoying the look on Carla's face. Naked, he straddled her, weighing her down at the hips, his cock pointing straight at her face. He unbuttoned her shirt and opened it.

'Luke Mallen,' he said, 'Luke Mallen, Luke Mallen, Luke Mallen . . . Once useful; indeed, useful for years; still useful, of course, but for how long? That's the question. Not long, in my opinion. And why? Because his usefulness depended on his bleak view of the world and of himself. He didn't care what he did because he didn't care what *came* of what he did. I used him from time to time; he was always ready for a little excitement, a little danger, a little risk.'

Her bra was just lace, so he lifted it away from her breasts and snapped the band where it joined in the centre.

'Now that's changed. Luke has grown difficult. And because difficult, dangerous. Why? Because now he *does* care what happens in his life. Why? Because he has started to think fondly of the future. Why? Because he's fallen in love with you.'

Carla's mouth was dry; she couldn't have raised enough moisture to spit. Ellwood shifted his weight to her thighs so that he could unbuckle her belt. He pulled the zipper on her jeans fraction by fraction, his head bent as he peered into the widening gap, his eyes bright.

'Green,' he said, 'apple-green underwear; how nice.'

It was early evening, but still warm; Carla could hear the sound of the ocean through the open window of the hotel bedroom; she could feel a breeze. Ellwood leaned forward and kissed her, briefly, his tongue nicking between her lips and wetting her gums.

'It's a mixed blessing, you see. For the first time, he's frightened and I can usually make use of fear. But the other side of the coin is that what makes him fearful is you – what you seem to offer. He wants his life back, and I can't afford to give it to him. Not at this moment, for sure; and probably never.'

He went to the end of the bed and took the legs of her jeans in either hand, then yanked them down and threw them across the room. A flutter of green went with them. He knelt by her feet and smiled.

'What am I going to do? How do I get what I want from him? How do I turn his fear to a fear I can use? There must be a way, mustn't there? In the meantime, it's all your fault, so open your legs, you bitch.'

Zeno took a torch and blew a streamer of flame, orange and black. He doused the torch in his mouth and drew out an endless string of flags, orange and black.

Everything he used came out of the big box and, when he'd finished, everything went back in; but when he tilted it towards them, they could see it was empty. Zeno stepped into the box and closed the lid.

Ellwood was all over her, frenetic, hungry, his tongue between her legs, his tongue in her mouth, his hands on

334

her breasts, in her hair, pushing at her thighs. He knelt astride her face, back arched with pleasure. He hoisted her knees and entered her, his eyes locked on her eyes, greedy for what he would find there.

Carla's mouth was wet; she could taste him at the back of her throat. The tendons from wrist to elbow stood out like wire rods.

'Untie me.' It was a howl, like an animal's cry.

Ellwood lay on her, his finger and thumb a pincer at the nape of her neck, his hips churning.

'*Untie me!*'

He yanked at the knots on both sides and set her free. At once her arms rose, circling his neck and his back, nails scoring his flesh. Her legs closed over his ribs and locked. Limbs wrapped round, she pulled him down, still howling, howling.

'Oh Christ, Wallace, Christ, fuck me, oh Christ, fuck, Wallace, Wallace, Christ, *fuck me, Wallace, Christfuck-ChristfuckChrist* . . .'

A long, fierce, famished litany of greed and need and pleasure too-long delayed.

They lay in a soup of their own sweat. Carla's hand was cupped between her legs, as if to hold in sweetness. Ellwood leaned over and smiled an inch from her face; when she smiled back, he licked her teeth.

'I didn't know,' she said, 'that he'd fall in love with me. Not like that. Not love like that.'

'No-one did. Not even the guy who gave us the profile.'

Carla remembered the careful preparation – Ellwood schooling her along with two other people chosen especially for the task. The others were both women; one a psychiatrist, one an actress.

'Waif and stray,' Ellwood had told her. 'You're a waif and stray.' Now he said it again, and laughed. 'You certainly got it right . . .'

They had been looking for a person, not a type. The psychological profile had given them someone lost, someone vulnerable, someone without a past; all that was good, but it wasn't enough. The fine tuning came in rehearsal. Together, Carla and the actress perfected the details of Carla's physical appearance – no make-up, dull hair, clothes that had a gypsy tattiness about them; and the limp as a brilliant grace-note. Carla and the psychiatrist put together the submissiveness, the devotion, the dependency – the blank page upon which anyone might draw his own picture.

'It was a perfect profile,' Ellwood said. 'Right on the money.' He remembered a phrase that had been used: 'Like someone washed up on a beach . . .' And that's exactly what they'd delivered.

'Who was it?' Carla asked.

'Was what?'

'Who supplied the profile?'

'Tom Carey.' Ellwood smiled. 'Father Tom; the Holy Father, Holy fucking Father Tom. Who better? That's what a confessor's for, isn't it? To know all the little sicknesses, the dark places. Well, you have to admit he did a hell of a good job—'

'Too good.' She anticipated what Ellwood was about to add. 'He's killed two people because of me; now he wants to quit – cut his losses . . .'

'And take you off to a better life,' Ellwood said. 'Yes; well, that's OK. It's all a matter of how you manage things from here.'

'He said a couple of days.'

'What?' Ellwood was suddenly alert.

'Here's what he told me. It came in bits and pieces: you know the way he tells me things and then thinks better of it. He's looking for ways to best protect the relationship, but—'

'Two days . . .'

'He mentioned a woman called Susan. Susan Hart. Something happened, but I don't know what. I think she was here in Longrock. I think they met. Someone from the past?' Ellwood nodded. 'OK, but he didn't kill her.

I'm sure of that. He mentioned Sam Pascoe and Sophie Lanner again.'

'Susan Hart was here, she saw him, then she went away.'

'That's how it sounded, yes.'

Ellwood frowned. 'I'd sooner he'd killed her.'

Carla didn't ask why. Her briefing had given her nothing more than she needed to do her job. Ellwood interpreted what she told him and made what use of it he could. A chain of separated links leads nowhere, and that was how everyone liked it to be: Ellwood, Hilary Todd, everyone . . .

'And he said a couple of days?'

'Then we go away, yes, that's what he told me.'

'He didn't say what the decision depended on? He didn't talk about some sort of a plan?'

'It wasn't to do with a plan. He didn't sound like a man who'd worked everything out. More that he'd given himself an arbitrary deadline. A couple of days – you know? – and if that doesn't do it we're off. That sort of thinking.' She rolled over and bit Ellwood on the shoulder. 'Frankly, I know how he feels. I'm getting tired of this Little Orphan Annie role, and I'm getting tired of him. He fucks me like he was doing a saint. I ought to get the Oscar for best simulated orgasm.'

She turned away slightly as she spoke, because what she was saying wasn't true. Carla wasn't even sure why she bothered with the lie. Was it to save Ellwood's masculinity, perhaps? Would it occur to him to care whether Mallen was a good lay or not?

Sex with Ellwood was everything she had guessed it would be – darkness and pain, dangerous games. It made her wet just to think of it. But with Luke there was something else, something more for Carla herself. It was power. It was the exquisite tension of knowing how much in love with her he was. His fervour, his devotion, his *worship*, was fiercely erotic. The other ingredient was her contempt.

The best ever, she'd said to Luke; and so it was. Not

337

him, not Luke Mallen, but *it* – sex as power, sex as control, sex as slave-maker.

It occurred to her that she might have lied to Ellwood because she didn't want him to detect that lust in her. It made her stronger than he would like.

She got off the bed and walked through into the main room, reappearing a moment later with some cigarettes. Her walk was even and lithe; not the trace of a limp. She used the business of lighting a cigarette to screen her gaze as she looked Ellwood up and down: the dry, lizard-like skin, the gun-metal slick of his hair, the thin, sinewy limbs.

Repellent, she thought, except I'm not repelled. She remembered her first sight of him in Hilary Todd's office. After he'd briefed her he'd said, 'Can you do that? You realize what it would entail.' She'd shrugged and said, 'I can do it, yes.' And when Ellwood grinned, she knew she'd found one of her own.

There are things you like that only some people can give. And there are things you feel that only some people can understand. Ellwood for some, Carla thought; Luke Mallen for others. She lay down again and watched her cigarette smoke laze towards the ceiling.

'Tom Carey's gone,' he said.

'Gone . . . ?'

'He just left. Who knows where?'

'Is that serious?'

'I don't think so. No, it's not serious. But everything that's happening means we have to move faster. A lot faster. Already, people have died in France and Italy. It's almost too late.' She didn't know what that meant, though she knew it must have something to do with Piper. Ellwood stared at the ceiling; he might have been talking to himself. 'I need a good result. I need a clean sheet. There's a European network still in place. Who knows about it? Who did that old man tell?'

Carla said, 'About what?'

'He started to talk last time.' Ellwood's eyes were half

closed, but his voice was far from drowsy. 'A couple more sessions and I'll know what he knows. Three people dead; three or four. We can still survive, we can stay inside, we just need to know who we're fighting.'

'This is Piper, right? You're talking about Piper.'

'If I can deliver that, if I can name names . . .' He looked at her as if he'd forgotten she was there. 'Piper, yes. I'll find a way into that old bastard's head.'

The clown came on stage and checked the fastenings on the box, shaking them to show how secure they were and wagging his head to and fro in a broad parody of despair. He hopped down from the stage and wandered through the audience, looking for a spare seat.

Sir Harold Piper's eyes were fixed on the clown. He felt dizzy and sick, like a child on a fairground ride. Don't sit here, he thought. Don't sit next to me.

The clown sat down and smiled a sad smile. 'He'll never get out of that . . .' He gestured towards the locked box at the centre of the stage. Piper looked at it and saw the terror of darkness, of no escape, of nowhere to turn. He felt a sudden wild surge of energy. He was sitting on his hands because the urge to kill was foaming in him like a black sea.

'I told no-one,' he said. 'Who said I did? Who said that?'

The clown had gone. The Great Zeno emerged from the box with a rattle of chains and a flourish of arms.

'Keep the pressure on,' Ellwood said. 'The trick is to make him want to get the job done quickly, but also to make him want to stay as long as I need him here. Hurry him up, but don't let him go – understand? You're the focal point. Wherever you are, that's where he'll want to be; whatever you want, he'll want it too.'

'It sounds like fun,' Carla said, 'and by golly, it *is* fun.' She got up on her hands and knelt astride Ellwood. She arrowed her tongue and flicked it at him like a snake.

'What do you want?' Already his hands were moving on her; a touch of pleasure, a touch of pain.

'All the things people don't like to do,' she said. 'Do that.'

Forty

The barman raised a hand as Pascoe approached. 'Still on the case, that right?' He wore a red blossom on either cheek – a row with his wife, Pascoe thought, or else he's drinking the profits.

'Still on the case.'

'It's old news now.' The barman had guessed that Pascoe would want a beer. He slid the glass across and scooped up the cash.

'Anyone can have news,' Pascoe said. 'Saddam fires the oil wells today, no-one cares tomorrow. I'm more interested in a story. Any messages for me?'

'Nothing.'

Pascoe took a sip of his beer and went to the phone. The number he called was busy, so he kept redialling until he got a ringing tone. Rob Thomas spoke his name and the name of his agency.

'Business must be good,' Pascoe said.

'Good enough. I get retainers from people who don't even work there any more.'

'Did you find him?'

'Yes, I found him. What I couldn't do was find you. You're not at that hotel.'

'Not yet,' Pascoe said. He gave the number of the bar. 'You can leave a message for me here. The barman thinks I work for a tabloid; he's waiting to see his name in print.'

The notion seemed to jog Thomas's memory. 'I saw that Anthony Stewart walked,' he said. 'A testament to mother-love.'

'George Roxborough's jubilant. Jubilant and drunk, when last heard of. I'd think you could safely double your bill.'

It could have been what Thomas was waiting to hear. He said, 'So . . . Wallace Ellwood . . . Is charging everything on Amex at a hotel called the Windrush, a couple of miles up the coast. You thought he'd be in the neighbourhood?'

'I thought it was worth a look. Did you have any trouble finding him?'

'Nah . . . He doesn't care who knows. Or else he doesn't expect anyone to be looking. The Amex is a company card, he isn't picking up the tab himself.'

'What company?'

'Lighthouse Distilleries.'

'Doesn't exist?'

'Doesn't exist.'

'Say thank you to your friend with the computer.'

'Well, listen,' Thomas said, 'the same to your friend with the cheque-book.'

The barman gave Pascoe directions. 'Out on the headland, you can't miss it.' Pascoe left without bothering to finish his beer and the barman poured it away with a little flourish of irritation. 'Expenses,' he said, 'every bastard's on expenses.'

A taxi took Carla home in the gathering dusk. Her eyes were closed. She was reconstructing her last half-hour with Ellwood – fingering her own lust, but also thinking of ways to use what she had, what she knew. Ellwood was important in the Department. Carla wanted to trade off that, and off anything that might put Ellwood in her debt – appetites, indiscretions, mistakes . . . She looked for advantage in the way he'd touched her, in what he'd said, in the way she had been able to draw him on. The combination of desire and deceit made her dizzy.

She opened her eyes – just for a moment or two as if the gods had directed it – and there was Luke, driving past in the opposite direction, on his way to Ellwood's hotel suite.

Carla almost cried out with pleasure. She closed her eyes

again, imagining him there, talking to Wallace, not knowing, *not knowing*, and Wallace with her smell still on him, *yes*! and Luke going into the bedroom, *why? Why?* To go to the bathroom, perhaps, yes, OK, and pausing, as if suddenly struck by a memory he couldn't place – a sense of someone, a voice still on the air.

And seeing, knotted on to the bedrail, the neckties that Ellwood had used for her wrists.

'I sat next to him. I was the clown: you know? Dressed up as the clown. He said, "I told no-one."'

'What else?'

'Nothing. Or if there was, I didn't hear. He was speaking very softly.'

'But he was speaking.'

'Yes.'

'Speaking to the clown.'

'It seemed that way. It could be. I don't know.'

'The clown, some sodium pentothal, one session more, maybe two; and we're there.' Ellwood was wearing a towel like a sarong, nothing else. He smiled apologetically. 'Sorry – I was entertaining a friend; you know? She's gone now.'

Luke could smell it in the room. Ellwood's smug grin stirred him to anger. 'I've told you – I want to get away.'

'That's right. And I've told you: your gimpy girlfriend suffers if you don't behave; you both suffer. Magic your way out of that. Great Zeno . . .' Ellwood chuckled over the name then, as if anxious not to push too hard, spread his hands in a mime of reasonableness. His tone grew persuasive. 'We've known each other a while, haven't we? Years . . .' He shrugged. 'A couple of days, that's all we need. Just a couple of days. Calm down, for Christ's sake.'

'A couple of days—' His own deadline. Luke felt as though Ellwood had switched sides. Suddenly, he could see the end of it. 'A couple of days is all right.'

A moment of intimacy lay between them, almost as if Carla had provoked it. 'What did you want?' Ellwood asked. 'When you killed them?'

Luke stared at him. 'How did you know?'

'What was it that you wanted?'

'Safety.'

'And if you saw the others now? If you could get to them –what would you do?'

Ellwood was trying to find a way of asking about Susan Hart – how much knowledge she had left with, what she and Luke had said to one another.

Luke was thinking of Susan too. He had stood over her for a long time. He had held the spike inside her ear, wanting to push, wanting to bear down as she slept. Finally, he'd left her there as if she didn't matter at all.

'If you saw the others,' Ellwood asked.

'I don't know,' Luke said. But he added, 'After we've gone from here, Wallace, after Carla and I have gone, don't look for me. Don't look for me ever again.' And Ellwood thought he sounded just like someone with a plan.

'A couple of days. Then you do as you please.' Ellwood dropped the towel on to the floor and walked naked towards the bedroom. 'Why not go home to – what is it? Carla?' Luke nodded. 'Go home to Carla. She'll probably be waiting for you by now, don't you think?'

Luke had gone to the window and was looking down. The evening trade had begun – people drinking on the terraces of five hotels, others coming in from the tennis courts and the golf course, fruit machines in the casino beginning to hum.

Sam Pascoe's face floated up at him and mingled with the cloud reflections in the pane. He was sitting there like any tourist waiting for the evening to come alive.

Ellwood stood in the bedroom doorway and scratched his balls absentmindedly, like a dog. 'I bet she'll be there waiting for you.'

Luke turned and looked the other man up and down, as

if suddenly offended by his nakedness. 'Get dressed,' he said.

Pascoe had left his car in the hotel car park and then had gone down a short flight of steps to the terrace below the main entrance. He'd ordered a drink and found a table to share with three other people – it was a warm evening and the terrace was crowded. Floodlights were on outside the hotels and the restaurants; between the buildings, strings of coloured bulbs glowed in the fading light.

Half an hour, he'd thought, just to look at things. To see what I might see. I'll sit here, a face among faces. Carla had stood under the marquee for a few minutes, waiting for a taxi. Pascoe had seen her but she'd meant nothing. A face among faces.

It wasn't possible to have a view of the hotel doors all the time – waiters were going back and forth, people would get up to leave, others would arrive. For that reason, Pascoe hadn't seen Luke as he'd gone into the Windrush, but he saw him as he came out.

Look in a crowd for someone you used to know. Look for the changes in a young man's face. Pascoe saw Luke, then saw a stranger. He looked hard and made the face become Luke's again: broad cheeks, a pale skin made paler by the harsh lighting, the jawline sharp at the angle.

A sweep of gravel drive went past the terrace and down towards the car park. Luke came within twenty feet of Pascoe's table. He seemed wholly in his thoughts, so preoccupied that he was muttering to himself. Pascoe remembered the empty house, the pine cupboard, that sudden terrifying presence in the room. He stared at Luke as he passed; but even though he knew the truth, Pascoe couldn't see Zeno there. He tried the face with make-up, red and black, and painted on a murderous grin; that was one person. Here was another: a friend from the past, someone he sort-of recognized.

Luke went out of sight, but Pascoe didn't move to

follow at once. He thought: I know where to find him – living an ordinary life in an ordinary house.

A man sat down at Pascoe's table and flagged for a drink. When the waiter arrived, Pascoe ordered another for himself. I'm delaying, he thought. Why? Perhaps because I've found Wallace Ellwood, but I don't know what that might mean. And I've found Luke, but I'm not sure what to do.

Get Ellwood's room number, knock on the door, confront him, say: What have you done to Luke?

Go to Luke's house in the woods, knock on the door, confront him, say: What have you done to Luke?

The waiter came back with a tray of drinks, put two on the table, and went away without leaving a bill. Pascoe called after him, but he didn't hear. The other man said, 'He thinks we're together; he's charged them to my room.' When Pascoe pulled out some money, he added: 'Forget it – really; it's just a beer.' He was wearing dark glasses against the floodlit glare and Pascoe could see his own face reflected there, framed in coloured lights, smiling in response to his benefactor's smile.

He had looked for Luke because Luke had tried to kill him. Had tried to kill Sophie. Had killed Nick Howard. Now here was the moment. Impossible to do anything else but stand before Luke and say, 'Here I am.'

He couldn't imagine what might happen next.

Pascoe finished his drink without hurrying. Now that he'd decided what to do, there was no need for haste; Luke would be there, waiting for him, among the ordinary things in the ordinary house. He walked between the couples making their way to restaurants or to the casino, almost rubbing shoulders, as if their lives might touch his and calm it. When he reached his car, the man in the dark glasses was behind him, still smiling the smile he'd offered earlier, and holding a gun half hidden in the crook of his arm.

'I will if I have to,' Ellwood told him.

Pascoe thought of Sophie's gun, locked away in his glove compartment like a really good idea gone to waste.

Luke appeared, and leaned on the roof of the car, his chin resting on his folded arms.

'I wondered where you'd been,' he said.

Forty-One

The lights up on the headland coalesced to a white glow, littered with points of colour. Every few seconds the beam of the lighthouse emerged from the rest and licked along the horizon, crossing Pascoe's eye-line. The blue clinker-built boat puttered across the bay, heading for the open sea.

Pascoe said, 'Susan told me about Ellwood. But why are you down here? What does he want from you?'

Luke was casual with the wheel; he seemed to know where he was going. Pascoe could hear the ocean, but couldn't see it. He said, 'Sophie knows I'm here.'

'Yes.' Luke's face was lit on one side by a lamp hanging from a cable below the canvas awning.

'If I don't go back, she'll guess why. She'll guess who.'

'Will she?'

'I know you saw Susan. You could have killed her, but you didn't.'

'This is different.'

'Why?'

'You're here. Susan went away.'

'I could go away.'

'Too late for that, Sam.'

'What about Sophie? In a day or so, she'll know something is wrong.'

'In a day or so, I'll be somewhere else.' Luke smiled, his face cut with shadow from the lamp. 'In a day or so, I'll be someone else.'

They had altered course to take them out of view of the lights. Pascoe realized there was darkness on all sides. Now and then he caught a glimpse of a line of white foam as the prow broke the wavetops. Luke twitched the wheel; the hand that held the gun was out of sight.

'They'll find my body.'

'Eventually, perhaps. Listen, Sam . . .' Luke paused, as if searching for a kind way of issuing a rebuke. 'Don't talk, OK? I don't really want to talk.'

'It was you in the boatyard.'

'Yes.'

'It was you in the empty house.'

'Yes. Of course it was. Yes.'

'A table set for two and you in your warpaint. A gentleman caller in top hat and tails.'

'A magic show,' Luke said. 'I don't want to talk.'

'Did you think you might be mad?' Pascoe asked him. 'Did you think of that?'

'What does it mean? Do you know what it means?'

'A magic show where people die. You in costume and make-up. Isn't that someone who's mad? Isn't that you?'

'Each to his own,' Luke said. 'What are you good at, Sam?'

'I'm a lawyer.'

'Ever defend a murderer?'

'Yes.'

'Did you know he was guilty?'

'Yes.'

'The thing is,' said Luke, 'I don't really want to talk. Shut up, Sam; OK? Shut up. Don't talk.'

'If I talk it's more difficult to kill me.'

'If you talk, it's easier.'

Pascoe wondered how far out to sea they were. Two miles, more like three. He could swim a hundred yards at best. He thought that if his life depended on it he might get two hundred.

'Turn the boat round,' he said, 'put me ashore. I'll go away and you won't see me again. You won't see Sophie.'

'You're right; that's what's going to happen. Shut up.'

Pascoe wanted to stop talking, but didn't know how to go silently to his death. 'What did you want with us – with

Sophie and me and the rest? Why those letters? Why the talk of Lori? Why try to kill us?'

'It's none of your business,' Luke said.

Pascoe started to laugh. 'It's what?' He laughed all the more when Luke didn't respond. 'Jesus Christ, you *are* mad. It's none of *what*?'

Luke turned, bringing the gun round. Pascoe saw its glint among the shadows from the lamp. He stood up. 'You don't have to do this,' he said. 'There are other ways out.'

'I want to do it.' Luke still had a hand on the wheel; he stood in profile, the gun pointing at Pascoe's knees.

'Why?'

'One less.' Luke said.

'You didn't kill Susan.'

'You're not Susan,' Luke said. He raised the gun, stiff-armed, and Pascoe went over the side as if he'd been shot.

Luke locked the wheel and fired into the darkness, leaning far out and aiming at the splash. The sounds of the shots rang in his inner ear like peals from a vast bell. He shut down the engine, and went back to the side, but there was nothing to be heard except the slow roll of the ocean and the slap of waves on the wallowing boat.

The glow of the lamp underneath the awning made everything round it blacker. Pascoe sculled away from the light, floating on his back and working his arms and legs as smoothly as possible. Luke's voice came at him across the water, conversational, and close enough to be startling.

'It's another way to die.'

The engine kicked in with a stutter and a thin stench of diesel. Pascoe saw Luke spin the wheel, a shadow moving among shadows. In a few seconds the light shrank to a vague cloud of phosphorus swaying above the water. Pascoe turned and swam twenty strokes, counting each one off. When he turned again, and trod water, the light and the beat of the engine were both gone.

In that wasteland of water, the sounds he could hear best

were his own: his breathing, his cursing, the floundering splash of his tired, inexpert crawl.

The plan was swim a few, then float, then swim a few more. He was conscious of a strong current that carried him no matter what he did. Swimming made things faster; it didn't change his direction, but it gave him a sense of control. Full-time floating was the more sensible option, but that made him feel helpless.

Swim ten, then float; he counted them out. On his back, he could feel the tug of the current more forcefully. He thought: It's like being in a plane when the engines fail. At thirty thousand feet you have time to know you're going to die. Same with me. I swim and then I float, and I know I'll never make it.

Already he felt tired. When Ellwood and Luke had taken him to the boat, he'd been dressed for the weather in just chinos and a shirt – light enough, but they dragged with each stroke. He trod water to shuffle them off. The shirt was difficult because he needed to raise his arms and that sent him under. He surfaced, gargling, and his clothes went past in the tide-race.

Swim ten, then float. His mind shuttled between terror and an eerie sense of inevitability. He saw himself, a jot in all that vastness – limitless darkness above, darkness on all sides, darkness below. No help possible, no deliverance, and death so close, so certain, that any minute he would turn and start to swim and feel his outstretched fingers touch the moment. The thought caused a terrible loosening in him, as if his entrails were unpicking, and he shouted out against it.

'*You bastard, you bastard, Mallen. I'll kill you. When I find you, I'll kill you.*' As if anger and the promise of another death might see him through.

But when he turned to float and felt the current's pulls and swerves, it seemed only sensible to give up control, to stay like that, face up to the dark, until his last strength had left him and he inched under. Since it was all a matter of time. Since it was on its way.

Swim ten, then float.

Each time it was more difficult to make the strokes. His biceps creaked. He was growing very cold.

Luke tied off the painter and walked the length of the quay to look for Ellwood's car. It was parked in a side-street. Ellwood was a silhouette at the wheel.

'OK?'

Luke nodded. 'Pascoe's dead.'

'Can you get Piper out tomorrow?'

'I can try.'

'Don't just try. Do it. There's no time left.'

'All right. Then I'm gone. Carla too.'

'I need him one more time.'

'One time,' Luke said, 'this last time. One more time. Make or break, kill or cure, and after that don't look for me, don't look ever again.'

What a fucking mess, thought Ellwood. Your fault, fucking Zeno, Great fucking Zeno, your fault, you stupid *fuck*. He said: 'Whatever you want. But give him to me tomorrow for the last time, OK?'

Luke asked, 'What did you think, Wallace, when Lori killed herself? What did you think about that?'

'I thought it was a pain in the ass. Lots of trouble and a good source stopped.'

'I thought that a great clock had started to tick.'

You mad fuck. Ellwood said, 'Just think about Piper. Concentrate on that.'

'It seemed to me that one death could make other deaths easier. Do you believe that, Wallace? Does that make sense to you? Sometimes death seems so easy, doesn't it?'

The silhouette grew eyes and teeth. 'Easy,' Wallace Ellwood said, 'that's right, yes, easy.'

Breathing was difficult because of the cold; and he was numb with fatigue. His eyes closed briefly, then again for five seconds or more, and he started to sink. He fought back, coughing water, and the current carried him on like a stick in a weir. He could hear the rush of it, the sea flowing in furrows, and felt his shoulders dip. Faint starlight showed him nothing but the sea.

He thought: Now would be all right. Yes, now's OK. I'm too tired to do anything else but die, so now would be fine.

But first – swim ten; because something makes you do that, even when it's better to die, easier to die, less painful to die. He turned with a terrible, weary cry and lofted an arm for the first stroke, counting them off, one – two . . .

A pleat of white lay across his eye-line as he turned in the water to breathe, and he saw that it was waves breaking. Not a weir, but breakers on rock. He felt the push of the tide, and swam with it as the seabed began to shelve.

Luke went through the house like a puma pacing a cage. His eyes were everywhere; he seemed to be counting their few possessions.

'Don't bother to pack,' he told Carla. 'You can leave this stuff behind.' He stared at the arrangement of pebbles, looking for bad luck. 'After tomorrow, none of this will be ours; nothing to do with us any more.'

In the bedroom, he was too restless to sit or lie. He crossed and recrossed in front of the open window. A breeze blew in, directly off the sea. The cage was eight paces long; he turned on his heel and passed the window again. Carla imagined she saw the bars flickering over his face, his eyes like drills. She got out of bed and went across to intercept him, smiling, calm, her limp made more poignant by her nakedness.

'Come on . . . Luke, come on . . .'

She took his hands and laid them on her breasts, and a stillness overtook him. 'I love you,' he said.

She backed off, holding the smile, and got on to the bed, up on her elbows to fetch him with her eyes.

'Come on . . .'

He was trembling, but she didn't know whether to take

it for audacity or fear. She wondered whether Ellwood was still pulling the strings, or whether Luke had started making his own decisions.

'Come on . . .'

She thought: Maybe Ellwood's losing his grip on this. Maybe there's a real advantage to be found.

Luke kissed her throat.

Come on, come on, come on.

He found a place in the dark.

First he managed a handhold where he hung for minutes, low among the wavetops, just breathing and spitting water, then he worked his way round until the rock seemed to level out. He heaved himself up on to the flat, travelling on hands and knees until he could go no further – five times his own length, perhaps. He crouched there rubbing his arms and legs, rubbing his torso. There was still warmth in the wind, but his teeth chattered. Some birds took off, unseen, and circled once before coming back to the roost.

A place in the dark.

Not dead, not quite. All a matter of time, perhaps, but not dead yet.

A great shudder ran through him, making his body quake, and he cried out in fury, a man with no future and everything to lose.

Forty-Two

It was a rock – scarcely better than that – a place for seabirds, more than two miles offshore. On one side, it was a massive pinnacle a hundred feet high. On the other, where the granite fell away to a low shelf, it made a tiny cove twenty feet or so across, that rose to form three broad lips of stone like a giant's altar. Dawn light showed Pascoe that he was backed up to the first lip. Behind him was maybe thirty feet of stone that ended where the curve of the rock made a natural shelter. Seawater had carved a shallow cave there, not much deeper than the kind of niche where a statue might stand. Flotsam was wedged into the crevice – a great curl of rope, thick as a man's arm, fragments of planking, a heap of rags, several plastic bottles.

Birds were circling the rock constantly, screaming and riding the wind. He watched the sun push through the hard line of the horizon – a dome and then a disc. There was nothing on the sea but sunlight.

By mid-morning the sky was cloudless. He knew there was a way to gather water by using the principle of condensation, but seemed to remember it involved sheets of polythene suspended over a trench. He collected one of the plastic bottles and used it to piss into.

There was a stench on the rock that was seaweed and bird shit and something rotting amid the bundle of rags. He wasn't sure about drinking piss, but he believed it was better than seawater.

A boat went past. Two hours later, another. Pascoe waved

and yelled, but neither had really been anywhere near him. Fishing vessels. He realized that even had they been close, the chances were he wouldn't have been seen. A fishing boat is busy and noisy; it would take someone out on deck and bothering to look twice at a rock where seabirds nested.

He thought: When I find you, Mallen, you bastard, I'll kill you for sure.

He thought about Sophie who carried his child.

He saw sails close to the horizon – red on one boat, he thought, another candy-striped, the others white or pale blue. Eight sails in all. He imagined the life on board: people judging the wind, reading charts, active at the tiller, active in the galley. No-one just out for the ride.

The sun was warm, its light bounced back off the surface of the sea to dazzle his eye and he could feel his skin tingling.

His tongue clacked against the roof of his mouth.

Two more hours, five more boats. He sorted among the broken planking until he found a strip about five feet long, then looked for a place to anchor it. He could attach some of the rags to make a flag; and he knew he must salvage something for a makeshift shirt: his shoulders were glowing where the sun had begun to roast him.

There was a jagged vee to one side of the rockface, just above the water line. Pascoe lodged the plank there, then pushed down hard. It wedged, but wouldn't stay put until he'd kicked it several times, leaving his heel and instep beaded with blood from a dozen cuts and grazes. The plank hung at an angle like a broken mast.

When he stirred the rags they fell apart like old turf – a fibrous, ripping sound; heavy clods of matter breaking up. He was holding a sleeve and inside the sleeve an arm. Among the ragpile, a shoulder bone glistened whitely. Now he could see tufts of hair; he could see legs, broken and twisted and swathed in weed.

*   *   *

Pascoe sat on the furthest part of the outermost lip of rock. From time to time, he basted his shoulders and back with seawater, but he could feel the burn spreading.

Luke had weighted Nick's body, but he hadn't weighted Marianne's; maybe that's how he'd come to realize his mistake – he'd offloaded her and she'd bobbed away like an abandoned raft. And fetched up on the rock – just as the prevailing current had carried Pascoe there.

He couldn't take anything off her for a flag, or for a shirt. He couldn't even push her back into the sea.

He had put a toe under the ragpile and turned it over. A great stench had risen, like a foul oven suddenly opened, and he'd seen the green-black hole of her abdomen, the ribs strung with flesh like bunting. She was blown with gas and putrefaction. Her face hung in black tatters, lips gone, eyes gone.

On the furthest lip of rock, and with his back to her, he could still smell her, still see her. He started to shake: sunburn, fear, and a sense of confinement so terrible that he almost slipped into the water and started to swim.

He remembered how he had sat in the Argentinian cell, waiting to be tortured, hearing the screams all around him.

The sea and the sky couldn't have given more space, more light. Pascoe sat, knees to chin, arms wrapped round, as if held by a block of darkness.

His cell-mate had travelled across twenty years to waft the scent of death towards him on the wind.

He closed his eyes and listened to the screams of gulls.

Forty-Three

Sir Harold Piper looked up at his window and saw a ragged line of crows go over. He saw a cloud like a long-nosed face and another in the shape of a dog.

The omens were indescribably bad.

A nurse carrying a tray of carefully set-out medication passed the clown in a corridor. He stopped and smiled: 'Are you on overtime rates, or what?'

'They seem to enjoy it.'

'You're not doing a show today?'

'Not a show.' The clown was anxious to get away, walking backwards as he spoke. 'Just some visiting. They seem to like it. Who knows . . . ?'

The nurse thought it was funny to see the real smile inside the greasepaint smile – scaled-down and slightly tawdry. He decided it was all better at a distance; the wig, the bright, baggy clothes, the painted teardrop. He said, 'We need more people like you. They're crazy, but they're not insane, you know? Not all of them, not all the time. I like the show myself.'

'That's great.' The clown was backing off, hand raised.

The nurse half turned, balancing the tray like a waiter – a dozen plastic beakers of pills. Over his shoulder he said, 'A cocktail each before an early supper . . .'

All day bad omens, and here was the bad event.

Piper sat on his bed with his back to the wall and refused to hold hands with the clown.

'We're going for a walk,' Luke said. 'Just as we did before. It's time to go.'

'I am Moloch,' Piper told him. 'I'm Omega.'

It was the time of day when nothing much happened, medication came round, people watched television or walked in the grounds.

Piper sat on his hands and said, 'No, no, no, no, no . . .' He was shaking his head and rocking slightly to and fro.

'Look at this.' The clown produced an egg from his ear; it flapped open and a little cloud of fireflies wafted into the room and settled on Piper's bed.

'My calculations are quite complete, thank you.' Piper brushed the silver glitter from his bedspread. 'I need no help. You can go now. I dismiss you.'

'A walk in the sunshine. The weather's fine and warm. A talk. I want to know the things you know – how you order the music of the spheres, how your calculations work. I want to hear about it.' Before, Piper had gone willingly with the clown; but even the mad have memories. A great tension was building in Luke. He sat next to Piper on the bed. The old man shuffled off until he was squatting on the pillow.

'Let's go for a walk.' The clown put out a hand and Piper shrank from it. His head hadn't stopped wagging to and fro. 'No, no, no, no, no.'

'I've made a bargain,' Luke told him. 'You're part of it. It's important, you see? My life depends on it. Carla's life too.' He stood up. 'Let's go.' He smiled his big, clownish smile.

Piper raised his arms above his head, fists clenched, moving slowly like someone miming a weight-lifter. He opened his mouth very wide. For a moment, there was no sound; then came a furious bellow: '*No-no-no-no-nooooooooooo!*'

Luke screamed with shock and alarm, his voice piercing the other man's yell. He stepped in and hit Piper hard, punching twice, then again, wired by anger and nothing else. Piper bounced against the wall, then rolled across the bed and on to the floor. He was up at once, his mouth bloody, his voice still booming.

Kill him, Luke thought. Kill him is the only thing to do.

Piper dragged all the clothes off his bed and threw them at Luke. '*Moloch*,' he shouted, '*Alpha and Omega*.' His strength was all madness. He wiped his face and shook a fist in the air. Covered in blankets, Luke felt a fist knock the side of his head. Piper was dancing and wagging his hands like a boxer. He backed off to the door and went out, leaving a bright red handprint on the woodwork.

The nurse with the tray looked in and saw Luke standing alone. 'What the fuck was that?' He paused, as if expecting an answer, then headed up the corridor.

Piper arrived in the television room bloodstained, terrified; an explosion of screaming. He ran this way and that, waving his arms. He howled, '*I don't like that clown*.'

Violence flickered round the room, going from eye to eye. People were crying, some were howling like Piper, some were laughing. Suddenly, everyone was standing up, dancing, running from place to place, overturning chairs, yanking curtains down, smashing whatever could be smashed.

Birdie crowed, head back like a rooster.

The Lady with the Flower stamped and shouted.

Mac the Cough put a fist through the television screen, shredding his knuckles. He laughed, *hek-hek-hek-hek-hek*.

Dog Face sat in a corner and watched it happen. All the time she screamed, rhythmically, one hand on her throat to feel the screams come out.

The Wandering Jew scuttled out after Piper as he went down corridors like a live fuse, taking the fear and fury with him.

Nurses were running towards the television room, but already there were cries coming from other parts of the asylum, together with the sound of breaking glass. Luke ran with the rest until he found the little common-room with its stage, where he always gave his show. There was a glass door in the room that let on to a lawn. It was locked, but Luke stood back and kicked at the frame close to the mortice, breaking a pane of glass, but breaking the frame as well. Two more kicks and the mortice splintered and dropped off. Beyond the lawn was tree cover, and beyond the trees, a curving wall. Luke started to circle on the inside of the wall, knowing that he would come to the driveway gates where his car was parked. When he looked through the trees, the building seemed as usual, apart from the faintest susurration of noise like birds waking.

Dog Face had taken her clothes off. She had rouged her nipples and powdered her pubic hair. She was using a lamp as a club, going from room to room looking for mirrors to smash.

Three men were setting a fire in the common-room. They had brought matches from the kitchen, and armfuls of paper, and a bottle of white spirit. The chairs for Zeno's audience were set out in rows. One of the men started breaking them up for kindling.

Sir Harold Piper ran out of the door and into the grounds. He was looking for the clown. He was looking for that other man who'd hit him, the man with the needle. He was looking for the priest. All Piper's madness, all his dismay, and all his anger ran together in one great charge of energy. He scouted the verge of the trees where the clown had taken him on the day of their first walk. He stopped and listened carefully, then ran on a few paces and stopped to listen again. What he could hear was Dr Harris, who had followed him out of the main door, his white coat flaring behind him.

'It's all right,' Harris said; he stepped up behind Piper and took him by the shoulder.

Piper screamed as he turned, pointing at the man accusingly. He wanted to say, Why wouldn't you listen? I told you I didn't like that clown. I told you so. Why wouldn't you listen to me?

'*Whylisseme?*' Pointing, turning, mouth wide. '*Dinlika-clun!*' Pointing, his arm hooking round. '*Whylisseme?*' All violent motion, his finger going up to the knuckle in

Harris's eye, a smooth slide, as if accidents depended on perfect timing.

Harris stepped back and Piper stepped with him. The doctor stepped back again. Like someone who's caught his button on another man's clothing, he was trying to disengage. They went up on their toes in a dance and Harris's shoulders rapped the trunk of a tree. He was screaming on an indrawn breath, as a child screams, and his fingers tapped vaguely at Piper's outstretched hand as if trying to call attention to the outrage.

Piper took out his finger and looked at it. Before Harris's scream could emerge, the man fainted, going down so hard that it seemed he'd been dropped from a height. Piper held the finger under his armpit and wiped it through like a blade.

'I told you,' he said. For a moment, he stood there as if some crucial task had escaped his mind; then he remembered and started across the lawn to the common-room.

The fire was looking for tinder. Low lines of smoke trailed on the floor, little orange tracers licking behind them like candles in a mist.

Piper hopped up on to the stage and looked into the wings on one side – just a narrow space hidden from view by an extension of the curtain that went across the stage. The clown wasn't there. Piper was breathing through his teeth: angry anticipation.

He crossed the stage and looked again on that side, half expecting to find the clown standing there, silently waiting for his cue. No-one . . . but he could see the box, unlocked, its chains lying alongside. Piper coughed and a wisp of smoke left his nostril. He went into the wings and lifted the lid of the box. It was empty.

He sniffed the smoke but couldn't find a meaning for it.

This is where he'll come, of course he will. A day of bad omens, and now this stroke of luck. And when he opens the box, he'll find me there. Piper laced his fingers together and squeezed, arms held straight down. It could have been gleeful anticipation at the surprise he was planning. It could have been the rehearsal of someone's death by throttling.

It was dark in the box when he closed the lid. Inside was a sour smell that filtered into his throat and made him want to cough, but he knew he mustn't give the game away. Crooking his elbow, he pointed a stiff finger at the lid of the box.

'I don't like you,' he said. 'I told you so.'

People were going back into their rooms. Everyone was jumpy, but the yelling had stopped. There were one or two short outbreaks of hysteria, one or two crying jags. A pair of doctors were doling out medication; little by little, the drugs were soaking through.

A nurse said, 'Where's Harris?'

His colleague shrugged. 'Did you see that crazy old bag with lipstick all over her tits and powder on her bush?'

'The duchess.'

'Is she?'

'Duchess, baroness, dame . . . Something or other.'

They checked each room in turn. The place was too expensive for wards, too classy for communal bathrooms.

'Where's Piper?' one of them asked.

The fire was like something disgruntled. It sulked along the floor, brightening suddenly when it found a line of white spirit that had been splashed along a skirting-board, then growing dull again. It snaked round, looking for something to latch on to. The chairs had burned briskly, then died down. The fire raisers had gone away disappointed. Now there were just low scallops of yellow under thinning smoke.

One of the men had tossed the bottle of spirit away as he'd left. It had spun an arc of fluid out into the middle of the room and the bottle had pitched up close to the stage. The fire knew what it fed off, but couldn't reach.

*   *   *

The clown walked in with the left side of his smile obliterated, the chalk-white make-up halved, the teardrop askew. He had been holding the steering wheel with his right hand, Kleenex and cold cream in his left. He had parked in the turning circle, too distracted to finish the job. There were tear-tracks down to his chin. Ellwood sat him down in the kitchen, close by the sink, and started to sponge away the happy face.

'He wouldn't come. I couldn't get him out.'

'What happened?'

'He started screaming. I hit him. He ran out. Then they all began.'

'What happened to Piper?' Ellwood was gentle as a wife, sponging slowly, bringing the sad face out.

'I don't know. They were chasing him – nurses. He was yelling and screaming. Everyone running around – the crazies, the nurses, Piper with blood all over, shouting . . .'

'Saying what?'

'It was just gibberish. You know – mad people's talk.' Ellwood rinsed the sponge and took flakes of white out of Luke's eyebrows.

Luke sat still as a statue, eyes front. He said, 'Wallace, I'm going anyway.'

'Did anyone see you there?'

'I talked to a nurse; other people must have seen me. Jesus, what do you think?' He spread his hands to take in his bright, baggy costume. 'I was the only clown up there at the time.'

Ellwood laughed. 'OK,' he said. 'But give it a day.'

'No. No more.'

'I'm not talking about Piper. Maybe that's a lost cause now; maybe there's another way. Whichever, you're out of it – I agree. But the last thing you need is unfinished business – no? The last thing you need is people looking for you with questions.'

'What will you do?'

'Talk to some people. Make sure you're off the hook.'

'If they ask me, I'll just say—'

'Best to be sure,' Ellwood told him. It hadn't quite worked with the sponge. He fetched a towel from a hook behind the door. Luke's face still bore streaks of white by the ears, traces of red above the cheek-bones.

'I can say he flipped, I can say . . .'

Ellwood dropped the towel over Luke's head and began to rub. He spoke to the shrouded head. 'You didn't do what I asked. You didn't keep the bargain. Never mind. You can't go back up there, I see that. But you owe me – yes? Now, don't worry; I'm going to let you go. But first, I'll talk to some people and make sure that things are OK. Not just your ass – my ass too. You understand?' He wiped Luke's cheeks gently, his voice was gentle. 'You stirred things up. Piper's the centre of attention now; the clown, too, for all we know. I'll do some talking, we'll wait, we'll get the OK. Then you'll be safe.'

Luke emerged from the towel clean, his mouth a line, his eyes glittering with mistrust. 'Tomorrow,' he said, 'tomorrow. Then I'm gone.'

'Listen, I like to be sure. Maybe I'm making too much of it. An old man falls down and hurts his face; he runs round shouting. He's crazy . . .' Ellwood went out of the kitchen and returned with two nips of brandy. 'But let's be sure that everyone's happy with that.' He drank. 'Tomorrow's fine.'

From the kitchen table Ellwood collected a syringe and a couple of phials of sodium pentothal.

Luke sat in the chair, unmoving, holding a towel with the muck of his old face on it.

The legs of the chairs were charred spillikins; when they collapsed, a little puffball of sparks went up and three or four discs of blue flame scattered on the floor like dropped coins.

One of them found a snail's track of white spirit and walked along it to the centre of the room. Little beads of spirit like stepping stones were there. The flame skipped across them to a tiny lake. There was a whispered *whoosh*.

The fire had found what it wanted. Flame leapt up on the spillage, crossing the room in a rush, the sound of canvas tearing. It hit the bottle of white spirit and blazed-up eight feet, winding into the stage curtain, laying down a carpet of fire on the planks of the stage.

Inside the box, Piper coughed. He could feel the heat.

A breeze came in at the open door and the fire turned like a wave, making its own draught; smoke streamed and curled in the doorway, drawn by the outlet, drawn back by the fire. The room seemed to be awash with red-orange light. A window exploded.

Dr Harris walked in at the front door, his hand over his eye like someone taking a sight test. Behind his fingers, the eye-crater wept red; his cheek was slick with blood and jelly.

Two nurses and a doctor were approaching the door – part of the search party for Sir Harold Piper. Harris walked past them, his good eye flicking to and fro like the eye of a fugitive.

The doctor went after him. One of the nurses said, 'Something's burning somewhere.'

The box stood inside a furnace. Already, its sides had begun to char, wisps of dark smoke spinning off the corners, a lacy beading of flame running to and fro on the underside.

The room was lined with flame, enormous rolls of it baling up and coiling across the walls. It made a noise like a massive engine. Smoke travelled in fronts, like weather, streaming through the open door and broken windows.

Harold Piper was baking like a trout, his skin beginning to pucker and pop in a rash of tiny blisters. Only the box had kept him from choking to death. Inside it, singed and wrapped in pain, he heard the roar of the fire and thought that, truly, this must be his hour. In a day of bad omens, of victory, of violence, of such conflict . . . His hour of death-in-life; his hour of rebirth as Anarch and as Judge.

He opened the lid and stepped out into the heart of light. Even as he emerged, his clothes ignited, his hair ignited. He turned and turned, arms raised, spinning towards the door. His mouth worked furiously behind its mask of fire.

'*Moloch! Omega!*'

There were faces at windows, faces behind hands, faces among the trees. Birdie whistled like a macaw; the Lady with the Flower turned her back. Doctors and nurses made a half-circle on the grass, standing way off where the heat was bearable.

He came out of the doorway into the day, not seeing the faces, not seeing the trees, wrapped in flame, arms raised like a prophet.

'*Moloch!*'

A great scorch enveloped him, stealing his breath, making clinker of his lungs.

The fire flowed up and crowned between his fingertips.

Forty-Four

Pascoe was conducting a conversation with Sophie, a castaway's fantasy.

'You'll never believe it, but I just drank some of this.' He rattled the bottle. His piss was amber and had a slight cloudiness to it.

'I'm not surprised.'

'Would you have done it?'

'I'd've had more trouble peeing in the bottle.'

He pinched his nostrils and took another gulp, trying to get it down before his sense of taste sent a message to his brain. 'I think it does harm to your kidneys.'

'So does Scotch whisky.'

'There's a choice?' He looked from side to side, playing the part. He didn't want to look behind.

Sophie said, 'You've already waited too long. It's afternoon – what would you think? – five o'clock? Your shoulders are pretty burnt. You should have done it earlier.'

'I can't.'

'It doesn't matter. She's dead.'

'I think I know that. You haven't had to look at her. You haven't had to smell her.'

'And, apart from the fact that you've barbecued your back, you have to make a flag.'

'No-one's going to see it.'

'That's right – unless you make one.'

'I could take off my shorts; I've still got those.'

'How unpleasant do you want your sunburn to be? Too small, in any case. Get on with it.'

'It's Marianne back there.'

368

'I know who it is.' Pascoe stared at the sea. 'How many boats went by?' Sophie asked.

'Saw fifteen; six were – not *close*, you know . . .'

'How many didn't you see?'

'What?'

'A flag's there whether you jump up and down and wave, or not.'

'I sense you're trying to tell me something.'

'Very funny. I want to get you off this fucking rock. There are things to talk about.'

'I know.'

'I just want to get you off this rock.'

She broke up in his hands. It made no difference how careful he was – working with tremendous stealth, as if he were trying to strip her without waking her. It was no good trying to imagine old sticks and garden refuse.

She was wearing a silk shirt and a dark, designer suit – tailored jacket and knee-length skirt. It was weird to know that – to be able to tell. The clothing looked as if a good laundry would be able to make all the difference. He unfastened the shirt buttons and tried the zipper on the skirt. It was jammed, but when he pulled the tab, the stitches unpicked all the way down.

Pascoe thought of all the women he'd undressed.

He took the shirt and jacket off as one, then pulled at the hem of the skirt. Marianne separated, disjointing like something cooked. Pascoe went to the very edge of the lip of stone and crouched down, elbow on thigh, his hand to his jaw, like Rodin's Thinker. Sophie said, 'Don't stop; it's worse if you stop.'

'You should try it on nothing more than a couple of mouthfuls of stale piss.'

'I didn't say you were going to like it, I said it had to be done.'

'Sophie, I don't feel good.'

'You're kidding.'

'No . . . I mean . . . The same as when I was in that

Argentinian cell and I thought that any minute they would come for me and torture me, and I could hear the screams.'

'They're just gulls.'

'I know that. No-one's saying it's a rational feeling. I know that I'm pretty sure to die anyway; I know that's a racing bet. How long can a man drink piss?'

'Some do it all their lives.'

Pascoe laughed. 'I keep thinking about how I felt when I sat in that cell. Crazy, isn't it? I'm washed up on a rock looking at death by thirst, or by exposure, or because I try to swim for it . . . I keep thinking about that cell.'

'Go back and do the rest of it,' Sophie told him.

Piece by piece he buried her at sea and stood on the rock, clutching her clothes like a grave-robber.

The jacket and the shirt would never fit. He tied their sleeve ends together and flew them from his flagpole. The skirt he wore like a poncho, head through the waistband. He shuddered and gagged, but kept it on through minutes of revulsion, standing up, sitting down, walking about, until he was broken to it, as a horse is broken to a saddle and saddle blanket. It smelled, he noticed, more of the sea than of anything else.

He said, 'I made the flag. I'm keeping the sun off my back.'

'That's good.'

Pascoe occupied the uppermost rock shelf now, his back to the curving wall of granite, his drink bottle between his knees. A boat went by, flying a flag of its own.

'How's the kid?' Pascoe asked.

'Fine,' she said. 'First rate. Missing her father.'

Forty-Five

Ellwood's anger was rich enough to choke him, but his voice was light and casual. He was trying for a tone of amused irritation.

'It wasn't what I'd planned for, we know that. The consolation is that Piper's dead.'

'What happened?' Hilary Todd asked.

'Piper got spooked. It looks like he started a riot up there. Several people hurt, and a lot of fire damage. Piper died in the fire.'

'How did it happen?'

'Who knows?' Ellwood was trying for damage limitation. 'Maybe we paid him a visit once too often, it's difficult to say. He was mad – what does that tell you?'

'You're in trouble, Ellwood. I'm glad to say. In shit. Can you smell it? Shit and quicksand.'

'No I'm not, Hilary. Local difficulty. I don't like it, and I wish it was otherwise, but not all operations succeed; everyone knows that.'

'You continued after you were told to stop.'

'Oh, yes? Who told me to stop?'

'I did.'

'No, Hilary; that can't be right. You're forgetting all sorts of things, aren't you? Forgetting Annie.'

Todd was quiet for a moment. Ellwood allowed the silence. Finally, Todd asked, 'You ran the operation. Someone was working with you – apart from Carla Jones?'

'A sleeper,' Ellwood said.

'We might need a sacrificial lamb.'

'For the Department.'

371

'The Department, the local police, anyone who needs to shake a stick. What was Jones? Bait?'

'I was given a free hand down here, Hilary. No-one's told me different. I report to you, but I don't have to apologize or explain. I know that pisses you off, which is lousy luck, but we stand in a relationship, you and I, of senior colleagues. Rank scarcely comes into it. I suppose it could be said that you've got an extra pip, but then I know that you quadruple your salary by creaming the stash-for-cash.' His voice was still light, but he'd already lost any advantage soft speech might have given him. When it came to Hilary Todd, Ellwood's anger was a bludgeon. 'So don't ask me questions you know I won't want to answer.'

'What's this phone call for?' Todd's voice was breathy. Ellwood fantasized that the man might have taken himself by the throat.

'I'm reporting, Hilary; I'm telling you what's happened. And I've a couple of questions of my own. If I decide to trade my sleeper for peace of mind, can we guarantee police silence, a trial in camera, the usual press blackout? I see the need for a culprit, but we'll have to bury him. I'll need that reassurance.'

'What else?'

'How do we cover my ass?'

Todd's laugh was like a retch. 'You bastard, Ellwood. You fuck up, you're ordered off the case, vanity forbids that, vanity and ambition and the fear of looking stupid, so you ignore the order and, *Christ*, you fuck up again. And you want to come out with clean hands and face.'

'So think about the answers to those questions, Hilary, and get back to me. Talk to whoever you have to talk to. I'll be here. You can call me day or night.'

Ellwood hung up, smiling. Fuck damage limitation, he thought. Bludgeons every time.

Pascoe could see a metaphor for life; whatever he put in to the bottle he also got out. He confided the discovery to

Sophie, who laughed. Pascoe laughed too. He said, 'I don't feel too bad, you know? I feel OK.'

'You're drifting,' Sophie told him. 'Don't drift.'

When he closed his eyes, the warmth from his skin, the sound of the sea, the cries of the gulls, all washed together to make a mood. The mood had colours. The colours changed. 'Just like a trip,' he said, 'with gentle acid.'

When he opened his eyes, the mood was there before him, lining the sky. The sunset was pink and vermilion, aquamarine and azure, primrose and ochre; brilliantly ironic. He watched it fade to lavender, then blue-black. Two planets rose: wet and heavy, not more than a hand-span apart. Planets or navigation lights.

Pascoe shivered. He shouldered his way into Marianne's niche and crouched there, elbows on knees, like Speak-no-evil.

Carla said, 'I'm really excited.' Earlier in the day, she had spoken to Ellwood, and knew what she had to do: *Just till tomorrow; keep him there until then. Don't let him run. Tie him down, get him drunk, fuck his brains out. Make him feel good. Make him feel it's really going to happen.*

She'd thought: You're in trouble, Ellwood; I was right. You need me badly, and one day you'll have to pay for that.

'Really excited,' she said. 'Where will we go?'

'Abroad, maybe. Greece, perhaps, or Turkey.'

Jesus, she thought, the hippy fucking trail. When you find them still in the sixties, you know they've got to be in their forties. She smiled and Luke saw genuine affection which, at that precise moment, was almost what Carla was feeling. Not quite.

'Show me something,' Carla said.

Luke went out and came back in tails and topper. The Great Zeno. He showed her an empty hand, then a Tarot card – the Lovers, whose sacrifice was over.

He turned a wrist, and the card was gone. On his open palm lay a tiny red heart, about the size of a dove's. He put it to his lips and it disappeared. When he opened his hand again, there lay a white feather to symbolize purity and flight.

He threw the feather up and it disappeared. In its place, like birth-in-death, a glistening egg. The egg flapped open, throwing brilliants everywhere, a cascade of tiny lights. Luke stepped forward and handed it to Carla.

The ring lay at the centre, shedding light; a setting two hundred years old, four concentric rings of diamonds with a rose cut solitaire at the centre. An engagement ring.

Carla looked first at the ring, then at Luke. In her face was everything he'd hoped to see: love, commitment, hope, acceptance.

Jesus fuck, she thought. Ohhhhh, Jesus *fuck*. She was dizzy with delight and horny as hell.

Sophie called three George Roxboroughs before she got George Roxborough. He said, 'Are you a close friend of Sam's?'

'Pretty close, yes.'

'Well, if you don't know where he is, what makes you think I might?'

'No: I'm worried, that's all. I wondered if he'd called.'

'Why?'

'What I mean is – you're the only person I could think of to ask. If I knew other people who might have spoken to him, I'd call them as well.'

'No,' Roxborough said, 'I haven't heard from him.' He fell silent and Sophie was about to say goodbye. 'He's a close friend?'

'I said that.' Sophie tried not to snap; her anxiety was emerging as ill-temper.

'Then you must know that he sometimes has odd moods, gets depressed, has a tendency to drink too much. Sometimes.'

'Yes.' Sophie was on the verge of saying, I'm sure it isn't that, but she stopped. She didn't want Roxborough's help or concern. She didn't want his curiosity.

As if sensing her caution, Roxborough asked: 'Are you the new woman in Sam Pascoe's life?' There was a little boozy leer behind the words.

'It's poorly paid work,' Sophie said, 'but someone has to do it.'

Roxborough laughed. He said, 'If you're anxious, I could—'

Sophie had her finger on the cut-off button. 'Don't worry, really; don't worry, I'll track him down.'

The clubs in Pall Mall are for men who like privilege and hate women. They're for starting and closing deals, for private favours and public patronage. They're for secrecy at all times.

Sir Rodney Bryden was nodding as he listened to Hilary Todd. Nothing he heard caused him much surprise or concern. He said, 'What are you asking for, Hilary? It doesn't sound too awful.'

'Doesn't it?' Todd wasn't sure why. 'Well, first, do we throw Ellwood's man to the wolves?'

'He won't work for us again?'

'Not according to Ellwood.'

'Ellwood's a good man. I'd tend to believe he'd got it right. If he says the man's dispensable—'

'And the rest?'

'Piper and so forth . . . ?'

'Yes.'

'Bit of a nuisance. I can see that someone's got to be found to blame. We can't have any sort of an *investigation* going on.' Bryden made it sound like an outrageous interference in private affairs. 'So we'll let them have the sleeper. But that aside, we can cope.' He read something in Todd's face and asked, 'You're happy enough with Ellwood, aren't you, Hilary? Nothing awry there?'

'No, nothing.'

'Well, pull him in and get him over to Europe. Piper's gone, so there's nothing else to pursue here.'

'We assume he was a double, don't we?'

'Do we?'

'The deaths in France and Italy . . .'

'It would have been nice to know. To be certain. It isn't pleasant to think someone might have the advantage of us, is it? But the fact is, we're pretty certain he was straight.'

For a moment, Todd didn't take it in. He had the look of a man who is the only one to have missed the joke. He said, 'Straight. You thought Piper was probably straight.'

'Naturally, we would have preferred to know for certain. Anxious to know, in fact. But the Insiders were blown in any case. Not the individuals . . . but the operation itself was common knowledge more than a year ago. We certainly wanted to know who Piper might have leaked information to if he *had* been a double. But as for the Insiders set up, that was a lost cause.'

Todd's bewilderment was turning to anger. 'But you think he was loyal?'

'On balance, yes.'

'I authorized an operation that Ellwood set up. Its purpose was to find out whether Piper had leaked information. I was told that the need to know was vitally urgent. That our people were at risk.' Todd was having trouble keeping his voice low. 'People have died. Insiders in France and Italy. The assumption was that Piper might have sold them out years ago and now they were paying the price. Why do you think I was pushing Ellwood so hard, giving him so much leeway?'

Bryden nodded. 'Yes, well, in a sense they were. Paying the price that is. But not of Piper's treachery, we think. Of Piper's schemes, perhaps – of the schemes of all those who devised the Insiders. It must have seemed a terrific notion at the time. War over, future uncertain, so leave behind a task force, a little secret army to be the first line of defence against the Commies . . . who wouldn't arrive at the border in tanks, it was thought, but as the enemy within. So – we needed people in high places; people who would become part of the hierarchies of those countries; people who could influence things – our way; and change them – as we chose.' Bryden paused and smiled. 'Well, it *was* a good idea, actually; it worked for a long time. Then it stopped working – mostly because it stopped being a secret. Europe's an open book now, Hilary. So we thought: Time to call a halt, before we become . . .' he shrugged, 'embarrassed.'

Todd said, 'But those who died?' And as he asked the question, he saw the answer.

'Ah, well, that was us, you see.' Bryden's tone was gently apologetic. He caught the eye of a club servant and raised his empty glass.

Todd felt ill. Bryden's calm smile said: *How grand did you think you were? How much in control?* For the first time, Todd knew the answers: *Not very; not much.* He said, 'Us. We killed them.'

'*Pour encourager les autres.* Not all of them: just three, strategically placed. The rest have gone to ground.' Bryden's fresh drink arrived. 'Perfectly judged, you see. The Insiders have gone before anyone but we knew who they were. But *they* don't know that – they feel hunted and at risk, so they're being tremendously cautious, staying out of the way. We're giving them limited help, but we'll let them get back in time. We didn't have to close them down, they did it themselves. So we avoided embarrassment without seeming to betray anyone – any cause. I expect they're having a good time, don't you? Disappearing, covering their tracks, zigzagging across Europe on false passports. Just like the old days.' He paused, feigning discomfort. 'We didn't tell you, Hilary—'

'Sure,' Todd said, 'of course. If I thought they were dying because of Piper, I'd feel under pressure; I'd do a better job.'

Bryden conceded with a turn of the head, then paused as if reluctant to apologize without seeking some new advantage. 'I heard about your assistant, Hilary. Are you happy about that?'

'Happy?'

'That there's no security problem.'

'Oh, yes,' Todd said, 'yes. Happy.'

Noises at two a.m. – yelling in the street, followed by laughter; the whip and whine of traffic on a red route; something breaking; sirens and bass-lines.

Sophie packed an airline bag and looked out of the window to check where she'd left her car. She was safer in her own place than in Pascoe's, but at two a.m. in the London zones there are creatures who are wide awake and hungry.

The roads out of the city were humming, mostly twelve-wheel artics flowing through a low haze of sodium and halogen. She put the radio on and found an army of wide-eyed insomniacs phoning in their problems to Dr Death.

She drove too fast, but rock-steady.

Here's my problem, Doc; I'm scared as hell. Someone I love could be dying. Have you ever thought that? Have you ever lain awake with that one? Could be dying at this very moment.

The worst thing.

Ellwood put the phone down on the pillow, and brought his mouth close to it. 'Yes?'

'You've got what you asked for,' Todd said. 'The people I spoke to agreed to your suggestions.'

'OK,' Ellwood said. 'Tomorrow – tell them to be prepared for that. Tell them to get me cover with the locals: full clearance.'

'Do you need any back-up?'

'I can handle it.'

'What about Jones?'

'Don't worry. She's briefed; she knows what to do.'

'Quick and clean. Make it trouble-free, then get out.'

'I'll bear your recommendation in mind, Hilary; that's a promise.'

The girl laughed silently, because Ellwood hadn't stopped fucking her to take the call.

'Hilary – where will I be in a week's time?'

'Europe,' Todd told him. 'You're going to Europe next.'

'Very nice; what a nice idea.'

After a long pause, Todd said: 'I'll find a way, Wallace. Remember you heard me say that.'

Forty-Six

The flag and flagpole fell into the sea. It was dark, but Pascoe heard them go. His body glowed and a fever burned his eyes. Where the material of the skirt touched him, his skin blazed. He tore it off, his shorts as well, and threw them after the flag, then walked to the edge of the furthest lip of stone and slipped into the sea, his fingers in crevices to anchor him.

He went to sleep twice while he floated there. The first time he woke he was swallowing seawater greedily, the second time he had lost contact and was twenty feet off the rock, kept up by instinct and plucked at by the tide. He swam back, groaning with effort, and went to the shelter of the niche.

Naked, he lay full length on the wet rock. He was hot, then cold; either way, he shivered. A great fit of anger took him, turning almost at once to weeping, and he struck about him with his fists, feeling the pain as his knuckles grazed and cut. It was loss that he felt, and sorrow and regret.

He turned his face to the granite wall and slept.

Pascoe's dreams would only deal with the severely practical. He was in a restaurant, waiting for someone to join him. He was hungry and very thirsty, but when he tried to catch the waiter's eye, the man wouldn't see him. Instead, he went to a nearby table and poured drinks for a man and woman seated there. Pascoe saw the wine in close-up, hitting the bowl of the glass and sluicing the sides. It was so cold that it shed a dew from stem to rim. The couple turned to him and offered a toast. Luke Mallen and Lori Cosgrove.

Luke said, 'It's another way to die,' and they drank every drop.

Pascoe closed his eyes on the sight and fell asleep. He dreamed he was on a rock far out to sea; three bare lips of granite backed up to a granite wall, the sound of waves breaking, the cries of gulls.

When he woke up, the waiter was standing there to take his order, leaning forward slightly, anxious to please. The man's face seemed a disc of shadow because the morning sun was directly in Pascoe's eyes.

A little way off, another man stood, hand held out like the spokesman of a welcoming committee. Beyond him was a man in a dinghy. And beyond him a small pleasure boat, where faces poured along the side, dumb with amazement.

They radioed ship to shore while they brought him in, and he told the story of how his sails turned turtle. They found clothes for him. He drank too much water and vomited it back, then drank some more. At first he couldn't connect with the voices, the sound of the engine, the planks under his feet; he kept looking back at the rock, until finally it was bigger in memory than in sight.

In the wheelhouse, he ate five packets of sweet biscuits and some cake. It was more than he wanted. He drank water until his stomach swelled.

Because they were all watching him, cheering for him, smiling at him, the crowd at the quayside seemed full of familiar faces.

He came ashore and went from hand to hand, famous and lucky, the blur of fever still on him and making the moment a mirage of sights and sounds.

The firm ground shifting underfoot, and gulls still crying to let him know he hadn't come far.

A voice asking, *Who was it?* as if anyone might know.

Masts and sails. Sunlight striking off the windows of

seafront buildings. A cigarette in his fingers, the first for eight years.

Sophie walking down the quayside towards him, just another face in the crowd.

Forty-Seven

Illusionist, Magus, Escapologist; now Soothsayer. When he looked into the mirror, Luke saw the future. His old face was on one side of the glass, a new face on the other; the features were the same, but everything else had changed.

Becoming someone else was both easy and miraculous. A new passport, a new name, bank accounts, birth certificate: that was the easy part. The miraculous was Carla.

He could hear her upstairs, the uneven step as she went to and fro. Just minutes before, Ellwood had phoned and said, 'Everything's fine. I'm on my way. Get ready to leave.'

'Get ready to leave,' Luke had said to Carla, as if passing on a coded message.

The mirror didn't show Luke the details of his future with Carla; that story would develop as they lived it. But he saw moments – images that welled up between the glass and the quicksilver.

They started with a picture from the past that was really the first minute of their life. He saw Carla huddled on the beach in the lee of a breakwater, her face blank and cold as the ocean.

He saw them walking together by another sea – the Mediterranean, was it? – her arm through his, the little swing of her limp making their hips knock gently with each step.

He saw the facets of an ordinary existence arranged like a still life: dull, domestic things that anyone could own.

The images came up, then faded; he and Carla were

383

never out of each other's reach. He saw a picnic on a hillside, then a garden at evening-time, where two people were having their first drink of the day.

He saw a room where all their possessions really belonged; and that was the last thing he saw before he finally noticed the reflection of Wallace Ellwood holding a gun.

'The thing is,' Ellwood said, 'I lied. And not for the first time.'

Luke turned and began to circle, instinct making him back off from the foot of the stairs where Carla would soon appear. He was like a bird, feigning injury to lure a predator away from the nest.

'Sit down,' Ellwood ordered. He wagged the gun at a chair close to the middle of the room. Both men heard Carla's footsteps as she crossed the floor. Their voices were low, like those of parents anxious not to wake a sleeping child.

'Wallace—'

'The trick is – don't lose. There's always a loser. Always. Don't be him. That's my only rule, you know? It's the only rule there is. Don't be the loser.'

'Wallace—'

'So this is how it goes . . . Not long from now – quite soon – some people who look a lot like policemen are going to arrive and take you out of my life. Goodbye.' He gave a sunny little wave; the gun didn't move. 'What happened at that place up on the hill has to be someone's fault; someone has to take the *blame*. Why? Because that's the way the world works. Don't ask me to explain – I've never figured it out.' Ellwood shook his head. 'Anyway, it's you. You're the patsy. Lousy luck.'

'Wallace, let Carla go.'

'Sure.' Ellwood scarcely seemed to have heard him. 'Once everyone knows that someone is to *blame*, things will ease off. The problem is, I don't think we can count on your discretion. Can we?' He paused as if he were expecting an answer. 'So the future isn't going to be what you'd hoped for.'

'Let her go. There's nothing she can say – nothing she knows. It'll complicate matters, won't it? Let her go.'

'Sure, OK. There's something I want to tell you. Something about the past.' A door opened and closed upstairs. Luke's head lifted sharply to the sound. When he looked back, Ellwood's eyes were still on him. 'About the past. About Lori.'

Luke's eyes started to flick round the room. He was looking for a way: anything to warn Carla.

'*Look at me.*' Ellwood's voice was a furious hiss. 'Blame. That's what we were talking about, isn't it? *Fault.* It seems reasonable enough that you should suffer for this fucking mess, Great Zeno, you *fuck*, because if you hadn't started to think about the past, you might have been able to concentrate on what *I* fucking wanted.'

Luke tried to picture what it was that Carla was doing. She was silent now; her footfalls had traversed the hallway and come to a stop in the bedroom.

'Well, here's something from the past that you ought to know.' Ellwood seemed calmer; he started to laugh, remembering something so funny that even the years couldn't take the edge off it. 'You thought I was a double. Maybe you thought I did it only for money, or perhaps I was hedging my bets. Or else you thought that it simply gave me a thrill. Well, that would have been closest, for sure – betrayal for fun. I like that. It's a terrific idea. It wasn't true, though.'

Carla crossed the bedroom, going towards the door, then went back again. Luke saw her standing close to the dressing table. He heard the stool in front of the mirror scrape the floor and imagined her looking into the mirror.

'You screwed Lori. Lori's husband could be indiscreet, God knows, and Lori would tell you things. Pillow talk. Things that might help the cause. A good idea – my idea. You would go to confession and tell Tom Carey what you'd heard. He'd pass it along. Chinese whispers . . .

Russian whispers, really. And everything organized by me for kicks, or money, or else for the good of the cause. Except—' Ellwood's laughter came back, a rill of giggles, a joke that was almost too good to share. 'Except that wasn't what I'd set up. What I'd set up was a great deal cleverer than that. Know how? Listen – the Colonel knew about you and Lori. He didn't care. Let me tell you something. Two nights after Lori killed herself, the Colonel organized a celebration party – just the two of us, some champagne and a little coke, and a couple of girls who got fucked until they stung, oh yes, we had a great time and the Colonel laughed so fucking much I thought he might split a gut.' So gleeful, the giggles sputtered across his lips in a little spray of froth.

Luke tried to imagine what Carla might be seeing in the mirror, then tried to forget – she would be seeing her own images of their future, summoned up like episodes from a dream.

'Got there yet, Great fucking Zeno, you stupid shit? See what that means? He knew. He didn't care. What Lori told you was what the Colonel told her. And what he told her was what I wanted you to hear. What I wanted Carey to hear. What I wanted all you fucks to hear, everyone in the whisper-chain. Disinformation – you know? Not just information that was crap, but *bad* crap, *damaging* crap. The kind of crap that sticks to people's shoes and comes off on the rug. And you passed it along, oh yes, and your friends, the baby revolutionaries, thought it was so funny you were screwing the military, and you thought it was so funny that they didn't know what was *really* happening, and I thought it was so fucking funny that I could hardly file a report on you without pissing my fucking pants.'

Carla got up from the stool – Luke heard the legs rasp on the floor again – and walked towards the door. The door opened.

Ellwood was watching Luke's face: peering at it; he seemed to be looking for signs of breakage.

Luke said, 'Why not just let her go?'

Ellwood frowned. 'Did you hear what I said just now?'

'Yes, I heard. I'm asking you, she's not part of this, why don't you let her go before anyone comes?'

'It was all a con,' Ellwood said. 'I set you up. Lori was just a channel for bad information.'

Luke said, 'What it was – Lori died; we killed her. That was the past. That was the worst thing. That was why I killed Nick and Marianne and Sam Pascoe. To obliterate the worst thing. You're telling me things I didn't know, but they're things I don't care about. I heard what you said – it was all a fake. You set us up. Brilliant. I thought I was taking secrets to Carey; I was taking lies. Clever you. Carey thought he was passing good stuff to East Germany; he was passing garbage. Hats off to Wallace. What I'm saying – I don't mind. I'd've minded then, but I don't now. Can you see? It's just politics and that sort of shit. It doesn't matter; it never really did.'

Carla's footstep was on the stair.

'Let her go – why don't you just let her go.'

Ellwood shook his head in amazement. 'I've never seen it before,' he said, 'and I can't really remember hearing about it that often.' He looked at Luke as a lepidopterist might look at a rare species in the killing-bottle. 'Selfless love – is that what it is? You killed to keep her, but now you'll let her go. *Selfless*. You'll let her go if I will. Is that right?'

Luke nodded. 'Whatever you want it to be. Just let her go.'

Ellwood's laughter overtook him now. He knew he couldn't shift his gaze from Luke, so he had to laugh like a man in chains. Head steady, gun steady, he shouted with laughter, mouth wide, eyes gone to slits, the muscles of his face puckered up round the joke.

'Oh, shit,' he said, 'oh, shit . . .' He cuffed a tear away with his free hand, the other eye keeping a bead on Luke's chest. Under the widow's peak of gun-metal hair, the forehead creased with glee; the grey skin seemed almost to glow for a moment. 'Oh, *shit*, have I saved the best till last with you.'

Carla came into the room and across Luke's eye-line, walking towards Ellwood and smiling broadly, as if a room full of laughter was what she had most expected.

There are models whose faces wait for the camera. Free of make-up, and free of ideas about their own beauty, they can seem pinched and plain. Then they stand in front of a backdrop, every cosmetic skilfully balanced, skilfully applied, hair tousled and flying, their features suddenly alive, jewellery, perfume, clothes stitch-perfect, their bodies lithe and full of energy.

Luke realized that what Carla had seen in the mirror wasn't a vision of a new life, but her beauty emerging under her own hand. As she crossed the room, she threw in a couple of limping steps as a cruel reminder.

Ellwood studied the expression on Luke's face and his bellows of laughter grew until he was almost fighting for breath. Carla stood next to him, her face bright.

Luke was still as a stone. He was looking at Carla like a man who has just seen a vision of his own death.

Ellwood's laughter came down the scale in broken fragments until a terrible silence settled on the room. Weeping would have been better; cursing would have been better. It was like the moment before an execution.

The moment made Carla breathless. She was watching Luke.

A pulse went through her temples, *zip-zip*, like tiny electric shocks: power making her dizzy; lust making her dizzy; the same thing. She moved closer to Ellwood, but she was watching Luke.

Ellwood's laugh returned briefly, making the gun barrel hop. He could feel her excitement like a heat-source. As she came close, he put an arm round her neck and let his hand drop on to her breast. She put her own hand over his, moving both; her tongue flickered between her teeth and her eyes half closed, but she was still watching Luke.

Carla and Wallace Ellwood. A side-by-side embrace, his hand moving on her, their bodies touching and nudging, like the happy couple posing for a last photograph in their going-away clothes, and scarcely able to wait until they could take their appetites to bed.

They both watched Luke; they didn't take their eyes off him for a second.

Forty-Eight

Pascoe lay back in the passenger seat of Sophie's car, eyes closed, and said no to everything.

No I don't feel good. No I'm not going back to London; not yet. No I won't just drop it, enough's enough, this bastard's tried to kill me several times and finally I'm angry. No I don't think going to the house is a risk-free move, but I'm going to do it anyway. No I don't know what I'll find there, but I hope it'll be Luke Mallen because I'm going to break his fucking back.

And no you can't come with me.

There were still people on the quayside, pointing out to sea, then back towards the seafront road – telling Pascoe's story.

Sophie asked, 'What about your capsized sailing boat?'

'I'm supposed to see some guy from the Coast Guard.'

'Will you?'

'Of course not.'

'What name did you give them?'

'John Kelly.'

'Who was that?'

'Grandfather on my mother's side of the family. I said you can't come with me.'

Sophie had started the car and was driving alongside the ocean. 'Yes, I heard you say that. I'm coming anyway.'

'Stop the car,' Pascoe told her.

'You know the way, you'd better give me—'

'Stop the car!'

'. . . directions.'

They drove for another ten minutes. Pascoe said, 'You should have turned right a mile back.'

*　　*　　*

There was a driver and two other men, both of whom sat in the back with Luke who was handcuffed to one of them. The priority clearance had stipulated no local involvement; the idea was to take the prisoner directly to London. They wound through the lanes, tall hedges on either side. The driver said, 'Shut him up, OK?'

The sunroof was jacked up to give air and the slipstream whickered against the rim. Above that sound, thin and steady, the sound of Luke's keening ran in the wind. He sat upright, eyes open, his mouth wide, and the cry came out of him unbidden.

It was the sound of unnegotiable despair.

Carla put some coffee on while Ellwood made phone calls. He said, 'Mallen's on his way.' Then, after a pause: 'No, better than that, tell them that he was picked up in London. Very soon, no-one will care. The local police can be briefed at any time.'

He hung up the phone, smiling; he said: 'You total asshole.'

'Tell me about him,' said Carla. 'About Todd.'

'You work with him. You know as much as I do.'

'No, Wallace, it's my strong suspicion that there are things I definitely *don't* know.'

'You're looking for an edge.'

'I'm looking for something. I don't know what it is. I'm hoping you'll help me find it.'

'What does it feel like – when you think of it?'

'A bit like money, a bit like power.'

Ellwood said, 'We're two of a kind – I can see that. I know what you want. I expect you'll find it, too. Be careful. It might belong to someone else.'

'I wouldn't take anything from you, Wallace. Do you imagine that? I wouldn't steal from you.'

Of course you would, Ellwood thought. And I'll be waiting for the moment. And when it comes I'll kick your tits off, *bitch*.

391

★   ★   ★

Luke was silent now. The man he was cuffed to had used
the free hand to slap his prisoner a few times. Luke didn't
mind the slapping much; he was thinking about something. 'The world is circular, did you know that?'

The man had a wormcast of scar-tissue running inwards
from his temple, making his eyebrow half-and-half. 'Say
what?'

'Circular.'

'Yeah; that's what I heard.'

The driver asked, 'What's he saying?'

'The world is round.'

'Oh, right . . .' The driver nodded, seeming to ratify
the opinion. All three men laughed.

'I did it to Lori,' Luke said, 'now someone's done it to
me. The bad things circle round, the past circles round.
You release something into the world, some awful thing,
the worst thing, and in time you get it back; you always get
it back.'

The third man said, 'Shut up, for fuck's sake. Go back
to squealing, all right?'

They were about three miles from Longrock, going
through a little town with a working port. The road fell
steeply to a littered quay where a stubby freighter was
putting in. The driver stopped at a set of lights on the
crown of the hill and watched the freighter's crew making
fast. 'Give him a pill,' he said, watching the lights. 'He can
sleep the journey away.' He looked over his shoulder,
fingertips to the wheel. 'Give him a knock-out drop.'

'Like an egg,' Luke said, 'but it doesn't mean new
beginnings.'

The third man turned, irritated now, and backhanded
Luke as if he were a dog. 'Enough,' he said.

'It means old things come round again, old sins come
round, old pain come round—'

A second slap made Luke's head rock back.

'Give the bastard a pill,' the driver advised, his eyes on
the red light.

'Like an egg.' The man turned in his seat, fist bunched, and Luke leaned towards him, and took an egg out of his ear. The driver heard the sudden silence but couldn't interpret it.

The two men in the back looked at the egg as if it were something they'd never seen before; as if they didn't have a word for it. Two seconds passed. The man with the split eyebrow realized that Luke had produced the egg with his handcuffed hand; when he tried to move, he found his arms were locked behind his back, a cuff on either wrist. He watched as the egg flapped open.

The third man said, 'Don't—'

The driver let the brake off and gunned the engine.

When the car filled with light, Luke was the only one with his eyes closed. There came a bang like a gunshot and the carbide-white light struck from the middle of the noise.

A standard thunderflash in a confined space – deafness and blindness ricocheting round the car. Luke crossed the lap of the handcuffed man in a dive, opening the door as the driver stamped on the accelerator; the door cracked against his shins and he went clear.

The driver hit the brake, but he couldn't see a thing. He glanced off an approaching pick-up and slewed sideways, falling across into the passenger seat. The car went on down the hill. In the back the third man had opened his door, but wouldn't jump into the white void that surrounded him.

The driver found the wheel, but didn't know where they were or what they were headed for. He swung it away from the slope and was broadsided by a delivery van. The three men flew round like broken-backed gymnasts. The car turned three hundred and sixty degrees and started its journey down the slope again. Now the man with the split eyebrow sat, cuffed and blind, amid the litter of the other two.

Every vehicle on the hill stopped. Faces at windows watched a car go past that seemed to have no driver and only one passenger. It hit wings and bumpers and headlights on one side, the kerb on the other, straightening itself up for the roll down to the quay.

It was Sophie's turn to say no.

Her 'no' was pretty straightforward; a singular 'no'. She had pulled the car in by the side of the road without warning – slamming the handbrake on and starting to cry before they had properly come to rest. She'd covered her face with her hands and wept like someone shouting – hoarse and loud – as if outrage and fear had been tracking her all night on the drive west, all morning as she waited on the quayside, and had finally caught up with her on this road above the ocean.

Pascoe had done nothing but wait and listen: 'You could have been anywhere, dead, anywhere, I didn't know, I drove for five hours not knowing what I'd find, and I didn't know if it was you, the man they were bringing in, and I stood on that fucking quayside among that crowd so fucking *busy* with it all, they were loving it all, and it could have been any fool that fetched up on a rock, but then it was you, and I'd been to the hotel and the bar and the fucking boatyard, thinking he might be there, thinking I might die, and you step off the boat like Robinson fucking Crusoe, you bastard . . .'

She had been turned away from him, rocking back and forth, sobs making her bounce in her seat, until he'd said, 'Do you want me to drive?' and she'd turned and hit him, closed fist on the boss of his shoulder, with all the anger she had.

'Do you want me to drive?'

'No,' Sophie said.

When they were travelling again, he said: 'I love you, but I'm not quite ready yet.'

Ellwood found Carla in the bedroom. He said, 'Let's go.'

She had arranged some items on the bed, like a little exhibition in the house of someone famous but long dead.

Three juggler's globes, a fan of throwing knives, a nest of brightly coloured silk scarves, two decks of cards, an egg that contained a ring. 'The rest must have been in the box,' she said. 'What shall we do with it?'

'Someone will come to clear up,' Ellwood told her. 'Technicians – you know? Waste and wipe. They'll take care of it.'

'Erasure,' Carla said. 'Is that it? Not a shred, not a jot, not a tittle.'

Ellwood looked at her and frowned. 'That's right. Problem?'

Carla laughed. 'It was a great performance, Wallace. You should have seen me. I was fucking *brilliant*. Now the show's over; I'm like an actress in a dark theatre.' She threw one of the globes into the air and clapped twice before catching it. 'No applause, no reviews, no stage-door Johnnies.' She set the globe down on the bed, carefully in place, and followed Ellwood to the door.

She turned a moment, her fingertips collecting kisses from her lips and flinging them towards a torrent of applause.

'Take something,' Ellwood said. 'Keepsake.'

Carla left the door open for the technicians. 'What in hell would I want to keep?' she asked.

Luke ran through the outskirts of the town, climbing all the time, putting the low areas around the quayside behind him, until he found the coastal path. He stopped to get breath and looked across the expanse of ocean that lay to the west. He could see Windrush Head and, just below it, the thin outcrop of Meer's Point like a raddled breakwater.

He started to jog. The thunderflash was still a high whine in both ears; it mingled with the sound of the sea like wind singing on outcrop rock.

He was thinking of nothing, which was the same thing as thinking of everything – a mind too full of the past, too full of pain, too full of loathing and misery and loss for any single image to come clear. He was working off instinct.

He ran better than two miles without stopping and came to a point on the cliff path that lay above the cove where two rocks were anchored in the shingle close to the sea's edge – one like a seal wading out through the breakers, the other like the arched back of a cat. He put a hand on either knee, then bent forward and spat. There was a pain under his ribs and the muscles in his legs had gone into spasm.

He waited, his chest ballooning with effort. Just instinct –nothing but that. There might be time later for thought. There might be time later to understand the little mysteries of life and death, the words that opened tombs, the magic moments.

Pascoe and Sophie stood at the door like friends come to call. He had circled the house twice and seen no-one because Ellwood and Carla were first going downstairs, then in view when Pascoe wasn't able to look in, then out of view again in the hallway.

Ellwood heard the door opening and took out his gun. As Pascoe stepped through, he fired reflexively – no time for thought, he could have been killing anyone. The bullet clipped Pascoe, passing through a fleshy inch just above his hip and causing him to sit down heavily on the hallway floor. Sophie was framed in the doorway like someone who's arrived on the wrong night, seeing the surprised looks on the faces of her hosts. Ellwood beckoned with the gun-barrel as if to say, Come in anyway; there's plenty for everyone. Carla shut the door.

'You're supposed to be dead,' Ellwood observed. 'Did he lie, or what?'

Pascoe cupped his hand and looked down at his side, expecting to see blood pour in. There was just a seepage; he couldn't feel much pain.

Carla said, 'Who's this?' Then her brow cleared and she said, 'I know; I know who,' remembering what Luke had told her of ghosts.

'He didn't lie,' Pascoe said, 'he tried as hard as he knew; I decided not to die.'

'Here's your chance to think again.' Ellwood wagged the gun towards the living room, ushering them in. He sounded as if he knew just what would happen next, but his eyes were dark with anger and confusion. To Carla he said, 'Close the blinds.'

'No-one comes up here.'

'Someone just did, so close the fucking blinds.'

Carla toured the room. Each window had a folding wooden panel on either side. She drew the room into twilight. Pascoe sat down, leaning against the upright pillar in the centre of the floor. Ellwood backed off to keep both of them in his angle of vision. He bit his lip.

Sophie said, 'If you don't know what to do, try doing nothing.'

Ellwood walked over and hooked the gun up under her ribs, hard; her lips stretched wide but she made no sound. She leaned forward like someone craning to listen, and Ellwood leaned forward too, his face so close to hers that his breath made her eyelids flicker. His rapid whisper filled the room, thick with murderous tension, the words running into one another: 'Do you want to die, you *fuck*, is that what you want? Because it could happen any moment, it could happen now, die *now*, it's easy you piece of *cunt*, it's very easy.'

Sophie put a hand to her side and sat down next to Pascoe. When the hand shifted to be under her heart, Pascoe knew she was thinking about the baby.

Ellwood backed off, still looking at them. His hand lingered by the telephone for a moment, then he sat down in a small wicker chair and crossed his left ankle on his right knee, looking for all the world like someone with a plan.

Carla watched him, then turned to close the final shutter and gave a big, glittering smile to the world outside. *You haven't the first idea what to do with them, have you Wallace? And you can't call the Department without looking bad – looking bad and having to start from the top with explanations and revelations and magic shows where people die and the*

397

strange disappearance of Father Tom Carey . . . And I can feel a little of your power leaking my way.

She crossed the room and patted Ellwood's shoulder, offering sensible advice like Martha Goodwife. 'You'll have to kill them, Wallace; it's a matter of how and where. The important things are no connection with you, no reflection on you. So make sure they're never found. There are woods out there and beyond the woods, the sea. We just sit here and calmly work out the best thing.'

No connection with *you*; no reflection on *you*. Ellwood thought: Ambition's your weakness. He stored the notion carefully. After a moment, he said: 'Wherever we take them, they'd travel better dead.'

Carla went out into the kitchen and came back carrying two heavy-duty bin-liners; she looked around and picked up a cushion from an armchair. 'OK?' she asked.

It was standard practice – the victim on one side, a cushion under the head to catch the shower from the exit wound, plastic over everything and down to the chest so that nothing leaked or stained. Most people simply went along with it, meek, almost anxious to please. Now and then, someone would force you to make a mess. Pascoe stood up, putting himself in front of Sophie. Ellwood got up too.

'It's your choice. I can shoot you a couple of times in the gut and there won't be much blood, but you'll be in too much pain to be a problem. Then we'll do her. Then you. It comes out the same.' Ellwood stood off six feet and lowered the gun to point at Pascoe's belly. Carla advanced on Sophie with the cushion and the bin bag, one in either hand, like a saleswoman showing the new style of the season. A globe of white light rolled out across the room, hissing slightly and glowing in the half-dark.

There was a silence in the room that seemed to last for several minutes. Two seconds, maybe. Ellwood turned and fired a shot that went into one of the shutters, opening a trough of splinters. He had bent slightly at the knee, like a tennis player winding up to serve, and Luke's knife took him in the face, going through the meat of the cheek and burying itself in the jaw. He screamed and stepped backwards, his torso arching away from the impact, and Pascoe simply took the gun out of his hand.

Ellwood stumbled off, feet tangling, but he stayed upright. His hands were wild at his face. He looked like an unsteady rope-walker being attacked by a swarm of bees. Pascoe swung the gun from one side to the other, not knowing who to cover.

Sophie said, 'Shoot him,' but Pascoe didn't know who she meant and, in any case, it was the wrong moment. He was looking at Luke; Luke was looking at Carla. Ellwood went backwards through the door, stiff with shock, his face running with blood like a terrible sweat.

Carla said, 'His car's parked in a lane sixty feet back from the turning circle. A blue Audi.' She was talking to Luke, hoping that Ellwood might draw him off. He neither moved nor looked away from her. Carla turned to Pascoe. She said, 'Shoot him.'

Ellwood leaned against the door of his car. The haft of the knife was jutting from his face beneath the left eye. He put up a hand to dislodge it, but the pain stopped him short.

He said, 'You fuck, you stupid *fuck*, know what you've done? Know what you've done, stupid, you want to die, or what?' It sounded as though he was chewing a mouthful of meat as he spoke. '*Stupid*, you want to die, you stupid *fuck*?'

He was talking to himself. He got into the car and gunned the engine, coming out on to the road above the ocean in a series of broad fishtails and a haze of blue smoke. Tears and blood ran off his chin as he drove.

In the house, no-one had moved. Luke hadn't bothered to look at Pascoe. He couldn't see how it was possible that the man was alive, but all astonishment had left him, all capacity for surprise. Here was Sam Pascoe who should be dead. Nothing was impossible, the past could unfold in the present, love could grow murderous and mad, the dead could walk.

'I'll wait with her till they come.'

'No!' Carla's plea went past Pascoe to Sophie. 'Don't do that. Stay here.'

The bin-bag and cushion lay on the floor close to Carla's feet. Sophie imagined herself lying down under the dark hood. She said, 'Are you OK?'

'More or less,' Pascoe told her.

'Let's go.'

'What will you do?' Pascoe asked Luke.

'Wait with her till they come.'

'Who is she?' Sophie was asking the question of Pascoe.

'I don't know.' Nothing made sense. Luke had attacked Ellwood. Now he was looking at this woman and holding a single thought. Pascoe could see what the thought was, but couldn't guess at a reason.

'Come on.' Sophie started to walk away.

'He'll kill her,' Pascoe said. 'It's Lori all over again. We can't go; we can't just go away.'

'It isn't Lori; it's not like that. We haven't done anything wrong. We don't even know who she is. It's not our business.'

'Walking away kills her. Do you want that?'

'How can you be sure?'

Pascoe sighed. 'Look at him. What's he thinking?'

They both looked at Luke. He only had eyes for Carla.

Sophie said, 'It's simple; if we stay here, we're involved. We'll never get clear of it – never survive. What do you want to do? Phone the police? And say what? Everything here is lethal to us, don't you see it? The past, who we are, what we've done, why we're here. But I'm not thinking about the past now, Sam. Fuck that. I'm thinking about the future.'

'A death preserves our future?'

Luke's head turned, as if someone had called his name in a crowd. 'One less,' he agreed. 'That's right; one less for you . . . I'll wait with her till they come.'

'Shoot him,' Carla said, 'and we're free.'

'You wanted to kill us all,' Sophie said. 'Everyone in the Group.'

'Yes.' Luke was just about able to transfer his attention to Sophie.

'Why?'

'Kill the past to preserve the future. You just said that – you said it yourself; you understand.'

Sophie looked at Carla and saw that the woman was shaking in every limb. 'She was the future?' Sophie asked. Luke didn't reply, but Sophie saw that it was true. 'What is she now?'

'Now . . .' Luke said. 'Now, she's the worst thing.'

Without speaking another word, Sophie turned and went through the hallway, then out of the door. Luke walked across to Carla and took her by the arm. When she pulled back, he held her more tightly, turning to face Pascoe and forcing her to turn with him.

'Here's the problem, Sam. What you lose matters more than the things you're able to keep.'

He opened the door and got in. Sophie started the engine at once, driving off before he'd got the door properly shut. She was licking tears off her upper lip. 'Enough of this shit, that's *all*, that's fucking *enough*.' She hit the wheel a crack with the heel of her hand.

Pascoe rolled from side to side as she took the downhill bends. He said, 'I feel pretty ill.'

She hadn't thought about that. 'What happens?' she asked.

'All gunshot wounds are reported to the police.'

'Can we do it ourselves?'

'I don't think so, no.'

'We'll have to.'

'At the least of it, I'll need antibiotics and some suturing. For all I know, it'll be surgery. Get me back to London, that's the first thing to do.'

'It's not the same,' Sophie said. 'Lori was everybody's fault; that woman is Luke's fault.'

'Not now,' Pascoe said. 'I don't want to think about that.' He leaned his head against the window and started to doze, but he was still thinking about his wound. 'Rob Thomas will know a bent doctor.'

'Are you sure?'

'I think so,' he said. 'Drive faster, I feel like shit.'

Luke turned to Carla as if he might kiss her and she backed off until her shoulders rapped the wall. He stood very close.

She said, 'What did you want? Why should it matter that much? It doesn't matter.'

He put his arm round her shoulders and fear made her want to faint. He laid a hand on her breast as if he might draw her heartstring.

She said, 'Luke . . .' and her eyes rolled up to show the white.

The globe still glowed in the dimness. It had rolled into a corner of the room where it shed a little neon puddle. Carla slid down the wall like a drunk, half conscious. She lay straight-legged, her head and shoulders in Luke's lap, and stared at the globe. She was shaking still.

'Let me go,' she said. 'Does it matter? Let me go.'

'I shall.'

He pinched her nostrils between finger and thumb. When she opened her mouth to breathe, he took from her ear the egg that held the diamond ring and pushed it into her mouth.

One of her arms was trapped against his body, the other came up, busy about her lips to remove the egg. He knocked the hand away. A coloured silk scarf shook out like a banner above her head. She tried to close her mouth against it, but already she was choking for air. The scarf went in with the egg, until her cheeks bulged. His fingers still pinched her nose and the other hand went across her lips to seal them.

402

Her fists beat against him, wherever she could reach. It made no difference; she might have been hitting stone. He knelt beside her, holding her head like a priceless bowl between his hands.

The house was still; the woods around the house were still. In the room there was the merest soft scampering, like tiny creatures running in the wainscot. It was the sound of Carla's heels scuffing the floor. Her back was arched so violently it seemed her spine must crack, each muscle pumped and rigid, sinews hard as thongs. Then everything in her came apart.

Luke kept his hands in position for a while, as if a word still lay in her mouth that had to be stifled. He took the scarf from her mouth and the word remained unspoken. Then he removed the egg. He took out the ring and slid it on to her finger.

'I'll wait until they come,' he said, speaking to no-one in particular.

A blood-bead lay in the corner of her mouth; he took it on the ball of one finger, then to his lips.

He closed her eyes. He finger-combed her hair.

Forty-Nine

Ellwood had gone three hundred miles, driving like a drunk. As he came into the city approaches, he was still weaving across lanes, overtaking on the inside, going hard and heavy between accelerator and brake. The car carried slashes in the paintwork where he'd nicked the central barrier at speed.

His entire face was numb. He couldn't get the knife free without causing more damage, but now he raised his hand to the haft from time to time, reflexively, like a man touching some gory token in the hope of finding good fortune.

For most of the journey he had felt like a wounded animal making for cover; his only objective was get back, get home, get away. Now he began to think a different thought.

A mistake. It was a mistake to leave. Go back and change things, go back and save yourself, go back and kill them all.

He saw them as though they were still standing there in the house – Luke by the stairway, Carla opposite, Pascoe and Sophie close to the wooden pillar, fixed in position as they were fixed in his mind.

The only way to save yourself. Go back and kill them all.

The motorway lanes were blocked by dawdlers – someone in the outside lane dribbling along at eighty. Ellwood made a diagonal across three vehicles, almost grazing their bumpers, and used the hard shoulder to overtake; then he made the reverse diagonal back to the fast lane. He touched the haft of the knife without knowing he'd done it. The flesh round the two inches of blade outside the wound was purplish and puffy.

Go back and kill them all.

In the lower part of Ellwood's vision, mostly to the left, there was an ullage of pearly light. It was blindness, seeping slowly upwards.

The traffic thickened where the road began to cut through the outer zone. With the early evening sun at his back, Ellwood hammered between trucks and cars like a man driving the mazy lines of a jigsaw. A dome of pollution hung over the inner zones of the city, jots and particles dancing in the air, borne up on thermals of stinging, ice-blue vapour. It ate ironwork. It brought rain like a soup of poisons.

Go back and kill them all.

Fired by fever, his imagination brought them to him one by one. Luke crossed from the stair; Carla walked forward sedately; Sophie followed, resigned, her head bowed; Pascoe shuffled up, clutching his wound. Each of them went under his hand, each died, and the future was clear.

He gunned the engine and changed down, using the hard shoulder again to take him round a vast container truck as he came up on to the elevated section. The sun over his shoulder made the windows of his tower block light up in red and white lines, top to bottom and side to side, shedding patterns like a vast kaleidoscope.

A car pulled over to take the exit road, found Ellwood on the hard shoulder, and took a side-swipe that peeled the hubcaps. Ellwood thought he was driving like a rock. In truth, he had lost better than half the vision in his left eye and was having trouble with perspective.

He put up a hand and touched the knife. *Go back and kill them all.*

He took the exit road at seventy, then fishtailed past the entrance level to the building until he hit a roundabout. He changed down viciously and came back towards the slope. The exit road was one-way, but had two lanes. Ellwood took the nearside, ascending into the sun, too dazed to register the traffic flow on the east-bound carriageway above him.

Everything on the exit road pulled over and tried to stop. He left a growing tail-back of rear-ended vehicles – a sound like iron doors slamming, one after another, in a long corridor. When he hit the hard shoulder of the elevated section, with three lanes of traffic bearing down on him, his speed was improving to ninety. He drove through a tunnel of noise – klaxons and engine roar – making almost a hundred yards on the shoulder before he saw a gap across to the outer lane.

A miracle took him through to it unscathed. Drivers coming eastward stood on their brakes, but that was pointless. They lost control at speed, some of them turning round completely, others going into wild skids that sent them back and forth across the lanes: first five, then twenty, then sixty cars, banging about the road as other vehicles slammed in from behind. Fire erupted in some of the cars, and flame raced across on a line of spillage to swarm round the wreckage. People got out of their cars and were killed where they stood – crushed by new impacts as other cars piled up, or hit by drivers still in motion. Some couldn't get out, but they could see the fire.

The opal in Ellwood's left eye turned crimson as sunlight flashed on the windscreen. Even so, he could see the road as a swim of colour; all he needed to do was keep his course.

The artic driver was high up and holding a bend. He could see the carnage ahead, but he couldn't see why. He took his foot off the accelerator, snapped on his hazard lights and began to look for a break in the traffic lines. At that point, Ellwood's car came into view on the crown of the bend.

The driver pumped the airbrake and swung the wheel, then Ellwood was on him, his car roof-high to the artic's wheels. He clouted a mudguard and veered a little, then took a more solid blow from the wheels of the trailer. The tail of the vehicle hadn't cleared at all; it was still snaking over from the outside lane. Ellwood side-slapped it at over a hundred miles an hour, rolled, came off his rear wheels like a diver and was airborne. The artic jack-knifed, going into a massive skid and tumbling cars with it, until the sheer clog of metal under the trailer made it flip on to its side. The driver came clear, but lay where he fell without moving. The only sounds were horns and the low rumble of fire.

Ellwood's car turned a complete somersault as it cleared the guard rails of the elevated section. It fell eighty feet into the crowded streets of Zone Two – cars, trucks, shopfronts, restaurant windows, pavements crowded with people – and turned twice more before coming to rest. All around it was chaos and pain.

Ellwood sat upright in the driver's seat. He was dead, but his last thought was still on the air.

Go back . . .

Fifty

It was a good wound, if wounds could be thought of that way, and Rob Thomas had sent Pascoe to a consulting room close to Harley Street where he was treated by a doctor who asked only medical questions.

'My car's in a hotel car park down there,' Pascoe had said, 'the Windrush.'

'Roxborough pays,' Thomas had guessed.

'Roxborough pays.'

'I'll fetch it. Listen, Sam, I didn't give you this address, I don't know about the gunshot wound, I haven't seen you for weeks.'

'You're right,' Pascoe had agreed. 'When you pick up the car, no fancy driving – don't get stopped.'

'Because . . .'

'Because there's a gun in the glove compartment that's registered to a junior minister in the Northern Ireland Office.'

Thomas had sighed. 'Thanks. You just saw the fee quadruple.'

Now it was time to leave, he looked back from the door and saw a place where he'd been both miserable and safe.

Sophie had lain awake most of the night and listened to the seismic clues from Pascoe's dreams: little grunts and howls, words scrambled like code, whimpers and unhappy laughter. They had eaten a meal, and the table still bore unused plates, some cutlery, torn bread, a pepper mill. An unfinished bottle of wine lolled in a silver cooling bucket.

'Let's go,' he said.

She saw that he had already opened the door. A small

suitcase stood in the hallway. Everything else in the apartment was unmoved; everything he owned still in place. The slow notes of a Beethoven cello sonata sifted on the air.

'Leave it like this?'

'Leave it like this.'

Sophie joined him at the door, but turned and looked round the room. 'Take something,' she said, 'for a keepsake.'

Pascoe shook his head, then turned and walked away, leaving her to follow. 'There's nothing I want to keep,' she heard him say.

Sirens and bass-lines.

'Where are we going?' She asked as if he ought to know.

The air scratched their throats and a greasy wind turned the leaves of the trees in the park, turned cans in the gutter.

'First, your apartment. Then a ferry port, then France, then just drive.'

There was a smell of charred wood. The sun was a yellow-white flush behind the haze.

'That sounds like a plan.'

'It is. That's just what it is. A plan.'

Sam Pascoe and Sophie Lanner, stepping out into the Dead Zone; and with them, their child, holding its breath and dreaming of the future.

Fifty-One

He put his hands to his mouth, like a man surprised, and began to unravel a cord from between his lips.

They had searched him, then taken away his shoelaces. He hadn't been wearing a tie. They had put a finger up his ass, then turned him round and lifted his balls to look there. They had shone a light into his mouth, and there had been nothing to see. Now here was the cord, arriving hand over hand. It was magic; just magic. It was easy.

They had rummaged in his hair and made him show them the soles of his feet. The cord reached to the ground, but still he kept bringing it out.

The Great Zeno.

The cell was dark apart from a ruddy glow at the barred window: the city's perpetual day-in-night.

He could see all that he wanted to see. A view from the cliff-top path, a running sea, and Carla crouching in the lee of a breakwater. Although she was far below, every detail of her face was clear. It was magic.

The cord kept coming, running between his lips, slightly damp. He stood on his bunk and tied it off to the bars, then made a running loop for his neck.

A gull slid down the wind, then another, then four or five together, fast enough to dazzle. Carla got up. She took a few paces towards him, and her hip swayed with the limp, worse on the pebbles, worse for going uphill. He could hear the drag and release of the sea loud in his ear. She raised a hand: to wave, perhaps, or encourage.

He would step down, step down to her now, the great drop from cliff to beach no more than the tread of a stair, the acres of air an illusion, nothing more.

Easy to step down and be with her now. Easy to step out of the cell, down on to the beach; it was nothing; just magic.

And everything would come right, step down.

And everything would be forgotten, step down.

And everything would be possible, step down.

Step down, now. Step *now*.

Abra –

THE END

SONS OF THE MORNING
by Jack Curtis

'Gripping . . . a superb book in all respects'
Express & Echo

Linda Bowman was the first. Nobody special, just a face in the crowd. Yet someone picked her out, someone with a high-velocity rifle, someone elated by his own dark power. Then there was the man on the train; then the young couple drinking at a riverside pub. It was every policeman's nightmare – a clever and remorseless killer choosing his victims at random.

Robin Culley is a policeman, and it's his nightmare, but his instinct tells him that, despite what they seem, the killings have a motive.

Culley's obsession with the apparently pointless slaughter leads him into worlds of fear and shadow; from the highest level of British politics – the Cabinet itself – to the world of assassins for hire and mercenaries on the run; from a sinister Arizona billionaire art collector to the dangerous secrets of the SAS. It threatens those closest to Culley; and it takes him, finally, to a heart-stopping confrontation wth a psychotic killer on the storm-torn wilderness of Dartmoor . . .

0 552 13592 5

CROWS' PARLIAMENT
by Jack Curtis

Simon Guerney plies a lonely trade. He specializes in the rescue of kidnap victims; his unrecognized skills the last resort of the rich and desperate.

At first the disappearance of David Paschini seems a straightforward abduction case and Guerney joins the boy's mother in New York to play out the usual waiting game. Once there he begins to sense inconsistencies in the pattern of events – but it is not until the unknown kidnappers demand that he travel to London that Guerney realizes the game has turned and that suddenly he is the prey not the hunter . . .

Strikingly original in its combination of power politics, the growing menace of kidnapping and the disturbing but very real world of ESP, *Crows' Parliament* will take its place amongst such classics of the genre as *Rogue Male* and *The Third Man*.

0 552 13081 8

BLOWBACK
by Denis Kilcommons

'If it is a blowback, who's responsible for the hits? The CIA? The Chinese? Or the KGB?'

The roll of film on the dead man's body set off alarm bells in MI6. What was the Home Secretary's daughter doing in Vienna, and in the arms of one of Europe's most wanted terrorists? Can the scandal be stopped before it goes too far?

Damage limitation or, as he calls it, cleaning up other people's messes, is one of Lacey's specialities. So debriefing Sara Mathieson and dealing with her lover seems pretty routine. That is, until Sara is killed in SIS custody and her death is linked to a series of assassinations in Europe. Then Lacey knows it isn't routine. It's something big; something that doesn't square with the Rules of the Game. Someone, somewhere is playing dirty. But is it the Wicked Witch of the East? Or of the West?

Set in the uncertain new world of East-West relations, BLOWBACK is a high-speed thriller of almost unbearable tension combined with an ingenious plot which saves its final nerve-jangling secret to the end. Following the promise of the award-winning THE DARK APOSTLE it confirms Denis Kilcommons as one of today's masters of the thriller genre.

0 552 13656 9

THE LUCY GHOSTS
by Eddy Shah

In the dying days of the Second World War many of Germany's rocket scientists traded their expertise for privileged treatment at the hands of both Russian and American invaders. For these scientists, bound together in a secret East-West brotherhood known as *Die Lucie Geister*, the war would never cease until Germany was united once more.

But with Reunification, sinister forces are unleashed. In a rash of assassinations, the scientists' records 'disappear' in the mysterious but systematic destruction of CIA and KGB files, and SAS captain Adam Nicholson is called in. A series of horrific murders leads him and his CIA sidekick, Billie Wood, from New Orleans to a neo-Nazi breeding ground in Germany. But it will be in Berlin, Germany's new capital, that her fragile democracy will be tested as never before, when Adam must gamble his life to unlock the final secrets of the Lucy Ghosts.

Eddy Shah's pulsating thriller transcends the pace and excitement of his first bestseller, RING OF RED ROSES (also available in Corgi), confirming his emergence as a remarkable new talent on the international thriller-writing scene.

'A BREATHLESS, RACY THRILLER'
Sunday Express

0 552 13918 1

A SELECTED LIST OF THRILLERS
AVAILABLE FROM CORGI BOOKS

THE PRICES SHOWN BELOW WERE CORRECT AT THE TIME OF GOING TO PRESS.
HOWEVER TRANSWORLD PUBLISHERS RESERVE THE RIGHT TO SHOW NEW
RETAIL PRICES ON COVERS WHICH MAY DIFFER FROM THOSE PREVIOUSLY
ADVERTISED IN THE TEXT OR ELSEWHERE.

All Corgi/Bantam Books are available at your bookshop or newsagent, or can be ordered from the following address:

Corgi/Bantam Books,
Cash Sales Department,
P.O. Box 11, Falmouth, Cornwall TR10 9EN

UK and B.F.P.O. customers please send a cheque or postal order (no currency) and allow £1.00 for postage and packing for the first book plus 50p for the second book and 30p for each additional book to a maximum charge of £3.00 (7 books plus).

Overseas customers, including Eire, please allow £2.00 for postage and packing for the first book plus £1.00 for the second book and 50p for each subsequent title ordered.

NAME (Block Letters) ....

ADDRESS ....

....